THE NEW FRONTIER

In hindsight, yes. It was the perfect decision. John F. Kennedy as Captain Jack Logan of the starship Enterprise. The man was perfect. Who wouldn't want to serve under him? But—at the time, who knew? It sounded crazy. Here's this old guy who's career is clearly fading fast—why cast him in *Star Track* . . . ?

—from "The Kennedy Enterprise" by David Gerrold

PLUS OVER TWENTY FASCINATING GLIMPSES OF DIFFERENT WORLDS AND *ALTERNATE KENNEDYS*!

ALTERNATE KENNEDYS

EDITED BY MIKE RESNICK

A TOM DOHERTY ASSOCIATES BOOK
NEW YORK

This is a work of fiction. All the characters and events portrayed in this book are fictitious, and any resemblance to real people or events is purely coincidental.

ALTERNATE KENNEDYS

Copyright © 1992 by Mike Resnick

Cover art by Barclay Shaw

A Tor Book
Published by Tom Doherty Associates, Inc.
175 Fifth Avenue
New York, N.Y. 10010

Tor ® is a registered trademark of Tom Doherty Associates, Inc.

ISBN: 0-812-51955-8

First edition: July 1992

Printed in the United States of America

0 9 8 7 6 5 4 3 2 1

COPYRIGHT ACKNOWLEDGEMENTS

To Carol, as always,

And to Ed Elbert,
a fine producer and a fine friend

NOTE TO THE READER

Contents

Contents

x

Camelot Redux
or,
Jack Kennedy Seen as an Alternating Current
by Jane Yolen

That was some kind of lightning storm, yes,
the first strike hitting the earth
in Washington D.C., 1960.
And he stood like an electric angel,
sparking America, charging us
with his dark corona of hair,
to do it for the country. Do it.
And he did it.
I love my country, I do.
I love my president, I do.
But there was some alternate current
running through the clan,
some dark changing force.
Perhaps it was Salinger or Sorenson,
copper and aluminum
wrapped around that steel Kennedy core,
who were conductors for the change.
Perhaps it was the lightning storm,
short circuiting all the lines.
But there he was, a different man
from the one we had elected.

Jane Yolen has discovered the secret of perpetual motion. How else does one explain a woman who has written more than one hundred books, has her own publishing imprint, turns out short stories by the bushel, produces some exquisite poetry, and still finds time to serve two terms as the President of the Science Fiction Writers of America and run a monthly workshop for writers/

When I asked her for a contribution to this book, she replied that she was too busy. Undaunted—she always says she's too busy the first time I ask her for anything—I went right for the jugular and told her that I would accept a poem. As Marlon Brando said under other circumstances, it was an offer she couldn't refuse.

Besides, what better way is there to begin a collection of Alternate Kennedys stories than with "Camelot Redux; or, Jack Kennedy Seen as an Alternating Current"?

of Glory," and heart-rending might-have-beens like Nicholas A. DiChario's "The Winterberry."

When I first agreed to edit this volume, I seriously wondered if there were enough quality Alternate Kennedy stories waiting to be told. I should have known better; the men and women who ask *What if?* for their livelihood could have filled another dozen such books.

—*Mike Resnick*

dy's sons lost a leg to cancer. The patriarch of the clan, Joseph Kennedy, Senior, the man who instilled the vigorous lust for life and power in his children, spent his final years as a paralyzed, inarticulate stroke victim.

And yet, John F. Kennedy, Junior, is an assistant district attorney in New York, and Joseph Kennedy III, one of Robert's sons, is a member of the U.S. House of Representatives, and nobody will be surprised if one or the other is running for President sometime in the next fifteen or twenty years, such is the family's power, resiliency, and charisma.

It is those three qualities—power, resiliency, and charisma—that keep the Kennedys in the public consciousness. Facts that had previously been hidden have been made public—Jack's hundreds of sexual liaisons during his presidency, Jack's and Bobby's dealings with the Mafia and their affairs with Marilyn Monroe, Teddy's seemingly endless personal scandals—and all they do is rekindle the public's interest in this remarkable family.

And always coloring the public's ongoing fascination with the Kennedys is the longing for a lost vision of Camelot: what if Jack had not been killed, if Bobby had not been killed, if Teddy had defeated Jimmy Carter for the nomination in 1980? How might things be now, what crises would have been avoided and what crises precipitated?

Well, when it comes to asking the question *What if?*, nobody does it better than those people who ask it for a living: science fiction writers. I assembled some of the best in the business, along with a few very talented newcomers, and asked each to give me an "alternate" Kennedy story, none of which had ever seen print before. Here you'll find realistic and powerful pieces such as Barry N. Malzberg's "In the Stone House," bittersweet fantasies like Susan Shwartz's "Siren Song," off-the-wall humor such as Jack Haldeman's "Short Count in Chicago," futuristic fables such as Laura Resnick's "A Fleeting Wisp held public office and acquitted themselves admirably. Senator Howard Baker learned the uses of power from his father-in-law, the great Senate Minority Leader Everett M. Dirksen. We've had the Doles, the Gores, and the Johnson/Robb families . . . and yet when one speaks of a political dynasty in America, when one looks at the covers of the weekly news journals and the weekly supermarket tabloids, there is only *one* family: the Kennedys.

Probably timing had a lot to do with it. They were young, they were handsome, they were vigorous, they were articulate, they were among the last politicians to be able to control the press (only Teddy outlived that particular power), and they seemed born to appear on television. Twenty years earlier, before the advent of television, half of the American electorate didn't even know that their four-time President, Franklin Delano Roosevelt, had been crippled by polio and spent most of his time in a wheelchair; the Kennedys needed television for their charisma to come across. Twenty years later, after Bob Woodward and Carl Bernstein's reporting had driven a President from office and given the press a courage and a bloodlust it had not previously possessed, men with a sexual morality similar to the Kennedys, such as Colorado's former Senator Gary Hart, could change from presidential front-runners to non-runners in the space of a week; the Kennedys' politics were subjected to criticism, but the press followed a hands-off policy concerning their personal lives.

Personal tragedy seemed to stalk the family, and this also created an emotional bond with the public: long before Jack and Bobby fell to assassins' bullets, brother Joe and sister Kathleen had already died tragically, and sister Rosemary had undergone a lobotomy. Jack had chronic back problems (his World War II exploits had nothing to do with it) and suffered from Addison's Disease; Teddy broke his back during a plane crash. Jack had a baby son who died in infancy during his presidency; one of Ted-

Introduction

The Kennedys.

What is it about them? Surely there have been more politically powerful American families. They have done nothing to equal the historical impact of John, Sam, and John Quincy Adams—and there is no question that the Roosevelts, Theodore and Franklin Delano, each accomplished more in given years than the Kennedy clan has achieved in its entire lifetime.

In point of historical fact, they weren't even that successful. Joe Kennedy proved to be an embarrassment to the United States when he served as our ambassador to Britain, and was forced to resign; Jack Kennedy was a relatively obscure Congressman and Senator who served only three years of what was, in truth, a historically undistinguished presidency; Bobby Kennedy began his political life as an aide to Senator Joseph McCarthy, conducted more wiretaps than any Attorney General in history, and held only one elective office in his life; and Teddy Kennedy, while he has been a distinguished lawmaker on the liberal side of the aisle, has had to overcome more public scandal than the rest of the clan combined.

During that same time, a number of Rockefellers have

When direct current is used
stable charges remain on the surface
and no effect on the transmission of power
is noticeable so long
as steady conditions are maintained.

Steady conditions—what president
can count on those, even with his power:
the missiles suborning the sea,
the Bay of Pigs,
the wall of shame that halved Berlin.

In alternating current
the overall transmission conductors
are constantly changing.

One day Jack woke a different man;
and the other one,
the one we voted for,
rode smiling past the Book Depository,
laying down his electric life
on the pink nubbled suit of his faithful wife.

Laura Resnick is the award-winning author of more than a dozen novels in the romance field under the pen-name of Laura Leone. She has recently turned to imaginative fiction, where she has sold eight stories in the past year, all under her own name. (She is also your understandably proud editor's daughter.)

When I asked for a contribution to this book, she replied that she was too young to write it, that she had been born the year before JFK was assassinated, and the only things she knew about his administration were the same cold, hard facts everyone else knew . . . plus, of course, this yearning on the part of so many people to return to those golden days of Camelot.

I suggested that the farther we got from 1963, the more like Camelot it would seem as memories grew hazy and myths grew stronger. She took that notion, ran with it, and came up with the following powerful little fable.

A Fleeting Wisp of Glory
by Laura Resnick

Jackie is fascinated by old Jonah, and she can listen for hours to the stories he tells. Me, I can take or leave him, though I still tag along after dark when there's nothing else to do and it's not safe to go alone to his cave. Not safe for Jackie, I mean. She's just a kid, after all. We're pretty isolated in these mountains, but that doesn't mean we never see Marauders, and there's no telling what they might do. Especially to, you know, a *girl*.

Jonah was named after a prophet who was swallowed by a whale. A whale is a big fish that breathes air. It's just a fairy tale, of course. I don't believe that anything like that ever existed, even before the Armageddon. Jonah insists that there were such creatures, though, and that they filled the seven seas with their songs before the waters boiled and the sky caught fire. He says they could get as big as the giants frozen in Rushmore's Rock. So Jonah—the one in the story, I mean—was swallowed by one of these things and lived to tell the tale, and then *our* Jonah was named after him.

Jonah is the oldest person I've ever seen. His skin is so loose it hangs on him like rags, and it's as dun-colored as his tunic. His wife and children were killed by Marauders a long time before I was born, and he's too old and weak to work now. In a lot of places, he'd just be left to die now that he's no use to anyone; it's hard enough to find your own food, let alone extra food for some broken old man. But these mountains are better than most places, and there aren't so many of us to feed as there are down below. So we bring Jonah food and water, and he tells stories and sometimes fixes things that no one else knows how to. Not useful things, dumb things. We found a little box one time, and Jonah fixed it so that now it makes an ugly growling noise when you push a button. It has a special part that's supposed to go in your ear, but why bother? I don't like to listen to the growling. It makes me think of Night Devils, with their glowing eyes and melting flesh, even though I know that's just a fairy tale, too.

Jackie thinks the box is really interesting, and she believes that stuff about the whales. She mostly likes to go to Jonah's cave, though, to hear about Camelot. That's her favorite story, and I don't think I could count how many times I've heard it. It's my mother's favorite story, too, and she even believes it's all true. Since my father can't speak or hear, I'm not sure what he thinks about Camelot, or if he even knows the story. That's all there is in my family now—me, my mother, and my father. I had two brothers once, but they caught the Sickness and died, one right after the other, blind, vomiting, and screaming. Sometimes I'm afraid Jackie will get the Sickness, but she says she's as strong as me and won't. She doesn't look that strong, though. She's sort of delicate, all blonde and pale and skinny, with blue eyes that water under the hot yellow sky.

I don't usually tell her that I worry about the Sickness killing her, or Marauders taking her, because she just gets huffy and tries to pretend that she's as tough as me, even though she's a girl. Anyhow, I'm a full year and a half older than Jackie, and I just know some things that she doesn't. I know that people die even when you don't want them to, and I know that the Sickness comes without warning and takes your mind away before anyone has a chance to say good-bye.

I also know that Jonah's stories are just a lot of toxic waste.

"If you don't want to listen, then don't *come,*" Jackie says as we approach Jonah's cave. The entrance is pretty well camouflaged. You've got to know right where it is, or you could stumble around the hill half the night.

I shrug. "I got nothing else to do."

"And be nice to Jonah," she adds, crawling between the branches that cover the mouth of the cave.

"I'm *always* nice to him."

"And don't look so bored when he talks," she whispers.

"Okay, okay." She can be really bossy sometimes.

It doesn't smell too good in Jonah's cave. Odors of sweat and blood have been trapped in here without a good breeze for as long as the moon has been red. Sometimes I sit very close to Jackie, who smells of grass and wet bark and the wind, and I forget that I don't like this cave very much.

Jonah has boiled a bunch of leaves again, and he makes us drink the brew, which he always says will stop our bowels being all yellow and runny. After we finish every last drop, he gives Jackie some more of the sweet-smelling salve he always wants her to put on her skin before going out in the sunshine. He tries to make me take some, too, and Jackie pokes me, but I don't want to go around smelling like that, so I refuse again. Jonah sets great store by these medicines, but most folks don't believe that there are secret colors in the sun that can kill you, though my mom always tells me to drink the brew in case you really *can* catch the Sickness from invisible spirits in the water.

Jonah finally asks if there's anything else he can do for us, as if he doesn't know why we've come, and Jackie says, "Tell us the story, Jonah!" She bounces a little and claps her hands. She's still pretty young.

"Which story?" he asks slyly, stroking his beard and looking all innocent.

"Tell us about Camelot," she insists.

"You want to hear about Camelot?"

"Sure," I say. "We've only heard the story a hundred times."

"Stop it, Bobby," Jackie hisses. She looks at him again and smiles, her teeth small and pretty straight. "Please tell us, Jonah."

But Jonah is looking at me, his eyes hooded and strange. "Do you think you've heard the story too often, Bobby?"

"Well . . ." Now I'm embarrassed. He's just a lonely old man, and my mom will be mad if she hears I've been mean to him.

"Do you think you've heard it so often that you know every word?" Jonah continues.

"Yes." I roll my eyes at Jackie. I don't know why she wants to keep climbing up to this smelly old cave every few days to hear the same old story again and again. Trying to be nice, I say, "But you know a lot of good stories, Jonah. Maybe you could tell a different one tonight."

"Do you think you could tell the story of Camelot as well as I can?" Jonah asks. "Without getting anything wrong?"

"I don't know." Who cares? "I guess so."

He smiles and looks excited. "Then tell it."

"Aw, come on, Jonah." He's punishing me for what I said before, I'm sure of it. "I don't want to. You tell it. Go on. I didn't mean what—"

"No," he says firmly. "I want to hear you tell the story tonight. I want to see if you can."

"Go on, Bobby," Jackie says. "You're so smart, *you* tell the story tonight."

I wish I'd let her come alone tonight. She *deserves* to get carried off by Marauders. Her cheeks are dimpled as she scoots away and sits near Jonah. They watch me in smirking silence, waiting for me to begin the tale. I *hate* this. It's hard to talk in front of a lot of people, and the two of them suddenly look like the whole clan.

I clear my throat. I open my mouth, but my tongue is too dry to talk. I feel silly as I swallow and start over, wishing Jackie would look away for a minute. "Once upon a time, this land here, and all the land as far as the eye can see, east, west, north, and south, was part of a great kingdom." I stop, already stuck, not sure what comes next.

"That was before the Armageddon," Jonah says to help.

"That was before the Armageddon, before the air burned our lungs, the waters burned our flesh, and the earth opened up to swallow our dead."

"Tell about the food," Jackie prompts. This is her favorite part.

"There was food for everyone in those days, and no one in this kingdom ever went hungry. There were juicy red meats, flaky white fish, and sweet-tasting birds that were basted in butter and wine and ... and ..."

"Cooked so that the flesh fell off the bone and melted

in your mouth," Jackie says, looking hungry all of a sudden.

"And there were a thousand kinds of fruit in as many different colors, with smooth shiny skins and firm, sweet flesh." Now I'm getting hungry, too, so I decide to get to the next part of the story. "But this kingdom needed a leader, and so a brave warrior came from the north, from the port of the Hyannis, and with the strength of his sword Excalibur, he made himself the ruler of this land from sea to shining sea."

I look to Jonah, and he nods to let me know I'm doing all right so far. "King Kennedy was young and handsome, and he took a beautiful woman to be his queen."

"Her name was Jacqueline," Jackie interrupts. I've been expecting this. She always interrupts Jonah at this point.

"Jacqueline was the daughter of . . ." I'm not sure, and Jonah doesn't help me this time. "The daughter of Lot," I say at last, hoping I'm right, "and she came from the north, too. Her dowry was a round table, and when Kennedy saw it, he invited knights from all over the land to come to Camelot, where he lived in a big white palace, and he asked them to pledge allegiance to the flag and join the round table. No one could sit at the head or the foot of the round table, and Kennedy said that made it perfect for a democracy."

Jonah once said that a democracy is like a family after the children have become as big as their parents and can argue instead of just doing what they're told.

"Many knights came to Camelot. Sir McNamara, Sir Rusk, Sir Galahad, Sir Warren, and Sir Bobby, who was the king's brother and most special advisor. Bobby and Kennedy were educated by a wizard named Merlin, so they knew more than other people." I stop again, thinking I've forgotten someone important.

"Who was the best knight?" Jonah asks softly.

"Oh! Sir Launcelot. He came from France, like Sir Salinger, but he was very brave even so."

"Tell about the Lady of Shallot," Jackie says.

"No, that part's stupid."

"Bobby!" She gets all huffy about it, so I decide to let her have her way.

"Her name was Marilyn, and she was a famous movie star." I'm not sure what that means. Jonah once said it meant Marilyn was a kind of storyteller, but she lived in a much better place than this cave. "She had hair the color of the sun, and she was every man and woman's ideal of beauty and grace. Kennedy and Sir Bobby both loved her, but she fell in love with Launcelot, like girls always did. But then she got half sick of shadows and . . ." I shrug. "And I guess she got the Sickness."

"No." Jonah shakes his head. "People didn't get the Sickness then. The Sickness came after the Armageddon."

"Oh, right. Anyhow, she died, and then Launcelot fell in love with the queen." I hesitate, feeling confused. I realize suddenly that the story hasn't always been the same. When I was just a kid, it was different somehow. Bit by bit, it's changed. "Have I got something wrong?"

"No, no, you're doing fine," Jonah says.

I guess he should know. "So Launcelot was afraid for his honor, because it was wrong to love the king's wife, so he went off to find the Holy Grail. All the other knights decided they should do good work, too, so they went off to far foreign lands like Africa and Asia and Thailand where they taught ignorant people to be just like them."

"And the women," Jackie adds. "Women went, too."

"Yes, and the women, too." She looks really impressed now, even though she keeps interrupting. "And the men and women of the round table taught people how to do all the wonderful, miraculous things that people in Camelot knew how to do. They taught them how to make water flow into their homes, how to build smooth shiny roads, how to make the Sickness go away—"

"Not the Sickness," Jonah says. "Just diseases."

"And they taught them how to make food like the people had in Camelot," Jackie says wistfully.

"I guess so."

"So everything was perfect in Camelot?" Jonah asks.

I know the answer to this. "It was perfect for a while, and people thought they were living in Paradise. Kennedy had many friends, like Sir Peter, who was a famous storyteller like Lady Marilyn, King Pellinore who came from ... the north, I guess. But Pellinore never stayed long, because he was always looking for the Questing Beast.

"Kennedy had an evil sister though, a sorceress named Morgause, and a child was born to their ... their ..." It's a big word, I know that.

"Their incestuous union," Jonah says.

"Their incestuous union. His name was Khrushchev, and he was a jealous, evil prince who grew up with Morgause's other sons, Gawaine, Agravaine, and Castro. He grew up to rule an evil kingdom, far, far, far away from here ... and I think he loved Jacqueline, too."

"Everybody loved her," Jackie says, touching her own hair, which is blonde but maybe not as blonde as they say Jacqueline's was. Or was it just Marilyn's hair that was blonde? I almost ask Jonah, but suddenly I wonder if he really knows the truth. Not that I believe any of it's true, of course.

"I don't think Khrushchev loved Jacqueline," Jonah says, but he doesn't sound very sure. "He might have loved the Lady of Shallot, but not the queen."

"Oh." He's so old. Is he forgetting how all the parts of the story go?

"Tell about the Holy Grail," Jackie says.

"Um, the knights of the round table were looking for the Grail, but instead they found missiles in Cuba, the kingdom of Prince Castro. The missiles were very powerful, more powerful than Excalibur or Merlin's magic or anything, and people were afraid. They knew they were in terrible danger." This is the part of the story I hate, and I don't want to go on.

"What happened, Bobby?" Jonah says. "Continue."

"Khrushchev wanted to rule in this kingdom, too, but Kennedy wouldn't let him. And so they began the war." I lick my lips, which are always cracked and sometimes bleed. "Armageddon." My stomach twists and burns, and I hope the brew Jonah made will work this time.

"You forgot the important part," Jackie says.

"What part?"

"Why didn't Kennedy want Khrushchev to rule in this kingdom?" Jonah asks. I know the answer, but for some reason I don't want to tell him. I don't really know what it means, and I think it should be left out of the story.

"Bobby?" Seeing that I won't say anything, Jonah sighs and says, "He wanted us to be free. You must remember that."

"Maybe he just wanted to keep the kingdom for himself."

"No!" Jonah looks agitated. "No, you mustn't say that. You mustn't doubt."

"Finish the story," Jackie says. "I have to go back soon." She's starting to look pretty tired.

I try to remember what comes next. "Armageddon," I repeat. "The end of the world. The end of Camelot."

I wonder, for the first time, if Kennedy knew about the Sickness when he started the war. Did he know the sky would burn like the heart of a fire? Did Merlin warn him that there would be nothing left when it was over, nothing to eat or drink, no place to live or sleep? Did he know that all the wonders they had in Camelot would be gone forever?

"No one can make water flow now, no one has a white palace . . ."

'You're skipping a lot," Jackie says, sounding upset.

"The sky burned, the air exploded, the sea boiled. . . . You know all that," I say. "Everyone died."

"But—"

"Everyone died, except for a few people who were . . . in good places. Like this place."

"And Kennedy?" Jonah prods.

I've heard this story a hundred times. I shouldn't feel so bad tonight. I don't want to finish it, but I can see that it's very important to Jonah that I do. "The king died and was carried off to Avalon, a secret place, where a magic spell was cast upon him. On the third day he arose and ascended into heaven. He is seated at the right hand of the Father, and he will come again, to judge the living and the dead."

"And so we wait for him," Jackie whispers.

"His sword, Excalibur rests at the bottom of the lake, and when he returns, he'll claim it and . . . Which lake?"

"What?" Jonah says.

"Which lake is the sword in?"

There's a long silence. Finally he says, "The lake near Avalon." I know he's lying. And because he's bothered to lie, I believe for the first time that some part of the story must be true. But which part?

"And he will use his sword to enforce right with might and to protect the meek," I say, finishing quickly, wanting to go back over the story and find out what's true and what's not.

"Well told, Bobby," Jonah says, crawling to his feet. "It's rough in a few places, but you'll soon know the story as well as I do." He's going to finish now, saying the part that's his alone to say. "This story is our past, and we must never forget it. My grandfather told it to me, as his grandfather's grandfather told it before him, as I tell it to you, and as you will tell it when I am gone. Each evening from December to December, we remember the wonders of Camelot and its brave king, waiting for him to return to us and make again the world that men knew then."

"He won't come back," I whisper suddenly, sure that this part, at least, isn't true. "Everyone dies, Jonah, and no one comes back."

I'm afraid for a minute that I've made him very angry, but then I see that the sparkle in his eyes is water, not anger. He slumps and looks older than he ever has before. "Then we must keep him alive with our stories," he says at last. A tear slides down his cheek, and I know my mom will beat me if she learns I've made him cry. "We must remember that there was a better world before this one, and believe that there will be a better one again. Otherwise, how will we go on?"

"You said you'd be nice to him," Jackie whispers angrily.

"I'm sorry, Jonah." But I don't really know what I've done wrong.

"It's all right, Bobby. You should take Jackie back now. It's getting late."

We leave the cave, and the smell of the night is a relief. I wonder what nighttime in Camelot smelled like? Did it smell of cooking fires and sewage like this night does? Did the rain sting, did the wind burn, did the air taste of dust? Was the moon fat, red, and streaked with orange? Did Kennedy and his knights fear the Night Devils? No, of course not—Jonah told me that Night Devils came after the Armageddon. What devils *did* they fear, then?

"Do really you believe it, Jackie?" I ask as we walk away from the cave.

"Enough of it."

"Enough for what?"

"Enough to know there was something better than this."

"But this is all we have."

"That's why we need the story," she says.

Something rustles past us in the dark, and she takes my hand. "You told it very well," she whispers.

Her hand is still so small. She was born without all her fingers, but I don't care.

"Will you tell it again sometime?" she asks.

I squeeze her hand and wonder why the twisting in my stomach is worse.

"Sure."

I guess it can't hurt to tell the story again.

Barry Malzberg, the author of more than ninety books, including such classics as *Galaxies, Herovit's World*, and the award-winning *Beyond Apollo*, has made the assassination of John F. Kennedy his own literary preserve, using it as the focus of numerous novels and short stories.

Usually the assassin is Lee Harvey Oswald; occasionally it is someone—or, since he is a science fiction writer, something . . . else. I suggested a possible guilty party for this story, and two days later Barry produced what I believe may be the best novelette he has yet written—and believe me, that covers a lot of brilliant novelettes.

In the Stone House
by Barry N. Malzberg

11/22/63 Joe Kennedy, Jr. wipes the stock of the rifle again, his hands shaking, then, dissatisfied, breaks it open for the third time, making sure that the shells are still there, that the trigger is properly positioned. He reassembles the gear slowly, cursing the damned M-1, cursing his own stupidity in putting so much dependency upon a weapon which was no damned good. He should have had better equipment, not relied on the old Army supply service. But then getting better equipment would have brought some attention and he didn't want that. You had to carry this on in secrecy. Joe Kennedy, Jr. knows all about secrecy now, has counted upon it, has made it his mistral and the source of all his splendor. Too late, Jack. Too late for all of this, Joe Kennedy mumbles. He positions the cartons on the floor, peers out the window. A scattering of crowd, good, the street cleared, better, no sign of the motorcade yet in the distance. A little behind schedule but nothing ominous. Jack and the powder puff would be along soon enough.

Joe Kennedy, once President of the United States, now reduced (in his own mind if not quite in the estimation of the press) to sniveling bum, sniveling potential assassin, perches on the sixth floor of the Dallas School Book Depository, waiting for the presidential motorcade. He will sight his rifle on his brother's tousled head, hope for the best, pull the trigger. It is a difficult business, assassinating your younger brother, crazier yet if you are an ex-President of the United States, 1952–1956, which raises fratricide to the level of lunacy but there you are. It is the last great service, Joe knows, which he can perform, not only for patrimony but for the country. Jack is out of control, the arrogant little bastard had never been trustworthy in the first place but to a certain point he had been manipulable, now he was no longer.

You had to save the plan, that was all: the plan was all that mattered and Jack had broken the plan, shattered everything, the bastard. Joe thought of this, thought of that, considered all of the dreadful but necessary implications of his position, watching the sun drop little pools of uneven light on the dusty surfaces of the cartons of books, feeling the old clarity coming back. It had been a long time since he had felt this level of control but here it was, at last he knew what he was after, what had to be done. In the distance, he thought he could hear the sound of shouting, the thin tremor of drums and then as he arched his body, peered awkwardly out the window, he could see the thin movement of the crowd which could only indicate, yes, that the motorcade was coming. His breath was high in his throat,

perched there like some enormous bird. Joe felt *alive*, felt
more in possession of himself than he had in this long,
dreadful exiled time. Well, he would wait it out, that was
all. This was a serious business. There was nothing frivolous
about it. The time for frivolity was gone.

11/22/46 I don't want it, Joe Jr. said to Jack, the big
strapping jock. I was never cut out for politics. This is
ridiculous. Jack laughed at him, winked riotously, hit him
on the back. You may not be cut out for it, Jack said, but
you *got* it. Mr. Smith goes to Washington. Shake 'em up
good, Joe. You're a fucking war hero.

Going to be a lot of war heroes down there, Bobby said.
War heroes are going to be a dime a dozen right through
the decade. Sure going to be a shake-up time there, right,
Dad?

Oh sure, Joe Sr. said, beaming at the three of them. Joe
hadn't seen the old man in this kind of mood on land
since before the war. This was what they called a family,
the four of them getting together after the election to figure out what the right move would be. But that was all a
bunch of crap, Joe knew, all the old man wanted to do
was to look at them and gloat. His three sons, the Congressman ready for his first term, everything lining up
after the war just as the old man had promised. Feels
good, doesn't it? the old man said. Well, it's a way to
welcome the boys home, right? I promised you a home-
coming.

I didn't want this, Joe Jr. said. Going up against the old
man was a losing cause but he had to go on the record,
if he had taken bombers out over Germany then he could
go up against the Ambassador to the Court of St. James's.
Couldn't he? But it was all crap, he couldn't stand up to
it. No one could, the old man rode you down one way or
the other and you just had to take it. I could get used to
it though, he said.

Oh, you can get used to it, the old man said. Power is

fun, even if a freshman Congressman hasn't got any. And the living is easy.

Lots of women, Jack said. Don't forget the women.

You never forgot anything, Bobby said. In your whole life you let nothing go by. I think I'll bail out of this, Dad, Bobby said. I have business downtown.

We have business to settle, the old man said. You'll go in a few minutes, when I say you can. Joe, I want a staff put together. You know the names, but I'd like to hear what you have to say if you have any ideas.

Oh, I have ideas, Joe said. I have lots of ideas. You'll never listen to any of them. Hyannisport, Joe thought. It always comes back to Hyannisport. Wherever you go, however hard you fly, whatever risks you take, you wind up in a room in a house on the beach where the old man tells you what to do. Why don't you just go ahead and fix it? he said to the Ambassador. I'm sure anything you want is okay with me.

I'll tell you this right now, Jack said. I don't want any part of it. I don't want to go to Washington and I don't want to be anyone's aide-in-waiting. I'm going to go back to school.

You think so, the Ambassador said. You think that's really the plan?

I'll get a graduate degree, Jack said. I always wanted to teach history. Maybe I'll go to law school. He yawned. No Congress for me, he said, no agenda, no roll calls, no quorums. I had enough of that on the high seas, thank you very much.

I'm too young, Bobby said. Don't look at me, Dad. It may be a young man's country again, but Joe can't have a twenty-two-year-old assistant. Besides, they'll just say that I got put on the payroll to keep me off the streets.

You see? Joe said to the Ambassador, it's a family revolt. Your sons are standing up and being counted. No aide-de-camp in the room, no assistant either. So just go ahead and get the Honey Fitz delegation, because I don't give a shit. It's all the same to me.

You're a defiant prick, the old man said. You know that? I give you everything and you shit on me. You think a few stripes, a couple of bombs, and you're hot shit. Well, you're the same little bum you were before the war, you know? Who do you think pulled you those assignments?

Joe felt the old anger. Hyannisport, Hyannisport, throwing sand at the beach, they could get you every time. That seemed to be part of the deal, you thought you could get away from it but the old man could always get you back.

Leave me alone, Joe said. Just leave me alone. You wanted me to run for Congress, I ran. You wanted me to make speeches, I made war hero speeches. You want a staff, appoint a staff. Just leave me out of it, you know? You don't give a damn anyway, so just have it your way.

Bobby said, Joe, calm down. It's okay.

He's just ragging you, Jack said. That's his way. You know that he means well. He's just kidding you, trying to get you to pay attention, right, Dad? But I think we should ease off, go for a swim or something.

You'll go when I say, the Ambassador said. Jack you're going to Washington with him. There's no time to waste and there's no time to screw around either. Bobby, you can go to law school, we won't need you for a few years but you're going to check in and stay close.

I don't want any part of this, Jack said. I want to study history, be a professor at Wellesley. Maybe Duke. Show the girls the way through the New Deal or maybe the Middle Ages. I've had all the goddamned politics I'll ever want. Jack paused, looked at the Ambassador, then took out a handkerchief and wiped his forehead slowly. I really *am* going to Washington, he said. You really mean it, don't you? The academy is just a dream, isn't it?

Just about, the Ambassador said. I told you, we have

no time for that. We have to get down to cases. There's a country out there.

Oh, there's a country out there, Joe Jr. thought, it's been out there for a hundred and seventy years now, waiting for us. And now the Ambassador figures it's about time that he took it. The sprawl of the land, the heat of the old man's need, the sense of injustice tilted within him, and for a moment it was as if the walls had come down and he could see *everything*, could see what was in store for all of them, the poor, foolish damned Ambassador too, but then mercifully the walls went up again and he could see only the bare surfaces of the conference room in Hyannisport. You really do mean it, don't you, he said, you meant it all.

From the start, the Ambassador said. Before you were ever born. Before *I* was ever born, I meant it. And you too, Joe. *You* mean it. Because you'd better.

11/22/63   It wasn't easy, Joe Kennedy, Jr. thinks, to progress from President to one-term President to ex-President to sniveling bum to assassin all in a seven-year period, it was an arc of history which refracted by opposites the old man's journey and might have been thought impossible if he, Joe Kennedy, Jr., hadn't proven that it *was* possible. But you had to work at it, you really did have to put your best attention to it because the country loved the few ex-Presidents it had so very much and paid such kind attention to them. But it helped if your younger brother had succeeded you as President and had found his own distinction and style in such a way as to absorb your own traces, and it also helped if you really needed to escape, if you needed somehow to sink back into the morass that his life had become since the Ambassador had looked at him in 1956 and had pulled the plug. You're through, laddie, the Ambassador had said, you've gone as far with this as you're going to go. You are not going to run in November, you are going to announce your withdrawal in Jack's favor right now, or things will get very hot for all of us. Do you understand that? Joe had understood it very well.

He had always understood the Ambassador. Maybe that was the problem, his father had been refractory of Joe Jr. from the start; Joe had felt not exactly like an extension of the Ambassador but simply a spare part, something extra that could be screwed in, unstuck, manipulated, it didn't matter, he was always around. Sometimes he had wanted to stand up to the Ambassador, he had given him a mild push in 1946 when he hadn't wanted to run for Congress, but that had collapsed pretty soon and then he had fought a little harder in '48 when the Ambassador had said that now was the time to go for the Governor's chair, a really shitty job then and now. In '51 Governor Joe Kennedy, Jr. had *really* struggled when the Ambassador had said, okay, now is the time, Truman is out of the way and we are going to stick it to this ignorant old general and take the presidency. For a few wild moments Joe had thought that he would beat down the Ambassador through simple expediency, make a speech in the Capitol like Silent Cal had in 1919 and simply pull down the temple, but he hadn't been able to do it then either. There was something very persuasive about the Ambassador, very tough, very ungiving. Ask Rose, ask Kathleen. Well, ask Rose now anyway. Ask Bobby if you could find him. That had been the worst of it, going out for the presidency, going through the worst imaginable campaign and the terrible events of the convention when he had had to break Adlai open right there in front of everyone, but since then it had gotten a little easier. It always got easier when you simply gave up, Jack had warned him and it was true, nothing had been as bad as that struggle in '52 and the convention, even '56 when Joe had had the plug pulled on him was easy in comparison. But once he had broken, once he had come down all the way to sniveling bum territory, it had been as if he had an entirely new perspective on things.

The perspective was new every day. Now Joe Jr. had a real grasp of the situation. More and more he was seeing it the Ambassador's way. Once you gave it up and gave the Ambassador his points, admitted what he was and that he had probably been right all along, everything else fell into line. Still, Joe Jr. knew that he was fucked up in his own mind. He couldn't figure out if he was doing this *for* the Ambassador or against him, whether it was his last great service for his father or a terrible act of defiance. It didn't matter, he supposed. This introspection, this wondering, this internalization, it just got you nowhere in the first place, you had to go on like the Ambassador himself and simply *do* things. The motorcade was in sight now, he thought he could see it, the lead cars of the agents. The crowd was straggling into separate ragged lines on either side of the street, the first advance patrol car came down the empty street between the barricades. It wouldn't be much longer now. Joe Kennedy, Jr. fondled the rifle and thought about this and that, thought about the nature of conditions and the question of his own sacrifice. He wanted one clear shot, that was all. One plug, one bolt of revenge, one pure thunderbolt, as Emily Dickinson said, to scalp his living soul. After that he would take his chances just like the rest of the world; he would come into a cause-and-effect world where things simply happened or failed to happen as a result of consequence. Oh Jack, he thought, it could have been different, but even as he murmured this he knew it was bullshit, it could have been no different at all. The old man had worked it out in his head long before any of them were born, had lain on a thousand pillows of resentment running the pictures through his head over and again, and by the time the four sons came along, they were nothing other than aspects of the plan like angels in the mind of God. The whole thing was determinism, that was all. One pure thunderbolt. To scalp his living soul.

10/22/63 I called you in, JFK said, because whatever has happened to us, whatever you've become, you're still a President and you're my brother. So I want you to know that I'm pulling the plug on all of this. Bobby is not going to get my endorsement. Bobby will never be President.

Joe looked at him. Past security, past the guards, past Salinger and O'Donnell into the Oval Office. Nobody had even looked at him. It had been as if he were dead. Only Caroline had waved at him when she saw her uncle go by. Caroline was probably the last friend Joe Jr. had in the family, now that he thought about it. What are you saying? he said. What does this mean to me?

It means that the dynasty is coming to a roaring halt, JFK said. He smiled at Joe. It means that Bobby is being dismissed from the Cabinet this afternoon. A press release has already been prepared. He is not being allowed to resign, he has been fired as Attorney General, *comprende*? And I will do everything within my power to make sure that he never runs for office again. The line is running out, Joe. There will be no more.

I don't understand, Joe said. I truly do not understand. His mind was as clear, as vacant as it had been the day he had been elected in 1952 and had come to understand that he had no agenda, not the shred of an agenda for the eight years of the presidency which stretched before him, and that the Ambassador had no real agenda either, they had been dumped by the wave of history but they were on the beach. Why are you doing this? he said to JFK. And why did you call me here to tell me that? What did you think I could do?

Well, nothing at all, JFK said. Call it a family courtesy. You can tell it to the Ambassador, that's what you can do for me. Tell it to Old Joe, break the word before he gets it from the radio. No Bobby in his future. The old man will shit a brick, but frankly, that's *his* problem. I have no concern for that now.

But why? Joe said. He seemed to be fixed on this point. He somehow couldn't get beyond it. That was what came from being your old man's first son, you had to take all of the mistakes, make them so that the others could have a smoother deal. Some deal they had. The deal was me, then you, then Bobby, Joe said. Now you're breaking the deal. There seemed to be a whining tone to his voice. In just a few moments he would cry. Then what? What did that mean? The crying Mr. President. I can't tell the Ambassador, Joe Jr. said. He'll go wild. He'll kill me.

You're fifty years old, JFK said. You've been the President of the United States. You're afraid some ancient fart with a cane is going to kill you? Is that what he's done to us? For what? For what purpose?

But why? Joe said again. Bobby was a good Attorney General. He never gave you any trouble. He got rid of Hoffa. He's got Hoover held down, the first guy in thirty years to do that. I couldn't do that. He's the next in line. So—

Because the country isn't our playpen, JFK said, because there has to be something else but the Ambassador's craziness and our own knee reflexes twitching away. Because it has to be broken sometime. I'm going to go for Lyndon. He's taken the shit admirably, he's kept out of the way, he's even been as polite as an ignorant Texan can be. Let *him* run the place for a while, I just want to go out and get laid which constitutionally I have to do now anyway. Maybe Lyndon will tame his sex life a little. Whatever he wants, it's okay with me.

It's crazy, Joe Jr. said, I've never heard such craziness. I can't believe that you're telling me this, that I'm here to listen. I wasn't a very good President. I fucked up, I admit it. The old man was right to tell me that I had to go. I admit it now, I never wanted to be there and the country was done a disservice. You did all right, Jack, in your way, up to a point. You kept Nixon out anyway, and that's a fact. But now you're betraying everything. I just don't get it. I don't—

Caroline, the President said. Caroline, honey. He extended his arms and the little girl bolted from the right doorway, ran toward him giggling. JFK leaned over, scooped up the six-year-old, bounced her in the air. Daddy, Caroline said. Joe could see the glint in their eyes, the same eyes really, the communion between the two. But it's best, still, he thought, it's best I didn't get married, didn't have children. It wouldn't have worked out. And I have spared a wife and children the disgrace of my life. I have at least kept the sadness to myself. Say hello to Uncle Joe, JFK said. Your uncle misses you.

I said hello when he came in, Caroline said. She squinted. Uncle Joe is tired, she said. He looks so tired.

We get tired earlier and earlier, honey, JFK said. He put the little girl on his lap, kissed the top of her head, spilled her off. That's enough, he said. We have to talk now. You can come back and play later.

I'll play later, Caroline agreed. She came over and kissed Joe on the cheek. I want to play with you later, she said and ran out. Joe stared at JFK, feeling the imprint of the little girl's lips on him.

It's enormous, he said, I don't believe it. This cannot be. This cannot be happening to us.

It was always meant to happen, JFK said. Now I told you. We can sneak you out the back way so that no one knows you were here.

How is Bobby taking it, Joe said, does he know?

JFK grinned. I guess he would know, the President said. I mean, I fired him face to face. It would be difficult to do that and for him not to *know*, right? Oh, he's in a ruddy gloom, Bobby is. But he'll get over it. We all get over it sooner or later. I've had my heart broken more times than you were up over Germany, Joe, and I've lived to tell the tale. You've lived pretty good yourself, and they could have shot you down anytime. Life goes on as long as you have it, that's all, you know? I'll get you down the back stairs. Anyway, that's the deal. How's your love life? I'll tell you, it's never been the same for me since the blonde did herself in. But that's another story.

Don't talk to me about the blonde, Joe said. How can you talk about the blonde? This is vile, do you hear me? It is enormous. It is impossible, it is the end of all of us, don't you see? You have destroyed us.

No, JFK said. He patted Joe's hand. That's why you're still trapped and I'm free now. Because you don't see it, you never got away, even when he made you quit you were still his property. But I see it and I tell you that this is the making of us. This is the beginning. It is the true beginning of the story. It is the beginning of the Kennedy story and someday you will see that. And now it is time for you to go, brother, but you may take a paperweight from the Oval Office as a reminder of why you no longer miss the place.

10/26/63   He hadn't been able to reach the old man first, of course. That was impossible. He had put in the call to the compound right after the conversation with Jack but no luck, the word was that the old man was getting physical therapy and couldn't be bothered. Not even by his son, the ex-President of the United States. Which meant that the old man was fucking or trying to fuck the nurse again. Half of his brain had been shut down, but the old man was still in there fighting and for all Joe Jr. knew he was having a kind of success. You had to give the old man credit, he was in there fighting until the end. In the second place, no one was really returning his calls or picking him up now, it was amazing how far an ex-President could fall if he had been out of office for almost seven years and if he had a brother-successor who was a real bastard. A real maneuverer, that was JFK. Thinking about it could get Joe sick so he tried not to consider

what had happened to him, how quickly it had all un-
raveled. Throttlebottom, wasn't that the name? the little
Vice President in *Of Thee I Sing* who gave guided tours
around the White House wearing a uniform and who had
lunch with his mother every day. Joe hadn't turned into
a Throttlebottom, not quite, he could probably seek paying employment and get it if he wanted (he didn't want
it) and probably half the adult population could name his
previous occupation, but it was still a hell of a thing.

So he had settled for trying to get through to Bobby.
Bobby at least would take his calls, would listen to him,
and this time maybe Joe could say a few words to the
Attorney General that might be of some comfort. It was a
hell of a situation, that was for sure. But Bobby wasn't
available, he was locked up incommunicado somewhere
in the Justice Department, maybe with Hoover for all Joe
knew, and there was no word on whether he would return the call if ever. So Joe had been absolutely at loose
ends, the first time it had been that way for him in years.
He literally did not know where to go. Surfacing, showing
up in public would be suicide now, the press would be
all over him, would want quotes, would want to know
what Jack had in mind. The city was exploding, absolutely on fire with this, with the unbelievable news that
JFK had ditched his younger brother, the Attorney General, and had announced that he was going to back the
Vice President for the nomination. The end of the dynasty, it seemed, the planned succession of Kennedys.
Ted had been smart, he was hiding out in the Senate well,
holding the gavel for the absent LBJ and denying comment of all kind. Besides, what the hell could a freshman
Senator have to say about any of this? Teddy was thirty-
one years old, he was in the Senate on a family pass,
everybody knew that they had used up every bit of credit
this time to sneak him in and if there was a next stop for
the dynasty it wouldn't be at his house for a long time,
maybe never.

So Joe stayed away from Teddy too. He hung out in the secret apartment on K Street, just him and his one Secret Service guy, sharing a bottle and telling stories about the war yet again, they had both been pilots over Dresden and Secret Service had had worse luck than Joe, had had to make an emergency landing and evade capture over land. It was kind of an interesting story, but Joe was sick of it. He was sick of the whole damned thing, that was the truth, the war and the hero stories and the dynasty and the old man's plans, all of it, the whole business. There was enough of it now, and with JFK pulling this rotten move there would be nothing but a recycling of all that stuff over and again.

There had been a time, just a few moments it seemed, after his discharge, when Joe thought that he might be free of it. Just as JFK had planned to go on and teach history at Harvard or Tufts or Haverford, hang out some place and be an academic, avoid the whole thing, Joe had thought that he might go to law school and then into pro bono work of some kind, maybe go into the down-and-out district around Scully Square and try to pay back some of Honey Fitz's debts. It wouldn't have been a bad life and somewhere along the way there might even have been a woman, one of the succession who would have stuck. He could have gotten a subscription to Friday Symphony, gone to Symphony Hall in the early afternoons and sat in the slant light of that cathedral and listened to Brahms, just Brahms and pro bono and one woman who would listen to him ... but that shimmering little moment had passed when the old man had sat them down early in the year and had laid out the situation. You and you and you. Joe would have tried to balk, but what was the point? No one got anywhere with the old man, Gloria Swanson had been the strongest-willed actress in the world, stronger than Marion Davies had been with the Ambassador's friend Hearst, and where had it gotten her? She was a slut on a boat, just gash for the old man and that's how she stayed. If Gloria Swanson couldn't beat this guy, then Joe who bore his name with the diminishing *Jr.* below didn't have a chance. JFK didn't have a chance, Bobby with his verve and his big eyes was down on the list but he was locked in too. Only Ted among them might have gotten through, he was fourteen years old then and the old man hadn't noticed him yet.

So Joe had capitulated. Run for Congress? All right he would run for Congress. Spring for the Senate because you had to keep on moving or get shot out of the water? That would be okay too. The presidency? Well, that had been a big leap, the biggest, but the Ambassador had put it to him bluntly. No one is going to beat the general unless *we* do it, the Ambassador had said, Truman is finished and the Democrats are done for unless they get a complete overhaul. And then what? Do you want that bastard Nixon just a heartbeat away, waiting for the old general to keel over? You know that the general is a figurehead, it will be Nixon and McCarthy running the show and we don't want that, do we? Joe Jr. had fallen for that, not Nixon so much, a thirty-nine-year-old shit who Joe had gotten to know in the Senate as too much of a nut case to ever be dangerous—but McCarthy in control . . . that was another story. (He hadn't known the Ambassador's full cunning, hadn't measured the Ambassador's plans.) So okay, he had run. He shrugged. What the hell? It was the presidency, there were people who had been forced to do far worse, like march to their deaths in gas chambers or take rickety planes high in the air to be open targets for every ground gunner in Dresden. You couldn't complain that being forced to run for the presidency was perdition. All right, Joe had said, all right then. We'll try it. There was the good possibility they would lose, the general had his points, and if he didn't lose, how bad could it be? He already knew that he was just keeping the seat warm for Jack, who the Ambassador was beginning to suspect was the real political guy here, the real son-in-waiting. Joe Jr. didn't care about that either. If they would just leave him alone, he could put it together. Sure he could. That was the plan.

Oddly, it was LBJ who took him out of this recursive brooding, this spiteful hammering at his history, the infinite and repeated measure of the betrayals which had become his post-presidential lot and now seemed in the wake of the Ambassador's unavailability, JFK's implacability, Bobby's invisibility, to be his complete fate. LBJ had turned him up at the secret apartment and had invited him over to Blair House for a confidential talk, just a courtesy he hoped he would get from the ex-President in hope of his continued support. That was LBJ for you, still maneuvering around, even when the maneuvering was unnecessary and made him look silly. But he couldn't get off the can. All right with me, Joe Jr. said. He told his Secret Service to take the afternoon off and went over on his own. No one seemed to care. Security had really been so lax with the ex-President for years that it was almost as if they had wanted him to get taken down, just end the whole problem. LBJ was full of courtesies, of winks and nods, of little pats on the hand and flourishes with the bottle of Jack Daniel's which he insisted Joe Jr. partake. I hope, LBJ said, that I can persuade *you* to put my name in nomination. It would be a great honor.

I don't know, Joe said, I haven't thought about it.

A *serious* honor, LBJ said. Or you can be a second if that's all you want. Anything you say. It would be a great unifying gesture.

I haven't thought about it, Joe said. I'm still in shock. I just haven't worked this out.

Yes, LBJ said, it is sure a shock. That is a boy of many surprises, our Jack, isn't he? He is one surprising boy in good times and bad. But certainly a good-looking boy and a *great* President. I hope that I can honor him in succession.

That was LBJ. Blair House, the sitting room, no one

there, Claudia knocking around somewhere upstairs, the staff dismissed or in hiding for the afternoon, an audience of one, then, and LBJ was still making speeches. You had to give him all kinds of credit, he never stopped. But wasn't that the Ambassador's lesson? You couldn't let go, you couldn't let down, not even once, because then you got led into bad habits and soon it would all unravel. So LBJ was still working the territory, audience of one, audience of a thousand, it was all the same. Still, Joe *was* the ex-President, that should count for something. So maybe he was an audience of a thousand.

Tell me, LBJ said. His cunning features, those of a hound, became even more shrewd, he leaned toward Joe. Fifty-five years old, he had the sudden, frightening ingenuousness of the thirteen-year-old kid in the schoolyard saying to the first grader, I sure could use your lunch money now, so why don't you pass it over? Why did he do it? LBJ said. What does he have up his sleeve?

I don't know, Joe said. I really don't know.

You talked to him. He had you in there the day after he did it, the day after he told me and Bobby what he was going to do. He must have told you something. What is the plan? Is he straight on this?

As far as I know.

Why would he ditch Bobby? Did Bobby do something bad? LBJ said, nudging Joe's elbow. Was that it, was it some kind of get-even, or to protect him? Because I've got to know that. If something comes out when I'm running, in mid-campaign, I ought to know that now. Why would he ditch his own brother?

I can't answer that, Joe said. I don't think there's anything bad, though. I just think maybe that he's had enough.

Who's had enough? The President?

JFK, Joe said. He's had enough of this. Maybe he wants to break the line, you know? My father—

Oh, that Ambassador is something, LBJ said, he is really

something. Fighting back from a stroke and all that. Still as stubborn as they come, a real guy. One of my favorite people. He paused. You say Jack has had enough of him?

Maybe, Joe said. Maybe that's it. I can't be sure. You have to draw a line somewhere. Maybe Jack has drawn that line.

I don't know, LBJ said. It's too deep for me, I'm just a simple son of the South, a man's man, a drinking derby of one. He lifted the glass. I sure would appreciate your support though, he said. And that's a fact. Your support would be very important to me. The Kennedys *are* this country, you know that, don't you?

Oh, I hope not, Joe said. I hope that's not the case.

But it's true. Sure you boys are. You put it together. You're in the movie magazines and the newspapers, you're on television and you're a soap opera too. You *are* America. A poor Southern boy like me, he hardly has a chance to get his name in nomination these days. Which is why Jack astounds me, why I can't figure this out.

Don't ask me, Joe said, I am the ex-President. If I could figure things out I would be in a different condition.

LBJ put a hand on his wrist. He wouldn't double-cross me, would he? he said. That's what I want to know. This isn't some slick maneuver, is it, and at the convention Bobby storms it and looks like an opposition candidate when it's really you all the same? That would be a bad business.

Joe shrugged. I don't know, he said, I'm out of all this. It's just headlines and memories to me now.

That stuff with Cuba, LBJ said, that was a pisser. I thought that Bobby was going to shit, I swear. I thought he was going to have a fit right in that office. But the guy went along with the plan in the end, didn't he? He fell into line. You boys, you all fall into line with each other, no matter how it seems. That's family, right?

Joe put down the glass, shook it, watched the ice revolve. Maybe, he said. I tell you, I don't know. You have me up here for a special reason, to pump me for information, and I tell you I can't give you what you want. I'm going to go now, I'm going to pack it in. Maybe you'll hear from me later.

A nomination would be a good thing, LBJ said. And there would be something in it for you. How would you like to be Secretary of State? How about that? Or UN ambassador? I've had enough of Adlai, I think, we all have. Or how would you like to be your old man and go to the Court of St. James's? You'd be the first ex-President to do some real government service. Why don't you think about it? You're a young man, younger than I, you still got it all ahead of you. We can work out something.

That was it. That was LBJ. He could always work out something, that was the way he saw life, everyone was stumbling around, looking to have an angle or to enact one, and Joe was just part of the party. Any man could be bought, any man could be sold. By all rights of experience, LBJ was on the ball, that was the way it happened. I don't know, Joe said, I'll think about it. We can talk about it next year. It's a long way to the convention.

It's going to be Atlantic City, LBJ said. That's where I want it. Jack said it was my choice and that's it.

Sure, Joe said, sure. There had to be a way out of Blair House. He had been over when he was in office a few times, Sparkman had shown him the corridors and hallways, he ought to remember. Sparkman was good at getting out of Blair House and so was he. He walked. LBJ sat on the chair at attention, his hands folded, peering at him brightly, letting him go unescorted. That was LBJ. Ferally alert, right through to the very end. It got you a reputation and you had to eat a lot of shit along the way, but at the end you were around all right, and there to pick up the pieces. All of the pieces. So much for the succession. Joe snapped back, came away from the parapet, looked no more at the imponderable, unspeakable future, felt himself hurled again and again into the hard wall of the past.

Somewhere back there were the conditions which if only understood could have changed all of this, even yet. Or so he thought. But you never knew. You never knew.

8/28/46 In the stone house at Hyannisport, Joe Jr. had sat with the girl, Rhoda, through the early afternoon and talked, talked through the soft dwindling light curling in the windows and into the early dark. They had made love through the morning, past stupor and into that high, fine, dense place which Joe had known only a few times in his life, most of them at high altitude and in dread of imminent death, but this was different. They had only known each other for three days but the connection was there, even a sense of possibility. The campaign was going all right, it was more than a safe seat, it was so easy that even the old man had slacked off on him and had allowed him to take a few days off for what the old man called with a smile, *rejuvenation*. The big push would begin right after Labor Day, but now there was some time for Rhoda. She was pretty in an unconventional, Wellesley-girl kind of way, the body wasn't much but she knew how to use it, and beyond that there was something else, something which touched Joe and showed him parts of himself which he had never been convinced were quite there. Knowing that they were there would have been too risky, dangerous maybe, but in this late August the Congressman-to-be didn't care. Rhoda was a secretary at the Worcester office, detailed to be on the road, just filling in the summer after college while she made decisions about her life, she said, but Joe suspected that she didn't much care either. Not caring was precious, there was so little of it in life and even then Joe must have known that it would never be happening for him again, that this was a weekend knocked out of eternity.

I don't understand, she said to him, I don't understand what it is with you boys. Young men. The three of you. I mean I haven't met Eddie yet, but it's probably the four of you. What is it with you and your father?

I don't know, Joe said. I don't know what you're asking.

I've seen how you talk about him. I've seen how you act when he comes to headquarters or gets up on that rostrum with you, I've watched Jack's face, and Bobby's too. You're afraid of him, aren't you? He really scares you, all of you, very badly.

This is not the way to make points with the Congressman, Joe said. You are not playing your cards right if you are looking for my heart.

I'm not looking for your heart, Rhoda said. She held his hand, looked at him with much intensity. I'm looking for *you*, don't you know that? I'm trying to find you, Joe, I'm trying to help us both see who you are. You were in the war, you flew planes, dropped bombs, you were a hero. Jack did Navy duty. Bobby didn't do much of anything but that wasn't his fault, the two of you boys though were out there making the world free for democracy. What does he have over you?

It's not fear, exactly, Joe said. It's not that. The Ambassador— He paused. The Ambassador is a very strong man. He is very insistent. He has big plans and has had them for a long time. Sometimes it is just easier to get out of the way and let him have his plans, you know? It is not worth opposing him.

This makes no sense at all, she said. You know that you're not a coward. So why are you acting like one? You saved the world for him, Joe. So why do you want to please him so? What is there about him that he holds over you?

Plans, Joe said. He has large plans. It's hard to explain. It's hard for anyone outside of the family to understand—

That's bullshit, she said and smiled at him when she saw him twitch. Bullshit, she said again. You don't have to be in the family to figure out what he has in mind. He wants you to be President. The first Catholic President.

Primogenitor, because you're the oldest. Then Jack. Then
Bobby. Then for all I know, Edward. One, two, three, four.
Those are his plans. He's always had them, from the time
his sons were born. He would have drowned his daughters if Rose hadn't taken on the responsibility for them.
Am I shocking you, Joe? You know it's the truth. Anyone
can see it. You talk of his big plans as if it's some kind
of sacred secret, but the fact is that everyone knows it. So
why don't you admit it and decide if you want to play or
not? You don't have to play, you know. You can go off
and have a nice life. She squeezed his hand. You're good-
looking. You've got lots of money, even if he cuts you off
you can make your way. You're not dumb. You can go
and be a professor of history.

That's Jack's ambition, Joe said. Not mine. But Jack's
not going to make that either.

So what's yours? Rhoda said. What do you want, Joe?

Congress, he said, I want to go to Congress.

No you don't.

Sure I do. It will keep me off the streets.

Then the Senate? The Governor's chair? The presidency? You want that, Joe? Is the whole package set with
Jack behind you?

He shrugged. I don't want to talk about it any more, he
said. You're supposed to be helping with the campaign,
not asking questions. You're very pretty, he said. When
the light catches you in a certain way—

Blarney will get you everywhere, she said. But you've
already been into the sacred trust. I think you have something to think about, she said. I think that you've got
some very serious thoughts ahead of you. Because this
isn't what you want, Joe, and it's not too late to pull out.

How do you know what I want?

I don't. But I know what you *don't* want and that's it.
Let Jack have it, she said. He'd have taken your place
anyway if something had gone wrong. If you had been

killed overseas, Jack would have been doing what you are right now. He will anyway. So you can get out of this.

You're persuasive, Joe said, pretty and persuasive. But I don't think you understand. There are centuries of family history here, generations of ignorance and slight, the Ambassador and all his forebears working—

I'm not interested in that, she said, I'm interested in *you*. I haven't been fucking the Ambassador or Jack all night and all morning, it's been you. You're the one I care about and I want you to see, want you to know—

He put a hand on her lips. All right, he said. I understand you. It's enough. I understand what you're trying to say. You don't have to say any more.

But you won't change, she said, will you? One pretty girl in one afternoon isn't going to make any difference at all. All those centuries of family history, generations of ignorance and slight, the Ambassador and his forebears working—

You got me, he said, let's go to bed. Let's make love. I want to see you. I want to enter you, I want to know—

She stared at him, her eyes round and full. In the stone house at Hyannis in that moment, he felt that he could have touched all the deepest parts of her. Maybe, he said. I don't know. I'll think about it. It's too much to think about. Maybe we have a chance, he said. You don't know where you're heading, what this has been, what has become of us. I can only tell you that there's more here than you can know. But we could try—

She put her arms around him. All right, she said, we won't talk any more. We won't say anything more now. I could love you. I don't love you. Maybe I do love you. I just don't know, can you see? We don't know what we are, we have to *dig* for it. You have to go inside, you have to understand.

Yes, he said, yes, we'll try, we'll try to go inside, and in the light and shadow they had come together in that room, not even leaving for the bedroom, and there had been that night and part of the next day too, and then Rhoda had left because her parents would want to know where she had been all these days and she had still been living at home. Then came Worcester and Boston and the tumult of the campaign resumed; it was not as if they simply fell apart, it was not that simple. They saw each other again and they almost came that close again several times, but as October went into November and then past the election and into the plans which had to be made for Washington it became clear to both of them, maybe Rhoda before Joe, that nothing was going to change, that he wasn't going to get out, not then or ever, that he was going to have to follow it through to the end and there was no room for her because she would have been part of the furniture. I think I'll always love you, she said. I don't think I'll ever marry. Me too, he said, me too, Rhoda, but that had all been what she would have called bullshit; Joe was the sincere one, Joe was the one who had never married (he sure had fucked around, though) but Rhoda was hooked up with a professor of economics in less than six months from their parting, went to UCLA with him, had four sons, a nice bit of collusion there, and had died at forty in San Bernardino in a crazy flood that had washed out a campground and drowned her and the oldest boy. So much for that. The stone house at Hyannis, the pinwheels of light, the soft sounds of her against him and the rising too, and then the end of it as they fell and fell and it was not Rhoda but his condition which embraced Joe as he lay there gasping by the cold fireplace, staring at the crazed and absolute configurations of his life. You kept on going, that was all, followed it through, and then on the beach at Hyannis or in the campgrounds at San Bernardino the waters came, the waters always came and they would take you. Take you up, take you down, take you to the castle of your life. Portraits of the Ambassador hung at every angle in every room, glinting, glinting with their spectral knowledge and absolute pity.

* * *

11/22/63 Joe checks the stock again of the M-l, feeling
it cold and solid in his hands, the trigger a little rigid but
it will yield in the clutch, he is sure. The trigger feels a
little bit like a clitoris against his index finger, he will
jiggle it a little, then take a firm grip and make the rifle
come. The thought of this, the analogy, makes Joe giggle
a little and there is a strange, whirring moment of descent
in which he wonders if he is really losing control, if this
act is truly as crazy as it might seem from the outside.
All of his life, he now sees, he has been surrounded by
ordnance, by gleaming machinery of one description or
another, the planes carrying him like an embryo in their
thin, shaking, gusty surfaces, then later in the open cars
and closed offices of politics, the experiments with hunting and high-caliber bullets which he had carried on at
Hyannisport over the weekends, just as a means of getting
away, then the years after the Presidency running around
the country in high-speed machines, sometimes with the
Secret Service in tow, more often not, tracking the highways of his doom, watching America stream by him. In
Las Vegas for a while in the late fifties there had been
some real peace, hurling himself against the distant to-
talizers, the green felt of the craps table, the roulette
wheel, feeling himself dispersed in these arenas of chance,
and in that machinery he had found for the first time
since Rhoda the beginnings of a frail if illusory sense of
himself . . . but that too had ended, Bobby had passed the
word, Las Vegas was just too touchy, mob-infested, in
the hands of the racketeers and it wouldn't look good if the
oldest son and the ex-President were seen at the gaming
tables, even if he was surrounded by Federal protection.

Worse if he were surrounded by Federal protection,
Bobby had said, because that made the government look
like collaborators, made it look as if they were granting
special prerogatives to the gangsters. Joe had made something of an issue of it, had even humiliatingly pleaded,

but Bobby had been firm, it wouldn't work out. He had to quit. At last the Ambassador himself had brought the word to Joe in a late-night phone call. They weren't talking much in those years, reconciliation had come later if at all, but the Ambassador made the call a special issue. You're entitled to some pleasure, maybe, the Ambassador had said, but you're fucking up things for everybody, Junior. So bury it. Come back East and play the horses at Bowie and Laurel with Hoover, but stay the fuck out of that Mafia trap. And that had been the end for him, he had never gone back since.

But the machinery had persisted, even to this moment when he cradled the M-1 and looked at its dull surfaces, feeling the power humming in the stock, feeling in his wrists the arc of the bullet which would tear off his brother's head. Reconciliation had come later if at all, that was true, but in a way *this* was reconciliation right now, he would be performing the one last great service for the Ambassador that no one else could have conceived, and that service would change everything.

See, you old bastard, I loved you all the time. I gave up everything for you because it was in you that I would find myself and that is what I have, Father, don't you see?

He didn't have to peer into the distance now, the motorcade was visible, clearly within the arc of his vision, it would be only a little while now. In the meantime, Joe Jr. thought, there was absolutely nothing to do but to stay calm, stay crouched amidst the cartons, let it happen. The worst thing would be to lose control now, to become emotional, to begin to think about it. The thinking had all been done. He had blamed the Ambassador for everything back then, had really fixated upon the Ambassador as being—how foolish, how stupid!—the force which destroyed his life, but then he had learned better, had come to understand that he who bore his name was if anything the Ambassador's greatest creation and now he would have to break the President to prove this to all of them.

In the end it all came simple, it was far less complex than anyone thought, one fine line carried through it all, and you simply had to follow that arc. The best part of being Throttlebottom was that you could put on a uniform and lead a guided tour and no one would notice, no one at all. Joe Jr. began to hum, hummed a little *marche militaire* in a cracked and insouciant tenor, waiting, waiting now for the cars to come. Getting out quickly, out the back way, that was going to be a tricky business. But he would work on it in due time.

11/22/55   Joe had gone ahead with everything up to that point. The Ambassador wanted to stock the cabinet with Massachusetts pols, that was okay with him; he wanted JFK in at HEW even with the nepotism angle, and that was okay too. He had a certain agenda, the Ambassador, and the best thing to do was to go along with it, otherwise he would take to reminding you of exactly who you were and how you had gotten there and what could be next.

So even putting McCarthy in at State, Joe had gone along with it. That had been the real shocker and he had taken plenty for that; it had looked in the beginning as if it would tear the party apart. But the Ambassador had been insistent. I want this and that's the way it's going to be, he said to Joe. Handle it any way you want, take it to the press, make any goddamned liberal excuse you want, but Tail-Gunner Joe is *in* there and that's the way it's going to be. What about the eighty-seven Communists he can't produce? Joe had asked mildly. What about that faked Tydings photograph? What about the loyalty oaths and that joke committee? The Ambassador had shrugged. That's all politics, he said, that's for show. The real thing is that I want him in there. He's an old friend and a good guy and we can keep an eye on him better there than in the Senate. Listen here, the Ambassador had said and maybe he was telling the truth, that was the thing about the old man, he could lie and lie and lie and then he'd pull something on you which was absolutely the truth and if you ignored it you could really get in trouble, would you rather have that guy over at State where we can keep an eye on him and control him all the time? Or do you want him in the Senate, skulking around with Nixon, making plans and working against us every minute? You'll see how much sense this makes.

Joe had seen it all right, had known what was going to come on him when he made the announcement, the best thing to do was to announce the Cabinet in a bunch in mid-December right around the tree-lighting ceremonies and kind of *sneak* McCarthy into the back of the pictures and hope that they could get away with it, but that of course wasn't the way it really worked out. The press had been too scared of Tail-Gunner Joe to really make a big issue of it, that had been left for Truman, who went half-crazy back in Independence, and to Alger Hiss, but they had certainly made it the story of the day, then the week. Handle it any way you want, the Ambassador had said, so Joe did just that, went on the radio the day after Christmas to talk about the New Unity Coalition which would come out of Tail-Gunner Joe being brought to State, even let the Tail-Gunner join him in the last ten minutes to make his own unity statement, and it seemed for a while as if it actually was going to work out. McCarthy liked his drinks and his boyfriends in secret and his prerogatives and really wasn't as much of a danger as everyone thought, the Ambassador had been quite right there, but then the situation had started to get really nasty when McCarthy all on his own decided to reconvene Un-American Activities and go after a whole flock of homosexuals and Communists who he said had been part of the old China group for years. A hundred were pitched out in October of 1955 in the first wave, and then Tail-Gunner Joe had taken some advice from Nixon and had gone on television, shaking his fists and crying and saying that he was standing up for an administration which was too cowed, just too scared to really face up to the degree of corruption, but the penalties had to be paid. Then Mc-Carthy had spoken about how the H-bomb plans had been shipped out to China and maybe the Soviet satellites by some of these hundred people and it might be too goddamned late to save security, they might have to deal with the possibility of a preventive strike against Peking, and looking at the shouting figure on television, looking at the grays and blues of the Secretary of State who was clearly drunker than he had ever been and absolutely out of control, Joe Jr., the President, had seen that he was going to take whatever risks were entailed, wherever they led, and he had fired the Secretary. Had simply called in Sorenson and told him to get the announcement out immediately and then had phoned the UPI himself at midnight to break the word. This is intolerable, the President had said. McCarthy does not speak for this administration, he speaks for no one. He was an attempt at a coalition which simply went wrong and he is out. Then he had gone to bed, alone as always, with the first solidity of conviction he had felt in more than a decade and had waited for all of it to sweep over him.

It had been even worse than he had thought it might be because McCarthy did not make a frontal attack, he sent up Cohn first and then Harriman (how he got Harriman to front for him was something that Joe could not figure out) and then amazingly Adlai had made a call and said that this was simply too extreme, that perhaps some compromise could be worked out. McCarthy might say that he had overstated the preventive strike issue and felt that the warning alone was sufficient. No, Joe said to the old trimmer, the Governor of Illinois who he had beaten back like a crutch at that rigged 1952 convention, there's no compromise. He's out. He is out as of thirty-six hours ago. He is crazy, Adlai, and I am crazy if I keep him. You don't understand the stakes, Adlai had said, and Joe understood then and only at that moment that Adlai was bought too, that Adlai was bent over and Tail-Gunner Joe had him cold. Adlai was a liberal who had spent his whole life waiting to be buggered and Tail-Gunner Joe had seen it and somehow done the job. It was the first insight the President had ever had which he thought might be worthy of his old man, the Ambassador, which he thought the old man might really have liked and respected, but of course it was too late for gaining respect that way.

At last McCarthy himself had come up alone, his eyes bloodshot, his head tilted, the scent of alcohol and frenzy coming off him, and something else, some deeper odor which Joe could not identify but which he knew was profound. Tail-Gunner Joe had already known that it was over, though. I'm not finished yet, he said. I'm not finished with you yet, Boston. There's plenty more to be said here. You aren't going to fuck with me like this. I came over to your side, gave you the advantage for years because I am a great American, but I see you for what you are now. You're part of them.

A Communist too, Joe said, is that what you're saying?

Never mind what I'm saying, McCarthy had said, you just remember that you're going to go down on this one.

If anyone crosses you he's a Communist, Joe said mildly. It played for a long time and it's probably going to still play, but I can't tolerate it at this level, Senator. The Chinese don't understand our politics, you understand, they don't know that it's all a game you're playing. They and the Russians are likely to do something which might go out of control and that's why you have to go. So you're gone. Except that you won't go easy. So go hard, but go away before I call the Secret Service and have you thrown out by all the powers of the office I have been given. I don't know how deep you're into all of this but I don't think you can compromise the Secret Service, at least not yet. Get out, he had said. Get out, you stinking, evil son of a bitch, go back to your boys and your press conferences and your glory holes but get the hell out of this White House right now and never come back.

So McCarthy had gone away then, something in Joe's face, certainly not the tone of his voice which was quiet, even choked, must have gotten through to him, but that wasn't the end of it, the Ambassador was up there in two hours, coming right in past Sorenson, past JFK, who was sitting with him, trying to calm Joe down. Get out of here, the Ambassador said to Jack and Jack got up and went, no argument, no response, just cleared out. That was the way it was done. The Ambassador closed the door and turned to the President. Just what the fuck do you think you're doing, he said, what is going on here? I want that man back, you understand. I want him back in office. I don't care how you handle it, a full retraction, a press conference, an arms-around-each-other bit, that's up to you. But you are not going to get this one by me. I have given you a lot of latitude, Junior, but I am not going to give you this one. The Tail-Gunner comes back.

No, Joe said. He's not coming back.

Must I—

No, Joe said. I have given in to you all the way. I have let you have one thing and the other thing, I have gone along with you from the first, I have given you primogeniture and the Presidency and I have not fucked with you, but you are not getting this one. McCarthy is out. He is not coming back. I will stand in the door of State before he ever comes back. I will go to the well of the Senate, I will make a joint session of Congress to hear an address, but he is out. I will get Hoover to release everything from every file on this guy if I have to, but he is *out* and he is not coming back. He will have us all in flames, don't you understand that? He will have a bomb put in Times Square and another in the Rose Garden here. Joe looked at the Ambassador, felt the tears hopelessly come to him. Dad, he said, he's crazy, don't you see that? He had not called the Ambassador Dad in twenty years, it shocked both of them. He wants us all dead for his own advantage, Joe said. That's the truth and you know it. It has to stop.

But it can't, the Ambassador said, it can't because I won't have it. Because I *said* so—

What you say goes almost all the time, Joe said, but it doesn't go this time and that's all. I will be impeached for it if necessary, but it ends here. McCarthy is out. Please, Dad, leave now. I won't throw you out, I can't do this to you, you're my father so I'm begging, but I want you to leave.

All right, the Ambassador said. He sat convulsively, took off his glasses, wiped them, stared at Joe. All right, he said, you'll make it stick. I can see that. You are that serious, you fool. You will stake everything on getting him out.

Yes I will. I must.

Then *you're* finished, the Ambassador said. Don't you understand that? You're all done for. I'll close the books on you. You're a one-term President.

I can't be concerned about that, Dad, Joe said. That's not the issue. The issue is—

The issue is that you can't give me this one. All right then, but it cuts the other way too. *I* can't give you this one either. You're finished, Joe. Jack is the next President. You're getting out. Ill health, inability to govern. You're going to pass it on to your brother, the Secretary of Health, Education and Welfare. You've got enough clout in the party to do it, you're the President. That's what is going to happen.

And if I don't? Joe said, what's going to happen then?

You will, the Ambassador said. He put on his glasses, stared precisely at Joe, rubbed his hands. You can make it hard or you can make it easy, it's up to you. I'll destroy you, Joe. If I have to I'll finish you off. So just get out. Make your announcement tomorrow. Otherwise—

Otherwise what?

Otherwise people are going to start to die, the Ambassador said. Maybe a housewife and college professor in San Bernardino for starters, maybe some other people. I'm not playing around, Joe.

Joe stared at him, swallowed, said nothing at all for a while. He tried to keep his mind blank. That was a trick his father had taught him long, long ago, if they hurt you, if you find yourself really bleeding, just shut up, keep your mind blank as a screen, allow them absolutely nothing. That was the only way to handle it until you got control again.

All right, Joe said, say I do it. Then what? Jack becomes President if he wins the election—

He wins the election, the Ambassador said. Don't you worry about that. He wins the election just like *you* won the election. We'll make sure of that. That's my department as of right now because *you*, Joe, you are finished. The election will be taken care of.

And so McCarthy gets back in at State, Joe said, so you'll reverse everything I've done here. I can't go along with that. You can take me down but I'll take you down too. Jack as well. You'll all go down, but McCarthy is never going to make a speech about preventive war again.

Okay, the Ambassador said. His glasses glinted, flashed in the light. No McCarthy. That's the deal. He won't be coming back. We'll keep him out.

And you say—

That's my word, the Ambassador said. You'll have to trust me just like I trusted you and got betrayed. Except that I won't betray you. McCarthy won't be Secretary of State.

Or Jenner, Joe said. Or Capehart. Or those swine McCarthy runs around with, I want them out too. That's the deal then. You make that pledge and I'll go quietly. Otherwise—

Otherwise you'll take us all down, the Ambassador said. Except you won't, you won't do that. Because you're a Kennedy, Joe, and that's part of the deal, the family first.

He limped toward the door. I want an announcement within forty-eight hours, he said. You can go on television live or call the press or sneak it out to the UPI the way you did the firing. That's up to you. But I want that forty-eight-hour business and that's all there is to it, you hear me? That is very definite.

And if not—?

We've been through that, Joe, the Ambassador said. We don't have to go through it again, do we? He opened the door, nodded at the Secret Service.

I'm your *son*! Joe wanted to shout, I'm your first-born *son*, how can you do this to me? If the door had been closed, if the Ambassador had still been there, he might have done that. But of course the Ambassador was too clever, he was gone already and he knew that the President wasn't going to make that kind of a scene in front of the security. So Joe just sat there, the way the Ambassador had known he must and after a while Jack drifted back in again from the side room where he had heard everything and they just stared at each other. There was absolutely nothing to say. This was another of those times, and there had been plenty in their lives where there was just not one brotherly word that could be passed.

Oh, the Ambassador had been angry at him! Joe had thought that it was irreparable. But of course as the years passed things cooled off. McCarthy died of drink not much later, meaning that he wouldn't have been around much longer anyway, and JFK had turned out in the long run to be an even bigger betrayer in office than Joe had been, in the estimation of the old man. And Joe had come to see after this one great confrontation that the old man had probably been right after all, McCarthy was just red meat for the troops, and backed off China and the Soviet Union with terror so that deals could have been made. Joe in any case never took issue with the Ambassador again; one way or the other that confrontation had been the end for him.

And here in Dallas at last and at least he could come back *all* the way, perform this one great service for the stricken, nurse-fucking, raunchy, devoted old Ambassador who had in the end proven in this circumstance as in so many others to have been absolutely right.

Son of a bitch, JFK had said in the Oval Office that afternoon, son of a bitch, I'm going to be President. Not even a thought of protest or uncertainty, that was how thoroughly the Ambassador had controlled them all. The fucking President, oh my God, I'm the next President.

Well, you'll love it, Joe said, you'll love the perks anyway. There are lots of interesting possibilities in this job.

I wonder if I should get married after all, Jack said, maybe this isn't the time to do it with the campaign coming up and all. Maybe I should wait.

Jackie won't let you wait, Joe had said, she's going to be First Lady now and no one is going to give that up. Except Rhoda, he thought, but that was another wench in another time and so dead, so dead to me. You might as well go ahead and have a big wedding, Joe had said. The voters will love that.

They had, they did, and Jack stormed in over Nixon with 472 electoral votes and Kefauver clinging onto him on the inaugural stand, holding him even tighter than Jackie. Joe Jr.'s instincts had always been good, even if his luck hadn't. One way or the other, the Ambassador had made him a first-class political animal.

A humble one too, and eager to get back under the umbrella. The real betrayal then had been JFK. JFK had broken the line.

11/22/63 The sounds of the motorcade drifting to his high seat in the depository, the sound of the crowd seeming to envelop him, Joe lifts the stock, sets the sight, puts the scope to the curly, tousled head of his brother, seeing the faint pink of Jacqueline's suit refracting an aura, takes off the safety then. With a precision he had never known to be within him, Joe sets the sight, aims the rifle and fires. The first shot is in the throat, Jack falls back, Joe can imagine the look of terror and surprise on his face. Second shot ... he cocks it again. Jackie is starting to scramble, casting wistful, hopeless glances over the back of the limousine. Joe puts the killing shot in, the shot that will come through the Governor's knee, enter Jack's head at a high angle and windage and blow off the skull. Bobby will storm the citadel in a wave of national horror and sympathy which will utterly repudiate the crude, the untalented JFK. For every plan there is another plan. Joe knows this. The Ambassador after all was absolutely right, there was *always* that alternative.

Giggling, Joe Kennedy, Jr. puts down the rifle, lurches for the door, yanks open the door and speeds down the steps toward the open air, leaving the concerns of the motorcade to the Secret Service and to Parkland Hospital. Later that afternoon the ex-President will be found cowering in a movie theater and later yet he will be taken away in what must be the most sensational story in all of American politics, but he will never tell. He will never tell. He will never tell. Only the Ambassador, should the Ambassador come to see him, he will tell the Ambassador everything. *Everything.* But that is a part of the saga, Joe Jr., assassin of the thirty-fifth President knows, which will have to be told by other than him. His time is done.

He wonders what Rhoda might have known.

The policeman, curious, sees him running and comes toward him. The rifle is back on the sixth floor but Joe still has the .38-caliber Smith & Wesson.

Would Rhoda have made any difference?

Flatly, the policeman comes toward him, then shouting.

Joe reaches for the gun.

David Gerrold is the author of *When Harlie Was One*, *The Man Who Folded Himself*, and numerous other books and short stories. But he is also a scriptwriter, and perhaps his most famous script is "The Trouble With Tribbles," which according to Paramount was the single most popular *Star Trek* episode in history.

Why do I mention that particular script/

There's a reason.

I suggested to David that his Hollywood background made him uniquely qualified to write a story in which a widowed Joe Kennedy actually married his mistress, film star Gloria Swanson, and moved his boys out to the West Coast. David agreed to give it a shot, and turned in a totally off-the-wall story that only he, by virtue of his experience, was capable of writing.

The Kennedy Enterprise
by David Gerrold

—Is that thing on? Good. Okay, go ahead. What do you want to know?

Kennedy, huh? Why is it always Kennedy? All this nostalgia for the fifties and the sixties. You guys are missing the point. There were so many better actors, and nobody remembers them anymore. That's the real crime—that Kennedy should get all the attention—but the guys who made him look so good are all passed over and forgotten. Why don't you jackals ever come around asking whatever happened to Bill Shatner or Jeffrey Hunter—?

Ahhh, besides, Kennedy's been done to death. Everybody does Kennedy. Because he's easy to do. But lemme tell you something, sonny. Kennedy wasn't really the sixties—uh-uh. He's just a convenient symbol. The sixties were a lot bigger than just another fading TV star.

Yeah, that's right. His glory days were over. He was on his way out. You're surprised to hear that, aren't you?

Look. I'll tell you something. Kennedy was not a good actor. In fact, he was goddamn lousy. He couldn't act his way out of a pay toilet if he'd had Charlton Heston in there to help him.

But—it didn't matter, did it? Hell, acting ability is the *last* thing in the world a movie star needs. It never slowed down what's'isname, Ronald Reagan.

Reagan? Oh, you wouldn't remember him. He was way before your time. He was sort of like a right-wing Henry Fonda, only he never got the kind of parts where he could inspire an audience. That's what you need to make it— one good part where you make the audience squirm or cry or leap from their seats, shouting. Anything to make them remember you longer than the time it takes to get out to the parking lot. But Reagan never really got any of those. He was just another poor schmuck eaten up by the system. A very sad story, really.

Yeah, I know. You want to hear about Kennedy. Uh-uh. Lemme tell you about Reagan first. So you'll see how easy it is to just disappear—and how much of a fluke it is to succeed.

See, Reagan wasn't stupid. He was one of the few wartime actors who actually made a successful transition into television. He was smart enough to be a host instead of a star—that way he didn't get himself typecast as a cowboy or a detective or a doctor. Reagan was a pretty good pitchman for General Electric on their Sunday night show and then— Wait a minute, lemme see now, sometime in there, he got himself elected president of the Screen Actors Guild and that's when all the trouble started—there was some uproar with the House Committee on Un-American Activities, and the blacklist and the way he sold out his colleagues. I don't really know the details, you can look it up. Anyway, tempers were hot, that's all you need to know, and Reagan got himself impeached, almost thrown out of his own Guild as a result.

Well, nobody wanted to work with him after that. His name was mud. He couldn't get arrested. And it was just tragic—cause he was good, no question about it. Those pictures he did with the monkey were hysterical—oh, yeah, he did a whole series of movies at the end of the war. *Bonzo Goes to College, Bonzo Goes to Hollywood, Bonzo Goes to Washington.* Yeah, everybody remembers the chimpanzee, nobody remembers Reagan. Yeah, people in this town only have long memories when there's a grudge attached.

So, Reagan couldn't get work. I mean, not real work. He ended up making B movies. A lot of crap. Stuff even Harry Cohn wouldn't touch. He must have really needed the money. The fifties were all downhill for him.

I remember, he did—oh, what was it?—*Queen of Outer Space* with that Hungarian broad. That was a real waste of film. Then he did some stuff with what's'isname—Ed Wood, remember him? Yeah, that's the one. Anyway, Ronnie's last picture was some piece of *dreck* called *Plan 9 from Outer Space.* Lugosi was supposed to do the part, but he died just before they started filming, so Reagan stepped in. I hear it's real big on the college circuits now. What they call *camp*, where it's so bad, it's funny. Have you seen it? No, neither have I. Too bad, really. No telling what Reagan could have become if he'd just had the right breaks.

Oh, right—you want to talk about Kennedy. But you get my point, don't you? This is a sorry excuse for an industry. There's no *sympatico*, no consideration. Talent is considered a commodity. It gets wasted. People get chewed up just because they're in someone else's way. That's the real story behind Kennedy—the people who got chewed up along the way.

Anyway, what was I saying about Kennedy before I got off the track? You wanna run that thing back? Oh, that's right. Kennedy had no talent. Yeah, you can quote me—what difference does it make? Somebody going to sue me? What're they going to get? My wheelchair? I'll say it again. Kennedy had no talent for acting. Zero. Zilch. *Nada*. What he did have was a considerable talent for self-promotion. He was *great* at that.

And y'know what else? Y'know what else Kennedy had? He had *style*. You don't need talent if you've got style. Mae West proved that. Gable proved that. Bette Davis.

Funny business, movies, television. Any other industry run the same way would go straight into the ground. A movie studio—you make one success, it pays for twenty flops. You have to be crazy to stay with it, y'know.

Okay, okay—back to Kennedy. Well, y'know, to really understand him, you gotta understand his dad. Joe Kennedy was one ambitious son of a bitch. He was smart enough to get his money out of the stock market before '29. He put it into real estate. When everybody else was jumping out of windows, he was picking up pieces all over the place.

He got very active in politics for a while. FDR wanted to send him to England as an ambassador, but the deal fell through—nobody knows why. Maybe his divorce, who knows? Y'know, the Kennedys were Irish-Catholic. It would have been a big scandal. Especially then.

Anyway, it doesn't matter. The story really starts when Joe Sr. brings his boys out to California. He marries Gloria Swanson and starts buying up property and studios and contracts. Next thing you know, his boys are all over the place. They come popping out of USC, one after the other, like Ford Mustangs rolling off an assembly line.

In no time, Joe's a director, Jack's taken up acting, and Bobby ends up running MGM. It's Thalberg all over again. Lemme think. That had to be '55 or '56, somewhere in there. Actually, Teddy was the smart one. He stayed out of the business. He went East, stayed home with his mom, and eventually went into politics where nobody ever heard of him again.

Anyway, you could see that Joe and Bobby were going to make out all right. They were all sonsabitches, but they were good sonsabitches. Joe did his homework, he brought in his pictures on time. Bobby was a ruthless S.O.B., but maybe that's what you need to run a studio. He didn't take any shit from anybody. Remember, he's the guy who told Garland to get it together or get out. And she *did*.

But Jack—Jack was always a problem. Two problems actually.

First of all, he couldn't keep his dick in his pants. Bobby had his hands full keeping the scandal-rags away from his brother. He had to buy off one columnist; he gave him the Rock Hudson story. The jackals had such a good time with that one they forgot all about Jack's little peccadillos in Palm Springs. Sometimes I think Bobby would have killed to protect his brother. Y'know, Hudson lost the lead in *Giant* because of that. They'd already shot two or three weeks of good footage. They junked it all. Nearly shit-canned the whole picture, but Heston jumped in at the last moment and ended up beating out the Dean kid for the Oscar. Like I said, it's a strange business. *Stupid* business.

Sometimes you end up hating the audience for just being the audience. It's not fair, when you think about it. The public wants their heroes to look like they're dashing and romantic and sexy—but they're horrified if they actually behave that way. I mean, could *your* private life stand up to that kind of scrutiny? I'm not sure anybody's could. Hell, the goddamn audience punishes the stars for doing the exact same things they're doing—cheating on their wives, drinking too much, smoking a little weed. If they're going to insist on morality tests for the actors, I think we should start insisting on morality tests for the audience before we let them in the theater. See how they'd like it for a change.

Oh well.

Anyway, the *other* problem was Jack's accent—that goddamn Massachusetts accent. He'd have made a great cowboy, he had the look, he had the build; but he couldn't open his mouth without sounding like a New England lobsterman. I mean, can you imagine Jack Kennedy on a horse or behind a badge—with *that* accent? They brought in the best speech coaches in the world to work with him. A waste of goddamn money. He ended up sounding like Cary Grant with a sinus problem.

You can't believe the parts he didn't get because of his voice. Y'know, at one point Twentieth wanted him for *The Misfits* with Marilyn Monroe—now, that would have been a picture. Can you imagine Kennedy and Monroe? Pure screen magic. But it never happened. His voice again. No, as far as I know, they never even met.

But that was always the problem. Finding the right picture for Jack. George Pal, the Puppetoon guy, gave him his first big break with *War of the Worlds*, over at Paramount, but Jack always hated science fiction. Afraid he'd get typecast. He saw what happened to Karloff and Lugosi. He thought of science fiction as the same kind of stuff.

The funny thing was, the picture was a big hit, but that only made Jack unhappier. He knew the audience had come to see the Martians, not him. That's when he swore, no more science fiction. And yeah, he really did say it, that famous quote: "Never play a scene with animals, children, or Martians. They always use the Martian's best take."

Hitchcock had a good sense of how to use Kennedy, but he only worked with him once. *North by Northwest.* Another big hit. Kennedy loved the film—he loved all that spy stuff, he always wanted to play James Bond—but he didn't like the way Hitchcock treated him. And he made the mistake of saying so to an interviewer. Remember? "Hitch doesn't direct. He herds. He treats his actors like cattle." That remark got back to Hitch, and the old man was terribly hurt by it. So, instead of casting Jack in his next film, he went to Jimmy Stewart. Who knows? Maybe that was best for everybody.

Jack spent nine months sitting on his ass, waiting for the right part. Nothing. Finally, he went to Bobby and said, "Help me get some of the good parts." By now, Bobby was running MGM, and this gave him control over one studio and a lot of bargaining power with all the others— he was the biggest deal-maker in town, buying, selling, trading contracts right and left to put together the right package.

Even so, Bobby still had to twist a lot of arms to get Jack into *The Caine Mutiny.* Van Johnson had already been screen-tested. He'd been fitted for his costumes, everything—suddenly, he's out on his ass and here's Jack Kennedy playing opposite Bogart. I can tell you, a lot of feathers were ruffled. Bogey knew how Jack got the part and he never forgave him for it. But, y'know—it helped the picture. Bogey's resentment of Jack shows up on the screen in every scene. Bogey should have had the Oscar for that one, but Bobby bought it for Jack. There was so much studio pressure on the voting—well, never mind. That's a body best left buried.

Anyway, in return, Bobby asked Jack to help him out with one or two of his problems. And Jack had no choice, but to say yes. See, when Bobby took over MGM, one of the projects about to shoot was a thing called *Forbidden*

Planet. Shakespeare in outer space. Dumb idea, right? That's what everybody thought, at the time. They couldn't cast it.

They were having real trouble finding a male lead, and they were about to go with ... oh, let me think. Oh, I don't remember his name. He ended up doing a cop show on ABC. Oh, here's a funny. At one point, they were even considering Ronald Reagan for the lead. Very strongly. But they finally passed on him—I guess Bobby remembered the McCarthy business. And that's why Reagan went and did *Queen of Outer Space*. Never mind, it doesn't matter. Bobby finally asked Jack to play the captain of the spaceship.

And I gotta tell you. Jack didn't want to do it—more of that science fiction crap, right?—but he couldn't very well say no, could he? So he goes ahead and does it. Bobby retitles the picture *The New Frontier*. And guess what? It's the studio's biggest grossing picture for the year. Go figure. But everybody's happy.

After that, Jack had a couple of rough years. One disaster after another. The biggest one was that goddamned musical. That was an embarrassment. The man should never have tried to sing. Even today, nobody can mention *Camelot* without thinking of Jack Kennedy, right? And those stupid tights.

You want my opinion, stay out of tights. Your career will never recover. It was all downhill for Errol Flynn after *Robin Hood* and the goddamned tights killed poor George Reeves. *Superman*'s another one of those unproducible properties. Nobody's ever going to make that one work. Or *Batman*. Tights. That's why.

Anyway, back to Kennedy—his career was in the dumper. So, when he was offered the chance to do a TV series, it didn't look so bad anymore. Most of the real action in town was moving to TV anyway. So Jack went over to Desilu and played Eliot Ness in *The Untouchables*. Y'know, that was one of J. Edgar Hoover's favorite shows.

Hoover even wrote to Kennedy and asked him for his autograph. He visited the set once just so he could get his picture taken with Jack. Hoover had to stand on a box. They shot him from the waist up, so's you'd never know, but the photographer managed to get one good long shot.

Meanwhile, back over at MGM, Bobby's looking at all the money that Warner Brothers and Desilu are making off TV and he's thinking—there's gotta be a way that he can cut himself a slice of that market, right? Right. So he starts looking around the lot to see what he's got that can be exploited.

Well, *Father Knows Best* is a big hit, so Bobby thinks, let's try turning *Andy Hardy* into a TV series. And how about *Dr. Kildare* too? The Hardy thing flopped. Bad casting. And it was opposite Disney on Sundays. It didn't have a chance. But the Kildare property caught well enough to encourage him to try again.

So, Bobby Kennedy's looking around, right? And here's where all the pieces come together all at once. NBC says to him, "How about a science fiction series? You did that *New Frontier* thing. Why don't you turn that into a TV series for us?"

There's this other series that's just winding down—a war series called *The Lieutenant*—Bobby calls in the producer, a guy named Roddenberry, and tells him that NBC wants a sci-fi show based on *The New Frontier*. Can he make it work? They've still got all the costumes, the sets, the miniatures, everything. Roddenberry says he doesn't know anything about science fiction, but he'll give it a try. He tells his secretary to rush out and buy up every science fiction anthology she can find and do summaries of all the stories that have spaceships in them.

What with one thing and another, it's 1964 before they ever start filming the first pilot. But all the MGM magic is applied, and they end up with one of the most beautiful—and most *expensive*—TV pilots ever made. Of course, Roddenberry put in all his own ideas, and by the time he was through, the only thing left from the movie was in the opening lines of the title sequence: "Space, the new frontier. These are the voyages . . . " et cetera, et cetera.

NBC hated the pilot—they said it was "too cerebral"—but they liked the look of the show, so they say to Bobby, let's try again, give us another pilot. Bobby says no. Take it or leave it. MGM bails out, so Roddenberry goes over to Desilu, where they make a second pilot. He changes the name to *Star Track*, and the show goes on the air in 1966. You know the rest.

Two years later, MGM buys Desilu. Bobby Kennedy strong-arms NBC to move the show to an eight o'clock time slot, and it's a big hit. But then, to settle some old grudge—Bobby hated being wrong—he fires Roddenberry. The rumor mill said it was women—maybe. I don't know and I'm not going to speculate. Dorothy Fontana takes over as producer, and surprise, the show just gets better. Meanwhile, *The Untouchables* gets canceled and Jack Kennedy is out of work again.

The timing was everything here. See, Shatner and Nimoy were feuding. Not only feuding, they were counting each other's lines. Nimoy threatens to quit. Shatner does too. They're both demanding the same thing: "Whatever he gets, I get."

Bobby agrees and fires both of them. He starts looking around for a new Captain.

He doesn't have to look very far.

In hindsight, yes. It was the perfect decision. John F. Kennedy as Captain Jack Logan of the starship *Enterprise*. The man was perfect. Who wouldn't want to serve under him? But—at the time, who knew? It sounded crazy. Here's this old fart who's career is clearly fading fast—why cast him in *Star Track*?

And Jack didn't want to do it. By now, he hated science fiction so much, he once took a poke at Harlan Ellison at the Emmy Awards. He didn't understand it. He had to have it explained to him. Once, he even called down to the research department and asked, "Just where is this planet Vulcan, anyway?"

And that was the other thing—Jack had already seen how Shatner got upstaged by the Vulcan. To him, it was the goddamn Martians all over again. The man was almost fifty—he looked great, but he was terrified of becoming a has-been, of ending up like Ronald Reagan.

But Bobby had a vision. He was good at that stuff. He promised to restructure the show in Jack's favor. Jack agreed—very reluctantly—to listen. That's enough for Bobby. He calls in the staff of the show and says, "My brother wants to be Captain. Make it so."

I gotta tell you. That was not a happy meeting. I'd just come aboard as story editor, so I just sat there and kept my mouth shut. Harlan argued a little, but his heart wasn't in it. Maybe he was afraid he'd get punched again. He didn't like the Kennedys very much. Dorothy did most of the talking for us—but Bobby didn't want to hear. He listened, maybe he just pretended to listen, but when everything had been said, he just answered, "Do it my way." We were not happy when we left.

For about three days, we were pissed as hell, because we'd finally gotten the show settled into a good solid working formula, and then suddenly—*poof!*—Roddenberry, Nimoy, and Shatner are gone, and Bobby Kennedy is giving orders. But then it sort of hit us all at the same time. Hey, this is an opportunity to reinvent *Star Track*. So we made a list of all the shit that bothered us—like the Captain always having to get the girl, the Captain always beaming down to the planet, that kind of stuff, and we started thinking about ways to fix it.

We knew Jack couldn't do the action stuff believably. He was already gray at the temples, and his back problems were legendary on the set of *The Untouchables*, so we knew we were going to have to introduce a younger second lead to pick up the action. That's where the Mission Team came from. So Jack wouldn't have to do it.

We really had no choice. Jack had to be an older, more thoughtful Captain who stayed on the ship and monitored the missions by remote control. The Mission Team would be headed by the First Officer. But this was perfect because it kept the Captain in command at all times, and it also made it impossible for the First Officer to become a sidekick, or a partner. Jack would be the undeniable star.

We also figured we'd just about milked the Vulcan idea to death, so we eighty-sixed the whole Vulcan species and brought in an android to take Spock's place as science officer. The android would be curious about humanity—kind of like an updated Pinocchio. The opposite of Spock; he *wants* to be human.

Just as we were starting to get excited about the possibilities of the new format, Jack suggested adding families to the crew of the starship to attract a family audience. Maybe the android's best friend could be a teenage computer genius . . . the kids would *love* that. We ended up calling the android REM—it means Rapid Eye Movement—and casting Donald Pleasence. Billy Mumy came aboard as Dr. McCoy's grandson, Wesley.

To be fair, Pleasence made the whole android thing work, but none of us ever really *liked* the idea very much. We tried arguing against it, but who ever listens to he writer's opinion? Whatever Jack wanted, Jack got. Bobby made sure of that. So, there we were—lost in space with Jack Kennedy.

And then . . . to make it even worse, Jack started reviewing outlines, sending us memos about what Jack Logan would or wouldn't do. Clearly, he was having trouble telling the difference between the character and the actor who played him. Jack killed a lot of good ideas. I had one where these little furballs started breeding like crazy—kind of like the rabbits in Australia? Dorothy thought it had a lot of whimsy. Everybody liked it. But Jack killed it. He said it made Logan look foolish. He didn't want to look foolish, said it wasn't right for his image.

His *image*? Give me a break. It doesn't matter much now, though, does it? He's got the best image of all. He's an *icon*.

Harlan quit the show first—which surprised all of us, because he was always the most patient and even-tempered of human beings. Y'know, he did that *est* thing and just mellowed out like a big pink pussycat. Ted Sturgeon used to come to him for advice.

Dorothy quit three months after Harlan. I tried to stick it out, but it wasn't any fun without them. I didn't get along with the new producer, and I finally tossed in the towel too.

The worst part of it, I guess, was that after we left, the ratings went up. It was pretty disheartening. I mean, talk about a pie in the face.

What happened to the original crew? I thought you'd never ask.

Roddenberry went over to Warners and worked for a while on *Wagon Train: The Next Generation*. Shatner showed up in a couple of guest spots, then landed the lead in a cop show; when he lost his hair, he took up directing—I hear he's pretty good at it. Nimoy, of course, gave up show business and ran for office. He's been a good governor; I guess he'll run for the Presidency. Walter Cronkite called him one of the ten most trusted men in America.

Dorothy was head of new projects at Twentieth for a while, then she started up her own production company. Harlan moved to Scotland. And me—well, my troubles were in all the newspapers, so I don't have to rehash them here, do I? But I'm doing a lot better these days, and I might even take up writing again. If I can figure out how to use a computer. Those things confuse me.

You don't need me to tell you anything else about *Star*

Track, do you? You can get the rest of it from the newspapers.

Yeah, I was there when it happened. We all were. I was as close to Jack as I am to you.

I dunno, I guess none of us realized what a zoo a *Star Track* convention could be. Not then, anyway. It was still early in the phenomenon.

I mean, we had no idea what kind of impact the show had made on the fans. We thought there might be a couple hundred people there. You know how big the crowd was? Nobody does. The news said there were fifteen thousand inside the hotel. We had no idea now many more were waiting outside.

We just didn't know how seriously the fans took the show. Of course, the Ambassador Hotel was never the same afterwards.

Anyway, Harlan was there, so was Dorothy. Gene came by, but he didn't stay very long. I think he felt disgraced. And of course, all the actors. De, Jimmy, Grace, Nichelle, Walter, George, Majel, Bruce, Mark, Leonard, Bill—all the also-rans, as they were calling themselves by then. I guess Bobby had put the screws on. Attend or else. There wasn't a lot of good feeling—at least, not at first.

But then the fans started applauding. One after the other, we all went out and chatted and answered questions, and the excitement just grew and grew and grew.

Of course, when Jack came out, the place went wild. It was like election night. There were people there wearing KENNEDY FOR PRESIDENT buttons. Like he was really the character he played. They loved him. And he loved being loved. Whatever else you might say about Jack Kennedy, he knew how to make love to an audience. Style and grace. That was Jack all over.

Y'know, I saw the Beatles at the Hollywood Bowl. All three concerts. And I never saw that kind of hysteria, not even when Ringo threw jellybeans at the audience. But the Trackies—I thought they were going to scream the walls down.

Jack was glowing. His wife had just turned to him and whispered, "Well, you can't say Los Angeles doesn't love you now"—when it happened.

At first, I thought it was a car backfiring. It didn't sound like a gunshot at all. In fact, most people were puzzled at the sound. It all happened so fast. Then Jack grabbed his throat, and I guess for a second, we all thought he was joking. Y'know how you do: "Augh, they got me—" But he had this real stupid look on his face—confused, like. Then the second and third shots went off—and it was the third shot that killed him. And that's when the screaming started. And the panic. All those people injured and killed, suffocated in the crush. It was terrible. Everybody running. I can still see it. I still get nightmares.

I've always been amazed they caught the little bastard who did it. Sirhan Sirhan. I'll never forget his name. Another one of those nerdy little geeks who never had a life of his own. He lived inside the TV. He thought it was real. Half a dozen of those really big women we see at all the conventions just jumped the poor son of a bitch and flattened him. They were outraged that someone would dare to attack *their* Captain. Sirhan was lucky to escape with his balls still attached.

Y'know, later some of the witnesses said that Sirhan kept yelling, "Wait, wait—I can explain!" Like you can explain a thing like that? It didn't make any sense then. It doesn't make any sense now, no matter how many articles William F. Buckley and Norman Mailer and Tom Wolfe write about it.

You know what it was? Sirhan never forgave us for replacing Kirk and Spock with Logan and REM. He said we'd ruined the whole show.

But that's not even the half of it. You want to know

the rest of the cosmic joke? Bugliosi, the district attorney, told me later on. Sirhan was aiming at Bobby and missed. Three times! Bobby was standing just behind Jack, but that kid couldn't shoot worth shit. I think if he'd have hit Bobby, the industry would have given him a medal. Instead, he got the gas chamber and a movie of the week.

But now—y'know, I think back on it, and I see how stupid we all were. We didn't know the power of television. None of us did. We didn't even suspect.

Jack knew, I think. Bobby knew for sure. He knew that you could change the way people think and feel and vote just by what you put on the screen. Bobby knew that. He had the vision. But he was never the same after that. How could you be? The whole thing scared the hell out of all of us—the whole industry. NBC cancelled the show, but they couldn't cancel the nightmares.

Y'ask me, I think that was the turning point in the sixties—the killing of Kennedy. That's when it all started going bad. That's when we all went crazy and started tearing things down. But, oh, well—that's old news. Everybody knows it.

Now, we've got the Kennedy mystique and *Star Track: The New Voyages*. And . . . it's all shit. It's just . . . so much merchandise. Whatever might have been true or meaningful or wonderful about *Star Track* is gone. It's all been eaten up by the lawyers and the fans and the publicity department.

Don't take this personally, but I don't trust anybody under thirty. I don't think any of you understand what happened then. It was special. We didn't understand it ourselves, but we knew it was special.

See . . . it's like this. Space isn't the new frontier. It never was.

What is the new frontier? You have to ask—? That proves my point. You're looking in the wrong place. The new frontier isn't out there. It's in here. In the heart. It's in us. Dorothy said it. If it's not in here, it's not anywhere.

Ahh—you know what, you're going to go out of here, you're going to write another one of those golden geezer articles. You'll miss the whole point, just like all the others. Shut that damn thing off and get the hell out of here before I whack you with my cane. Nurse! Nurse—!

Kristine Kathryn Rusch, Campbell winner, Hugo and Nebula nominee, editor of Axolotl Press and *The Magazine of Fantasy and Science Fiction*, and the author of a number of recent novels such as *Afterimage* (with Kevin J. Anderson) (no, I don't know how she gets through the day either), presents us with a grim, hard-bitten story of politics, murder, and the road not taken.

The Best and the Brightest

by Kristine Kathryn Rusch

... what we discussed about Martin Luther King—the reason that President Kennedy and I, and the Department of Justice, were so reserved about him during this period of time, which I'm sure he felt ... We never wanted to get very close to him just because of these contacts and connections that he had, which we felt were damaging to the civil rights movement. And because we were so intimately involved in the struggle for civil rights, it also damaged us. It damaged what we were trying to do.

—Robert F. Kennedy
in an interview with
Anthony Lewis, December, 1964.

Fame is an elusive thing. Some men spend their lives chasing it. Others have it thrust upon them. But those who touch it and lose it seem to be the most bitter men of all.

Fame visited my neighborhood once. And we flirted for a few hours ...

Cold Chicago morning. I stood on the street corner, watching the morning traffic pass, my hands tucked under my arms, shaking foot to foot for warmth, breath fogging the air around me. Waiting. Feeling out of place near the gutted-out buildings, and the abandoned cars, in a world where I once felt at home.

"Well, if it ain't the *Tribune*'s token nigger boy."

I whirled, saw someone I didn't expect. Harold Washington stood behind me, dapper in a slim gray suit. Washington always managed to look older and more powerful than his thirty-some years. He had been running for alderman for four elections straight, and even though every black on the South Side claimed to have voted for him, he still lost by a sizable margin thanks to Mayor Daley and the graveyard vote.

"Harold." Anger as deep as the cold shook through me. I thought I was going to meet some secretive little informer, not a politician. "You could have met me in my office."

"No, this one's too big. Besides, I already been to your boss with it."

Wasted morning. And my fingers were numb. "Jesus, Harold. You think a beat reporter can buck the editor in chief?"

"I think a *brother* can right an injustice."

I sighed, closed my eyes. Remembered the jobs, the money slipped to me, the entire community hoping that once their boy left Northwestern he would overthrow the entire system. Instead, I covered neighborhood meetings.

"What's so important to drag me out in zero-degree weather?"

"You know the boy they said shot Martin Luther King? I found him."

Remembered that night as if it had happened a moment before. King was down here, on this very street corner, arm around Washington, making promises into the mike. *We will fight for our rights! Fight for our brothers! We will have black men represent black men instead of white folk representing death—*

Then the report of a gun, screams, a frantic crowd. I saw Washington turn, King clutching his arm, the people nearby parting so Washington could drag King by. They hid in a building where King's blood still stains the floor. Later discovered there were two bullets, although most of us only heard one shot. One grazed King's shoulder. The other nicked his spine.

The Reverend would never walk again.

And no one saw who did it.

Washington hustled me into a small restaurant around the corner. Grime streaked the wall. The plastic booths were ripped, and the entire place smelled of bad cooking oil. Only one other customer sat inside, twirling a dirty water-glass between his fingers. A thin white boy, freckle-faced, jug-eared, starving. Hands shook as he moved.

"Where'd you find him, Harold?" I kept my voice soft.

"He came to me. Turned in the gun, confessed. Wanted me to kill him, I think."

I started. Washington was tough, but not a killer. Interesting thought. "This'll probably kill him anyway."

"Papers aren't going to touch him, unless you do." Washington put his hand on the small of my back, propelling me forward. The boy stared at us, green eyes wide in his too-narrow face. Washington forced me into the seat opposite.

"Willis here is a reporter." Washington remained standing. I had a sudden fear that he would leave me with this kid. "I want you to tell him everything you told me."

Color patches splotched the kid's cheeks. "Everything?" he whispered.

Washington nodded. He grabbed a chair, spun it around and sat on it, arms resting on the back, just far enough inside our circle to control the boy, but outside enough to make me feel like I was going to get an honest tale.

The boy gazed at his grimy fingers. In a halting voice, he told about searching for a gun, paying too much cash; how his hands shook as he pulled the trigger, scared, the second shot an accident when he realized what really was going to happen; the money bulging in his pocket, already gone to a skipped-out mother, and a dope fiend sister.

"Who hired you?" I asked.

The boy frowned. The question he'd been waiting for. The question he wanted to avoid. "Big guy, black suit. Talked like some rich guy, and didn't want to be near me."

"Was he alone?"

"No. Three other guys were with him, including the guy who sells my sister dope."

"Why'd they pick you?"

The kid looked out the dirt-streaked window. "Because they knew they could get me. Because I said I'm the best."

"Are you?"

"No." A whisper. Teenage grandiosity. Enough money to survive. Now it was gone, and the kid had shot a man, caused a national incident.

"Did you ever see the guy who hired you again?"

"Two nights ago. On TV. Standing behind the President."

* * *

Two nights previous. The news clips were of Bobby Kennedy on the way to an official dinner here in Chicago, surrounded by his bodyguards, the Secret Service, and a handful of cabinet officers. I was shaking. I never liked Bobby Kennedy: thought him too zealous, too serious, too scary. He went after the mob with single-minded zeal, but used civil rights as a voting platform, using it only when he couldn't avoid it. I often wondered what would have happened had Bobby not decided to run in '64. Maybe LBJ would have made a better President. Maybe he would have avoided Southeast Asia, and the deadlock in the Senate.

But he would not have done anything for civil rights. Not a good ole boy like LBJ. Neither would Goldwater.

And now King, stirring up trouble, gaining such a following that he was about to turn the country on its ear, overturn all the strong white traditions that the nation had held so long, and overturn Bobby Kennedy in the bargain.

It was no secret that Bobby Kennedy thought King was hurting the civil rights movement instead of helping it. No secret that the administration saw King as a threat.

Had Kennedy learned something from the mob?

Murder had never been the Kennedy way.

Before.

"I know what you're thinking." Washington scooted his chair forward. "Can't be true, can't possibly be true. Right?"

I didn't answer. He pulled a manila envelope out of his briefcase, and tossed it at me. He nodded at the kid, who slid out of the booth and ran into the back.

"Wait a minute," I said.

"I know where to find him." Washington's voice was soft. He indicated the envelope. "Open it."

I did, hands shaking. A black and white glossy sat on the top. The scene I remembered from two days previous,

Kennedy and his men. Washington pointed to a man on the sidelines. "This is the man who met with the boy."

I let out the air I'd been holding. A Daley thug. Just what the press had been predicting. Daley had gone after King, and Daley had nearly destroyed him.

"Why didn't the *Trib*—?"

"Because of these." Washington threw documents, memoranda, down in front of me. I thumbed through them. This was Chicago. Daley didn't care if he kept a paper trail. He was in charge, in control, Only the *Trib* could come out against him, and even then it suffered at times.

But these. I recognized the names. Assistants, undersecretaries, aides to the President. And Kenneth O'Donnell, JFK's right-hand man, Bobby's favorite advisor. On the most damning document of all.

> ... *U.S. Government cannot tolerate situation in which power lies in King's hands. The Civil Rights Movement must be given chance to rid itself of King and his coterie and replace them with best political personalities available.*
>
> *If, in spite of all your efforts, King remains obdurate and refuses, then we must face the possibility that King himself cannot be preserved.**

"Where did you get this?"

Washington shrugged. "Daley's government is corrupt. Sometimes that works for him. Sometimes it doesn't."

I pushed the documents away from me, hands shaking. "You showed this at the *Trib*?"

He nodded.

"What do you want me to do?"

"Break it. Run with the story. You're our boy, Willis. We can't let this get away from us."

I stood, paced. The inside of the grimy restaurant was

cold. Pans banged in the back. I couldn't believe that anyone ate here. "What if the *Trib* won't take it?"

"Then somebody will. The *New York Times*, the *Washington Post*, hell, even the *Milwaukee Journal*. Somebody."

I pictured myself peddling the story. The threats. The career. All those years, climbing the ladders, playing politics so that I could be the *Trib*'s token nigger boy.

"If this goes out, it could ruin me."

"It could make you."

"People would call it lies. Black vengeance."

"Black justice," Washington said. His voice was soft, but his hands shook as he gathered the documents together. "It could save a man's life."

"Or it could cost me mine."

We stared at each other. Maybe I would fight Daley. Maybe I would fight the administration. But not both, and not along with the white world. "A reporter can't face a President, and win."

Washington assessed me. Some kind of light went out in his eyes. "I thought you had courage."

"I do," I said. "But I only fight fights that I can win."

"Then you need to go into another profession," he said, tucking the manila envelope back into his briefcase. "The good reporters tilt at windmills."

"That windmill nearly destroyed Don Quixote," I said.

"But even today, people remember him." Washington turned his back on me, and walked away.

I remained in the ripped booth, staring out the dirt-streaked window for nearly an hour, the boy's half-full water glass across from me. I was shaking, top to bottom. What happened if a reporter could topple a President? Wasn't that what free press was supposed to be about?

I shoved the glass aside, leaned back. Pans continued to rattle in the kitchen, but no one waited on me. Any journalist knew that a free press was a lie made up for schoolchildren. Economics, politics, power, all restrained the press. I would take this story to paper after paper, get turned down, and end up working as a janitor somewhere, hiding in some basement, trying to forget the things I knew. The community believed in me. I couldn't let them down. And with that thought, I too left.

Every morning, as I cross to my desk at the *Trib*, that day haunts me. Washington showed me a little glimpse of fame, just a taste, really. But I didn't realize it until the events began to unfold . . .

Three months after I had met with Washington, a two-paragraph story about the man behind the assassination attempt appeared in the *Washington Post*, bylined by their token black reporter, Stevens. A year later, Bobby Kennedy announced he would not run for another term. Six weeks after that, hounded by the press, he resigned. The boy I met has relocated—federal witness protection program. Stevens won a Pulitzer. Washington became mayor of Chicago. Martin Luther King is running for President.

Me, I dream about that envelope now, holding it in my hands, taking it through the backwaters of the *Trib*, facing down my boss. Washington would be speaking to me still. I would be writing books, giving lectures, going on TV as a resident expert, instead of covering these damn meetings. They've grown dull since Washington became mayor. Aboveboard. And I write them dutifully, thinking about 1960, when I graduated from college, when JFK was elected. When the world seemed clean, and fresh, and new.

And the future was the best and the brightest it could ever be.

---

* With fictional name substitutions to make it relevant to this story, the language in this document was taken from a top secret telegram from the Department of State, sent on August 24, 1963, recommending the assassination of Vietnamese President Diem. (Taken from *Kennedy in Vietnam: American Vietnam Policy, 1960–1963*, by William J. Rust, published by Da Capo Press, New York, 1985.)

Jack Haldeman, co-author of such excellent works as *Bill the Galactic Hero on the Planet of Zombie Vampires* (with Harry Harrison), and *Echoes of Thunder* and *High Steel* (with Jack Dann) was too busy the first time I sent out invitations for contributions to this book.

When he caught up with his deadlines, he asked if there was still time to write a story for *Alternate Kennedys*, and did I have any suggestions/ I said yes, that I would love to see him give his sense of humor free range and write one about the Hyannis Kid versus the Trickster in a story entitled "The 1960 Presidential Campaign Considered as a World Wrestling Federation Steel Cage Match."

He replied that if I was crazy enough to conceive it, he was crazy enough to write it.

And sure enough, he was.

The 1960 Presidential Campaign, Considered as a World Wrestling Federation Steel Cage Match

or

Short Count in Chicago

by Jack C. Haldeman II

The packed house in the Stockyard Wrestling Arena couldn't believe it. Their howls of protest rattled the walls. The Castrato Brothers, Fido and Shay, had just upset the long-established team of Bobo Batisto and the Sugar Daddy. It was the last preliminary event before the Match of the Century. The Hyannis Kid was taking on The Trickster; one fall for the championship belt and all the bucks. Because of the potential danger they posed for the outside world, they would be fighting within the confines of a specially-designed steel cage.

"What do you think, Willie?" asked The Hawk, hunched over his microphone and speaking loudly so the national television viewers could hear him over the roar of the crowd. "Are the Castratos in it for the long haul?"

Wee Willie Manchester, the 400-pound color announcer, adjusted his tie, knowing they had to stall until the steel cage was set up. "I like Fido," he said. "But speaking as an ex-wrestler, I feel that Shay's guerrilla style of combat is risky."

"Fido should do something about his beard," said the

Hawk. "It's too long, and untrimmed. Makes him look like a wild man."

"Fido knows what he's doing," said Willie. "That's more than you can say for The French Ticklers."

The Hawk winced. He'd long been a vocal champion for the French Ticklers, who had been defeated in a Far East Championship tag-team bout last weekend by Mousie Tongue and the Hoochie Men.

"Who would have thought Mousie would have had such staying power?" said the Hawk. "I can't figure him out."

"Inscrutable," said Willie. "I don't think the Far East title will be clear for a long time."

"I understand there was a big confrontation between The Hyannis Kid and The Trickster at the weigh-in this morning," said The Hawk, rapidly changing the subject.

"It was more of a debate," said Willie. "If words were enough to win the big fight, The Kid would have this thing sewed up."

"The Trickster's a scrapper," said The Hawk. "He's been against the ropes a few times in his life, and he always lands on his feet."

"This time he doesn't have The General in his corner."

"True enough," said The Hawk. "But The General practically hand-picked The Trickster himself when he retired."

"That and a nickel will get you a phone call," snorted Willie. "Regardless of how popular The General was, The Trickster still has to win it in the ring."

"Here they come!" shouted the Hawk.

The fans in the arena went wild, stomping their feet and yelling.

The Hyannis Kid entered first, shadow-boxing the air in front of him and flashing his famous smile. He was trailed by his brothers, Gorgeous Bob and Ted Terrific, both decent wrestlers and heavy contenders in their own divisions.

An instant later, The Trickster appeared from the opposite ramp, hands held high in his trademark V-for-Victory salute. Rubbing his sweaty back with a towel was his sometime tag-team partner, The Baltimore Geek. His manager, Hank Kiss-My-Finger, was whispering last-minute instructions in his ear.

The crowd seemed equally divided between the two fighters. If either one had an edge in popularity, it wasn't apparent. A lot of people were swayed by The Kid's boyish good looks, while others opted for experience over good looks and intelligence.

"Ladies and gentlemen, they're approaching the cage," said the Hawk. "We're about to—wait! The Trickster goes to a ringside seat to shake hands with The General. In a rare show of sportsmanship, The Kid goes over too, but The General refuses to shake his hand. Snubbed, The Kid vaults through the door into the ring. The cage door closes behind him with a clang and they're locked in now."

"The referee for tonight's match is the Windy City's own Chicago Dick," said Willie as the fighters stared at each other. "This is his home turf, and he rules the canvas with an iron hand."

"There's the bell!" shouted the Hawk.

The fighters circled each other. The Trickster made the first move, a bone-crushing roundhouse called the Checkers Chop that caught The Kid by surprise. He was stunned by the Trickster's sheer audaciousness in starting with such an obvious ploy and barely ducked in time. As it was, the Chop caught him a glancing blow and he fell to the canvas. The Trickster was immediately on top of him, gouging his eyes as he tried to get him into the deadly Vicuña Vice Grip.

"What skill!" cried the Hawk. "The Trickster can really manipulate an opponent!"

"Forget skill," said Willie. "He's rubbing resin into the Kid's eyes. The Trickster's jabbing him with something he smuggled into the ring."

"The Trickster knows his tricks," said The Hawk, nodding sagely.

"Dirty tricks," grumbled Willie.

The Kid was in trouble, serious trouble. Luckily for him, The Trickster was nervous and sweaty, which kept him from completing the Vicuña Vice Grip. Somehow The Kid managed to roll to the edge of the mat, but when he touched the edge of the steel cage, Chicago Dick turned away, and instead of safety, The Kid found himself in the grip of The Baltimore Geek, grabbing him through the bars while The Trickster pummeled him unmercifully. A low-rent wrestler called Nikita the Chef whonked him on the head between the bars with his shoe and another would-be champ named Pops Doc threw a bloody frozen chicken into the ring.

"The Trickster has a lot of friends," said The Hawk.

"It's more like The Kid has a lot of enemies," said Willie. "But here comes the cavalry!"

Gorgeous Bob and Ted Terrific had joined the ringside fray. They were holding their own against the invaders until Hank Kiss-My-Finger waded in with his tomahawk and petrified German sausage, counting coup and bashing heads.

"It's all over but the shouting," chortled The Hawk. "The Trickster's got this one locked up!"

"Wait!" yelled Willie. "Here comes The Kid's mother."

"Gardenia?" asked The Hawk. "What good is Gardenia going to be?"

"She's a tough old lady," said Willie. "Raised a whole family full of wrestlers, didn't she?"

Sure enough, Gardenia waded into the battle with an umbrella in one hand and a folding chair in the other, knocking the hell out of anyone who wasn't related. The Kid managed to roll away from the edge of the mat.

The Trickster was on him in an instant, tripping him with the Kitchen Debate Shuffle and pinning him with the Great Wall Belly-Flop.

"One," said Chicago Dick, pounding the canvas, then getting to his feet and leisurely lighting a cigar.

"What's happening?" cried the Hawk. "This is the slowest count I've ever seen!"

"Two," said Chicago Dick, wandering over to a neutral corner to talk to some ward bosses in the front row.

"I can't believe this!" yelled the Hawk. "How can he get away with this?"

"It's his town," said Wee Willie Manchester with a smile. "They do things his way here."

The Kid broke loose and in a stunning reversal, pinned The Trickster to the mat with a subtle variation of the Boston Bash.

"One-two-three," said Chicago Dick in one breath, pulling The Kid to his feet and raising the new champion's hand into the air.

"Now I've seen everything!" moaned The Hawk.

"No you haven't," said Willie, watching Nikita pound the bars of the age with his shoe. "I think this means war."

"What?" asked The Hawk.

"War," said Willie, watching Pops Doc pull another bloody frozen chicken out of his ice chest and toss it into the ring. "A long, cold war."

Susan Shwartz, author of *The Grail of Hearts* and numerous other fantasy novels, plus such memorable novelettes as "Suppose They Gave a Peace . . . " and the Nebula-nominated "Loose Cannon" and "Getting Real," here presents the youthful captain of *PT-109* with a harder choice than he ever made as President, in a hauntingly beautiful and bittersweet parable.

Siren Song
by Susan Shwartz

Don't let the bastards get you down, Jack told himself as he slipped on the coral once again. It scored his hands, and they bled. His lips were cracked and bleeding from the salt water, his stomach ached, whether from hunger or his usual ulcer he didn't want to know, the sun turned his body into a barbecue, and his back felt as if the god-damned *Amagiri* had rammed *him,* and not that plywood wreck of a *PT-109.*

Damn, he hurt. He hurt forever. When he still had a ship, he'd slept on a plank. It wasn't easy, but he always had an out. He knew his buddy Lennie Thom—if he ever had a sick day in his life it didn't show—made mother-hen noises over him. More to the point, he knew that one message could get him off the PT boat, out of Espíritu Santo, away from the New Hebrides, and back to a place where people appreciated Jack Kennedy. Where there were bright lights and clean uniforms and women.

Now, he was out of fast ways out.

All he wore now were his shoes and his lifebelt. Damn good thing he had both of them. The shoes kept his feet from being cut to rags on the coral, and the lifebelt—well, if he ever got out of this mess, he didn't want to be singing soprano, like the jokes they'd told at Choate. "I think there are SHARKS IN THE WATER . . ." with the words before "sharks" in a bass voice, and everything else cheeped in falsetto.

It wasn't funny. Because there *were* sharks in these waters. All the guys said so, even McMahon, whom he'd towed onto that damned atoll when the *109*'s bow finally sank. They'd raised hell about his coming out alone. There were sharks in the water. He didn't know jackshit about water currents in Ferguson Passage. And if he swam out there with a lantern and a pistol, some PT men might think he was some sort of Jap.

The day before, he'd swum for four hours, towing McMahon. The other nine men swam behind them or clung to a plank that was all that was left of the forward deck of the *109*. Good thing he'd used it to mount that 37mm gun, or more would have died than the two he actually lost. A man with three kids and a guy who was just a kid himself, sleeping with the fishes. He wasn't going to be able to forget them any time soon.

But it wasn't he who'd lost those two. It was those other bastards, the other skippers of the other PTs. Who could have turned and picked them up, but they didn't. His father the Ambassador would have their guts for that, but first the old man had to know he was alive. He and the rest of his men. That was up to him. There was no Ambassador, no big-shot Joe Jr. to pull him out of hot water— or salt water—this time, not when the water was the Pacific, and the heat was burning gas.

The heat was other stuff too. He could hear it now. "For Chrissake, Kennedy, how'd you lose your fuckin' *ship*?"

Or "God, trust Crash Kennedy. First he crashes into a

dock. Now he crashes into a damn *destroyer*! Daddy's going to cut off his allowance for sure."

Fifteen boats sent out to attack four destroyers that carried nine hundred troops and seventy tons of cargo, and *his* boat had to be the one that got rammed. Had a Jap ship ever rammed a PT boat before? All wood and gas tank, the things were floating bombs. He was damned lucky to be alive.

Hail Mary Mother of God ... his mother would have liked it if he prayed. *His last thoughts were of the Blessed Virgin* ... yeah, but there was no chaplain to write the letter, and if he had anything to say about it, there wouldn't be a letter to write.

And he had a more useful prayer than the Rosary.

Illegitimi non carborundum, Domine, salvam fac.

Don't let the bastards wear you down, the way they sang it at Harvard, with the pious *Domine, salvam fac* pronounced like "fuck," though they'd haul you to the Ad Board if they caught you singing it like that. Swimming was about the only sport he was half good at at Harvard. God knows he tried. Roomed with a football letterman at Winthrop House. Went out for every scrimmage. But even if he got into a game, he usually got sick. As opposed to his brother Joe, who had been a starter at Dexter and at Choate and at Harvard. With Jack following in his wake. Sickly Jack. (Kee-rist, why couldn't he have stuck it out at Princeton?) The disappointment.

Gaudeamus igitur. Veritas non sequitur. Therefore, let's rejoice, like something out of the goddamn *Student Prince*. The truth doesn't follow.

Domine salvam fuck. This time, he actually said it, and he got a mouthful of seawater. He snorted and spat it out, and said fuck again, stumbling along in the dark and hoping the coral didn't just drop off into some kind of pit, or jag him, or trap him here.

Admiral Halsey was going to tan his hide and hang it out to dry. That is, if the coral and the sun and the Japs left anything of it. One consolation—once the admiral got through with him, there wouldn't be anything left that his father could chew up and spit out.

Right now, though, if he could close his eyes and then open them and see the bleachers around the pool . . . no, make that the place in Florida because of the hot, jungly feel of the air and the water, it would be worth having to face everyone and see in their eyes that Jacky boy had let the side down once again.

And to think he'd been so proud of the chance to beat Joe to a medal, too. Only medal he needed now was St. Christopher.

Domine salvam fac.

How long had he been swimming since he left the atoll where his men were trying to get through the night? Christ, McMahon had bad burns, and he wasn't the only one. If he didn't get help soon, he might as well not bother at all. It would be a toss-up whether they'd die of infection or thirst first. *Water, water, everywhere.* He had a book out, his senior thesis turned into a best-seller—and most of the "sales" stacked up at home, such as it was. Books impress a high-class crowd, his father said. But this poetry stuff . . . aside from the occasional song or the skits at the Pudding . . . *Illegitimi non carborundum* . . .

How long, Lord, how long?

A plane flew by, flying real low, and he ducked into the water, warm like a baby's bath, not that he knew much about babies except they weren't cheap once the girl said it was yours.

He'd told the guys to hide out from planes. Might be Zeros. Damned if he wanted to swim his ass off and come back to find them all bled out on the beach.

The horizon opened up. He'd reached the passage. Thank God. And he meant it. The water got deeper, and he didn't have to worry about the coral anymore. Sharks, maybe. Japanese, maybe. His own side, maybe that too. But no coral. Thank God for small blessings.

He had his lantern out, Diogenes looking for an honest PT boat.

C'mon, you bastards, he wished at the empty water. *C'mon and find me!* He had to be found. He was the Ambassador's son. He couldn't die like other people—like his two men who slept with the fishes. It just didn't make sense.

Jack floated. God, he floated for hours while his skin puffed up and wrinkled and the southern sky wheeled overhead and the occasional plane scared hell out of him.

"Anyone out theah?" The broad Boston Irish accent sounded so funny out here in the New Hebrides that he had to giggle, then stop himself before he lost it.

They'd be waiting for him on the atoll. They'd raised holy hell about him swimming out here. He was too tired, they'd said. And they were right. Thom had looked at him as if he was personally planning to tackle him and tie him down. Mutiny, that would have been. He was still the skipper. Skipper had to look out for his men. He was trying his best. Wasn't his fault if there weren't any PTs in the water.

Maybe the Japs had got all the PTs in the world. Maybe they'd never be found. If he got back . . . *when* he got back . . . he'd have to move the men to a place where there was water, maybe trees, and some food.

Maybe natives.

Was that a boat out there?

"Hey!!!!!!"

No boat. No nothing. He was seeing things.

His stomach burned, but at least the water held him up so his back was okay. For now. It would have to last till he got back to his men.

The sky was getting paler. If he didn't move soon, he'd be out here at dawn, just bobbing in the sea for anyone to pick off.

One last look around.

No boats. Never any boats. Shit.

A plane flew overhead. He dived and held his breath till he was sure it was gone.

Time to turn around. Time to swim out of the Passage and back to the atoll. His lantern and his pistol weighed a ton each, but he didn't dare toss them away. At the very worst, he could at least try to shoot a shark. Or a Jap. Riiight. The way they expected PT boats to attack destroyers.

The sun hadn't come up yet, wouldn't for hours; but his sunburn twinged. The salt in the water was going to hurt like hell once his blisters broke. And he was hungry, too. He could feel his stomach, eating itself away.

Well, at least this time he had something to worry about. The men he'd come out here to try and save. He was sort of surprised he cared about his crew so much.

After all, there wasn't a single one of those men back on the atoll who was in a position to do him a damned bit of good once he got back to civilization, was there? Or was that true?

Clearly as if the Ambassador sat across the table from him spelling it out, he could see things from his father's point of view.

If he got back . . . there was a Negro, a Jew, McMahon was from the Old Sod like him . . . his father would have the PR people out pounding the table, and he'd be a fuckin' hero.

If they didn't court-martial him first for losing goddamned *PT-109*. If his father and Joe, the fair-haired boy, didn't write him off the way he always thought they'd do.

You're a real shit, he told himself. *First things first. First you get those men safe. Then you worry about running for President.*

Senator, more likely. The way his father set it up, Joe was supposed to be President. First Irishman and first Catholic to be President. And the first Kennedy. "*That'll* show the bastards!" his father always said. He always wanted to show the bastards, but he insisted his boys go to school with them.

So would Jack, if he could get back home. If he could even get back safe. The acid juices poured into his stomach and didn't find anything to work on. God, that hurt. He hawked and spit. No blood. Thank God for that, fasting, which is exactly what he'd been doing. Priest would be pleased.

Now, which way? Hard to tell. He sighted along the waning stars. After a while, the water got shallower. His foot scraped bottom—damn coral again—and he got to a place where he could wade.

Stomach cramps brought him to his knees in the water. He doubled over and retched bile till he was dizzy. His forehead touched the water and his own sickness. He jerked back upright, splashed over to a clean spot, and ducked his head to clean himself off.

If he was real lucky, he'd make it back to the atoll by dawn. He'd want to move the men, find water. Maybe someone else could do the swim tomorrow. Barney Ross, most likely.

He was trudging through the water now, and his back hurt worse than his stomach. One day they'd cut him open and find nothing but ache in between the skin of his back and the skin of his stomach.

Don't let the bastards wear you down. *Illegitimi non carborundum* ... damn it all, he'd always been lousy at Latin. Didn't think it mattered once he got out of school. Stupid song. Wasn't even good for walking to.

If nothing else had gone wrong when he got back, maybe he'd even let himself sleep for a little. He'd always said he couldn't sleep till he'd gotten himself laid first. Didn't work that way out here, did it? Unless he found himself some kind of fish ...

He found himself laughing about that. When the laugh turned into a hoot, he got worried and put a lid on it.

Anyone could hear him. Come hear the crazy man. Hell of a way to die, shot because he couldn't button his lip.

He laughed again and found himself falling. The water, blood warm now, brought him around. His hands were bleeding.

Move it, Mister.

He forced himself to his feet. They were swollen, and they pressed against the waterlogged shoes. Probably have to be cut away. Probably lose half the skin on his feet, and then where'd the men be? Keep moving.

By the time the sun rose in the sky—brilliant bloody ball of sun like the way the *109* had exploded when the *Amagiri* hit it, he knew it. He was shit out of luck lost. Out of his range. Almost out of his head. And damned thirsty. All that water. All he had to do was bend down and scoop it up . . .

And he'd be on his knees puking his guts up, too.

The sun was shining over one shoulder, then over another, then over the first. He was going in circles, he knew that. He'd gotten himself turned around. He'd never make it home now, and the guys would think he was dead. Sleeping with the fishes. They knew that was the only thing that would keep him away from them.

At least, *try*.

He kept on going on wobbling legs. *Illegitimi non carborundum* . . . something more cheerful.

How about *"The freshmen down at Yale get no tail, get no tail . . ."* This time his laugh cracked into a schoolboy giggle.

Another laugh joined his. He spun around and promptly belly-flopped into the water. Again that laugh . . . beautiful, silvery laughter like the most expensive hooker in the world.

Right. In the desert, you saw mirages and they were full of water. In the water, did you see mirages that were full of dry land?

He dashed his hair—stringy and crusted from the salt—

back from his forehead. God, his head ached, and the sun was going to fry it like an egg in a couple hours.

It took as much guts for him to open his eyes as it had the night before, when he'd had to order everyone to abandon ship. He didn't want to do that either. What would he do if he saw dry land and it was a mirage?

Die of a broken heart?

Again the laughter. Definitely, an expensive woman's voice. Definitely, the sun had got to him. He was crazy.

He said so.

"No, you're not."

It *was* a woman's voice.

He peeled his eyelids apart and blinked. Well, hel-lo sailor! He pursed his lips to whistle, which was a very bad idea.

Try again, Jacky. *"The freshmen down at Yale get no tail, get no tail . . ."*

"No tail? What do you call this?"

He had to be out of his fucking mind. Because, directly ahead of him was either an atoll, a nice big one with trees and fruit maybe, not like the little reef he'd left his men on, or the most unbelievable dry-land mirage he'd ever dreamt of. And between him and the atoll . . .

She was blonde. Long, long fair hair bleached greenish white by the sun. It ought to have looked cheap against her tan (though cheap usually got the juices flowing), but it didn't That long blonde hair flowed down her body. It was already half dry at the ends, where it fluffed out nicely over her breasts. He'd like to brush it away from them, then . . .

He let his eyes follow the long hair past those awesome breasts. Hmmm, we may be out of our stinking mind and about to drown here, but let's check and see if she's a *real* blonde, shall we?

Ho-ly shit!

It wasn't just that this woman he'd found sitting on a rock in the middle of the Pacific was one fine piece of

tail, though that was true. She looked better than anything he'd had in Hollywood, or Inga Arvad, his Inga-
Binga, tastiest piece of Danish he'd found Stateside.

But talk about tail. This babe *had* one. Was wearing
one.

Like a *mermaid*?

Never mind that. God, just look at her. Primavera? Bot-
ticelli's Venus? Those two babes looked like librarians
compared with her. That hair, those breasts, curving out
over a tiny waist, with the generous hips and soft belly
and the glistening triangle . . .

Glistening with scales?

Jack found himself rising to the occasion, which didn't
at all surprise him seeing he was who he was—if he
couldn't salute a gorgeous woman, he might as well be
dead. Then he went limp, which was a bit of a disappointment. Her loss.

"I would not have let my friends eat you," said the
mirage . . . mermaid . . . what the hell. She had a soft,
wispy voice.

In another life, he'd have had the right, teasing answer
for that. *You'd do it yourself, right?* God, yes.

He couldn't keep it up, though. Not anything; and certainly not his dignity.

He was sinking to his knees, blacking out . . . He heard
a murmur of dismay and sympathy, felt himself caught
by soft arms that smelled excitingly of woman and salt
water . . .

Damn shame, thought John Fitzgerald Kennedy, and
blacked out.

Water ran down it—fresh, sweet water—and he lapped
at it without opening his eyes. Funny, he didn't hear any
rain. Imaginary water?

You're a sick, sick boy, Jack, he told himself. Nothing
new in that. He'd always been sickly and always pushed
himself too hard to make up for it. Look what happened

this time. His big chance to be a man and a hero, to make people proud of him, and his eyes start playing tricks on him. At least, it better be just his eyes. The Ambassador would never stand for one of his sons going crazy. Mermaids, indeed! Nurses, maybe: the kind in white coats, with mustaches and lots of muscle even on the women. He'd done that once already.

Again, he lapped at the water. His head was cushioned on something smooth and cool. He moved his cheek experimentally and felt his beard rasp over ... it wasn't fabric, but he didn't expect it to be. Leaves? Had to be it. He must have staggered out of the water to black out under a coconut palm.

Then he heard laughter. "Like a shark's skin, but so warm!"

He had heard that voice before he blacked out, too. It was the hallucination. The mermaid. Gentle fingers turned his chin. "You would say, 'that tickles!' I watched you drink the water. You're awake. I have better for you than water. Come open your eyes and look at me."

He opend his eyes in shock, then opened them wider. He lay half on the sand, half across the lap of the mermaid who had told him she would not let her friends the sharks eat him. Her scales ... After a party, he had once napped briefly, his head in the lap of his date, who wore a sequined gown. He had had more satisfactory pillows, and the dress had been a real bitch to get her out of. This was altogether different. The scales were only faintly warm, but they were very smooth, and they slid into new patterns of comfort with every move she made.

And right above his head ... sweet Jesus, all he had to do was put his hand up and cup one of the most beautiful breasts he had ever seen. Round like melons, full, with veins the color of the sea, rising and falling with her breathing. You couldn't expect him not to.

A hand batted his away. "You're still very tired. Drink this."

One of the most gorgeous things he'd ever seen, and what did you know? She had to make noises like a nurse.

She raised his head with one hand and held a coconut shell, brimming with thin sweet milk, to his lips.

Thirst and the surprising strength in those hands left him no choice. *Good thing I didn't grab. She may not need those sharks to help out.*

"Better, isn't it? Now, sleep."

Her fingers brushed over his eyelids. He smelled salt and water and flowers, and then he slept . . .

. . . to wake with a start.

"My crew!" He sprang up as quickly as if a hired detective had crashed open the door to his hotel room.

The mermaid was seated a few feet away from him, her . . . her flippers dangling in the water of a glistening stream. Its water reflected the sky, iridescent, as if he lay between two halves of a shell. It looked like no sky he had ever seen.

"I told you I would not let my friends harm you. They will not harm your friends, either. Seeing that they are yours. Soon, they will be found. Others of your kind know where they are and are coming to help them."

"Lady, if you think I'm going to let a bunch of goddam . . . " He was getting his Irish up. He'd never let a woman take the lead yet, and he wasn't going to stand for it from this one. Even if she was half fish. His lifebelt and his pistol lay right to hand. All he had to do was pick them up and be on his way, right?

He strapped the belt about his waist. Odd. The cuts and scrapes and burns that had bothered hell out of him since the *PT-109* sank didn't trouble him at all. And the underlying troubles were gone too. If asthma didn't have him gasping, between his back and his ulcer, he should have been doubled over in pain. But he wasn't. God, if he'd felt this way in college, he'd have lettered in football and won a Rhodes scholarship.

"Are you angry at me?"

He paused. Was *she* responsible for his well-being?

Her eyebrows arched. Beneath them, her eyes grew impossibly large and sad.

"I wanted to help you," she said. She sounded like a sad little girl, but none of his sisters had voices that sweet when they were kids, and they were likelier to scream or hit back than cry when hurt. "I brought you here. I never brought anyone else here, not even my cousins."

He had a sudden, weird vision of blacking out and being scooped up by the mermaid in a cross-chest carry that would have done any lifeguard proud. And being brought here.

Wherever *here* was. Now he spared time for more than a glance around. The familiar marks of channel and island were gone. He saw water and sky, both iridescent, both reflecting each other, with only this island between them. And the island itself was impossible: more a garden than an atoll, with its swaying coconut palms and its lavish stands of tropical flowers, some of which grew only a thousand miles away. Statues, some perfect, some half-ruined and crusted with dried weeds and shells, stood arranged by huge branches or coral. And near the mermaid's hands rested a white marble shell, in which glimmered water as strange as the sea that surrounded them.

He had heard a story once, about a mermaid . . . Nah, fairy stories were for girls. Even Teddy never listened to them. They made you soft.

"Now, you think I might be in the pay of your enemies. What could they give me that I could possibly want? All the treasures in your world come from the sea, and storms, or carelessness, or your wars return them to us. Life comes from the sea, I tell you. I promise you your friends are well. Would you see?"

She held out a hand in a gesture as graceful as plants beckoning underwater. He knew he should have backed off, should have headed for the shore and his friends, wherever *they* were. Instead, he found himself drawn toward her. He loomed over her, naked and armed. But she ignored that.

"It is good you care about your friends. See?"

She waved a hand over the water-filled shell. The water turned milky, then went clear. In it, he saw ... Jesus, Mary, and Joseph, there they were, like a newsreel in a movie theater. McMahon, Ross, Harris, Thom ... all the men who had survived. McMahon seemed to be sleeping easy. He wouldn't sleep that easy if his burns were infected.

The water went opaque once again.

"No!"

Once more it cleared. Now he saw the cone of a volcano. Washed up on a beach— "That's my ship!" He must be looking through someone's eyes. But whose?

A man with the pinkish burned, rangy look of an Aussie lowered his binoculars. The skin around his eyes was very white because his binoculars covered it for so much of the day.

Jack sighed. Even if Thom and Ross couldn't get help, even if *he* failed, the Aussie had to report to someone. And once that was done ... he could see uniformed men holding telegrams; his father moving heaven and earth all the way to the President, if need be, to get his second son back.

"Thank God!" he said and meant it. Since he'd gone to school, Mass had always been something for Mother and the girls. Now, though, he crossed himself. His eyes filled and welled over. His tears dropped into the shell basin, dissolving the vision of the Aussie observer who was going to save his men's lives.

The mermaid laid gentle fingers on his hair and stroked the thick unruly waves back from his forehead. Her hand slipped from his hair to his face.

"So much pain," she whispered. "I thought it was a simple thing, like the statues I pulled from the water, cleaned, and restored. I saw you bleed and fall. And when

I picked you up, I sensed that you were in greater pain than that. And now . . ."

Jack cradled her hand against his cheek, then kissed it, and wept into it.

"No . . . no . . . this is not foolishness, to weep for love." The mermaid's voice was very gentle. Her arm went around his shoulders and drew him close. He rested his head against her neck and breathed in her scent: flowers and the sea and woman. When he was a boy, if he fell, he was expected to pick himself up. Even by his mother. And as for his father . . . *Damn blubbering fool.* He could hear the Ambassador. *Stand up! Be a man! Make me proud of you.* He had always tried. He had mostly failed. Unless you counted the times when the Ambassador had gotten into the act.

He had succeeded in this much. His crew was safe. They had been found. They would live. He wept for that; and then he wept for the times he had hurt, and no one had comforted him; and then he wept for sorrow at the idea of children growing up as he had, with every comfort but love and forbearance.

He cried with no thought of shame, and she cradled him against her, skin against skin. And when he was cried out, he raised his head, and she kissed him.

Her lips were like the rest of her—cool, with the possibility of heat beneath the surface. They were not practiced, but they were very sweet. Very sweet indeed. He felt himself warming to the kiss. This would be easy.

To Jack's own astonishment, he was the first to break away, unmoved by her little cry of disappointment.

"I don't even know your name," he said.

"Name? It is the Great Ones, the whales, who give us our names. You could never sing them. Give me one of your names."

Calypso. Circe. Names from textbooks he'd browsed through came to mind. For the first time in his life he understood them. This was no witch who held him. A witch would be more knowing.

"Miranda," he muttered. "Oh, you wonder."

"That's a pretty sound. I like it. I like this too." Her hands tangled in his hair, trying to pull his face back down to hers. He resisted.

God, scruples? *Him?*

"Do you know what you're doing?" he asked, as if he were in a clinch with some girl he'd met at a roadhouse and suspected of being jailbait.

"Your skin is so warm," she said, running her hands over his shoulders and down his back. Thanks to her, his pain-free back. "I had a great-great-uncle who swam where the water is cold. He took a bride from those who live on land. And one of my cousins . . ."

A shadow crossed the perfection of her face.

"Yes?" Before Jack knew it, he had raised a hand to stroke that frown away.

"She loved a land-dweller. A . . . a prince, you would say. And more than anything, she wished to walk on land herself. So she bargained . . . I remember, she had had the sweetest voice, but she traded her music for feet and legs. I have heard that every step she took hurt her as if, once again, the wizard had cut out her tongue in payment. I asked her once if she thought the price worthwhile. She could not speak, of course, but she shook her head 'yes.' '

"I've seen your cousin," Jack told her before he thought. The whole damn family had been dragged through the Gardens to look at it, and some sentimental Mediterranean types had sniffled at the pack of ruddy American children—until the girls had started a kicking and hair-pulling match.

"There's a statue of her . . . far away." How could he make her understand how far? "The water is cold, and in the summer, the sun doesn't set until very late."

"She vanished. They say we have power, but no souls,

that when we cease, our bodies dissolve into seafoam, and our memories linger."

"Her memory lingers," Jack told Miranda tenderly. "In my world, every child knows of her."

Even he.

"I would not like to cease like that, even for love," said Miranda. "And yet, like my cousin, I have seen a man from the shore and . . ."

His throat tightened, the first pain he had felt since Miranda had taken him up and brought him to her island.

Jack tightened his arms about the mermaid. His Miranda, God, what would they say if they could see him now?

They wouldn't get a chance, he told himself. Miranda wasn't like the others, to be hidden away like a guilty secret or flaunted like a sports car. She was so precious . . . *God, you sound like you swallowed a bowl of sugar, don't you?*

Well, she was! he told himself.

Jack, think *what you're doing!* His father's richly accented voice pierced through the haze of pity and desire that wreathed him just as surely as clouds ring the base of an island volcano. *Think of your mother.* That was a good one; his father never did. *Think of your church.* Right. He'd pay good money to see their parish priest baptize a mermaid. Probably take a special dispensation from the Pope. *Think of me.*

I'm trying not to, sir.

He held the girl . . . Miranda . . . against him as if her cool flesh were a shield against such memories. She tightened her arms about him.

The feel of those soft, full breasts against his chest made his head spin; but before it spun out of control, he broke away from her opening lips to ask, "What do you want of me?"

"What my cousin wanted from her prince," Miranda whispered. She leaned forward to touch his mouth again with her own. "Love that does not die. Stay with me. Stay with me forever."

The shock was enough to make him jerk away from her lips, but not enough to stop him from running his hands down her sides and onto her breasts. They filled his hands. And Miranda shivered and pressed the length of her body against his. A mermaid? *Well, Jack, it's probably the only thing you haven't* ... His mind shied away from the joke.

His body wasn't shying away at all. In fact, as she moved her hips, murmuring with pleasure, he found himself rearing up, seeking entrance to her body. He slid his hands down onto her hips and touched the scales he found there gingerly. He had feared it would be like touching a fish. It wasn't. Not at all. In fact ...

"Do you know what you're doing?" he asked her.

"You do," she said. "You are so warm. Stay with me. Never grow old. Never hurt any more. And I will love you."

From the way her hands, innocent but learning fast, began to explore his body, he had no doubts of it.

"And if I want to go back?"

"I will send you, of course." The great dark eyes filled with tears. "I do not want a prisoner. No more than my cousin did. You are free."

She dropped her arms with a sigh and pushed herself a little away from him. Seeing how his eyes dropped to her nipples, which had turned pink and hard, she wrapped her arms about herself. The shell garland she wore lapped over them.

Just one woman—one mermaid—for the rest of his life, which was likely to be very, very long—unless the Japs could find him here?

He didn't think they could. After all, she had called the sharks her friends. Thank God he hadn't run into any, let alone had to shoot one.

He lifted the shell garland from around her neck,

thinking fast. To buy time, he made himself smile and put it over his own neck. She laughed, her tears turning the sound into a watery gurgle. He wanted to please her. When had he wanted to please anyone but himself?

And, of course and always, his father.

Think, Jack. For Jesus' sake, think!

His friends were safe. He needn't go back. And he could even please his father, who'd be able to say he had a son who was a war hero. He could probably get as much political mileage out of a dead hero as a live one. Let Joe Jr. have the burden; their father had groomed him to be President since he was old enough to throw a football. It wasn't as if he were the only one left, either. There was Teddy. Granted, he was spoiled rotten and wouldn't know what to do in a crisis to save his soul; but he'd have to learn just like all the Kennedy men did.

An heir and a spare. Like royalty. What more could his father want? He'd be rid of the runt.

"I could send you back," she whispered. "I could. Any time. Any place. Just look in the shell. And when the water changes, say the word, and I will send you."

She might speak of sending him away, but her voice had grown even huskier and deepened in a way he knew well. If he didn't know when a woman was ready by now, he might as well take her up on that offer or become a priest. In his own world, he'd have accused any woman who talked like that in his arms of teasing, laid her anyhow, then gotten up and left.

But he believed Miranda. Maybe it was some of that second sight that the Irish were supposed to have coming through.

And maybe it was a miracle. She had saved his life and healed him, body and soul—down to his cynicism.

It would have been a wonder if he didn't love her as much—sweet Jesus, what those scales felt like against his cock!—as he wanted her.

They could have their dead hero. He'd choose the living creature who reclined half in, half out of the stream that ran beneath the coconut palm. She clasped him with her arms and twined her lower body about his legs. The sun seemed to stroke his back and buttocks where her hands could not reach. And the lapping of the stream and the more distant flow of the sea rocked him as surely as the pliant body beneath his own.

How am I going to manage this? he thought as he slid his hand down past the mermaid's waist.

All in all, he managed fine, Jack thought later, as he drowsed by Miranda's side. For one thing, he hadn't fucked her: they'd made love, a distinction he had never thought too much about. Now, it didn't need thinking about. It just happened. Her body wasn't always cool from the salt water. It had heated up under his hands and lips as eagerly as he could have wished. And if the neat little slit within her scales had been hard to find, the scales were softer than they looked. Rubbing against them made him even harder, and her body welcomed him as if he plunged into deep water.

He raised his head. The sky had darkened. Even as he watched, the green flash exploded like a flare at the horizon. All around the tiny atoll, seafire sprang up. Some of the phosphorescence even touched Miranda, spreading up her fins and along the swell of her hip.

She opened her eyes and raised a hand. "Your face is wet." She brought her fingers to his lips, and he tasted salt. He touched her cheeks.

She shook her head. "We do not weep."

God, talk about count-your-blessings time. He had all but promised to be faithful to one woman—but she was a woman who didn't cry.

He hoped he'd never make her wish she could.

And that was a famous first.

She was watching him a little tentatively, so he laughed

and kissed her. That was far more important than famous firsts or anything else in the world.

Dusk slid into dawn—dark mother-of-pearl bleaching to white. This island floated on the breast of time like a sealed bottle on the water. Time made the island rich—time to love, time to rest, time to catch the fish or pluck the fruits, time even just to sit and gaze out into the strange sea that bounded Jack's new world, while Miranda sang.

Gradually he remembered some of the ballads she sang. They were very old, if age had any place here. She promised him that it did not, that they would never age, never die. For her, truly, the world of Tom under the hill, or the maid who loved a silkie, were as real today as when they were first sung.

Did time truly make that much difference? All his life, he had been subject to clocks and timetables, waiting only for the time when he could replace other people's schedules with his own. Now, for the first time, time held no such pressures for him, and so he listened as the mermaid sang to him.

He could well imagine how men, hearing that song as it pierced the veil between Miranda's world and the one he had left behind, hurled themselves from their ships into the water. Did their bones still rest on the ocean's bed, or did they too sit beside Mirandas of their own, listening to the piercing sweetness of their songs?

He could wish everyone to be as happy as he was. Sometimes, he would think of his crew on the atoll. By now, surely, they must have been rescued. By now, surely, they were on their way home. By now, too, every church in Boston was probably draped in black and echoing with requiem masses. His mother would be sorry. So would his sisters. Buy out every damn veil in town. Maybe even his father and brothers. He saw them grim-faced, fighting the easy sentimental Irish tears. Briefly, it occurred to him to regret it; and then Miranda sang again.

"I am a man upon the land . . . and a silkie on the sea . . ."

Scots, not Irish; but it gave him goosebumps anyhow, and then Miranda's hands did even more.

Gradually, ballad melted into ballad. Hero melded with hero, and ship with ship. It didn't truly matter if a man sailed in sight of land on a small ship with a blue eye daubed for luck at the prow, or on a vessel carved like a dragon or hung with shields, or on a galleon, looming high above the waves—or even a destroyer as deadly to ships as a killer whale was to living sea creatures: it was all the same story. In the end, a seafaring man was lucky if he had a home to return to, or, far more rarely, found someone like Miranda.

Day by day, her beauty grew warmer, and her song grew richer. It was love, he knew, and he set himself to please her, to tend the little wild garden she had made on the island, to extend it to places that the stream did not flow to, and to carry her to see those spots, then back to the water that brought life and health and eternal youth to her.

But always, the spot she loved best was the place where he had wakened, under the large coconut palm where the stream glinted in the sun and chuckled as it flowed by the marble shell into which Miranda had looked that first day, when she had told him that his men were safe.

As the days drew on and on, Miranda introduced him to more and more of her world: the great creatures and the small, who came when she whistled or sang to them. Even the mighty sharks curved their fearsome backs to her; though Jack was certain that they eyed him as a cat might eye a pet bird.

By day, Jack worked at the garden or at gathering wood that was cast up upon the shore. To his amusement, once or twice, he saw wood that might have come from a PT boat, weathered as if it had been long at sea. He had no pain, thanks to Miranda.

At night, he burned the wood. Soaked in salt, then a long time dried, it sent up fires of remarkable and vivid colors. Though Miranda kept a good way back from the fire, Jack observed how fascinated she was by it.

"Can you see pictures in the flames too?" he asked her. He stretched, warmed on one side by the fire, and on the other by Miranda's presence. "That's what you do when you live on land, you know. When I was a child, we used to make up stories about what we saw in the flames."

Burning fuel on the water . . . men swimming through it, crying in pain . . . that all seemed a distant nightmare that someone else had had. His own burns had healed without so much as a scar.

"We draw our visions from water, not fire. And they are true."

"True?" Lazily, he leaned back.

"Didn't I show you your men? And you believed me, and so you stayed?" She rested her head against his shoulder and ran a hand questioningly down his side.

"You some kind of witch, lady?" he asked lazily. He knew the answer to that. Witches had ice-cold tits. Witches were old and ugly. His Miranda was no witch.

He expected her to laugh, but she went grave, quiet like she did when she was going to talk about her world.

"Witches steal their power, no? Or they tell lies. But my power is part of what I am. What I showed you is true. You knew that, or you would not have stayed. Would not have been the man I love."

She bent and kissed his forehead, then his mouth, and he had better things to worry about than a shell full of salt water.

Miranda served dinner that night in its own shells. After Jack slurped up the tasty morsels, he stared first at the shells he'd eaten from, then into the fire, where the dreams leapt and danced in the brilliant colors that you got when you burned wood that had steeped a long time in the salt of the sea.

"You sing for me," Miranda asked.

He settled himself comfortably, head on her lap. He didn't know many songs except hymns, and somehow it didn't seem right to sing them. How about a Christmas carol? So what if it was out of season? There weren't any seasons here anyhow.

Miranda laughed at the partridge in the pear tree and chimed in on the five gold rings, swooping her hand like a white bird between him and the fire so he could almost imagine she was wearing them, one on every finger.

He ran into trouble on the later days of Christmas when the numbers started mounting up.

Nine ladies dancing, ten lords a-leaping ... Wasn't right, was it? *Ten pipers piping, eleven lords a-leaping* ... And there were drummers in there too.

He broke off, laughing. "I always *did* get it wrong. Part of the fun."

"We can see them in the fire, dancing," Miranda said.

"It's all illusion, what the fire shows," Jack said.

"*We* are real, though. *Here* is real. And the fire is real, and in it, the ladies are dancing in their fine gowns. As my cousin danced. I cannot dance with them—except in the sea. Come ... dance with me there."

She started to tug at his hand. They would dance in the warm, phosphorescent water; and she would buoy him up. Afterward, he would lay her down on the beach and they would dance another way too.

For all the days of his life, however long it was likely to be. He was abruptly, blackly down, with the Celtic gloom that hit like a sou'wester. Hadn't even had a thing to drink, either.

"How do I know it's not all a dream? That *you* aren't a dream and that I'm not lying on a rock or in a hospital somewhere?"

Now *that* would be the real joke, wouldn't it? Miranda said his men were safe. May as well believe that was true. What if they were all back—and there he was in some VA hospital, drugged out of his mind and dreaming of mermaids?

What is truth? asked Pilate. The advantages of a good Catholic education. Damn.

Jack raised his head from her lap so fast she murmured in protest. "Show me what's real. Show me."

He had her wrist in his hand and was pulling her over to the marble shell.

"What good will it do to look? You have said you are not going back."

He smiled at her and felt the old lust to dominate rise within him. "Because I asked you, baby. Because I asked."

She shook her head, and the bright hair flew about her lovely face. "This is no good time to look, when you feel the way you do. It will make you feel no better. Why don't we . . . ?" Her lips were parted, and her hands were reaching out to touch him, but he held them away from his body.

"I'm telling you, I want to see!" The old command voice was back, the one he'd used on lots of women. The way his father spoke to them because that way you got results. Never thought he'd turn down a lay in favor of some hocus-pocus, though. Well, maybe, afterward, after he saw what he was missing.

Miranda sighed, but not even the spectacular view of her breasts, rising and falling with her worry—it was *real* worry, too, no telling why—made Jack think twice. Bull-headed like his father. Call it decisive. He'd floated long enough. Time to take back control.

The mermaid bent over the marble shell. Her long hair dropped over her body and into the water. Ordinarily, he would have brushed it away for her. Now, he waited. She pushed at it, and held her hands, shining in the red fire-light, out over the water. It shone, then went silvery, like a movie screen. Jack had always wanted to see himself on one of those, with the turning globe, and the announcer proclaiming NEWS OF THE WORLD and the march music rising up to inspire the movie audience, the ones who weren't too busy trying to get their hands up someone's skirt up there in the balcony.

And there he was! Tanned, weathered even, with a truly admirable modest-but-proud grin, balancing on crutches; standing before men in uniform, receiving handshakes that told him not just that all is forgiven, but all is just fine. Like falling into a pile of pigshit, and coming up covered with gold.

He saw faces ... the big shots his father had always admired ... and now he stood among them, grinning, standing tall despite the back that he knew had to hurt like hell.

The water flickered, and he saw himself with a black band on his sleeve. Joe Jr. Oh, damn! Shot down. Wouldn't wish it on a dog, let alone his brother. But *he* was the heir apparent now, and his father stood at his shoulder, watchful, able, deadly competent. His mother and sisters wowed 'em in Boston at the rallies, and South Boston was dancing in the goddamn streets—all for him.

And there he was in the Senate. War hero. Pulitzer-prize-winning author. Senator. A very big deal, not some bare-assed beach bum shacked up on a desert island with a crazy broad.

Miranda let her hands drop. She moaned faintly in dismay, which wasn't the way he liked to hear her moan at all.

"This isn't like you," she whispered. Then, almost as if she was singing to him, "Johnny, I hardly knew ye."

"It's me, all right," he told her. "The me I was born to be. *Show* me. I have to see. What would have happened? Do I get to be President?"

She glanced into the water, eager as always to please

him. Then she flinched and cried out. "Don't ask me, oh don't!"

"Dammit, show me!" She wasn't Miranda now, the beloved, magical creature who had saved his life and who sang him into desire and then into sleep. She was just another blonde who needed to learn that when he said jump, you just asked how high. Maybe not just another blonde. All the women he'd known before would have cried. She didn't.

"As you wish." Her voice was lifeless.

Once again, the water in the marble shell shone and went silvery . . .

. . . *They were playing "Hail to the Chief" and it was for him. Damn, he'd beaten out that shifty bastard Nixon, not by much, but enough to win, and here they were riding up Pennsylvania Avenue. He had on a morning coat and a top hat because you want to look classy when you're riding next to a five-star general and lame-duck two-term President. It was cold, and it was sunny. That old poet Frost couldn't see to read the poem he wrote . . . Damn! If we weren't careful we'd have the guy crying on the platform. No, he was tougher than he looked, he was pulling himself together. Show some class, Jack; they'll love it. Give the old man his arm, smile it off, and wait for the Bible to be brought out, with— who was that tall woman with the sleek dark hair? His Jackie, deb of the year even if her old man drank—his wife standing there beaming at the idea of being First Lady.*

Pride made him shake, though the night was warm.

Jack drew himself up from where he had lain stretched out on the sand, mouthing the words, more potent than any prayer, after the Chief Justice and along with himself-as-might-have-been in the water . . . "I . . . John Fitzgerald Kennedy . . . do solemnly swear to preserve, protect, and defend the Constitution of the United States. So help me God."

And God, his father's face!

He could feel the cheers in his blood. This was the

payoff. It was better than sex, better than the rush some damn fools bragged they got in battle ... there he was in Washington, the focus of everything. His father was proud of him, and he was President. He took out his speech and started to read it in the bright cold glare of a D.C. January with the most important people in the world shutting up as he started to speak. Bet no one would ever make jokes about his accent again.

". . . and therefore I say, 'Ask not what your country can do for you, but what you can do for your country . . .' "

Damn! It was jackpot. It was Hollywood. It was all the old bastards who'd ruled countries standing at his shoulder, centuries of leaders, saying, "Good stuff! Keep it going."

Part of him really believed it. And part of him just had to have the rush of power and adoration that swept the grandstand like a tidal wave.

"Did you see that?" he asked Miranda, sweeping her away from the shell and kissing her. In a minute or two, she was going to be one very lucky girl.

Her lips were passive under his, and she pulled away with the strength he'd forgotten she had. He wondered why she'd let him push her around if she were that strong.

"I saw." She didn't squirm or protest, but moved quite firmly out of his encircling arms.

"I saw everything. Will you see the rest?"

Not waiting for his answer, she spread out her hands.

He was riding in an open car, and that twisty S.O.B. Johnson was somewhere behind him in the motorcade, not that you ever really wanted to turn your back on him for a moment. Jackie was beside him in some pink thing or other, looking beautiful now that she was coming back, thank God, from little Patrick's death ... and the sun was shining, and he was grinning, and people—these big, hearty Texans—were cheering him ...

... Fire exploded at the back of his skull and he pitched forward ...

And in the white water, he saw the tiny figure—himself as he might be if he were in the world and not on this island—fall, his skull blooming into an impossible mess of red and gray that seeped out into the water and blotted out its light.

Miranda threw herself between him and the vision. Then she fell forward in a dead faint. He had just enough time to catch her before she cracked her skull on the marble basin in which he had seen his glory and his death.

It took some time to bring her around. And even longer before she would do more than turn away from him, that gorgeous body of hers curled up into a ball as if he didn't exist. She lay in his arms, trembling, as the dawn came up. Another perfect dawn in this island between the worlds where sky and sea looked like two halves of the same precious shell and no one ever grew old or died.

And where no one would ever know what had become of the man who would otherwise have helped rule the world.

After a long while, Miranda's arms came up to encircle his neck, drawing him down beside her for what they both knew had to be the last time.

The sweat had barely dried on his body when he raised his head from her breasts. Overhead, the sun was shining in the shell-like sky, empty of all excitement or ambition.

"I have to go back."

She nodded. "I knew you'd say that. I can send you back. They'll find you on the island, you'll be a hero like the ones in the ballads we've sung, and it will all happen the way you saw it. And you'll be dead, when you could have lived forever."

The question of the sleek, black-haired woman never even came up. The world he craved was no place for Mirandas. It would make a spectacle out of her, use her up, cast her away—not that he could have her with him, in any case.

It wouldn't be a place for him, not for long, once he stood at the top of it. He looked at his Miranda. If only he hadn't wanted to know, hadn't asked. Loving him, trusting him, she had shown him his future, and the lust for power had waked in him once more. It was an ache she lacked. It was an ache she could never understand. It was bigger than both of them, as they said in the movies.

"But it means your death!" She hurled herself against him, and they both went sprawling. *My God, she's immortal—she must think of dying the way my mother thinks of hell.* "Is it really worth that much?"

The craving to be out, to be meeting people, to be chasing and mastering the power he now knew he'd win was pounding in his blood. With it came impatience—it wasn't as if there weren't lots of women, and you couldn't let them stand in your way.

But only one Miranda. (Besides that, he told the ache within him, he needed her to send him back in time for him to take his place as the hero of the rescue of *PT-109*.) Then, carefully, he stroked her hair.

"Do you remember," he asked, "the stories we told each other? The ones you told me about the black ships with the eyes painted at their prows? We have those stories, too. Did you ever hear the one about Achilles?"

"A blind man ..." Her own eyes went dim. "In the Inland Sea ... yes. Something about a choice."

Over his own voice and the lapping of the tide, Jack heard the sounds of a Harvard lecture hall, of the Master of Eliot House lecturing on how Achilles walked on the sand and had to choose between a short and glorious life and a long and happy one, while his mother—a water goddess—mourned for him as if he were already dead. His voice and the professor's seemed to sing together, like holding up a shell to your ear, even as the tide came in.

"And you are another one like this Achilles?" Miranda asked it innocently enough, but Jack was stung.

"Yes. Yes, I am. After you send me back, they will make stories about me."

She held up a hand. "I will send you back. And they will make the stories about you. And, here on my island, I will hear them. And I will, no doubt, hear when you have died. And in the end, as your people know it, it will be those stories that are true. But *I* know truth too. And what I see as truth is the man who helped me build my garden. The man who loved me, but loved . . ." Her voice broke.

I thought mermaids couldn't cry! Tears tracked her pale cheeks. Jack put out a hand to wipe them away, then, mercifully, let it drop.

"I had another cousin who loved a man. He knew this hero of yours, this Achilles, too," she added as if telling a story of old friends. "For ten years she kept him, and she swore to me that he was happy. In the tenth year, he came to her and clasped her knees and begged her to send him home.

"She did, of course. She wanted a man, not a prisoner. So I will send you back," she said. "Now. No use delaying. Get your things. You will take back all that you came with. And my love, too. And I will pray that the gods of the sea are kind to you, and that you do not remember this, except in dreams."

"But you will remember." It came almost as a demand. Even here, he could not bear to be forgotten.

"More faithfully than your own people will. And with greater love."

"How do I get back?" Jack asked.

"Walk into the sea. Swim away. *Will* yourself away. Leave the rest to me."

"Miranda . . ."

"I give that name back to you." The gray eyes begged him to understand. "Go *now*."

He walked into the water. When it reached his thighs, he turned to wave. The mermaid sat as he first had seen her, upon a rock, her hair covering her breasts, beautiful—but not of his world.

He leaned forward into the water's embrace and began to swim. A wave splashed into his face. When he emerged, sputtering, his sunburn and blisters stung, his back ached fiercely, and bile from his ulcer threatened to come up on him.

He kept on swimming. It had taken him hours, he recalled, to swim out. He returned to the atoll and to the dawn he had escaped in much less than that. His men were on the atoll. He stumbled out into their arms.

"My God, he's burning up!"

"Thank God you made it back, sir!"

"We were about to send someone after you."

He let himself sag into their arms. "Tomorrow night," he told Barney Ross, "you swim out. Do it!"

They pulled him from the water, half-carried him into the camp they had made.

"Sorry, there isn't much water," they told him.

"Then we'll move," he said. Through bleary eyes, smarting from the brine, he saw the doubt on their faces. "I'm telling you, we'll make it."

He saw their eyes brighten with faith. That was the kind of thing power could do for you. But it couldn't keep him standing. His knees gave way, and they eased him down. It felt good—or as good as he got to feel—to be lying down.

Something brushed against Jack's chest, and he raised his hand to touch it. A necklace of shells, so fragile he had barely noticed it. Even as an undertow of sleep tugged him away from consciousness, he pulled it off.

Some damn fool was clamoring in his ear. "Do you think we can make it, Lieutenant?"

He cupped the shells to his ear and heard not the sea, but the roaring of applause. Right.

"We'll make it. I've done harder things," said John Fitzgerald Kennedy.

He dropped Miranda's garland onto the beach. No memories, she had said. A wave picked it up, and it was gone.

Judith Tarr, the best-selling-author of such books as *Alamut* and *Lord of the Two Lands*, has a delightfully warped way of looking at things. (Who else would make a nasty book review the murder weapon in a mystery story?)

She took this book's title as a mandate and gave us the four Kennedy brothers as they might have been had Fate taken a totally different turn—and then, just for good measure, she balanced that with her choice for President.

Them Old Hyannis Blues
by Judith Tarr

Jack was late again. "Who is it this time?" Marilyn wanted to know. She still had that voice, all breathy and sweetsy-nice. That body, too. She swore it didn't owe a thing to modern medical science. As far as Bobby knew, she was telling the truth.

He was dead bone-tired of running this road show. Jack late. Young Joe toked out in a corner. Sometimes he giggled. Most of the time he just let the makeup maven take off the last ten years or so of living high, Kennedy Brothers style. Teddy made great stone-faces in the dressing-room mirror. Sweet Tammy was home with the kids, singing hymns by the fire and waiting for Daddy and Uncle Joe and Uncle Jack and Uncle Bobby to show up on TV—Live from the Valens Center for the Performing Arts: The Inaugural Gala.

Marilyn was looking particularly voluptuous in a Halston silk suit. It was her new look, she'd informed Bobby last year, along about the time she passed the bar. She'd had it with being a sex object. She was going to realize the power of her femininity, burst out of the patriarchal power structures, and become a new woman.

She was certainly bursting out of that suit.

"Bobby, you're not listening to me," she said. Breathy. Sweet. Iron underneath. "I want a divorce."

"Ten minutes!" from outside.

"Later," said Bobby.

"I said," she said, "I want a divorce."

Bobby ran through the checklist. Secret Service codes all over it. Times down to the minute: "1800 hours, arrive Valens Center. 1806, pass checkpoint. 1820, secure dressing room. 1833, order dinner. 1854, consume dinner." Right up to "2200, arrive backstage" and "2216, begin rendition: 'Hail to the Chief.' "

They should have added, "2143, Jack still missing." Jack did what Jack damned well pleased.

"If he doesn't show up," Bobby said, "Joe, you take keyboard."

Joe stopped giggling. "Jack always shows up."

"One of these days he won't," Teddy said. He was all ready, every sequin in place. He'd called Sweet Tammy precisely at 2135, and talked to her for precisely two minutes and fifty-nine seconds, doling out twenty seconds apiece to each of the offspring. "I'll take over for him. I have the parts down."

Bobby's teeth hurt. "You stay at bass. We need that line. You know Joe can't play bass and sing at the same time."

"Can," said Joe.

"I want a divorce," said Marilyn. "I've done the paperwork. I'm filing tomorrow. Lee says it should be final just in time for me to matriculate at Yale."

Bobby jerked around. "Yale? What the hell do you think—"

"International law," she said. "I'm going for the doctorate. I'm thinking that with the new administration and the New Direction President Presley has promised, there should be room for a few good women."

"A doctorate," said Teddy, "takes at least four years. More like eight. Or ten. He'll be out of office before you get the degree. And you'll be almost sixt—"

She flashed the smile. Like the body, it hadn't dimmed much with age. "I'll do it in four. When he comes up for his second term, I'll be ready for him."

"God," said Bobby. "Yale."

She wouldn't divorce him. She'd threatened before. He'd always got her to come around. But this looked serious. The law degree had been bad enough. "What's wrong with Harvard?"

"You went there," she said sweetly. She touched up her lips—none of this no-makeup, no-bra, hairy-legs crap for her, he gave her that much—and shut her compact with a sharp click. "I'm going out now. Break a leg, boys."

"That's for stage actors," Teddy said, as usual.

"Shut up," Joe said, also as usual.

"Am I late?" Jack asked.

The forecast had been for sleet. It must be falling: it was in the famous hair. The famous smile was turned up to max. A blonde hung on the famous arm.

Forty years of voice lessons and he still couldn't sing. The girls didn't care. They collected the old albums. They swooned over the old movies. They bought every single one of his hack best-sellers, even his "serious" shtick, *Profiles in Charisma*. They screamed when he went by.

Hiding him behind a piano hadn't worked when the Kennedy Brothers were the big band to end all big bands. When Bobby saw the future in a pounding beat and switched the act to rock and roll, Jack got himself a keyboard and taught himself some moves, and it was his name they screamed, even with Joe at lead vocals. Joe had It, said *Tiger Beat* and *Groovy* and *Rolling Stone*, but Jack had It cubed.

Jack and Marilyn together were death on the synapses. The blonde on his arm pouted, dulled to dishwater and knowing it. Marilyn patted her on the shoulder. "There," she said. "You realize of course that you're succumbing to the lies of the patriarchal system? Come on now, they're due onstage and we have some talking to do."

"We do?" the blonde asked.

"Of course we do." Marilyn got a grip on her arm. They hadn't got past the door before she started talking. "You think that there's no way to obtain power in this society except through a man. But if you consider—"

Jack laughed. "She said she wanted to meet Marilyn," he said. He looked around. "I thought we were going formal tonight. What's with the attack sequins? Are we trying to upstage Liberace?"

"We are trying," Bobby said through gritted teeth, "to perform at President Presley's inaugural ball."

"One of them," said Teddy. No one paid any attention.

The makeup maven started on Jack. He was moving stiffly, Bobby noticed. The back was out again. That meant he'd try something stupid in the performance, soldier through it with the famous bravery, and end up in the hospital. Bobby had figured it in. They weren't playing Vegas till March, and the filming wouldn't start till May. *The Road to Saigon.* Joe was the war hero this time. Jack got to be the handsome good-for-nothing who discovered himself in the last ten minutes, and saved the world for rock and roll.

"One minute!" from outside.

"Let's boogie," said Jack.

The Ritchie Valens Center for the Performing Arts smelled like a new car. Looked like one, too, shiny and new and every piece in its place, not even threatening to fall off. This was its first major gala, not that they got much bigger than the main inaugural ball. What Bobby saw was mostly glitter. Glitter hanging in sheets from the ceiling. Glitter inset in the floor. Glitter on the people packed as tight as fans at a rockfest. There were globes floating everywhere, glowing pearlily. "Alabaster," sighed Joe. "Alabaster globes." He wasn't looking up. A woman waited backstage—one of the acts, Bobby supposed; he didn't recognize her offhand. She was wearing a square yard, just about, of silver lamé, and a lot of pearls. They went nicely with her endowments, which were considerable.

Jack was over there already, flashing the grin. Joe was content to giggle. Teddy pursed his lips and disapproved. Bobby sighed.

"Time!" from the curtain.

They leaped into place: Bobby at drums, Joe at the mike, Teddy at bass. Jack sauntered. He inspected the keyboard. He frowned. "I'm not sure—"

The curtain sank through the floor. Crowd-roar rocked them back. A chord thundered out of the keyboard. The bass howled a split second late. Then they were into it: "Hail to the Chief," as arranged and performed by the Kennedy Brothers in honor of the thirty-seventh President of the United States.

"El-vis! El-vis! El-vis!"

He came in waving and smiling, looking just a little sultry in white tie and tails. The First Lady was radiant in clouds of white tulle, with her platinum hair done up just this side of extravagant, and a spray of orchids for a tiara. His nibs had lost some lard, Bobby noticed, and her FirstLadyship had gone ahead and got that breast-reduction surgery. Too bad. In her heyday she'd have outdone the bosom in the wings by a good six inches. She was still magnificent. There'd been a few nights, and that weekend in Malibu . . .

He'd forgotten it, of course. Until he needed it.

They ended the old standby with a new riff that took

all of Bobby's concentration. Then they swung into something light and easy, mill-and-swill music for the President's ball. Joe crooned into the mike. "Them blues, them
old Hyannis blues. . . ."

They'd cover the country tonight, from Hyannis to Malibu, Grosse Pointe to Galveston, and end up with the
President's own personal theme, "Graceland on My Mind."
Teddy was back on track after doing half the first number
a half-note behind. Joe was in good voice, for once. Jack
hadn't missed any notes yet. Bobby let the rhythm play
through him and, for the first time in months, thought
he might relax.

Vice President King came backstage at the break, towing a nicely integrated pair of teenage gigglers. The redhead would be something when she was a few years older.
The Veep's daughter already was. Took after her mother,
Bobby noticed. "And how's Coretta?" Teddy was asking.

"Glowing," said the Veep. "Just glowing."

"Alabaster," crooned Joe. "Alabaster globes."

"New song," Bobby said quickly. He slashed a hand
behind his back. One of the roadies boxed Joe in and got
him talking about, as far as Bobby could tell, the High
Sierras.

Jack had wandered off again. He wasn't interested in
potential. He wanted his beauties ripe, and now. After a
while he wandered back. Teddy and the Veep were swap-
ping road stories—the campaign trail wasn't much different from the rock circuit. The gigglers were giggling and
sliding eyes at Jack, who made their year with a grin and
a platitude. They'd never know they'd had the brushoff.
"Take a look at this," he said to Bobby.

Bobby started to snap back, but Jack had pulled him
over to the edge of the stage. There was a gap in the
curtain. Bobby got a wide angle on the audience, milling
and swilling as frantically as ever. The President was in

the middle, and the First Lady's platinum 'do glowed as brightly as one of those damned ambulating beach balls.

"Look over there," said Jack.

Marilyn still had the blonde in tow, but they'd picked up a third weird sister. This one looked like a very genteel horse.

"She's British," Jack said. "Amazing how a woman can look like hell in chiffon."

"The dress isn't bad," said Bobby. "The hat is the problem."

"The hat is always the problem," Jack said. "Just ask the Queen." He paused. He wasn't grinning as much as usual. "You know, it's funny. Remember that crazy we had to ask Frankie to help us get rid of, back in L.A.? She looks like that."

"That crazy was male, filthy, and wouldn't know chiffon if you wrapped him in it."

"Not that, damn it," said Jack. "Look at her eyes."

Jack couldn't read a newspaper at less than three feet, but give him a hundred yards of packed ballroom and he could count the sequins on Liberace's cummerbund. Bobby squinted. Marilyn was holding forth. The blonde was either rapt or shell-shocked. The woman in chiffon— God, a face like that and she wanted ruffles—wasn't looking at either of them. Marilyn was about twenty feet from the President, just outside the security perimeter. The President would be standing, from the woman's angle, just behind Marilyn's right shoulder.

Bobby didn't shiver often. "Tough," he said, "and mean. What's she got against him?"

"The Revolutionary War?" Jack shrugged. "Maybe the War of 1812, though we've got grudges of our own, there."

Bobby curled his lip. "Egghead," he said.

Jack punched Bobby on the shoulder. It was nicely calculated. Just hard enough to bruise, not hard enough to knock him sideways. Smiling all the while. "She does look like old dad, doesn't she?" He crossed himself devoutly. "May he rest in peace, if there's peace in downtown hell."

"Downtown," Joe twanged behind them. "Downtown hell."

There was one good thing about Joe's getting loose. The Veep wasn't there anymore to hear him.

Outside, onstage, Secretary of State Lennon was going on about New Directions and Brave New Worlds and When It's '84. He'd smoothed out his accent for the occasion.

Bobby happened to glance toward Marilyn. She hadn't moved. Hadn't stopped talking, either. But if the Brit in chiffon had looked mean when she looked at the President, she looked murderous as she listened to the Secretary of State.

Bobby shrugged. She wasn't his problem. Keeping this show on the road was.

They got through the medley—"Rocky Mountain Sighs," "California Babes," and the wall-thumping, teeth-rattling crescendos of "Niagara Falls." Then, while the floor was still rocking and the crowd still rolling, Jack grabbed the bass right out of Teddy's hands and leaped off the stage.

Bobby had been in between chords somewhere. He came out of it with a snap. Teddy goggling and empty-handed. Joe at the mike, starting in on "Manhattan Lovers." Blurs out beyond the stage, with smudges for eyes. Jack bounding through with Teddy's custom axe high over his head, heading right for President Presley.

People goggling. His nibs looking sultry. Suits closing in. Over on the edge, winter-white Halston and dishwater blonde and too damned much pink chiffon.

The chiffon had a gun.

So did the tux heading for the President.

The axe caught the tux's hand. Bobby didn't hear the gun go off. Too many screamers. Teddy's bass came back around and lobbed the tux right into the oncoming suits.

Jack was grinning like a maniac. He might have been singing, too. Bobby didn't envy anybody who could hear him.

The chiffon braced her wrist with her other hand. Bobby's eye followed the line of her aim. Vice President King was somewhere in the muddle, suits all over, women shrieking, men hitting the floor. Secretary Lennon hadn't moved. His silly little glasses gleamed. His long egghead face looked more interested than anything else. Even when the red flower bloomed all over the front of his clean white shirt.

Halston tackled chiffon. Marilyn's timing was just a little off. It did keep the second shot from hitting anything but one of those damned globes. It shattered. The shrieking hit banshee volume.

Bobby slammed the cymbal. It brought Teddy around. Bobby jerked his head toward the keyboard. Teddy did a fish-take, but he went where Bobby told him. On the way by, he pulled at Joe's arm. Bobby signaled. Joe, bless his pickled brains, wrapped his hands around the mike. Teddy kicked a chord out of the board. Bobby set the beat. Joe started to wail. He had lungs on him, and the amps were cranked just short of feedback. Without the bass line it wasn't the gut-buster it could have been, but it outhowled anything the crowd could come up with. "Bay-*beeeeeee*, you just kill me, baby, do . . ."

Jack landed himself in the hospital. It wasn't the backhand that did it, though it finished off Teddy's bass. It was the pileup afterward, with the tux on the bottom and Jack on top of him and the Secret Service six deep on top of that.

The tux was Brit, too. "Name of Jagger," said President Presley in his best corn-pone drawl. "Front man for the Unified United Kingdom Front."

"The one that wants to take over Free Ireland and make it safe for tea and crumpets?" asked the hero of the hour.

He was flat in the hospital bed and white as the sheets, but it didn't stop him from turning on the grin.

"That one," the President said. "The other bastard, though, who got John Lennon—God rest him—" he said, looking more sultry than usual, damn near smoldering, "that was their fearless leader herself."

"Iron Maggie," said Marilyn. Makeup just about hid the black eye, and she didn't limp when she thought anyone was noticing, but she carried herself with a certain air she hadn't had before. Satisfaction. "The Friedrich Engels of the underground. She'll take over Britain, she says, and make it a world power again."

"You've been talking to her?" Even Jack sounded surprised.

"She's supremely wrongheaded," Marilyn said, "and she's convinced herself that the only way to overcome male power structures is to dominate them and then destroy them, but she does agree that violence was not exactly the best way to go about it. I've sent her Betty's book, and Gloria is going to see her tomorrow."

"She'll be deported," said Teddy from where he sat by the window. His voice seemed to be coming out of a basket of gardenias. "If she's lucky, she'll get out of prison in about sixty years."

"Oh," said Marilyn, "I don't know. She did feel that she was executing a traitor. He was, if you look at things that way. He should have dedicated his genius to the cause of his own country, not to a pack of jumped-up rebels."

Bobby rolled his eyes. The President looked a bit glazed. Marilyn had that effect on people.

His nibs mustered up a smile. "You certainly saved us from a very unfortunate situation," he said. "We'd have lost more than John, without the two of you."

"And the boys, too," said Marilyn. "They kept the crowd calm."

"They certainly did," said the President, shaking hands

all around. Joe wiped his hand on his pants. People pretended not to notice.

Jack traded grins with the President. "You know, Jack," his nibs said, "with a little help from your friends, you'd be a smash in politics."

"I'd need help?" Jack asked.

Everybody laughed. Jack just kept smiling.

"Think about it," the President said. "You saved my life—and the Veep's, too. You know how to work a crowd. I can just see the ads: Mad Jack with his bass guitar, saving the world for democracy."

Bobby's face hurt. So did his stomach.

"What do you say?" said the President in the fast patter of politicians and used-car salesmen everywhere. "There'll be a House seat vacant, you wait and see. Then maybe the Senate."

"I don't know," said Jack.

"It's the least I can do," said the President, "for the man who saved my life."

"What about the woman?"

Maybe no one heard that one but Bobby. Marilyn was smiling as sweet and empty as a pile of cotton candy. Until you saw her eyes. Bobby wondered just how much she'd been teaching Iron Maggie, and how much she'd been learning.

"Oh," Jack said again, "I don't know. I'm not much on speechifying, or on keeping my nose clean. Now, if you wanted to ask Teddy . . ."

Not Bobby, Bobby noticed. Teddy was already blustering, the old I'm-not-worthy shtick. The presidential focus turned on him. A minute more and they were an act, his nibs leaning, his purity protesting, and everybody else closed out.

"Clever," said Bobby.

Jack grinned. He looked gray under it. Soldiering on. Bloody fool.

"I wonder sometimes," Bobby said, "if politics might not have been the way to go after all."

"Not me," said Jack. "Not till hell freezes over."

"Downtown," Joe sang to himself from among the gardenias. "Downtown hell. Hot time, hot time in downtown, downtown, downtown hell."

"Washington," Jack sang in his just-off-key tenor. "Washington blues. So hot in August, we can't—you can't— Hell," he said. "I never could get a line to come out straight."

"Straight down," sang Joe, "straight down, go down, to downtown hell."

"I sent the papers in," said Marilyn, "yesterday. For the divorce."

Bobby grabbed a piece of paper. It was part of Jack's chart. He flipped it over and fished out a pen.

"You can keep the house," she said. "I've rented a cottage in Westport—Katherine was so sweet about it, she even threw in the maid and gardener. I'll commute to Yale from there."

"Hell," sang Joe, "hell so hot, so hot . . ."

Jack fingered imaginary keys on the tight white sheet. Joe sang nonsense, but nonsense with a beat. Bobby pulled it all together. Arrangements—bigger group for this one. Backups. Chicks in red, devil babes, lots of glitz. Teddy needed a new axe, got to get that straightened out, and Vegas, and the *Stone* interview, and maybe Jack should do the hero in the *Road* movie, after all, the ads for that, now, what his nibs said about Mad Jack wasn't a bad idea at all.

"I may even," she said, "now that I think of it, try politics myself."

Politics, Bobby thought, scribbling words and music. Who needs politics? We've got a song to write.

Leave it to best-selling horror writer Alan Rodgers, author of *Fire*, *Night*, and *Pandora*, and his collaborator, James Macdonald, author of *The Gathering Flame* (with Debra Doyle), to choose the lobotomized Rosemary Kennedy as their subject.

This exceptionally strange story is told from Rosemary's point of view. Depending on your point of view, it's either science fiction or horror. Or perhaps both.

Rosemary: Scrambled Eggs on a Blue Plate
by Alan Rodgers
and James D. Macdonald

"The family experienced its first misfortune when Rosemary was found to be mentally defective."

—Encyclopaedia Britannica

"Partial separation of the frontal lobes from the rest of the brain results in reduction of disagreeable self-consciousness, abolition of obsessive thinking, and satisfaction with performance, even though the performance is inferior in quality."

—Psychosurgery,
Walter Freeman and James Watts,
Springfield, Ill., 1942

The thing about Rosemary was that they cut out her brain the year she turned twenty-three.

Oh, not all of it; if they'd took it all she'd have had nothing to think with or feel with or know with at all. That would have been a blessing, if they'd took it all. If they'd took it all it would have spared her knowing what she was, and feeling what she was; and maybe if they'd took enough her body would've shut down and died.

But no; instead of taking it all and giving her dark to escape the light they took the part that gave her the will to get up in the morning and *live*.

They took the part she needed to think two thoughts in a row.

The part that would've let her tell . . . !

But the thing that they didn't take, that she really wished they had, was her *remember*.

Oh, how she wished they'd took her *remember*! If they'd took it she wouldn't have to *remember* over and over again. *Remember* what happened that afternoon on the green hill beneath the too-blue sky; *remember* the angel-hair worms and Jack and Bobby and Joe running for his life, which was no use in the long run; *remember* the diamond-green-eyed doctor who wasn't any doctor even if Daddy and everybody else thought he was; *remember* the clamp and the light in the hospital where they cut up her brain even though she tried to scream at them to let her go go go let her alone get away *get away!* She screamed just like she always screamed when she thought about—

About.

Worse than the hospital and the doctors who weren't doctors but something infinitely more terrible; worse than being stuck in now with no past and no future, *remember* gave her the vision of John.

And the thing that took him.

John John John.

Her brother John.
John F. Kennedy! President of you and me! John F. Kennedy!

Sometimes when she watched it happening over and over again in her head, it seemed to her that she was seeing through someone else's eyes. Not just the someone else who was her before Space Aliens cut her brains out because she knew too much. The eyes of *lots* of someones! Lots and lots! That was stupid crazy scatterbrains like everything about Rosemary now, but it was true, it was true, her memory was a movie on late-night TV, a camera moving switching jumping from scene to scene till she wasn't sure who or what or why she was, but then Rosemary confused easy nowadays anyway.

John was her brother and he was her President, and that made her very proud. Except when she *remembered*. Which was more often than she liked to think about.

She could remember John even when he was still John, could remember back before he was President. That was the trouble, wasn't it? The trouble was about—

About.

The door opened and the shade flapped as the wind pushed against it and the pretty lady with the diamond-green eyes walked into the room.

So pretty pretty pretty, that lady. Pretty and hateful and mean.

She wasn't any lady neither.

Time for your medication, Rosemary, she'd say in a minute. Rosemary didn't know this by deduction the way ordinary folks do—she didn't have it in her to think about how the lady was here yesterday and the day before and the day before into forever, and if she always came around this time of day with medicine then she must be here with medicine again—

No.

Rosemary knew it like this: A vision of a woman, and the woman looked just like this one except Rosemary could see her as what she looked like down inside, with diamond-green skin and lizardy to match the eyes she always had on the outside; and Rosemary watched amazed to see the alien evil beautiful horrible mouth open to say, *Time for your medication, Rosemary,* just as this woman the real woman so beautiful just now came through to door and said,

"Time for your medication, Rosemary," as she smiled *so* wide. "Rosemary? Time for your medication."

So evil, that beautiful woman. Rosemary just ignored her.

It was the evil beautiful Space Alien women who stole John and Bobby and maybe Ted, maybe not. It was! Rosemary saw them when they came to take him and switch him for a doppelgänger made of strange fleshlike clay from beyond the stars!

It was true it was really true true true and Rosemary knew it because when she told about it the UFO Aliens pretended to be doctors and cut out her brain.

Rosemary *remembers* as the medication overwhelms her. That's the way *remember* almost always starts.

When the *remember* camera is someone else Rosemary can think almost clear. Like now through the eyes of the scrambled-egg lady in the big institutional kitchen that services the convent—now and here in the graying dark she can *remember* how sometimes when she looks in a mirror the face she sees isn't her own, but then she wasn't standing in front of a mirror anyway. And when she touches her face with her hand it isn't her face and it isn't her hand but she can *look* and she can *see* when no one else can look *or* see.

And she can *do*, too.

Sometimes when she finds eyes that aren't very crazy (and it's the crazy people whose eyes she shares—it always has been) it occurs to her to wonder how it happens she can see cameralike this way. Is it some strange effect from the worm that tried and failed to take her? Is it some uncanny psychic power come to her by equal and opposite reaction when the doctor reached in her brain with his sharp tool and *stirred*?

There isn't any way to know; in the end it's a silly question. She knows; she sees; she's Rosemary; she *is*.

Remembers.

Remembers the dark in the convent kitchen that isn't dark but bright bright like the light that shines from the sky against the blue sky! In the morning bright blue light she's making scrambled eggs *Green Eggs and Ham* no blue not green blue—

No. That's the way it looks to *Rosemary*. These eyes see it differently.

Making scrambled eggs for the patients (but she *is* a patient!) and the kitchen walls are blue with all the color washed away like black-and-white TV she knows, she remembers, she *knows* gray eggs because she *is* gray scrambled eggs. . . .

Blue most of all. Blue, blue, blue.

Rosemary seeing through the camera that was the scrambled-egg lady in the kitchen knows why she draws fine wormlike strands of egg out across the griddle; knows what the worms did and what they are. Knows what they mean and what they mean to do.

And even if the hands, the eyes, the brains of the morning cook don't know from worms or angel hair or why Rosemary makes the hands draw egg out wormlike across the griddle, Rosemary knows.

Rosemary hates worms like angels' hair. Hates them. Rosemary.

Rosemary was found to be mentally defective. That's what it said in the encyclopedia. Rosemary read it one day when they left her in the doctor's office for half an hour and she'd had a chance to play with his bookcase. She couldn't read good no more, no more no more couldn't think couldn't read could cry too well when she needed to, but she could read that sentence! And she could never forget it. *Rosemary was found to be mentally defective.* Those were exactly the words it said. Defective! Like she was a tire with a hole in it when it came from the factory. And who was it who found her that way, huh? The Space Aliens, of course.

Rosemary.

Deeper, deeper Rosemary she goes till it's summertime, the summer just before the war after the war to end all wars *War of the Worlds* world of the wars world war too when Joey died that war that war where they killed him. (They killed Rosemary, too. But they left her alive when they were done and she's still mad about that.)

The doctor has a pretty pretty voice, just like the voice of the medication lady still singing echoes inside Rosemary's skull. "I'm sorry, Mr. Ambassador." He's hungry as he says this, Rosemary can hear it hear it there's hunger in his voice like lust she remembers lust just barely just enough to recognize it in the doctor's voice. "Rosemary suffers from *dementia.* There's hope—that surgery can make her happy and normal. . . . Well adjusted." Rosemary can feel him smiling inwardly as he as he holds his face slack-still. "This is my recommendation."

A high clear blue-sky day, and they're on a picnic. Jack and Bobby and Joe and Rosemary, all of them together now when everyone stands still alive, alive to walk the emerald-green hill beneath the sky so clear so impossibly clear blue. . . . Even now the blue that was only color and light no sinister no alien no hate no hunger just-the-color blue would send her screaming if she had wits to scream.

Today they served her scrambled eggs on a sky-blue plate.

Just to remind her.

Remind her.

Remind.

Remember.

This is a *remember*, isn't it? Rosemary has trouble telling which from which sometimes. Sometimes she thinks even the medication is only a *remember*.

It doesn't matter. All that matters is the high-blue New England autumn day.

Bobby saw it first, Bobby the little boy saw it first, great white blinding light in the sky that wasn't the sun, wasn't the sun or fire nor any artifice of man nor woman. . . .

They call it angel hair that falls from the sky.

What do you know about lobotomies? The word comes from the Latin *lobus*, which comes in its turn from the Greek *lobos*—any rounded and projecting part of an organ. And -*tomy*, from the Greek *tomē*—a cutting. The word is of modern coinage. It means "a cutting into or across a lobe of the brain, usually the cerebrum, to alter brain functions, especially in the treatment of mental disorders."

Rosemary lost *now* from *when* a long time ago—she remembers words like *date* and *time*, but she isn't sure what they mean any more. But she could never lose the blueberry bushes, no matter what they cut away from her. The blueberry bushes and the too-blue sky, and the light that came and the people after, and how they came for her and John and Bobby and Joe and hunted them down.

How she ran.

How she screamed.

She remembers what screaming was like, and wishes she could again. Like before she felt the hard cold thing that pressed pinpoint-sharp at the corner of her eye.

> *"Even though the fixed ideas persist and the compulsions continue for a while, the fear that disabled the patient is banished. How much the relief means to the patient suffering from doubts and fear, morbid thoughts, hallucinations and delusions, and compulsive activities, may easily be imagined."*
>
>   —Psychosurgery

She's looking through the trees as green as lizards' eyes, waiting for something to appear.

The eyes she sees through aren't her own.

Remember wedges into *remember*: They stuck something in her eye. Rosemary who is not Rosemary shudders involuntarily, terrified of the *remember* as she cannot be when she sees through her own eyes. She cries out softly, almost loud enough to hear, almost loud enough to give herself away. And reaches up, and rubs her eyes.

The eyes that are not Rosemary's blink and blink, confused and afraid at the unknowable *Rosemary* cascade of motion and emotion.

What goes in through the eye can come out through the eye. Stands to reason.

They took Jack and they took Bobby, but Joe ran the other way and they didn't get him. She saw them try she saw them hunt but they never got him never ever ever that Rosemary saw. The sky was blue and the angel hair kept falling falling falling and she took it and she tried to save it but it melted melted all over her hands and blouse and dried to vapor, traceless, stainless, nothing to show, to prove, no way to say *it isn't me I'm not crazy or am but what's it matter!?* They wouldn't believe a word she said, she knew that knew it so why even open her mouth? Crazy Rosemary, go talk to yourself.

It's a beautiful day and nothing happened. Nothing at all or she'd remember, and she'd tell.

Wouldn't she?

Time for your medication, Rosemary.

"No, Mr. Ambassador. There won't be a scar. She's such a pretty girl. There won't be any scar."

The ship was big and bright and full of who knows what with lizard skins and eyes so green and even with the light so blinding she could see they weren't people at all, but they came and took Jack and Bobby and was Ted there? She can't remember. Maybe they got him that day, maybe it was another. She wasn't sure. That's why she had to try. On the days her *remember* worked, when she could scream if she wanted, she didn't so they wouldn't know. When the light came she put the angel hair in her pocket because she was clever then. Clever before they stirred her brains with a knife. But inside the ship, she sneaked in there too when they weren't watching and saw what they did with Jack and Bobby and she told Joe later and he said don't tell anyone they'll think you're crazy.

Joe had a way with words, he did. And he was always right.

She's holding something hard against her cheek and squinting, squinting, looking through her eyes that aren't hers, waiting for something to appear through the trees. She rubs her eyes again, rubs her left eye with her free hand, only this time the arm doesn't want to do what she wants, it doesn't like her, it's confused, it's afraid, it doesn't know where it is or what it's doing or why the hardness on her right cheek, and Rosemary's hand did what Rosemary wanted—the hand didn't care and what do crazy people know about what you think of them?

What do crazy people know?

The angel hair all melted before she got home, and no one believed her. They never believed her. They all thought she was crazy. Rosemary understood and no one ever believed her.

"Shall we schedule the operation, Mr. Ambassador? The sooner the better, if you'll follow my advice, sir. She isn't going to get any better, and delay could only worsen her condition."

Bones and blood, they turned them inside out but then they came walking out they came looking just the same, but they weren't, she could tell, not the same, not the same down deep inside where the *you* was, where the *me* was, where the *they* was not not not the same where the *I* was. Only she could tell no one else no one, and who would believe *Crazy Rosemary*? The angel hair was gone, hair covers the head, inside the head was different. Alien Clay, it formed, she watched and no one believed. Of course not! She was *Crazy Rosemary*! That's what makes them strong, you know. What makes them strong is how no one no one no one ever believes her.

At the autopsy, when the doctors at Bethesda cut open and dissected what was left of John Kennedy, the thing that amazed them most of all was the way his brain came so easily away from his skull. At least one conspiracy theory is based on that fact—that for all the world it looked to the doctors at Bethesda as though someone had *already* dissected the President's head.

Who could have suspected that it happened before he died? Assuming, of course, that alien clay is alive at all.

* * *

Wealth goes with power, power with wealth, and she was wealthy, wealthy as any Kennedy. So why wasn't she powerful? Strong enough to stop it. To stop them.

What was the question?

The sky was blue and they all walked home together and was Teddy there and why can't I remember but Bobby and Jack were there and Joe too and he held her hand and squeezed so hard it hurt and I remember. With wealth comes power. But not to the simple and meek, and who would she tell because here comes the nasty lady to say *Why won't you take your medication, Rosemary? It's for your own good, you know.*

The prefrontal lobotomy cuts off—what else?—the prefrontal lobes of the brain. The place where the self lives, if you believe some of the theories. There's even an expression that's so common it's a cliché: *a lobotomized smile.* Because people with lobotomies are always happy. Maybe because they can't remember what made them sad.

In the old days, in the first half of the twentieth century, lobotomies were done the hard, messy way. The patient was anesthetized with electric shock, the skin above the forehead cut and the scalp drawn back to reveal the skull. A small hole, about an inch in diameter, was drilled in the coronal suture, carefully, to avoid damage to the very sensitive organ that lay beneath, and the prefrontal lobes were separated from the rest of the brain with a single stroke. Then the scalp was returned and sewn together. A difficult, dangerous, and lengthy procedure.

The first surgeon to have done a lobotomy must have had balls of brass, to dare cut up a living brain like that. Either that, or he didn't care if the patient lived or died or spent the rest of her life in diapers.

Either that, or someone told him that it would work.

Did you know that most, maybe all, of the brain surgeons who did frontals were men? And that most, though not all, of their patients were women? Stands to reason: women get hysterical, and nothing calms them down like a good lobotomy.

Talk to them talk to who, who are they let me talk to them? Scrambled eggs on a sky-blue plate, the sky was blue that day and Jack looked like scrambled eggs only red red and blue and red white and blue bunting the inauguration saw that on television couldn't let her out in public where the press could see her because that might mean questions about how *stable* the *President* was wouldn't it? Bad enough he's a *Catholic* and owes allegiance to a foreign power. They'll never know how foreign how alien the power is, or how deep the allegiance I pledge allegiance to the flag red white and blue scrambled eggs. Bless me Father for I have sinned, I don't know how long it's been since my last confession but she hasn't sinned.

Green leaves green like lizard eyes.

Here they come. Squeeze.

Crazy people can't sin because to sin you need total consent of the will and crazy people don't have consent. Or will either. And she's crazy isn't she or they wouldn't need to give her medication.

Would they?

"The operation was a success, Mr. Ambassador. A complete success."

The new method of performing a lobotomy is quite simple. It's called an orbital lobotomy. The patient is restrained, since some can become quite agitated and might hurt themselves. The head is immobilized. A local anesthetic is given, which is much safer than general anesthesia—with general anesthesia, there's always a chance that the patient will never wake up. A tiny mistake with the gasses, and she never wakes up.

* * *

Let's see, Jack was there and she's sure of him and Bobby was there and she's sure of *him* and Joe was there, and she's sure it wasn't him, but she isn't sure of Teddy. Maybe he wasn't even there. The angel hair melted and her eyes should have melted from looking on the light like the light of God that you can't look on and keep your wits after and some run mad and some prophesy, and some never return. No, none of them ever return the way they were. And that was when she *decided*, when she *knew*, when she had to do something but was it before or after Joe died?

The instrument used to perform the orbital lobotomy is called a *leucotome*. Long, flat, and thin, it looks like nothing so much as a stiletto made of surgical steel. The leucotome is introduced at the midline of the orbit, below the upper eyelid, and pressed inward. That's where the name comes from: *orbit-* from the Latin *orbitis* (meaning a wheel or circle), in anatomy the bony cavity of the skull containing the eye and its appendages (muscles, glands, etc.), the eye socket; and the *-al* genitive ending, meaning "of or pertaining to." In the orbital lobotomy, the instrument is passed up above the eye, through the socket and into the brain, and then moved slightly from side to side. Performed properly, the sharp end of the probe separates the prefrontal lobe.

A mark is placed on the instrument, the leucotome, the probe, the stiletto, the knitting needle, the ice pick, so that the surgeon will know when it's gone in to the proper depth. For the slice.

In contrast with the original method of lobotomy—which required the surgeon to wait for his patient to recover from the anesthesia to learn whether or not the procedure met with success—orbital lobotomy allows the surgeon to see the result of his efforts almost immediately. The moment he makes the cut, his patient relaxes. Often she will smile.

The entire procedure can take as little as fifteen minutes.

They put her head in the clamp and it was cold and she faced into the blinding light like the light against the pure blue sky and she screamed and it didn't stop and there were bites, pinpricks, like the mosquitoes that bit her on the picnic around her eye, top and bottom and right and left and she looked into the light like the light that shone against the blue blue sky. And she squinted against the light looking hard, waiting for it to appear. And there was the pressure against her eye, and a cold feeling inside and her eye was taped open and she couldn't blink and there was more pressure and the cold went inside and she could *hear* it as it scraped along the inside along the bone and the light wouldn't go out. And then it didn't matter anymore and everything was fine and what was it about Jack anyway? *Rosemary, it's time for your medication.*

The *remember* is still there but time's gone away and it's always now. Remind. Mind again. Never mind. She's half a mind to tell someone but who'd believe her? Was Teddy there? Joe was there but they didn't get him. No he got himself so they wouldn't get him because they were following him or maybe they wanted him out of the way so that Jack could do it, be president of the most powerful country in the world and get people into space and into space space is where they come from and the sky is blue when you look up but they're green—

—and how can you have power you can't use and use it anyway because they have to be stopped and they're cruel and if you could only see them like they are you'd stop them too—

—and never leave the green earth to go where they want you to go into space by the end of the decade to the moon which shines bright at night but not as bright as the bright bright light in the operating room against the blue blue sky when the angel hair fell.

"Welcome home, Rosemary."

"Hello, Daddy."

"I'd like you to meet Nurse Larson. She's here to help you, to make sure you take your medication."

"Thank you, Daddy."

She looks *out* through the eye where the ice pick went *in*, and she sees through eyes that aren't hers.

You can't stop them by shooting them. Rosemary tried that a long time before the School Book Depository and through the eye of the one with the beard and the running sores on his left arm. Jack only got a bad back. It didn't help to shoot them in the human parts—you had to find the clay. Alien clay. Brain. Alien clay brain.

Joe was gone gone gone in the war. And who was there besides Rosemary? Who? Nobody. Nobody but Rosemary and God! Does she hate scrambled eggs and they always serve her scrambled eggs on a blue plate to make sure she knows even if she can't remember. And is that alien clay in her head? Why is she trying to dig into her head with her fingernails? I thought I told you to make sure she took her medication.

No time no time at all only now and the light and the sky and the brain and the light there at the same time light the sky is blue there's something wrong with his brain but the brain is missing in a bottle on someone's desk not buried with the rest of him and now it's missing and no one knows where it is and she's watching TV again because she can sit in front of the TV and smile and everyone seeing her smile thinks she's enjoying the show and then they break and the pictures are from somewhere called Dallas and someone shot him in the head when his car came out from behind the trees and she's still smiling and they say she doesn't understand.

But she does. She does, she does, she really does understand.

He's dead now.

Jack just like Joe because she saw him in the sights and she squeezed.

Later on they get confused, ask her about smiling again and again because they know she knows she saw Jack! *John F. Kennedy! President of you and me!* saw him dead in the convertible in Dallas she won't answer she won't ever tell them the walls have ears and someone says she's hysterical but she isn't really, isn't even though they give her more medicine she doesn't need it, really, really doesn't need it Rosemary couldn't be happier she couldn't.

So take the medicine, and *remember* takes her and she's standing on the hill with Bobby and Joe and Jack and maybe Teddy maybe not, she thinks about Bobby. And she thinks: if Bobby ever gets *near* being President she knows just exactly what to do. It's all now. The now before, the now after, remind.

Remember.

Scrambled eggs on a blue plate.

"*Not always does the operation succeed; and sometimes it succeeds too well, in that it abolishes the finer sentiments that have kept the sick individual within the bounds of adequate social behavior. What may be satisfactory for the patient may be ruinous for the family.*"

—Psychosurgery

"*Rose bore her husband nine children and taught them love, compassion, and serenity.*"

—Encyclopaedia Britannica

Brian Thomsen, editor of Questar Books, has recently started writing science fiction as well as purchasing it. As a not-very-proud-of-it former editor of precisely the kind of source material he used for this version of John F. Kennedy's life, I'll vouch for its authenticity (if not its veracity).

•

The Missing 35th President
by Brian M. Thomsen

REPORT   5673097
DATE: 04132731
TO: Professor M. Chandler, Director of Research &
             Reintegration, Wolper Inc.
FROM: Malachi Sanders, Consultant
RE: MISSING PRESIDENTIAL REMAINS #35

As we approach our final deadline for the full implementation of Operation Inaugural Clone two years hence, I have grown quite discouraged. It would be a shame to have the entire Millennium celebration of American Independence's Night of a Hundred Presidential Clones suffer for the absence of one of the first hundred leaders of our country. Though PDC[1] information is scarce, we have nonetheless solved over the past forty years of the project's history such problems as "Grover Cleveland—#24 or #26?," "John, Sam, and John Q.—which two?," "Nixon—why was he deleted?," and the now famous plot to substitute J. Edgar Hoover's DNA for the Herbert Hoover sample by a radical minority fringe group called the New Republicans. At the present time all ninety-nine clones are healthy and happy in preparation for their big day on July 4, 2776. At the present time, only the remains of the 35th President, John F. Kennedy, have not been located for processing.

The official federal records concerning his demise are as follows:

11221963 John Fitzgerald Kennedy assassinated in Dallas, Texas, by Lee Harvey Oswald.
Body transported to Washington, D.C., for funeral.
11251963 Body interred at Arlington National Cemetery. Memorial commissioned with eternal flame by act of Congress.
03172001 Eternal flame goes out due to federal bankruptcy.
01162700 Section G7[2] removed samples from grave.
01302700 Test results confirmed—no DNA/human remains (residue) present.
02102700 Section G7 removed larger sample from grave.
02242700 Test results confirmed—no DNA/human remains (residue) present.
03012700 Entire contents of grave and surrounding area exhumed and transported to RCGRF.[3]
06022700 Test results confirmed—no evidence of DNA/human remains (residue) present for at least nine hundred years.

Conclusions:
1. The Presidential remains were removed prior to research project (conclusion dismissed upon examination of Arlington security records.)
2. The Presidential remains were never interred in this location (confirmed by EPA[4] soil analysis).

* * *

Recent archival records unearthed at the West Palm Beach Archaeological Dig have provided a substantial amount of evidence suggesting that Kennedy did not die in 1963. After evaluating several thousand pages of newspaper (circa 20th century) that somehow survived the data collapse of the early 21st century[5] we have pieced together the following post-Dallas Kennedy information:

Articles #1–7 JFK ASSASSINATION FAKED (NI 7867)[6]
• Joint Castro-Giancana plot to kill the President foiled by assassination hoax.
• Kennedy accidentally wounded by Secret Service during staged shooting.
• Kennedy convalesces on the island of Skorpios.
• Alleged assassin Oswald killed by CIA operative Jack Ruby to complete cover-up.
• Kennedy, reunited with lost love, decides to retire from public life (see: JFK WEDS MM).

Articles #8–9 MARILYN LIVES (GWN 6301)[7]
• Marilyn Monroe (formerly Norma Jean Baker) still alive after her death was faked on August 4, 1962, following a nervous breakdown believed to be precipitated by ongoing FBI surveillance/harassment.
• Accompanied by former lover Robert Kennedy and confidant Peter Lawford, Monroe is whisked away to a private sanitarium in Hyannisport to recover from breakdown. Later retires from public life saying, "I never wanted to be an actress—I just wanted to be loved."
• Signs agreement in 1970 to collaborate with Norman Mailer on her posthumous autobiography.

Articles #10–16 JFK WEDS MM (SSMWR 371)[8]
• July 7, 1969, John F. Kennedy weds

Marilyn Monroe after five-year romance following their reunion on the island of Skorpios during JFK's recuperation. Inside sources cite the death of JFK's brother Bobby as removing the last hurdle from the nuptial consummation of their undying love.

• Wedding hosted by the Shah of Iran at his private palatial estate.

• Rumors concerning Marilyn's pregnancy are thought to be unfounded.

(also see Article #97, THE KING SINGS AT KENNEDY-MONROE 20TH ANNIVERSARY BASH)[9]

Articles #17–70 THE POST-ASSASSINATION ACCOMPLISHMENTS OF JFK

• At a private Hollywood party, JFK calls upon old Rat Pack buddy Sammy Davis, Jr., to infiltrate the international Satanist conspiracy. A 45-rpm single of their duet version of "The Candy Man" is privately pressed for distribution among their friends.[10]

• JFK revealed as Bob Woodward's "Deep Throat" contact during Watergate investigation.[11]

• Before a secret Vatican court, JFK clears Pope John Paul II of any connection to the mysterious death of Pope John Paul I. Kennedy is quoted as saying, "We Catholic leaders have to stick together."[12]

• JFK attends third Roswell summit meeting with extraterrestrials as official U.S. delegate to Galactic Congress.[13]

• JFK persuades Jimmy Hoffa to turn over State's evidence in exchange for a place in the Federal Witness Protection Program.[14]

• JFK signs deal with Random House for two new books tentatively titled *Profiles in Valor* and *Profiles in Immortality*.[15]

• All other articles available on file.

Evaluation of all available materials would indicate that Kennedy's remains were either buried on the island of Skorpios[16] (therefore unobtainable), or jettisoned into space in honor of his contributions to the aforementioned Galactic Congress[17] (therefore also unobtainable). In either case, his cloning must be no longer considered viable.

It is therefore my recommendation that an alternate subject be substituted for Kennedy without the public's knowledge, so as not to jeopardize the entire project.

Recommended candidates have already been found. See file coded MEADER, VAUGHN FF 33.333.

Notes:
1. Pre Data Collapse
2. Genetic Reclamation Team
3. Riddley Cameron Genetic Research Facility
4. Environmental Protection Agency
5. At the present time we have no evidence to suggest why these periodicals were never converted to reference disk data (and subsequently lost due to EMP) as such other publications of the time as *Time*, the *New York Times*, the *Wall Street Journal*, and *TV Guide* were.
6. *National Inquirer* File 7867
7. *Global Weekly News* File 6301
8. *Star Sun Moon Weekly Report* File 371
9. Ibid. File 906 (The exact identity and affiliation of "the King" seems to be a mystery as current research fails to reveal a monarch contemporary to Kennedy by the name of Elvis Presley).
10. *Personalities* File 55
11. *The Rivera Review* File 4
12. *National Inquirer* File 9331

13. *World Weekly Report* File 745
14. *Global Weekly News* File 6534
15. *Publishers Clearing House* File 666
16. Sunk by tidal wave March 16, 2401 during Hurricane Patricia.
17. *SF Chronolog* File 23

Barbara Delaplace has made quite a reputation for herself since bursting onto the science fiction scene with close to a dozen stories in the past year.

In "Freedom," she explores the conflicts within the oldest of the Kennedy brothers, Joe Junior, and re-examines his fate with the insight and compassion that have come to typify her work.

Freedom
by Barbara Delaplace

Freedom.

He loved the sea and sky. The vast expanse of empty air and water filled him with an oddly thrilling sense of his own unimportance. Not for him that terrifying insignificance his fellow pilots felt as the ground disappeared beneath them. Here, all things shrank into their true, proper proportions, and freed him.

He smiled wryly to himself. They'd laugh at him if he told them that.

"Free?" they'd ask. "What d'ya mean you feel free out there? Don't you feel free right now? Man, I wish I had what you've got, J.J.: status, money, family connections ... If those are problems, I could sure learn to live with 'em."

Sure they could.

But if they had all those, they'd also have his father, and he wouldn't wish that on anyone.

He shifted slightly in the cramped, noisy quarters of the cockpit. This was no limousine, that's for sure. But *he* was the one in control here. The powerful engine did *his* bidding, took him to where *he* told it. Took him to where there was just him, the sky around him, the sun above him, and the ocean below. To freedom.

He was never free at home. He always felt like an appendage. Even his nickname, J.J. Short for Joe Jr.: Joseph Kennedy Junior. *He didn't even give me a name of my own.* He clenched a fist. *Just a continuation of the family bloodline, that's me.* The family was more important than the individual.

No, that was wrong. The wishes of Joe Kennedy Senior were more important than the individual, particularly if that individual was his eldest son, for whom he had plans. That's how it had been all his life it seemed—living out his father's plans for him.

"But I don't like to play football."

"Nonsense, young man—every red-blooded American boy loves football. You'll sign up for the team."

"Sir, I'd really rather sign up for swimming. Coach Roberts says I've got a good chance . . ."

His father's eyebrows lowered, a dangerous sign, but he kept his voice level. "I said you'll sign up for football. And I'll phone Coach Roberts and tell him you're not going out for swimming."

"But sir . . ."

"Enough!" His father's voice was thunderous. "You'll do as I tell you!"

And he did. Coach Roberts got the phone call, all right, and suddenly showed a distinct lack of interest in the swimming abilities of one Joe Kennedy, Jr. He learned an important lesson then: it didn't matter what his thoughts, his wishes, his dreams were. What counted were his fa-

ther's thoughts and wishes. And later on, his father's
wishes had included Harvard and law.

"Law?"

"Of course. What else?"

"But I planned to go into journalism."

"NO!" His father was furious. "No son of mine is going to
waste his time scribbling words on paper! You're going to
learn a proper skill, one that's going to be useful to you in
the future—not fritter away your time at writing! Lawyers
are important. They meet important people, make contacts,
contacts you'll need when you go into politics."

He tried to assert himself. "Father, I've already applied at
Columbia."

"Irrelevant. I decide what's best for you! You're going to
follow my wishes. That's the end of this discussion."

And once again, as always, he'd done as he was told.
His friend Dick once asked him, over a cup of coffee in
the mess, "But J.J.—why didn't you just go ahead and go
to Columbia?"

He grimaced. "Dick, you don't know my father."

"So what? With your marks you'd be guaranteed a
scholarship. A place to live is no problem—you'd have
frats stumbling over themselves to rush you. And even if
he cut off your money, there's lots of on-campus jobs.
You'd get by."

He sighed. "My father has friends in high places—lots
of friends—and that includes university presidents. A few
phone calls, and I'd be out on my ass."

"You're kidding!"

"Oh, they wouldn't expel me. They'd just call me aside
for a quiet chat to explain the situation, how they knew
I wouldn't want to go against the wishes of my father. 'A
fine man, your father. And important to us here at the
university.' You get the picture."

Dick looked at him with a tinge of envy. "I guess I do. Imagine having that sort of power—just a phone call."

He smiled grimly. "Trust me, you wouldn't enjoy it. It comes with price tags, big ones."

"They might be worth it. I might be willing to give it a try."

He smiled to himself. Dick might, too. There wasn't a man in the military who could work harder when he had a goal in mind than Dick Nixon. He checked his compass heading for the umpteenth time. Reconnaissance wasn't especially exciting, and a flier could easily get lost: too much featureless, empty ocean. You had to stay alert. But at least it got him up here where he could be free in the vault of the sky.

Not that he minded much being down below—much to his surprise, he loved life in the Navy. He admitted it: one of the main reasons he'd enlisted was to get away from the all-pervading presence of his father. Then he'd gone to tell him what he'd done, apprehension gnawing at him. But for once his father approved of his actions.

"I joined up today."

"Well done, Joe. Every American must do his duty to his country. I know you'll bring glory to the Kennedy name. What service?"

He felt his heart lifting—his father was pleased with him! "The Navy."

"Excellent! That will look impressive on your record after the war, when you go into politics. Help garner votes."

His joy suddenly evaporated. Of course, he should have realized. "I hadn't thought about that. I suppose it will."

"Of course it will. We'll make a point of playing up your service record. Make you a war hero."

"Sir, I don't think you can make a hero."

"That will be quite enough, young man. I won't tolerate impertinence."

Impertinence. He sighed inwardly. As if he was still a schoolboy, not a man of twenty-five.

"Yes, sir."
What else could he say.?

Even then, Joe Senior had been making more plans for his son, planning to exploit whatever he could to improve his chances of being elected.

Never mind that I have no interest in politics. Never mind that Jack is the one with the charm, the looks, the drive for glory. He'd be a natural, and he'd love every minute of it. He'd make a fine politician, a fine President. *Not me.*

Somehow he just couldn't seem to gather enough courage to defy his father. He was powerless against that supreme self-assurance. *Yeah, I'd make a fine leader for the most powerful country in the world. Some man you are, Junior. How can you stand up to Hitler and Hirohito when you can't even stand up to your father?*

He found himself idly wondering if Hitler or Hirohito could stand up to his father, either.

"The Bouviers have a daughter. Pretty girl named Jacqueline. Blue-blood family. It'll be a good match. We'll arrange a few get-togethers, make sure it gets in the society pages."

He won't even let me choose my own wife!

His father was a monster who wouldn't be denied. That familiar feeling of helplessness surged over him yet again, the feeling of things moving beyond his control.

"Face it, Joe, you're a weakling." He suddenly realized he'd spoken aloud; his words would be heard by the entire flight. "Ah, sorry about that, guys. My mind was wandering."

No response. "Den Mother, this is Alpha Foxtrot Three calling. Come in please."

The radio remained silent. "Den Mother, this is Alpha Foxtrot Three calling. Come in."

Nothing. The radio set had been misbehaving for three days now, and each day the mechanics thought they'd got it fixed. He shrugged. Right now, it didn't seem to matter.

He could see the rest of his life stretching before him, all planned out. Planned out by a man who didn't care a damn for Joseph Kennedy Junior, but only for his own ambition to make the Kennedys the most powerful family in the land. Royalty in a country that had proudly defied royalty.

He laughed bitterly. It wouldn't even matter if he died right this moment. That wouldn't stop his father. After all, he had more sons. He'd put on a black armband and mourn, and then shift his attentions to Jack.

He'd make his dead son a hero who gave his life in the service of his country. He'd make certain the death of Joseph Kennedy Junior would bring even more honor to the Kennedy clan, who never asked (in public) what their country could do for them, but only what they could do for their country.

I'm powerless. No matter what I do, my father will make it serve him.

He craned his neck, glanced down at the immense vista of water. How peaceful and clear everything seemed here. Above was the incredibly blue dome of the sky set with the blazing sun. The firmament created by God, with the greater light that ruled the day.

I wish I could stay here forever.

Never again to worry about his father's plans, but simply glory in the stark simple beauty of air, fire and water all around him. The thought of having to become earthbound again, of having to carry out all those plans made him feel unutterably weary. Down through all the years of his life, fulfilling someone else's dreams, never his own.

Then it came to him.

A way to thwart his father. A way to carry out his own wishes. A way that could set him free forever.

The one choice *he* could make, and his father couldn't stop him. He could make it right now. A last flight to a blessed oblivion.

He set the controls, lowered the nose of his plane. It

rocketed toward the wrinkled metal surface of the ocean. His hands clenched the arms of his seat. As the furious drone of the engine grew louder and louder in his ears, he kept his eyes raised to the heavens. In a few seconds, he would finally be at peace. The force of the impact would kill them instantly. He was sorry, truly sorry, about Dick and the others, but as his father had pointed out so many times, once you know what you want, you never let anyone stand in your way. You go out and you *take* it.

And he finally knew what he wanted.

Freedom.

Harry Turtledove has been doing his own thing—
science fiction—for a number of years now, and
has built up a considerable following with such
books as *Noninterference* and *A World of Difference*. I was a bit fearful, when he told me the title
of his story, that it might bear too great a resemblance to Mark Twain's *A Connecticut Yankee in
King Arthur's Court*. I apologize, Harry: I should
have known better.

A Massachusetts Yankee
in King Arthur's Court
by Harry Turtledove

Duncan Morris was glad he was tall. Though several rows
back from the curb, the shaggy-haired young man in a
robe had enough inches to be able to see over most of
the people ahead of him. He'd have a good view of the
motorcade when it passed.

A rising murmur announced its coming. Morris's head
swiveled to the left. In the lead were motorcycles with
hard-faced bobbies—or would they be SAS men? he wondered—atop them. Then came limousines full of minor
dignitaries: MPs, Cabinet subministers, and the like.

Behind them was the Prime Minister's car. Harold Macmillan stood stiff and straight, nodding to the crowds that

lined both sides of King's Road as if he were what they'd turned out to see. His white hair blew in the breeze.

A few people did cheer Macmillan. Others shouted things like "How's Christine in the sack?" and "Where's Profumo?" If the Prime Minister heard the taunts about the sex scandal that had rocked his government, he gave no sign of it. He kept on nodding, like a machine.

The hum of excitement rose to a crescendo. Schoolboys and grannies waved little Union Jacks and American flags. With its jutting fins and grille full of chromium teeth, the open Cadillac seemed more like a prehistoric monster than something that belonged in London in 1963. Far easier of manner than Harold Macmillan, President Kennedy grinned to the throngs of Englishmen and waved as if they were old friends.

A few more cars full of lesser lights, another squadron of motorcycles, and it was over. One of the matronly types in front of Morris sighed ecstatically. "Oh, Madge, 'e's so 'andsome."

"That 'e is," Madge answered, sighing too. "The telly and the papers are right—seeing 'im is like Camelot come again."

With Kennedy gone, the crowd began to thin out. "Camelot!" Morris snarled to his friend Andrew Llewellyn as they walked toward the nearest Underground station. "Did you hear those two fat fools? Fat lot *they* know about Camelot!"

Llewellyn's robe was the twin to Morris's; their sandals went *swish-slap, swish-slap* at every step. "Fat bleeding lot Master John Prettyboy Kennedy knows about it either, come to that."

Duncan Morris stopped dead in his tracks. "Andrew, you're a genius. He ought to find out what it *was* like, he should—he deserves to, you might say, for wearing the name in vain. Let's try giving him a bit of a lesson, shall we?"

"What, us?" Andrew Llewellyn stared at Morris.

Duncan struck a pose, right there in the middle of the street. "Who better? Are we druids, Andrew, or not?"

"Well, we are, but—"

"But me no buts." Morris looked down his long, thin nose at Llewellyn. He'd always wondered if the other were in it more for a game than from conviction, and now he had his answer. It saddened him; the old gods of Gaul and Britain and Ireland had too few followers to spare even one. But he truly believed. "I swear by the gods of my people, Andrew, I will magic a magic that shows the upstart American what life in the olden times was like."

"You can't really hope to do such a thing," Llewellyn said. But his skepticism wobbled, as did his voice when he added, "Can you?"

"I can try. Past that, if the gods favor me, I'll succeed. If not, I've lost nothing."

Llewellyn was shaking his head when they went into the Underground. Morris didn't care; he was already planning how the magic might go. Pity he couldn't sacrifice a man to fuel it— He sat silent beside his friend until Andrew got off. His own stop was farther out.

He ducked into a pet shop not far from where he emerged from the Underground—*from the Underworld*, he thought, pleased at the analogy. He bought a white mouse and a small wicker cage a songbird might inhabit. "You don't want to keep that little fellow in there," the shopkeeper warned, perhaps thinking from Morris's robe that he was a simpleton. "He'll gnaw his way out in no time."

Morris nodded, walked out. His flat was a couple of blocks from the shop. When he got there, he let the mouse run around in a tin bucket while he went to his books. He scowled as he read. So much ancient Celtic lore came down through enemies like Caesar and Pliny; who could say, after so long, what they'd corrupted?

But the druids of old, the druids of power, had known souls traveled from one body to the next in an endless chain of being. Looping the chain back upon itself was clearly within natural law as they understood it. Through proper ritual and sacrifice (he did hope a mouse would be enough, but could not bring himself to hurt any larger beast), the gods could be compelled to do his will. He studied and planned till evening twilight gave way to full darkness.

A little before midnight, he took the mouse, the cage, lighter fluid, and matches down to a little park close by. The streets were quiet and still. In the center of the park stood a clump of old oaks—not old enough to reach back before Roman days, but old. He stood in the clearing at their heart. His own heart pounded.

He took the mouse out of the bucket, stuck it in the wicker cage. Then he squirted lighter fluid on both cage and mouse. The little animal rubbed frantically at its fur and eyes, trying to get the stinking, stinging stuff off. Duncan lit a match. He tossed it into the cage.

The blast of flame almost burned off his eyebrows. He sprang back, but not before he heard a despairing squeak from the mouse. He almost forgot the invocation he'd labored long to prepare: "Esus of the savage shrine, ruthless Teutates, Taranis the thunderer, Cernunnos the mighty horned one, Dagdá the good god of the earth, Brân and Gwyn and Mider of the underworld, come to my aid against one who would usurp the place of your glorious heroes of old. I pray you each and separately, let him learn of his presumption. Let it be so, let it be so, let it be so!"

He was proud of the eclectic spell, summoning the gods of Gaul and Ireland and ancient Britain all together and using the common Celtic pattern of threefold invocation. The wicker cage burned so hot and fierce—as the Gauls had once burned criminals—that it left only a smear of ashes on the ground: nothing, he hoped, to bring down the wrath of the RSPCA.

He hurried home, went to bed. When he got up the next morning, he switched on the BBC news service, hoping to hear of wild consternation. Nothing, though, was in the least out of the ordinary. His faith didn't shatter, but it bent.

He felt guilty about the mouse for years.

John F. Kennedy woke up in bed with a redhead. For a second or two, he just smiled. It must have been quite a night. The pounding headache back of his eyes said he'd been into the bottle deep enough to drown.

The girl had her back to him. Her hair was really spectacular, bright as the early morning sun that peered through the window. She was snoring a little. He chuckled and swung out of bed.

His bare feet came down on bare ground.

The damp, gritty feel of the dirt, utterly unexpected, brought full awareness flooding back to him. No matter how drunk he'd been, he couldn't have been crazy enough to go off and spend a night with a woman not his wife, not when he had to meet the Prime Minister again at ten this morning.

He looked around. Where the devil was he, anyway, and how could he manage, as inconspicuously as possible, to get back to where he was supposed to be? The room offered few clues. The walls were plastered (not very smooth); a rickety wooden chair, old as the hills, stood a couple of feet from the bed, with clothes carelessly tossed onto it. And the floor was dirt. Had he met the proverbial farmer's daughter? Did even the poorest farms in England still have dirt floors? He doubted it.

The wool blanket he'd shrugged off was scratchy enough to belong on a poor farm. The mattress was wool, too, stuffed into a sack of linen ticking and set on top of a wooden bed frame—not a spring anywhere in sight. It was probably good for his back, but it was a long way from comfortable.

He drew in a deep breath, preparatory to shouting angrily. The shout turned into a strangled gurgle as the symphony of smells hit him.

Hit was the operative word; they had an almost physical power to them. Some were pleasant: cooking food, fresh grass. But they were only notes in the greater composition. Wood-smoke and horse rang louder. So did horse dung, a minor-key variation on the theme of grass. Nor was horse dung the only dung around; the cool morning air gave the impression that a dozen cesspools had all overflowed at once.

Cautiously, Kennedy breathed again. The outhouse stink was not all that told him of other human beings besides himself and the redhead. Sour sweat smelled staler and stronger than in any locker room after a big game.

His grunt of astonishment woke his bedmate. She sat up and smiled at him. She was a beauty, her eyes forest-green, skin so fair and pale he could see the tracery of veins beneath. Generous pink nipples tipped her breasts. She spoke to him—in a language he did not understand.

"I'm sorry, what was that?" he said.

She tried again. Again he recognized no words, though the rhythm seemed familiar. He needed a moment to find the memory. When he'd visited Ireland as a Congressman, he'd gone into a pub once for a pint and found the background chatter to be Erse, not English. It had sounded so much like a brogue that he'd not even noticed till his Guinness was almost gone. The girl's voice held the same lilt.

Kennedy ruefully shook his head. Celt though he was by blood, his tongue was incurably Sassenach. He said, "I'm sorry, but I really don't follow you."

The girl frowned a little. If the unbelievable stench bothered her, she didn't show it. She shifted languages, speaking more slowly. Now the words she used were mouth-filling and guttural. They sounded more like German than anything else. Aside from the phrase *Ich bin ein Berliner*, which he'd practiced all the way across the Atlantic, he had no German. This wasn't quite it, anyhow, or he didn't think so.

He must have looked dreadfully puzzled, for the girl's frown disappeared. She laughed at him, then spoke again, in yet another tongue. At first he thought it was French, though it was no more the French with whose sounds, at least, he was familiar than the other language had been German.

A light clicked on in his head. Not French—Latin! It was oddly accented (not at all what he was used to hearing in church) and had its endings slurred, but it was Latin. The Jesuits had drilled Latin into him in his prep school days. He hadn't used it since, or even thought much about it, but pieces of it, he discovered, remained in place. If the only way to talk with this beautiful naked redhead was in fragmentary Latin, he'd do his damnedest.

"Qui urbs est?" he asked: "What city is this?" He knew he'd do horrible things to his cases and numbers and verbs, but he didn't care. He wasn't trying for a grade or to pretend to be Cicero, just to make himself understood.

He succeeded—the girl's face lit up. She rattled off a long sentence, most of which was gibberish to Kennedy. He did manage to catch the name of the place. It sounded like *Cam'lod'n.*

It wasn't familiar to him. *"In Britannia est?"* he asked. The climate felt British, and the girl looked like someone from the British Isles, though more likely from Scotland or Ireland than England.

"Britannia," she said, and nodded. Her bare breasts bobbed up and down too, enchantingly. She laughed again, spoke some more. Again, he couldn't follow all of what she said, but by repeating herself and pantomime she got across that she thought he was a merchant from Gaul—and that he really must have been drunk last night if he couldn't remember what part of the world he was in.

Fear knotted Kennedy's guts. If he was stuck back in Roman times ... His first appalled thought was that that made Lyndon Johnson President of the United States.

Then he decided that wasn't number one on his list of worries. If he'd somehow been sent from 1963 London to ancient Cam'lod'n, that implied he also might make the trip in the other direction. But he needed more information. He asked, *"Quis est imperator Romanorum?"* Genitive plural, by God! The fathers would have been proud.

The girl's shrug was as appealing as her nod had been. She backed and filled until he got the idea no Emperor ruled Britain right now, and none had for some time. He shivered, though the room was no worse than cool. He hadn't read Gibbon in a long time either, but— He shook his head. No. He couldn't believe it.

The girl leaned forward, ran a gentle forefinger along the scar that seamed his back. *"In bell'?"* she asked—was it a war wound?

He nodded, not so much to impress her as because he didn't think anyone however many hundred or thousand years ago this was would believe in disc fusion surgery. A light fuzz of golden hair covered the girl's forearm; beneath it, from elbow to wrist, ran a track of small red welts. They were all the more obvious because of her milk-pale skin. As with so much whenever this was, Kennedy needed a few seconds to recognize them.

"Bedbugs!" he exclaimed, startled back into English. And he'd spent the night with her! If she had bedbugs, she probably had lice and fleas and God only knew what else. He wanted to scratch himself all over at once. Then another thought struck him: if she'd given him the clap, the Romans had never heard of penicillin.

He forced himself back toward calm. For the moment, no matter how much vermin disgusted him, he couldn't do anything about them. He still needed information from the girl, too. A word at a time, he shaped another Latin sentence: *"Si non est imperator Romanorum, quis est rex Britanniae?"*

Everything he said seemed to amuse the redhead. He couldn't do anything about that; he was a stranger here, from farther away than she could imagine. Again she spoke too quick for him to understand everything she said, but he got the gist: Britain's current ruler (she called him *dux*, duke, not *rex*, king) was somebody named Artorius.

He started to take that as just another fact: in its Latin disguise, the name didn't immediately seem familiar. Then he stopped and stared as a couple of pieces to his puzzle fit together. "Artorious of Cam'lod'n?" he said, imitating her pronunciation as well as he could. A moment later, he used the one more familiar to him: "Arthur of Camelot? This is Arthur's Camelot?"

She nodded cheerfully, pleased he'd followed her. She must have understood his words, too—maybe just the names, but maybe not. What was that second language she'd tried on him? Old English, perhaps, or something like it?

This, Camelot? Kennedy wanted to throw back his head and roar hysterical laughter. This, the center of Arthur and the Round Table and knights in shining armor? A town that, though he hadn't set eye on any of it yet save one room, smelled like a city dump on a hot summer day? All that chivalry and romance, sprung from a garbage heap?

"I can't believe it," he said, more to himself than to the girl. But now his curiosity was kindled. "Camelot," he muttered. "This I have to see." He laughed a little himself, breathed in some more of the horrible stink, laughed again. "It sure as hell isn't Lerner and Loewe."

He walked over to the chair, took his first good look at the clothes there. On top lay two sets of linen drawers, one bigger than the other. He put that one on, tossed the other to the girl. She came all the way out from under the blanket. He admired her legs, though she'd never heard of shaving them.

Beneath the drawers were long woolen tunics with hoods, the bigger one a deep blue, the smaller the creamy color of natural wool. When he pulled on the one that was obviously his, he felt a weight to one side. That was how he discovered the tunic had pockets. He reached in, pulled out his wallet and the maybe dollar and a half in change that had jingled in the pocket of the trousers he'd worn the night before—or more than a thousand years later, depending on how you looked at things.

The girl put on her tunic, too, then reached under the bed and got out her sandals. He squatted and discovered another pair, big enough to be his. They had more complicated straps than he was used to, but he managed to fasten them. They felt good on his feet, as if he'd worn them a long time.

Beside his sandals stood a glazed brown pot. He didn't think anything of it until the girl took it out, pulled down the drawers she'd just donned, and squatted over it. He felt himself turning red. She didn't seem to think anything of it, and chattered away in her odd Latin till she was done. Then she got up, put her drawers back on, and offered the pot to him.

He decided he didn't need to urinate that badly, shook his head. Shrugging, she flipped the pot's contents out the open window, then replaced it under the bed. Kennedy knew he was standing there with his mouth open, but couldn't help it. He cast about for something, anything, to say. At last he managed, *"Qui nomen est tuus?"* He knew he'd made a hash of the sentence, but he didn't care.

"Eurolwyn," she answered, and then added something that he thought meant he'd known her name the night before. By his headache, he'd been drunk enough to keep him from arguing. Eurolwyn added, *"E'tu e' John."* In her mouth, it came out halfway between *Sean* and *Ioan*—certainly prettier than the blunt monosyllable he was used to.

As he nodded, he wondered if he owed her anything for the night. He also wondered what money was worth hereabouts: a buck and a half might not take him far. But when he took a few coins out of his pocket, Eurolwyn's eyes got enormous. And when he offered her a silver dime, she kissed him passionately (he wished she'd brushed her teeth any time lately, but his own mouth was none too fresh), then flipped the tunic off over her head and started to peel her drawers down again.

"Wait!" he said. She glared at him. He could read her thoughts perfectly: *Wasn't I good enough for you to want me again?* Just then, by luck, his stomach rumbled. He rubbed it and said, *"Alimentum? Panis?"* He turned the last word into English: "Bread?"

Hunger was an excuse she understood (he wondered how often she went hungry herself). She dressed once more, pulled a bone comb out of her pocket, ran it through her hair. Before she put it back, she used a thumbnail to crush something crawling on it. Kennedy's appetite threatened to disappear. But she took him by the hand, unbarred the door, and led him down a hall to a large chamber with a fireplace, several hand-hewn tables, and a by-God bar behind which stood a big blond fellow with a big blond mustache who had the patient eyes of a by-God bartender. A dead hare hung head-down from a nail pounded into the wall in back of him.

Eurolwyn sat Kennedy down, spoke to the bartender in the Erse-sounding language. He nodded and brought over a roundish, lumpy loaf of bread and two mugs that looked like miniature versions of the chamber pot. Kennedy displayed another dime. The bartender grabbed as if to get it before Kennedy changed his mind. If he'd had a forelock, he would have tugged it. He hurried away, came back with a big bowl of oysters, which he set on the table with a flourish.

Raw oysters and chunks of bread weren't Kennedy's idea of breakfast, but weren't bad, either. The mugs held beer—flat, room temperature, and unhopped. Since there was no point asking for coffee, Kennedy drank it without complaint. Like the rest of the meal, it wasn't what he was used to but could have been worse.

Three or four other tables were occupied by people dressed much like him and Eurolwyn. Some ate bread, others spooned what looked like oatmeal from wooden bowls. They spoke the tongue Eurolwyn had used with the barkeep.

Kennedy asked, *"Ubi est castellum Artorii?"*

Eurolwyn's directions on how to find Arthur's castle were so long and detailed that he lost her after about the third sentence. He didn't worry; if he found the biggest building in town, that was likely to be it. He smiled. Maybe Merlin would help him get home. Of course, if the real Merlin bore the same resemblance to the one of fable as this town did to legendary Camelot, he wouldn't be much use.

When he was full, Kennedy got up and headed for the doorway. The bartender bowed himself almost double. Eurolwyn was still munching bread and sucking oysters out of their shells. She fluttered her fingers in a wave.

Kennedy's first step outside was into mud; though the day was bright and sunny, it must have rained recently. His second step was into something more unpleasant. It oozed through the holes in his sandals onto his feet. He jerked his leg like a dog that had walked into something sticky.

To his surprise, streets ran north-south and east-west in a regular grid. That much of what they said about Roman towns was true, then. If, however, the streets had ever been paved, it wasn't recently. Here and there, in ragged patches, covered colonnades still stood by the roadside to shield walkers from the elements. Most of them were gone, though.

A man leaned a ladder against one of the surviving stretches, clambered up to the top, and pried off a couple of red clay roof tiles. Carrying them in one hand and the ladder under his other arm, he walked back to the house across the street. He got onto the roof there, placed the tiles over a hole, cemented them into position with mud and straw, and descended with every sign of satisfaction.

Kennedy wanted to scream at him, first for desecrating an antiquity and then for using public property to private advantage. But he had to feeling neither was against the law hereabouts (if there was any law hereabouts), so he kept quiet.

He spotted the tallest building in town, off to the northeast, and made in that direction. No one paid him any special notice; with his red-brown hair and Irish features, he fit in well enough. A lot of men favored beards or mustaches, but some didn't. He was taller than most, but the barkeep had been his size or bigger and so were some people on the street.

The horses that added so much to the pungency of the air were hardly larger than ponies. Some of the men atop them almost dragged their feet in the muck. Nobody, Kennedy noticed after a while, used stirrups. Nobody had heard of axle grease, either; squealing cart wheels replaced blaring auto horns in local traffic noise.

He suspected Camelot, or Cam'lod'n, or whatever its name was in proper classical Latin, had been a more prosperous town in pre-Arthurian times. Some of the old houses and public buildings still stood. With walls of stucco and red tile roofs like those of the colonnades, they reminded him of nothing so much as the "Spanish"-style ranch houses common in the Southwest.

Other such buildings, though, were ruins that gave signs of having been quarried for building materials. *Takes less work to rob graves than make anything new,* Kennedy thought, and a chill ran through him. Perhaps one lot in four was empty, with weeds and wildflowers growing in riotous profusion and, here and there, saplings taller than a man. Yes, Cam'lod'n had seen better days.

A few plots of land empty of Roman housing had newer buildings on them, but hardly of a sort to give Kennedy hope for the future: the round huts with walls of wattle and daub supporting turf or straw roofs seemed more like an intrusion from the past, as if Indian teepees suddenly sprang up beside Faneuil Hall in Boston. But the people who chased chickens and scrawny hogs in and out of those huts seemed no different from anyone else.

One piece of stonework still stood strong: the town's Roman wall. Its gray crenellated bulk defined the horizon, and few crenellations showed missing chunks of rock. Somewhere out there was an enemy who made it worthwhile not to plunder the fortifications even to maintain houses and shops within the circuit. Arthur had done a lot of fighting, Kennedy remembered.

Hardly had that thought crossed his mind when he turned a corner and came face to face with a couple of men he presumed to be that enemy. For one thing, they spoke the German-sounding language Eurolwyn had tried on him instead of either the Celtic tongue that most people here used or the Latin that still appeared on signs over an inn, a smithy, a fish market that added its own stink to the many in Camelot. For another, they wore tunics and trousers of a tighter cut than those of the locals, and trimmed their hair shorter. And for a third, they were looking around with expressions halfway between those of country boys marveling at the big city and crooks casing a joint before they knocked it over.

Had Kennedy been a cop, he would have run them in for loitering. As it was, he found himself unarmed while both Saxons—or would they be Angles? Jutes?—had swords swinging on their left hips and knives on their right; one, for good measure, also wore an iron helmet with cheek pieces and several rusty spots. He gave them a wide berth. They were too busy eyeing a tanner's shop to pay him any mind.

A tumbledown building in the shape of a semicircle puzzled Kennedy until he realized it must have been a theater. Through fallen portions of the outer wall, he could see rotting wooden seats on banks of gravel. The mute tale of lost—no, forgotten,—happiness made hot tears sting his eyes till he angrily tossed his head and willed them away.

The big structure to which he'd been heading was only about a hundred yards past the theater. By then, he'd already seen it was half a ruin, too. Nor was it a palace or a castle or anywhere else a *dux Britanniae* might want to live; it looked more like a Roman temple than anything else.

A broad stairway led up to a portico fronted by eight marble columns. Bits of gilding still clung to their capitals. Bronze wreaths had once been affixed to the low walls on either side of the stairs; Kennedy could see the verdigris stains they'd left behind. Time and people seeking stone had reduced the reliefs on the architrave to meaninglessness. Only a fragment of the inscription below survived: TI·CLAUDIO·CAES·AUG· The rest was gone.

"Claudius," Kennedy said softly. Wasn't Claudius the Emperor who conquered Britain? Once upon a time, either he'd dedicated this shrine or it was dedicated to him. No one worshiped here any more. A skinny brown dog lifted its leg against a column.

Kennedy looked around. He didn't see any other imposing buildings in this part of Cam'lod'n, so he headed back toward the west. He didn't take long getting from one end of town to the other; the walls enclosed a stretch of land only about half a mile from east to west by a quarter-mile from north to south. *And to the Romans, this place was a city,* he thought. He wondered how many people it had held in its heyday. No more than a few thousand, surely. Anything that deserved to be called civilization, then, had existed on the thinnest of margins. No wonder it was failing.

When he nodded to a pretty woman on the street, she smiled back. That encouraged him to try his half-remembered Latin on her. She spread her hands and gave back the Celtic dialect he didn't understand. He shrugged, walked on.

He came up to a shop where a gray-haired man in a leather apron was smoothing a board with a plane that looked as though it could have come from the Sears hardware section. A neatly lettered sign above the shop read FABER LIGNARIUS, which Kennedy assumed meant *carpenter*. Since the sign was Latin, he hoped the carpenter spoke it, too. He asked where Artorius's *castellum* was.

The man with the plane looked up from his work. He paused to think before he answered. As he did so, his mouth came open; Kennedy saw he had only three or four teeth in the front of his jaws. At last he said, "*Ad*, er, *portam*, uh, *occidentalem*."

Kennedy smiled. Here was somebody with Latin worse than his. He bowed his thanks and tossed the carpenter a penny. Even the little copper coin was enough to win him a gap-toothed smile of gratitude.

He headed for the western gate. It was an impressive piece of fortcraft, a double-arched gateway flanked on either side by a stout stone roundtower. He wouldn't have cared to attack it with anything less than a tank. The Romans had built both big and strong. Today, the only traffic through the gates was a herder in a ragged tunic driving eight or ten sheep ahead of him into town.

The buildings close by the gateway were better preserved than those elsewhere in Cam'lod'n. Kennedy tried to figure out which one was likely to be Arthur's residence. He was about to buttonhole someone in the street when he turned a corner and saw a big house with a couple of armed men lounging in front of the door. They weren't nearly clean and spruce enough to get into the Secret Service, but it was the first guarded residence he'd come across. That made it better than a fair bet to belong to somebody important.

He walked up to the guards. One of them had a mug full of what he'd bet was beer; no, the Secret Service would not have approved. Instead of the usual long, hooded tunics, they both wore mail shirts and helmets over checked wool trousers. Neither reached for his sword as Kennedy approached, but both followed him with their eyes.

He stopped about six feet away, let them see his hands were empty. Dipping his head in what was half a nod, half a bow, he said, *"Hic est domus Artorii?"*

"Yes, this is Arthur's house," one of the guards answered in slow Latin. "What can we do for you, stranger?"

"I want to see Arthur," Kennedy said. He wished he didn't have to be so blunt, but his memory of the subjunctive was as one with the snows of yesteryear.

"That cannot be." The guard also spoke in simple declarative sentences; maybe he didn't know how the subjunctive worked, either. He went on, "Arthur is not here. He is away in the southwest, fighting against the pagan Saxons." He could use participles, which put him one up on Kennedy.

"Damnatio," Kennedy said. *"Pestilentia."* The guards smiled and sympathetically shook their heads. Shoulder slumping, Kennedy turned to go. *Hell of a thing*, he thought, *to end up in Camelot and find Arthur's not home.*

The door to Arthur's residence had a little filigreed opening so people inside could see what was going on outside. Kennedy caught a flash of motion behind it. The door opened. The guards didn't come to attention, but they did salute with outstretched arms and clenched fists. Kennedy first thought of Mussolini, then of the Roman legions from which Benny the Moose had stolen the gesture.

The man who came out into the watery sunshine was like no one else Kennedy had seen in Cam'lod'n. He was slight and swarthy and shaved his head. With delicately sculpted features, thin-to-gauntness, and fathomless black eyes, he looked more like someone from the Middle East than the strapping, ruddy Celts who peopled the town.

"Wait, please, Excellency," he said to Kennedy. "You

are of interest to me." His Latin sounded different from that of the locals, too. It was also clearer. Kennedy could hear the carefully pronounced word endings the people of Cam'lod'n often swallowed.

"Who are you, Excellency?" Kennedy asked.

The other man bowed. A smile touched his mouth, but not those eyes. "No Excellency I," he said. "I am but a humble priest of God." A red light went on in the politician's part of Kennedy's mind—people who called themselves humble usually weren't. The dark man continued, "I left my native Egypt many years ago to preach the Gospel in this distant land where many knew it not. Though my parents were Christian, they named me Horus, after the hawk god of old who gave his name to our nome, our district."

"Horatius?" Kennedy said, trying to give the name a proper Latin twist.

The other smiled that half-amused smile again. "No, Horus," he said, and ran through the declension of his name. "But it is of small import, because the men here long ago translated my name into their speech. These days I am mostly known as the Merlin."

Kennedy stared. Maybe Arthur wasn't home, but running into Merlin had to be the next best thing. In fact, his earlier joke to himself aside, maybe it was better than the next best thing. Merlin was supposed to be a magician, after all. If anyone had ever needed a magician, John F. Kennedy was the man.

Magician or no, Merlin knew how to watch people. "You have heard of me. This is also of interest, for I am not known outside these parts—and you, by the way you speak Latin, are from far outside these parts indeed. That is the reason I came out to speak with you: never have I heard (forgive me, I beg you) such poor and slow pronunciation combined with an educated man's command of word endings. If you would be so kind, please tell me whence you have come."

As usual, Kennedy needed repetition and backing and filling before he understood all that. He knew a moment's pride that he hadn't been too ungrammatical talking with Arthur's guards. He pieced together a sentence in his mind, then spoke it: "Priest Merlin, I come from so far, I know not how to tell you."

Merlin crossed himself. So did the two guards. After a moment so did Kennedy. "I see you are a Christian, at any rate," Merlin said. He gestured in invitation. "Come in, if you care to, and we shall speak of these matters."

Kennedy was sure Merlin would think he was crazy. Maybe he was. What had he to lose, though? "I come in with you," he said; he'd forgotten how to form the future tense. The guards took a couple of respectful steps back as he followed the Egyptian priest into Arthur's residence.

The outer wall of the house, but for the door and a couple of slit windows, had been unrelieved stucco; Kennedy expected darkness and gloom within. But the house proved built around a courtyard, and open doors and large windows admitted abundant light. Furniture was spare and roughly made, except for one elegantly carved table just inside the doorway that looked old, old. None of the floors had rugs; that of the chamber to which Merlin led Kennedy was enlivened by a mosaic of hunting dogs pursuing a stag.

"Are you hungry?" Merlin asked. At Kennedy's nod, the priest called, "Morvudd!" When a middle-aged woman poked her head in a few seconds later, he spoke to her in Celtic. She nodded and left, returning with a tray that held cakes, two mugs, and a pitcher.

The pitcher contained beer. Merlin poured it into each mug. The cakes were sweetened with honey. The two tastes clashed in Kennedy's mouth. If Merlin found the combination strange, he didn't show it, so Kennedy also held his peace. Though not perfectly to his taste, the beer was stronger than what he'd drunk this morning at the inn. Warmth spread from his middle.

He'd finished two cakes and got halfway into his second mug of beer when Merlin said, "If you are somewhat refreshed, excellency, perhaps you will now give me the tale of how you came to be in Camulodunum. Also, how shall I address you?"

"My name is John," Kennedy answered, filing away the full pronunciation of Camelot's name. "How I came to be here? ... My home is in a land west across the ocean—"

"Hibernia?" Merlin asked.

"No, west even of Hibernia, though my father's fathers came from that land. I was leader"—he found no better word than *dux* to explain his title—"of my people, the Americani, and came here to Britain to talk with its leader, who is our friend."

Merlin lifted an eyebrow in elegant skepticism and said, "I hope you will forgive my saying that I have never heard of the Americani, and that Artorius the *dux*, to my certain knowledge, has no dealings with them."

"Yes, I know that," Kennedy said. "I am of a time more than a thousand years from now, come to your, ah, Camulodunum I know not how. You think I am a madman, but—" He pulled coins from his pocket, shoved them across the table at Merlin. "Here is money of my people."

The priest picked up a quarter, bounced it off the tabletop. It rang sweetly. "Good silver," he murmured. He looked at the reverse. "United States of America." In his mouth, the first two words sounded like *oonneeted stahtees*. "You have an eagle like Rome's, I see, and even a Latin motto—from many, one. But Latin is not your tongue."

"No." Kennedy didn't want to admit English was the name of his language, not when the Angles and Saxons Merlin knew were at war with Arthur.

"A time more than a thousand years from now," Merlin said musingly. He looked at the coins a while longer, then crossed himself again. "It was a powerful magic that sent you back among us, John of America."

"Yes, it was. The books we have, Merlin, name you master magician." Kennedy would have got style points from the Jesuits for *magnus magus*. "Can you make a magic to send me back to my own time?"

"I? I am but a mere priest who has perhaps read more widely, in Latin and in Greek, than most in these sorry times." But Merlin didn't sound as if he were saying no. As it had before, his profession of being but a mere priest rang false: he had pride under the humility his vocation enforced. Kennedy smiled—he'd known plenty of Irish priests like that. Merlin went on, "Let me pray and consult the holy scriptures and such other volumes as I possess, and I shall essay to do as you ask. I make no promises of success, you understand."

"Yes, I thank you, holy sir." Kennedy refused to let hope rise too high, lest it fall and shatter.

Merlin waved a hand in a graceful, almost feminine gesture. "You do honor me by entrusting to me this challenge to both faith and knowledge. I—" He looked up, scrambled to his feet. "Good day, my lady."

Kennedy's back was to the doorway. When Merlin rose, he turned, then quickly got up himself, bowing. The woman standing there was worth bowing to. He guessed she was in her mid-twenties, old enough to have her face show she'd seen the world but too young for it to have marked her. Her hair was strawberry blond, fairer than Eurolwyn's. It flashed as brightly as the garnet-studded gold brooch she wore just above her left breast. That, the embroidered border to her tunic, and Merlin's deference said she was something special in more than looks.

Her laugh, a generous contralto, sounded sweeter than any silver coin. As Merlin had, she used Latin: "Sit priest. I'd thought you were alone. Who is your guest? I've not seen him before."

"His name is John, my lady; he comes from a distant land called America." Merlin turned to Kennedy. "John of

America, allow me to present you to Guinevere, wife to Arthur the *dux*."

Kennedy bowed again. Why not? Of all he'd seen in Camelot, only Guinevere lived up to legend—and then some. She smiled graciously and extended her hand. When he took it, he held it a second or two longer than he would have for a fiftyish, lumpy male bureaucrat.

She noticed—he saw the pupils widen slightly in her cornflower-blue eyes. All at once, he knew he was going to try to lay her. It wasn't so much that she was beautiful, though that didn't hurt. But the idea of going to bed with *Guinevere*—it would be the here-and-now equivalent of sleeping with Marilyn Monroe, exciting not just for that delicious body but because of who she was.

And if legend didn't lie (and it sure hadn't lied about her), she put out, too. There was the whole business with Lancelot, and something about Mordred he half-remembered from the musical. So why not with John of America? He hammered a sentence together in his halting Latin: "The wife of Arthur decorates his house." That didn't lay it on too thick. If she wasn't even a little interested, she could just let it pass.

She smiled. "Wherever America may lie, its men are well-spoken." Instead of modestly lowering her eyes, she kept looking straight at him. Her lips seemed to grow fuller. Just for a moment, the tip of her tongue peeked out between them. *By God, she is interested*, he thought. His heart beat harder; he could feel the blood surge through him.

Merlin was as learned a man as this age and place knew. Of that Kennedy had no doubt. Merlin was, however, also a priest; everything about him shouted *ascetic*. Now, proving indeed that he was blind to the flesh, he said, "My lady, this John of America has set me a problem of considerable complexity, one which requires study and contemplation before it can be solved, if indeed it be soluble at all. Perhaps you might in your graciousness conduct him through the rest of the *dux*'s residence while I retire for the time being with my books."

Guinevere smiled again. "What would you like to see, John of America?"

How you look under that tunic, he thought. Aloud, he said, "Whatever is pleasing to my lady." His eyes held her as he hoped his arms would.

Merlin said, "Pray, both of you, for the success of my efforts." He dipped his head once more to Guinevere, then not quite so deeply to Kennedy, and headed off to whatever little monastic cell he called his own. *Leaving the fox to guard the chicken coop,* Kennedy thought. He gave Guinevere his most foxlike grin, the one that got him votes (and sighs) every time it showed up on television.

"Since you are assuredly a man, John of America," she said, coloring very slightly, "I shall show you a man's things first. Come with me to the armory." She turned and walked slowly across the courtyard, looking back to urge him to follow. He needed no urging.

Maybe in Roman times the courtyard had held a flower garden. Now vegetables grew there. An old man was down on hands and knees, weeding. He glanced up at Kennedy, then returned to work. *Just another visitor who doesn't matter to the likes of me,* his bent back said.

"Many of the armaments usually stored within are now in use against the Saxons," Guinevere said as she opened a door and waved Kennedy into a shedlike storage room. "By what remains, though, and by the empty pegs on the wall, you shall be able to judge the might my husband commands."

Kennedy didn't think he'd care about that; what mattered more to him was the way his arm accidentally brushed hers at the doorway. His eyes flicked to her face to see if she'd noticed. Hers were flicking to him in the same instant. That made him wonder whether he'd caused the accident or she had.

Despite not expecting to care a Boston baked bean for

a room full (or, at the moment, mostly empty) of swords and shields and armor, Kennedy found himself impressed. Even in the dim light inside the armory, the swords' sharp edges glittered; he suspected he could have shaved with any of them. Some of the round shields bore brown splotches—old blood. You had to fight face-to-face here and now. It didn't happen rarely and by accident, as it had with *PT-109*.

The sight of the cutlery also made Kennedy wonder what Arthur would do if he came home and found somebody between his wife's legs. Nothing polite, he suspected. But Arthur was off fighting Saxons. Surely he wouldn't come back at just the wrong time.

"Your husband has good armaments," Kennedy said. "He needs good armaments, to protect his ornament." It wasn't great wordplay, but his Latin wasn't great, either. The hungry look in his eyes told Guinevere more of what he had in mind.

"Come with me," she said. *I'd love to,* he thought, but that didn't translate into Latin at all.

They brushed against each other once more as they left the armory. Guinevere let out a throaty little laugh that made Kennedy want to pull her down to the floor then and there. *Be patient,* he told himself. *If you're wrong and if she screams, they won't wait for Arthur to get back. They'll kill you themselves, likely an inch at a time.*

"The kitchen," Guinevere said.

The kitchen looked like a kitchen. A girl plucked the carcass of a goose. Another one kneaded a fat mound of bread dough on a table. Pots, most of them clay but a few metal, hung on shelves to one side of a raised platform that housed a charcoal fire. A pot on a gridiron bubbled above it. It smelled good. Kennedy walked over to see what was cooking. It turned out to be pease porridge. It was all he could do not to recite the nursery rhyme.

A woman with strong, muscular forearms worked a quern, which puzzled him until he realized she was grinding grain into flour. Judging by those arms, she did a lot of that. Even if the kitchen looked like a kitchen, this wasn't the twentieth century.

"Here is John of America, a traveler from a distant land," Guinevere told the kitchen help in Latin. Then she used the Celtic speech they probably followed better; the only part of that Kennedy understood was his name.

The women studied him with lively curiosity. The girl who was plucking the goose looked from him to Guinevere and back again. She whispered something behind her hand to the older woman making flour. The older woman chuckled under her breath. Kennedy wondered what they knew about their mistress. He hoped he'd find out.

The room past the kitchen held a loom and a spinning wheel, with women working at each of them. That brought home how far from the twentieth century Kennedy really was. If you wanted clothes in Camelot, you couldn't zip round the corner and buy them. You had to make them yourself.

Guinevere muttered something that sounded annoyed. She hurried back to the kitchens. When she returned, she was carrying a little clay lamp with a lit wick. *She couldn't just flick a switch to start it,* Kennedy realized. *She had to go back to where there was fire.* He wasn't used to thinking like that. With some help from Merlin, he wouldn't have to get used to it.

Like the armory, the next room had a door. Guinevere opened it, saying, "This is where we store the cloth we make. Step in, that you may see how much we produce."

Kennedy didn't care about bolts of cloth. For politeness' sake, though, he walked into the storeroom. Some of the bolts were heavy, nubby wool, others smoother linen. Some were dyed the same dark blue as his tunic (the word *woad* floated up in his memory), others plain. None was what he called exciting.

Then Guinevere closed the door behind them.

He turned in what wasn't quite surprise. In the dim, flickering glow of the lamp, Guinevere's eyes were enormous. She licked her lips. He took half a step toward her, paused one last time to make sure he wasn't wrong. He wasn't. He put his hands on her shoulders.

"Not only are the men of distant America handsome as the old false gods," she whispered, "but I see they are masterful as well." She slid away from him, but only for a moment, so she could pull a fat bolt of wool down from its shelf and set the lamp there in its place. Then she unrolled the cloth on the floor. "Now."

Stooping beside her, Kennedy bit his lip so he wouldn't howl with laughter. She'd wanted him as much as he wanted her. She'd been the one who set this whole thing up. She'd even been the one who went back for the lamp. And now she was saying he'd overmastered her! Well, some women were like that—they didn't want to admit, even to themselves, that they got horny, too. They had to be "swept away." *I'll be your broom,* he thought.

He ran his hands down the length of her body. She was every bit as full and ripe as he'd figured. Her eyelids half-covered her eyes. She gave a snakelike wriggle and moaned softly, deep in her throat. He nodded to himself. Even hot, she had the good sense not to be a screamer. He didn't want anybody opening that door, not for a while.

They had to sit up for a moment to help each other off with their tunics. She lay back on the wool, reached up for him.

Taking her proved repulsive and exciting at the same time. He was more fastidious than anyone in Cam'lod'n dreamed of being. He noticed that she wasn't perfectly clean, that she had several strong odors, that she'd never thought of shaving her armpits or her legs. She probably had bugs, too, like Eurolwyn.

Somehow, though, none of that mattered. Part of the

reason was that she took dirt and smells and hair (and probably bugs) for granted. Part of it was who she was—as with Marilyn, he wasn't just having her body, he was actually doing something millions of men only dreamed of. And part of it, as he rapidly discovered, was that she was one hell of a sexy woman in her own right.

Just as she gasped under him, just as he made himself swallow his own outcry though pleasure almost blinded him, the closed storeroom door opened. Guinevere gasped again, this time in horror. Kennedy's head whipped around. He started to scramble to his feet. At worst, he'd go down fighting. Better that than letting the locals think up something slow and creative for him.

But no outraged bellow came from the doorway, nor even a feminine shriek of discovery. Merlin stood there, too full of his own affairs to notice Kennedy's for a moment: "Good news, John of America! I have found a way to send you back to—" Because he was full of his own affairs, and because the storeroom was dimly lit, a few seconds went by before he really noticed what had been going on in there. His jaw dropped like an anchor. "Mother of God!" he whispered.

He was still crossing himself when Kennedy grabbed him by the front of his robe, yanked him into the storeroom, and shut the door behind him. "If you have found a way to send me back to my own time, use it now," he ground out.

"No," Merlin said, though Kennedy could have broken him in half. "Gladly would I aid a good man, an honest man, but an adulterer who seduces the *dux*'s wife deserves all the punishment that may descend upon him. I shall not help you, John of America."

"Oh yes you will, priest," Guinevere snarled. Merlin sounded stubborn, but the menace in her voice frightened Kennedy, and she was on his side. "If you know a way to aid him, you will use it, and use it at once."

Merlin *was* stubborn. "I shall not, my lady, nor shall I aid you in your adulteries."

"No?" She took a step toward him. Like Kennedy, she was still naked. From the way Merlin cringed, that bothered him worse than any threat she might make. When she chose a threat, though, she knew the one to pick: "If you do not aid him, priest, I shall tell Artorius my husband that you put *your* hands on me, here and here and *here*. Shall we see which of us he believes?"

"You will spend eternity in hellfire for your sins, my lady," Merlin whispered. But in the lamplight his swarthy features had gone as pale as they could. Though the storeroom was cool and drafty, sudden beads of sweat glistened on his shaven skull. Kennedy knew a beaten man when he saw one. Merlin said, "All right, then, my lady, all right, but only because, if successful, I shall put this man out of your lustful reach forever."

"Whatever you say," she answered indifferently. "Just get on with it."

Merlin flashed Guinevere a look full of hatred. Kennedy put his tunic back on. Guinevere didn't bother. Her body remained a weapon against the Egyptian priest. From the way Merlin stared and stared at her, Kennedy got the idea he might have wanted to put his hands there and there and especially *there*.

"I must be pure," Merlin whispered, as if reminding himself. With what looked like a deliberate—and difficult—act of will, he tore his eyes away from Guinevere, raised them to the heavens. He began a slow chant; Kennedy wasn't sure whether to call it prayer or spell or both at once.

He spoke first in Latin. Kennedy heard him invoke all three Persons of the Trinity, the Virgin, several archangels, and more saints. The storeroom felt closer, more confining—or was that just imagination?

Merlin shifted to another language, more rapid and

musical than Latin. Not until Kennedy heard *"Kyrie eleison, Christe eleison"* did he recognize it for Greek. He'd managed to avoid Greek in school. He thought Merlin summoned the spirits of Plato and Aristotle to his aid, but wasn't sure. He was sure the lamp flickered oddly.

He heard some kind of commotion through the storeroom door. Guinevere heard it, too. She snatched up her tunic, swiftly covered her nakedness, and hissed to Merlin, "Hurry, priest, damn you! If I fall, I drag you down with me!"

Looking harassed, Merlin changed languages again. Kennedy had expected him to use Celtic, but needed to hear only a few words to know this wasn't it. Maybe it was Egyptian or Coptic or whatever they spoke along the Nile these days.

At the front door of the residence, somebody boomed something in a voice that echoed like a big bass drum. A voice like that could belong only to a leader of men. Kennedy didn't need Guinevere's horrified expression to figure out it was Arthur, saying something like, "Hi, honey! I'm home!"

But Merlin was still chanting. He pulled a little brown lizard out of a pocket, threw it on the ground, and crushed it under his heel. At the same instant, he pointed a bony index finger at Kennedy and called out a Word. Kennedy heard only the first syllable. Everything around him went red, then gray, then black . . .

As he had before, he woke up in bed with a splitting headache. Ever so cautiously, he rolled over. The woman sleeping beside him had dark brown hair. He sighed in heartfelt relief—so far, so good. He rolled back the other way. An electric cord ran from the base of the lamp on the nightstand by the bed into the wall. He sat up and felt of himself. He was wearing his own pajamas again.

"Back where I belong," he whispered, and sighed again. He looked around in the dark, quiet hotel suite. Had he really left it? He shook his head. He didn't, couldn't believe that. Too bad. Guinevere was quite a piece. "What a hell of a dream." He lay back and went to sleep.

Harold Macmillan wore a dark blue pinstripe Savile Row suit that defined British reserve. After the greetings outside 10 Downing Street for the press, he led Kennedy into his office. "One advantage of dealing between ourselves," the Prime Minister said. "No need for interpreters."

"True enough," Kennedy agreed. Something ran through his mind: *I don't have to try and speak Latin any more, either*. He scowled. No, that *had* been a dream. It couldn't have been anything else, therefore it wasn't anything else. "Shall we get down to business?"

"You Americans. So impetuous. Always trying to get everywhere at once." Macmillan smiled to take the sting out of the words. He tapped a copy of the *Times* of London on the desk in front of him. "I suppose that accounts for this little item."

"What is it?" Kennedy leaned forward, tried to read upside down.

Macmillan saved him the trouble. "An archaeological team just unearthed an American dime in what otherwise seems to be an undisturbed post-Roman level at Colchester. They can't for the life of them imagine how it got there."

"Colchester?"

"North and east of here. It would have been Camulodunum in those days, I imagine."

"Yes, it would, more or less," Kennedy said, with such certainty in his voice that Macmillan gave him a rather surprised look. How had he come to know anything at all about post-Roman Britain? Though he wanted to, he couldn't tell the PM; wouldn't do to have your chief ally think you were off your rocker.

He remembered the feel of Guinevere in his arms. No, he'd never had a dream *that* good. And he'd gotten away with it, too. He grinned. It was a fine day. "However it got there, it was a long time ago. How are we going to deal with the Russians tomorrow . . . ?"

This is Mark Aronson's first professional fiction sale, but he is hardly unacquainted with either the written word or the field of science fiction. As one of Chicago's hottest creative advertising directors, Mark has a shelf full of awards for his writing, including several Addys and one from the International Film and TV Festival. As a science fiction fan, he and his wife Lynne founded Windycon, one of the largest and most prestigious science fiction conventions in the country.

As everyone knows, Richard M. Nixon became our thirty-seventh President in 1968. Now prepare yourself for the damnedest account of exactly *how* it happened.

President-Elect
by Mark Aronson

There has never been a moment like this one in your life. The surge of energy that electrifies you is completely unexpected, even though victory was certain. Everyone in the ballroom of the Hotel Ambassador leans toward you, or so it seems to you, like trees before a gale, and in a moment of clarity brighter than the blinding lights of the network television cameras you see triumph—inevitable!—in the New York primary two weeks hence, a first-ballot victory at the Democratic Convention in Chicago, a sweeping win in November, a mandate for change. All this between one step and the next as you press toward the hallway, the crowd rippling behind you, around you. You have put Gene McCarthy away in the California primary, and Humphrey has polled a distant and dismal third, which must be giving Lyndon fits. The thought pleases you; with a broad grin you turn to the cameras. "On to Chicago," you say, "and let's win there."

Through the door and down the corridor, cameras live, coast to coast. You think about the victory party at The Factory, a Los Angeles nightclub. Ethel will meet you there, Pierre Salinger is doubtless already oiling the guests; perhaps you'll have a moment for a quick word with Teddy White, see how his '68 book is going. Sorensen will propose a toast; you've had a nap, you're good for the night.

You turn right and enter the hotel's kitchen; you may be able to lose some of the hangers-on before you get to your waiting car. Eyes turn from stoves and stacked dishes as you enter. Behind you in the hallway someone—Mankiewicz? It's hard to see past the lights—gestures broadly. A telephone call. You hesitate. He points toward the phone on the kitchen wall to your left. He'll have the call transferred. And yes, it's important.

You shrug. Why not? And as you turn toward the phone you feel the bullet rip through the air past your right ear and watch it bury itself in the shoulder of a bodyguard. It makes a sound like a fastball in a catcher's mitt.

The picture that floods your mind is one you have lived with for almost five years, of your brother slumped forward, a bullet in his brain, already dead, in an open limousine in Dallas. No. It will not happen twice. NO! It is an image that leaves no room for thought, and so you turn on instinct alone. Others reach for the hand that fired the gun, but it seems to you that they move with a dreamlike quicksand slowness, and you reach Sirhan first, one hand clamping his wrist, the other his throat. He fires twice more, into the ceiling, before you twist the gun from his hand, and you are close enough to see the hatred, fear and shock in his eyes; it isn't fair, he seems to be saying, you weren't supposed to move, you should be dead, I want you dead.

They have to pull you away from Sirhan; you have been choking him and slamming him against the wall. There is a rage within you beyond expression or understanding. The fate of a nation cannot rest on a madman with a gun, and yet it does, and now you must act. You are not the person you were when you walked into the kitchen fifteen seconds ago.

The cameras are still rolling, and across a darkened America millions of people have seen you escape assassination. You are Robert Francis Kennedy, and late in the evening of June 5, 1968, you have become the most popular political figure of the twentieth century.

The view from Lawrence O'Brien's hotel suite framed seven billion dollars' worth of Manhattan's choicest real estate.

The curtains were drawn.

Technically speaking, O'Brien ranked no higher than third in the Democratic party hierarchy, after National Chairman John Bailey and National Treasurer John Criswell. Fourth if you counted Lyndon Johnson. And everyone counted Lyndon. But O'Brien's job was far more important.

As Johnson's point man, he controlled the campaign of Johnson's anointed candidate. And one week before the New York primary, Hubert Humphrey was in serious trouble.

Every flat surface and most of the floor in O'Brien's suite was stacked with newspapers from New York, Chicago, Los Angeles, Topeka, Des Moines, Dallas, Phoenix, Tacoma, Bangor. Every headline bannered the Kennedy name.

From the *New York Times:*
Kennedy Proposes Sweeping Crime-Control Initiatives

Envisions End to
"Era of Violence";
"Our War Is in the Streets of America,
Not the Jungles of Vietnam."

From *Midnight*:
JFK RUNS BOBBY'S CAMPAIGN FROM GRAVE

On the air, the story was the same. Replays of the near-miss in Los Angeles dominated every news program. Humphrey was all but invisible.

Bobby Kennedy sat in a comfortable chair opposite O'Brien's desk. He looked well-rested legs crossed, the cigar that was never seen on camera resting in an ashtray on the arm of the chair.

O'Brien hated cigar smoke.

The room looked disheveled, burdened by seventy-two hours of continuous meetings, room-service meals and deferred housekeeping. O'Brien looked much the same.

"Lyndon sends his regards."

Kennedy took a deep drag on his cigar, let the smoke out slowly.

"I'll bet. Cut the crap, Larry. Lay it out."

"All right. After New York, Hubert steps aside, defers to 'the will of the people,' throws his support to you, not that you need it. You sail through the convention on the first ballot with Lyndon's blessing. Nice, neat and ready to eat."

"What happens to Hubert?"

O'Brien shrugged.

"I see. 'Well done, thou good and faithful servant. Now get lost.' No wonder Lyndon gets along so well with Hoover. And I imagine there's a price?"

O'Brien rubbed his eyes; for a moment he had no idea what time of day it was. He gestured at the nearest stack of newsprint.

"Pick any one you want. 'Kennedy Vows Viet Pullout.' 'Kennedy Hits Street Violence, Proposes Law And Order Plank.' Ever since L.A. you've been sounding like a cross between Clean Gene and the goddamn Republican National Committee. If you want the nomination the easy way, back off a little, that's all. Nobody wants to hear about street crime. We're the party of civil rights, empowerment, entitlement—you remember, huddled masses? You want out of Vietnam? Fine. But talk about a negotiated settlement first. Think about national pride ..."

" 'National pride' my ass. National PR is a lot more like it. Lyndon knows something's wrong with his Great Society—he just doesn't have the guts to face it. It took a bullet to teach me what was going on. And I spent three years as Attorney General! I put Hoffa away, I saw Jack get cut down, and still I didn't know what the hell any of that meant until I was on the receiving end last week. But there are millions of people out there who do. And they're scared.

"There's no pride in death, Larry, no empowerment. Exactly how many civil rights do you have when someone sticks a gun in your ear? Or when your government sends you ten thousand miles away to stick a gun in someone else's ear? There are people in this country who live with those questions every day of their lives. And no one speaks for them. That's the difference between you and me, Larry. I'm one of them now. You're not. I represent them. And you can't. Those are the issues I'm running on, the issues I'll be nominated on, the issues I'll be elected President on."

Kennedy stubbed out his cigar and strode to the window, pushed aside a curtain and stared at the choked traffic thirty floors below. O'Brien spoke so quietly that Kennedy almost missed his first few words.

"Then you'll do it on one hell of a write-in campaign, Bobby. Because if you don't walk a little closer to the mainstream line, here's what will happen. You'll come to

Chicago with a million delegates in your pocket. You'll feel good. Mister Destiny, Mister First-Ballot. Then things will start to go wrong. Credentials fights. Favorite-son candidates pulling your numbers down. Delays, questions, doubts. On the first ballot, you'll come up a little short. There'll be floor demonstrations, some long, pointless speeches, it'll get to be four in the morning, everyone's beat. Maybe you'll get some of your delegates back. Maybe not. If you do, if you manage to grab the nomination, you'll find the big boys in the states are very unhappy. In fact, I wouldn't be a bit surprised if they found it hard—maybe impossible—to get your campaign moving in the general election. In '60, remember, Jack won because he won in Illinois—by about two votes per precinct. It's just as easy to lose by two votes per precinct.

"Politics is the art of compromise and favors—favors especially. And if favors were nickels, Lyndon would be a billionaire. I'm telling you he's prepared to call them all in if you don't toe the line. No matter what it does to the party."

Kennedy continued to stare at the traffic.

"Lyndon would do that." It wasn't a question.

"Lyndon *will* do that. So it's up to you. The way I see it, you've got two options: Compromise, or find out what it feels like to be mud under a tank tread."

On your way down in the elevator, you discard both of O'Brien's—Johnson's—options. You cannot compromise. You are quite certain God did not spare you to make a deal with Lyndon Johnson. And you must not lose. By the time you reach the lobby, you have settled on a third option. You need a phone number. Surely Salinger has it; he knows everyone, even someone as unlikely as the man you now must call.

New York, as predicted, fell to Kennedy the Democrat and Nixon the Republican. The turnout was unusually large. And certain voting patterns were so odd that both parties commissioned expensive national polls to verify them.

Two days after the primary, the results of the Republican survey were neatly summarized in a handful of manila folders on a coffee table in the suite of Republican National Chairman Ray Bliss.

Bliss's suite was handsomely appointed with expensive reproductions of Louis Quinze furniture; it was as manicured as O'Brien's had been unkempt. The folders stood out starkly against the rich, contoured wood of the table.

Bliss sat in an amazingly uncomfortable chair opposite Richard Nixon, who occupied a deep sofa. The coffee table was between them. Nixon's briefcase rested against the front of the sofa, and he had kept his suit coat buttoned.

Jesus, thought Bliss, he's still wearing those constipated three-button suits. If the guy would just loosen up a little . . .

Actually Nixon had loosened up considerably for his 1968 campaign. He welcomed reporters, joked with them, held frequent press conferences and generally made himself available for interviews. His style had become much freer than that of the dour, reserved Nixon of 1960.

But on this July afternoon, it was the old Nixon sitting opposite Bliss.

Bliss was in an unusual position. Nixon had built his own campaign from the ashes of political defeat, forging a brilliant strategy that had muscled him past rivals Rockefeller and Reagan in the early primaries and that promised to gain him the Republican nomination in Miami without incident. Bliss, selected as nominal head of the party after the Goldwater fiasco of 1964, deferred to Nixon, clearly recognizing where the party's true leadership lay.

But today he had to confront Nixon. All because of one phone call.

It was simple, really. Bobby Kennedy wanted the Republican presidential nomination.

"O'Brien's right," he had said to Bliss on the phone, "I'm running on a platform that would do Dick Nixon proud. And Lyndon will wreck the Democratic party before he lets me do that.

"I want to be President. And kick Lyndon's ass along the way. And I'd rather have a party organization behind me than go it alone. But let me make one thing perfectly clear: I *will* win in November. Not as a Democrat. Think it over."

As Bliss recounted the phone call, Nixon drew even more into himself. Bliss tapped the folders on the coffee table.

"All the scenarios are right here, Dick, black-and-white. Bobby's a national hero because he ducked a bullet. By the time November rolls around he won't be down more than two, three points in the polls. Not enough. Not nearly enough.

"First scenario." Tap, tap. "Bobby runs as a Democrat— fragmented party and all. You're his opponent. He beats the crap out of you—seventy to thirty percent, plus or minus three.

"Second scenario." Tap. "Bobby runs as an independent. You're the Republican. Hubert's the Democrat. This one's closer. First time there's been a good chance for a third-party candidate since Teddy Roosevelt. Either Bobby wins outright—just—or it's a runoff between him and Hubert, and the House decides it. Either way, you're out of it. And this time you're out of it for good, Dick. You're deader than Goldwater. A pariah. Because one miracle political comeback is all you're allowed."

Nixon still said nothing. But sweat was forming on the back of his neck.

"Third scenario. Bobby runs as a Republican. He beats Hubert very clean, very big. He spends eight years in the

White House making trouble for the bad guys. He retires to write his memoirs or play touch football or some goddamn thing and his veep rolls on into office in 1976. And that's you, Dick."

Nixon remained silent. There were beads of moisture on his forehead.

Bliss tried to sound conciliatory. "Yeah, it's lousy. But it's your only chance to stay alive. Hell, Dick, you'll only be sixty-three. A good age for a President.

"Listen, think it over. It's got to be your decision, yours and Pat's. This isn't a case of bad luck. This is history. At least according to these polls. Why don't you check them out yourself? Better yet, let Haldeman check them out. He's your captive adman; they'll make more sense to him."

Haldeman had already checked out the polls; copies were in Nixon's briefcase, even though Bliss thought he had the only set. And Nixon the practical politician had already considered his options.

Richard Nixon continued to sit quietly on the plump upholstery of the sofa, his hands folded comtemplatively, knuckles growing whiter and whiter.

Larry O'Brien had spent the day arguing with Hubert Humphrey, first over the phone and now in person. Lack of sleep and lack of leadership—Lyndon Johnson was hiding out in the White House and communicating only through his staff—had worn his patience as thin as an old sweat sock.

"Hubert, shut up. Sit down and listen."

Humphrey, shocked into silence, sat in the armchair in front of O'Brien's desk. Someone had cleared away the newspapers, and all that could be seen on the desk top were several blue folders; the Democratic pollsters favored blue for their report covers.

O'Brien slumped into his own chair, suddenly drained of energy. He stared at Humphrey for a moment.

"It's partly your own fault, you know. If you had distanced yourself from Lyndon's position on the war a little sooner, Bobby wouldn't have had an issue to run on. You'd be ahead in the primaries—hell, he probably wouldn't have run at all. Then Sirhan couldn't have taken a shot at him and we wouldn't be in this mess."

He placed one hand on the small stack of blue folders.

"Anyway, here's what it comes down to. Against a Kennedy-Nixon Republican ticket—can you believe it?— you lose, sixty-five to thirty-five percent, plus or minus three, no matter who you choose as VP. We've got only one chance—just on the low side of even, according to the numbers. But it means someone else heading the ticket, with you as VP. If you want it."

O'Brien pushed one folder toward Humphrey. Humphrey opened his mouth as if to argue, but spoke only one word.

"Who?"

O'Brien smiled—a rare event, these days.

"Kennedy."

"But Bobby's . . ."

"Not Bobby. Teddy."

It is a fact that the organs of democracy are rarely democratic within themselves. The power brokers of the Democratic and Republican parties quietly lined up the support necessary to nominate their candidates without incident at their respective conventions. And in general without the elected delegates realizing how they were being manipulated.

In Chicago, Mayor Richard Daley and Connecticut Senator Abraham Ribicoff struck a deal to maintain order at the Democratic National Convention. Daley ordered his police force to extend every courtesy to the media and to avoid confrontations with demonstrators. On the first night of the convention, network news viewers were treated to the sight of a mixed quartet of hippies and police officers in Grant Park, opposite the Conrad Hilton Hotel, all flower-bedecked and singing anti-war songs. A forty-three-year-old patrolman played the guitar.

Ribicoff kept potentially disruptive speakers away from convention microphones, smoothing the way for the orderly—some said dull—nomination of Edward M. Kennedy and Hubert H. Humphrey as standard bearers for the Democratic Party in 1968.

The Republican National Convention in Miami was more boisterous. Robert Kennedy's student following—the vanguard of the Kennedy Movement—erected a tent city on the beach near the convention hall whose population, according to the Associated Press, exceeded 17,000. Clashes with the police were frequent, but few were violent. And in due course Robert F. Kennedy and Richard M. Nixon were nominated to represent the Republican party in the general election.

Kennedy and Nixon got along surprisingly well as running mates, each developing a mutual, if grudging, respect for the other's strengths. Kennedy was impressed by Nixon's pragmatic view of world politics, while Nixon privately admitted to friends that Kennedy's domestic policies got the public's pulse racing faster than his own ever could have.

Kennedy's stirring nomination acceptance speech set the tone for his entire campaign: ". . . and to the last, I believe that the vanguard of freedom is justice. Justice in America, that none might live in fear. Justice for Americans—for all Americans equally. Justice by America in its dealings with the peoples of the world."

But even more surprising was the success of the Edward Kennedy-Hubert Humphrey campaign. His brother's abdication as crown prince of the Democratic party left Ted Kennedy with the freedom to run an old-fashioned, pulpit-pounding, barnstorming, whistle-stop campaign based on the legacy of New Deal politics and the mystique of Camelot.

People ate it up—which was reflected in the polls. Even Humphrey became a believer.

The grueling pace of the campaign seemed to energize Ted Kennedy; he had never looked healthier, never spoken so compellingly. Although there was nothing new in the 1968 Democratic platform, no candidate in twenty years had articulated the traditional Democratic virtues with such fire.

In the end, it was too close to call.

The voting on Election Day, November 5, was the heaviest in the nation's history. Over 104,000,000 cast ballots—fully eighty-seven percent of those eligible to vote. Fistfights erupted over voting irregularities as polling places ran out of materials. Voting hours were extended, and lines reached around city blocks.

The three networks, arrogant in the accuracy of previous computer projections, were frustrated by tight races in every state. Numbers on the video tote boards changed with agonizing slowness due to the sheer volume of the vote. Well past midnight, no one was willing to project a winner.

Perhaps speaking for all of his colleagues, a bemused and exhausted Walter Cronkite signed off at four A.M.: "We who report the news are trained to listen when the people speak. Today the people of America have not only spoken, but have shouted—and I hope we can all be pardoned for being a little deaf, and more than a little tired. This is Walter Cronkite for CBS News. Good night."

In the composing room of the *Chicago Tribune*, a pressman pulled a proof and grinned.

"Hey, Chuck, I guess we can't screw up like we did in '48."

Chuck looked up from the negative he was stripping

and peered at the dummy front page through the bottoms of his bifocals. Smoke spit up from his pipe as he let out a cynical grunt.

"No argument."

The headline read, KENNEDY WINS.

It took two days to sort out which Kennedy had won: Kennedy-Nixon, 271 electoral votes; Kennedy-Humphrey, 267 electoral votes. Third-party candidate George Wallace failed to carry his own state.

The popular vote was even closer, with a bare 100,000 votes separating the two tickets—less than a tenth of one percent of the total.

In the weeks that followed, the inevitable challenges failed to alter the results, and in the letdown that always occurs after a national election, the attention of the media drifted elsewhere.

In the Manhattan apartment of a mutual friend, two brothers sit in identical chairs as the short December day draws to a close. Through the picture window, the George Washington Bridge is outlined in lights against a fading sky of pale orange and blue-black. In another room a radio plays "Love is Blue." The day has been warmer than normal, and a light fog coats the city—in fact, the entire Eastern seaboard.

You are the President-elect. You are calm, peaceful for the first time since your brush with another destiny six months ago. There are plans to make, agendas to be formed for the architecture of your administration. But others can take care of that for the moment.

The campaign was exhilarating and devastating both. Brother versus brother. A highly localized Civil War. And now it is time to make your peace.

Teddy, you observe, is hardly a broken man. On the contrary. Facing impossibly long odds, he rallied the Democratic party from a certain rout and nearly pulled off a stunning upset. His political future is secure, and even you see him in a new light.

But you have much to talk about. And you find it hard to begin. Still, you are brothers, a tie stronger than political differences. An impish grin crosses your face.

"Teddy, let's get the hell out of here and talk."

"Where?"

"Let's just drive. Drive and talk. Up to Massachusetts— Martha's Vineyard. Remember where we all used to hang out when we were kids?"

"The island? It's, what, a six-hour drive? Plus the ferry— you know the ferry doesn't run at night this time of year. You're nuts!"

But Ted smiles anyway.

You continue. "Okay, I'm nuts! Besides, we both know the harbor master—we'll charter the ferry if we need to. Come on, let's do it!"

"What about Joan and Ethel and the kids?"

"We'll call them from Chappaquiddick."

For a moment, the years melt away, you laugh and like bad little boys you figure out how to elude the Secret Service men. Teddy is tired; you'll drive.

Hours later, in the fog on Martha's Vineyard, you regret your decision. You're very tired. Perhaps you should have flown directly to Edgartown. But you're almost there.

Teddy is asleep in the passenger seat as you approach the bridge to Chappaquiddick Island. You seem to remember that the road veers to the right, and so you turn. And drive off the bridge.

Black water is the last thing you ever see.

From the *New York Times*, Monday, December 16, 1968:
Robert Kennedy Killed in Automobile Accident

Misses Bridge in Fog;
Edward Kennedy Hospitalized
After Futile Attempt
to Rescue Brother

On January 20, 1969, Richard M. Nixon was inaugurated as the thirty-seventh President of the United States of America.

Hugo and Nebula nominee Pat Cadigan is the author of such powerful novels as *Mindplayers*, *Synners* and *Fools*—and with stories such as the memorable "Dispatches From the Revolution," she has staked out 1968 as her private literary preserve as surely as Barry Malzberg has claimed November of 1963.

Here she presents a typically searing vision of 1968, with perhaps the least likely Kennedy of all serving as the Senator from Massachusetts, and an even less likely priest numbered among the Catonsville Nine.

No Prisoners
by Pat Cadigan

Of everyone in the family, Senator Kennedy thought, staring at the TV screen, Bobby was the most photogenic. Or perhaps the word was telegenic. The camera loved him in a way that surpassed even Jack. Jack's charisma and confident leadership had always lent his image great warmth, but the fact of his attractiveness was more of an afterthought. The press routinely referred to Ambassador Kennedy as glamorous, and that was certainly true. The Senator's own press adjective was *striking* and the thought brought a wry smile: some kind soul with a thesaurus, as some other less kind soul had said once. But Bobby—the first thing you saw was his pure physical beauty. As if he were a movie star. To the press, he was the Golden Kennedy.

The old man had always thought the press was just rubbing it in. Perhaps he was right, in a few cases—Joseph P. Kennedy was hardly the beloved figure of American politics that poor, lost Jack had been. Not that Joe had ever sought that for himself, nor, really, for his children—not as such, anyway. But everyone in the family knew that the old man had believed, deep in his secret, idealistic heart of hearts, that if his children did what was right, the love of the American people would follow.

The Senator sat back in the easy chair, still smiling, though the smile had become somewhat wistful now. And so, had that come true? For Jack, it was certainly so now. Jack was forever frozen in 1963. It would be a long, long time before any other U.S. President inspired the affection that Jack had. Never mind his enemies—they had all been more or less neutralized by an assassin's bullet. Martyr status conferred sainthood, rightly or wrongly, and Jack would be a near-impossible act to follow, even for the other Kennedys themselves. If any of them had any presidential aspirations, anyway.

And who was there? The old man himself had all but come right out and said the dream was over. That would have been galling, but they all knew it wasn't a statement of no confidence on his part, just an assessment of reality. Joe Kennedy had always had faith in his children; they all knew it and had worked hard to justify that faith. In the end, the old man had been as much bewildered as gratified. Only Jack and Jean had fit the scheme of things.

We always loved you deeply, Dad, thought the Senator, *but you taught us too well.* The former Attorney General, now *Senator* Kennedy, wasn't supposed to have been named Eunice. Ambassador Kennedy wasn't supposed to have been Patricia. And Father Robert Kennedy wasn't supposed to have *been*, at all.

Father Robert Kennedy, S.J., if you please. The old man

blamed their mother for that. He'd wanted all the children to have a public-school education, so they'd be able to get along with all kinds of people. But Rose had insisted on sending Bobby first to St. Paul's and then to the Priory, and when Joe had tried to send him to Milton Academy, Bobby had dug in his heels and refused.

What's the matter with you, don't you want to go to Harvard? the old man had demanded.

No. I want to go to Poughkeepsie. Like a silly child's smarting off.

And what in God's name is in Poughkeepsie? the old man had thundered at him.

The seminary. In God's name, yes.

You could read the old man's thoughts in his face just as clearly as if they had appeared over his head in a neon word-balloon. *Now we'll never have a Kennedy in the White House!*

He had turned his anger on all of them, but the Senator and Patricia had borne the brunt. *You middle children— always looking out for each other! You've been in collusion from the beginning!*

Well, truthfully, Dad? Yes. From the moment we all knew what we wanted, we knew we'd have to stick together because half the battle would be you. That was the answer she never made aloud because she hadn't dared speak to her father that way then (or even now, even if he hadn't been so ill). But she really hadn't had to. She'd have just been telling him something he'd already known, and Joe Kennedy wasn't one for wasting words. Privately, she thought that, on some deeper level, the old man felt a certain ... contentment, perhaps. He could blame Rose for Bobby's entering the priesthood, and he could blame her and Patricia for igniting the feminist movement. That satisfied his need for visible causes.

How he had howled when she had declared for the Eleventh Congressional District back in '46! His girls had been raised to be good wives to politicians, not politicians themselves. Her win had shut up him, though, and paved the way for Patricia. Thank God—if she had not run, Patricia might have decided to suppress her own aspirations. She might even have married that British movie star who had been chasing her so earnestly. But she and Bobby had managed to put the kibosh on that by convincing Jack to take Patricia as well as Teddy with him on the trip from Israel to Japan in 1951. If Patricia had ever been considering giving it all up, the encounter with Nehru had clinched her decision to enter diplomatic service. Sandwiched between Jack and Teddy, she alone had commanded Nehru's attention with her intelligence and her incisive questions on Vietnam and Communism. "He snubbed us for Pat," Teddy had written home. "We bored him; she fascinated him. Upstaged by a pretty girl."

Not hardly, Teddy, Eunice thought, still amused. So much for Teddy Kennedy, Boy Diplomat, and just as well. He made a much better businessman than he ever would have made a politician. The boy just liked to entertain too much (*way* too much); better that he did it in his own chain of resorts than in public office. When you paid your staff off to keep quiet, it was called *Christmas bonuses*, not *bribes*.

Poor Teddy. Bobby would have disapproved of her thoughts and called her uncharitable, as he did whenever she made even the faintest criticism of the so-called Wildest Kennedy's behavior. *Teddy never could get enough attention, let alone approval,* Bobby had once said. *He came along too late. He couldn't be a war hero like Joe Jr. or Jack. You and I and Patricia were busy taking turns making the old man mad. Kick died and Rosemary . . . well. Jean had the Good Child spot sewed up. All that was left for Teddy was getting sick, hurting his back in accidents, and going to parties.*

Family, Eunice thought. *The gift that keeps on giving.* Well, she'd make some allowances for Teddy, but she was never, *ever* going to like that Leona Helmsley woman he'd married after divorcing Joan, and not just because the woman was twelve years his senior. Teddy had to know that had been a terrible mistake and thank God he'd waited until after Jack's election to make it.

The TV screen snapped her back to the present by showing her a close-up of Bobby's smiling, laughing face. The Golden Kennedy, indeed—he had never looked more so. Black smoke suddenly obscured his face, which gave her a start; it always did, even though she had seen this footage dozens of times, or so it seemed. The way the smoke went in front of him made it look as if he, too, were burning.

The camera drew back to show Bobby standing next to Daniel Berrigan. The image froze, became the page-one snapshot that was the latest marker on the Kennedy landscape. Like her own victory speech after her first win, like Jack's inauguration, like the Zapruder frames and Jackie standing next to LBJ as he was sworn in, like John-John saluting at Jack's funeral, this one would never die. The Picture From Catonsville, everyone called it. Like the Creature from the Black Lagoon, a monster you couldn't tear your eyes away from.

Anti-War Priest-Activist Kennedy Assists in the Burning of Draft Records With Homemade Napalm.

If that sight hadn't killed the old man, Eunice thought, he would probably live forever.

She hadn't been terribly prepared for it herself, though she had seen some kind of big demonstration coming, given Bobby's activism with the Berrigans & Co. Looking back on it, she should have seen something coming as soon as he'd fallen in with Daniel Berrigan back in Poughkeepsie. Philip had come a little bit later, but as soon as he had, it had been as if a circuit had been completed. As if Bobby had discovered in them his true brothers.

Well, they were a little closer to his own age, but that was only part of it. Because the Berrigans *were* brothers, they were to Bobby the epitome of what he had missed being the odd man out in a (mostly) political family—brothers in fact as well as brothers in Christ.

The Berrigans had been equally drawn to Bobby and this had made her suspicious at first. She had cultivated suspicion during the time young men had pursued her—young men with big political aspirations, all of them, looking to grab the brass ring by marrying into the Kennedy family. Actually, she hadn't had to cultivate much suspicion about her own desirability; she'd have had to have been in a coma not to see. But the Berrigans ... what could they possibly want? They were the furthest thing from Vatican game-players that existed; they made headlines now, but that hadn't been the case back when they had hooked up with Bobby.

You just don't understand yet, Bobby had told her gently. *Maybe someday you'll meet other senators who stand for all the things you stand for, and then you'll see. Philip and Daniel don't just talk human rights. They live human rights.*

Sure did. She'd had them investigated, discreetly but thoroughly, feeling glad of that Kennedy power advantage and yet at the same time, a little bit guilty for some reason. And the Berrigans had turned out to be what they appeared to be—a couple of do-gooding priests who had come out of hardship, acting on their beliefs. No aspirations to be cardinal or bishop or even official Kennedy chaplains. Philip's order, the Josephites, were dedicated to serving the needs of American black people, while the Jesuits were, as ever, the Jesuits.

In the end, she'd had to conclude that Bobby's alliance with the Berrigans and, subsequently, the peace movement, had an awful lot in common with her own alliance with the feminist movement—they were both getting what their family had not, with few exceptions, been able to give: acceptance.

Well, that was mostly Joe; Rose, too, to a certain extent, though she seemed to make more of an attempt to understand her wayward children. As for the rest of them—

it wasn't really that Teddy hadn't been accepted as much as his being just too distant in age; he'd been too young to be an ally. Jean had never expressed disapproval, but she was the next youngest and vying to be everything Joe and Rose wanted her to be. Jack had had to distance himself from Bobby for the sake of the election—the fact of his Catholicism had been handicap enough, and without Joe Kennedy's machine, he probably could never have brought it off.

By comparison, she had been much less of a thorn in the campaign's side. She had been expected to deliver the women's vote, and she had, by God—done it and done it big. Jack had had to tread very cautiously around some of the more explosive issues like abortion, however; it had helped that Jackie had been pregnant.

And then Jack had surprised her by offering her the Attorney General's spot. It was unheard-of, unprecedented, unbelievable, and her first impulse had been to turn it down flat, feminism be damned. It was one thing to stand up for what you believed in, but quite another to face down the whole country with something it might not be ready for.

"I'd be like the cricket that attacked the lawn mower," she'd said to Jack. "Incredibly brave, completely lacking in judgment."

"You think *I'm* completely lacking in judgment?" Jack had asked her with a smile.

She'd looked around the Oval Office. "Up till now you've been batting a thousand, I guess. But this is no time to go kamikaze."

He flashed the smile, that famous Kennedy smile that she had seen on every face in her family, including her own. "The Kamikaze Kennedy—this could be a whole new image for me. After all, we have to look ahead to '64."

"*Jack.*"

"All right, all right. Look, I'm serious, Eunice. I can't think of a better person for Attorney General. You know what Dad used to say about you? He used to say that if you'd been blessed with balls, you'd own this country."

She'd burst out laughing at that one.

"He was right, too. Of all of us, you were the one with the best head for politics, and you still are."

Her laughter wound down. "Maybe that's true. And maybe I know when the time isn't right to force the issue of a woman Attorney General. Maybe after the '64 election—*if* you win—"

"That's not the way you thought back in '46, Eunice. Was the time right to force the issue of a woman candidate for the Eleventh Congressional District? You didn't even have the feminist movement backing you up then, because there was no such thing! *You* brought it about— the first strong Kennedy woman who wasn't somebody's mother or wife or sister, *you* made that happen. You won the Eleventh with a lot of Rosie-the-Riveters raising hell for you. And you can carry off the Attorney General's office now. If you'd been thinking like this back in '46, there probably wouldn't *be* any feminist movement now. Not the way we know it. You want to live in a country like that?"

His vehemence had startled her. She'd told him she'd have to sleep on it and went straight home to call Bobby.

"Jack wants you for Attorney General? He's a very smart man. What's the problem?" he'd said.

"Well, what do you *think* the problem is, Bobby? Don't you think he's jumping the gun?"

Even through the tinny phone receiver, his laughter had been musical. All that chanting in Latin, she thought, nonsensically. "Now you sound just like Dad, circa 1946!"

"That's what Jack said."

More laughter. "Now, what did you say the problem was? Eunice, what happened to you? With an attitude like that, you could set the feminist movement back twenty years! Don't you remember your own fair-housing-fair-pay speech from '47? 'No quarter given, no compromise, and *no prisoners*!' Are you a leader, or aren't you?"

It had burst out of her then before she could stop it. "Bobby, I'm afraid!"

Silence. Not a stunned silence, or a horrified silence, but a reverent silence. The silence of church, of the confessional. Those Catholic reflexes, Eunice thought: talk to a priest, spill your guts.

"I *am* afraid," she went on. "You're the only one I could tell that to. I've stood up to a lot of opposition over the years, I should be used to it by now, I guess, but ... I don't know. Maybe it's not the kind of thing you can get used to. And what will Dad say?"

"*Hah!*" Bobby said. "That's the *real* problem, isn't it? Well, after he says all the things he usually says after one of us middle-children troublemakers kicks over yet another applecart, he'll probably say something like, 'What better person for Attorney General than someone Jack can really trust?' He doesn't really *get* feminism, Eunice, but he's not a caveman."

"No, not compared to some senators and congressmen I can think of."

"Don't be scared, Eunice." He paused. "Or, go ahead and be scared, but do it anyway."

God, but suddenly they were all so idealistic. Where was it coming from? "Easy for *you* to say," she'd said with a weak laugh.

"Call Patricia, she'll tell you the same thing. What time is it in New Delhi, anyway?"

"I'm not going to call Patricia. I'll be all right, I'll think this out on my own."

"Do it, Eunice. If Jack didn't think the country could take it, he wouldn't have asked you. He needs you. Things are going to get rough in the next few years."

There had been a little more conversation after that, but she had hung up with those words echoing in her head: Things are going to get rough in the next few years.

What could he have meant by that? she had wondered. Things had always gotten rough; fate would have to go to some length to top Joe McCarthy and Roy Cohn.

The next day, a telegram had arrived, from Patricia at the American embassy in India: BEHIND YOU 900 PERCENT STOP STAND TALL STOP NO PRISONERS. She had called Bobby back immediately.

"Is that what you do with the money from the collection box—blow it on phone calls to the other side of the world?"

"No, normally we buy limos with the collection box money, but I figured you were worth the sacrifice. I can do without a new limo for a month if it means my big sister will take the Attorney General's job. Then she can fix all my parking tickets." Pause. "Well?"

"Suffer," she'd said, and hung up. And waited all of five minutes to call Jack and tell him yes, she'd do it.

And it had been tough going at first, but her record and her image had pulled her through. Eunice Kennedy had always been someone to take seriously and those who opposed her on the basis of gender came off looking antiquated and ridiculous.

That had been the good news, Eunice reflected. The bad news had been that the clever ones changed their tactics and found other ways to oppose her. But she had persevered, drawing on reserves of strength she'd never known she'd had, all the way up to November 22, 1963, when the world as she'd known it had shattered into a million pieces.

So much for idealism. Johnson's accession to the Presidency had been a return to hardball politics reminiscent of the stories she'd remembered her father telling. It was all politics, all the time, and sometimes she wondered if Johnson's insisting—practically begging—that she stay on had been his way of trying to break her back and, by extension, the Kennedy power.

"If politics is now a matter of trying to determine what

form the other fellow's paranoia is taking, then become an expert on paranoia," Bobby had told her. "Whatever you have to do to get the job done. And if it's too much, get out and go back to the Senate."

"Sometimes I think I just want to walk away from the whole thing," she'd told him. "Go into private practice. Or teach."

"Whatever your conscience tells you," he'd answered in that maddeningly serene way.

"Thanks a lot, little brother. I hate you."

"I love you, too, Sis."

Of course her conscience had not let her walk away. She'd caught the idealism disease from Jack and Bobby. It had killed Jack; if Bobby was suffering any ill effects, he wasn't saying.

And the feminists had gone from dancing in the streets to marching in the streets, this time to demonstrate against the war in Vietnam—those that weren't enlisting and demanding to be sent into combat, anyway. She had viewed this development with much alarm. It was only logical, if equal rights were real, but there was something unsavory about it, something sick. Perhaps she was finally meeting the limits of her beliefs as a child of her generation, she'd thought, watching footage of anti-war demonstrators juxtaposed with demonstrations of pro-female-combat demonstrators at the enlistment centers. The country was going schizophrenic and maybe, she'd thought at the time, she was going schizophrenic right along with it. If no compromises, then combat: check one, yes or no. She wavered, trying to find the trick in the question.

And then she went to Bobby and, for the first time, fetched up against a brick wall. "It's not a trick question, Senator," he'd said. "It's just plain wrong to send *anyone* into combat. You know that, and that's why you can't resolve it. You *won't* resolve it until you stop denying that this war is wrong."

"It's not that simple," she'd said and had been about to say more when he cut her off.

"I'll pray for you, Sis." The next thing she'd heard was the buzz of the dial tone. Apparently, she had just found Bobby's limit, too.

His pictures had already started turning up in the news, and the press always singled him out for recognition. *Father Robert Kennedy, the Jesuit-priest brother of slain President John F. Kennedy, etc., etc., etc., along with the notorious priest-activists Daniel and Philip Berrigan* . . . The Berrigans would have drawn a crowd by themselves, but Bobby could draw a mob the size of a small village.

"I'm just God's instrument," he'd told her in a subsequent phone call. "As God's instrument I must do His work." She could always hear the capital letters in his voice when he referred to the deity. "If the name 'Kennedy' enables me and the others to do God's work more effectively—well, His Will be done."

The phone conversations were becoming less frequent now. Bobby was taking part more and more in anti-war actions and he and the Berrigans were getting arrested now. For her, there was the war to think about constantly, and with '68 coming up, she was being pressured two ways: on one side to push for the vice-presidential spot on the Democratic ticket, and on the other, to announce as early as possible that she had no aspirations to the White House, so as not to muddy the issues and split the voting in Chicago. Hell, if Johnson could understand how important it was for a Democratic victory that he not run, she should be able to understand, too, or so she was told.

She found herself going around in a rage most of the time. Her advisors were no help—they all seemed to have their own agendas now and she felt as if they were viewing her more as some kind of tool they could put to use to get what they wanted. Not all of them, certainly, but the fact that they were all so polarized on every issue was yet another source of trouble for her.

While for Bobby it was so damned simple. The war is wrong, discussion closed. In torment, she had called him one night late last year. Instead of the Brother Confessor with the willing ear, she had found a Bobby that was preoccupied, even short with her.

A few weeks later, she had heard that he was to go to Hanoi with Daniel Berrigan. Some American pilots taken prisoner were to be released on Tet, and two Americans had been invited to take them back to the States. Immediately, she made calls. It didn't surprise her when the men refused any and all help from the government with their journey, but she felt she had to make the effort for them. For Bobby. The prospect of the trip had raised the specter of tragedy; for some reason, whenever she thought of it, the picture of blood-drenched draft-board files rose up in her mind—Philip Berrigan's felony in the name of peace, committed with three others. Why she associated that with Bobby's trip to Hanoi she had never been able to figure out—Bobby hadn't been involved in that action and Philip Berrigan had been jailed.

Not the act of protest itself, but the blood, she thought; All she could see in her mind was the blood, independent of anything. Blood spilled. It had the feel of a bad omen to her.

Jack . . .

And then she'd been unable to shake the conviction that Bobby was going to die in some kind of attack. Maybe he would expose himself to danger deliberately—

She'd tried to stop him, but he'd been unmoved by her pleas. Duty; conscience; instrument of God; His Will be done.

Alternately cursing God and Daniel Berrigan, she had seen Bobby off in New York, convinced it was the last time she would ever see him alive. Then she'd gone back to Washington and, for the first time in years, called Sargent Shriver. He was long married to someone else by then, some other woman who had been raised to be a politician's good wife and was glad to do it, but their own parting had been on good terms and they had remained professional as well as personal friends.

Sarge, bless his heart, had come over immediately and sat up almost all night, listening to her rant, talking her down, and then letting her rant some more and talking her down again.

When footage of the Tet Offensive had come on the news, she had accepted tranquilizers from Ethel Skakel. Ethel had been her right arm almost from the beginning of her political career, but that had been the first time she had ever taken Ethel up on an offer of anything stronger than a vitamin pill. It wasn't lost on her that Ethel took some herself. She'd always suspected that Ethel had had a secret but ultimately futile crush on Bobby.

And what the hell: Bobby had come home after all. She'd gone early to meet his plane, watching the sky with angry defiance, thinking, *You missed, God! You missed!*

But the man who had stepped off the plane wincing under an onslaught of flashbulbs and bright TV lights was a faded shadow of the Golden Kennedy. He looked more like many of the returning combat veterans she had often been called on to welcome home personally—devastated, drained, permanently changed for all time.

For once, she had gotten her way and managed to whisk him away to a borrowed townhouse for rest and recuperation. She'd had to take Daniel Berrigan as well, but she hadn't minded. Nor had she cared that the press was already speculating that her actions meant that Senator Kennedy might possibly be about to align herself with the anti-war movement, unduly influenced by her brother.

While Daniel Berrigan had slept, or tactfully pretended to sleep, they had sat together in the townhouse's shiny kitchen, drinking the tea that Bobby had said a Vietnamese grandmother had given him. It was a bitter brew that she'd had to force down.

She had been braced to hear all about the trip, but oddly, he was not as forthcoming as she had thought he would be. "I cannot tell you," he said over and over. "I cannot begin to describe . . ." His voice trailed off so that she didn't know what it was that he couldn't describe. "But you saw it on the news. A good part of it. Now if you can imagine, say, Jean's kids, our nieces and nephews, running through the streets, trying to find shelter from the blasts and the fire, the napalm . . ."

He became a little more animated, expressing his anger at how the American ambassador had intercepted them in Vientiane, Laos, and insisted that the recently-released airmen return to the States on an Air Force plane.

"Politics, Eunice," he said darkly. "You should recognize that. The government war machine could not allow a humanitarian mission. The men had to go home on a *military* plane, the only kind that gets the stamp of approval. Why don't they just stamp 'FDA-Approved' on all the soldiers as well? That's what you do with cattle bound for slaughter, isn't it?"

She rubbed her eyes. "For a minute, I thought that was Daniel Berrigan sitting there."

"Do you know what Daniel calls Vietnam?" He sipped his bitter tea. "The Land of Burning Children."

"But they're killing our boys as well, Bobby," she said. "You said it yourself. You *saw* it yourself."

"They kill us ad we kill them. Show me where is the right in that. Show me where the good is."

"It's not that simple!"

"When did it get so complicated, then? Show me the exact point in time where people suddenly became disposable for the sake of—of *anything*. Show me when and where that became right." He'd looked at her with an expression so sad, she'd found it shocking. "You can't, Eunice. No one can. And I cannot stay with you here, under the auspices of this death-dealing government. Remember, Sis? No prisoners." With that, he had awakened Daniel and they'd left together. And she'd known that his departure had been a final thing between them, that he had not just left her presence but left *her*, as a person, as his sister, as anything and everything she had been to him. Her, and the rest of the family as well.

She had not called anyone that night. Though it had seemed like the longest night she ever had to get through, she could not remember a thing about it afterward, whether she had watched television, or tried to read, or just sat at the table until dawn with the dregs of that bitter Vietnamese tea.

The full force of 1968 had hit right after that. The explosion of racial violence after King's assassination seemed to melt into the campus unrest and the anti-war demonstrations until it seemed like there was no city anywhere that was not burning, and she could not tell news footage of Baltimore, Chicago, or even Washington itself from the footage of the cities of the Mekong Delta.

Land of the Burning Children ...

Burn, baby, burn ...

People continued to fill the streets, marching against the war and for abortion rights and a national day-care system, for the right to take part in combat, for civil rights and integration, for fair housing and a better welfare system, for a fetus's right to life, for truth, justice and the American way. There were so many of them in so many different groups, so many that came to her because she was Senator Kennedy, came to demand an answer for everything they saw that was wrong.

Go to Church! she wanted to scream at them. *Go to Church where all the answers are simple, where right and wrong never change places and everybody always knows which is which!*

And then Catonsville. Nine Catholic activists armed with prayer books and consciences and homemade napalm—soap-flakes and gasoline. Who would have thought the recipe for *that* would be so simple?

When she had seen the film of it on television, her first thought had been that Bobby looked almost like his old self again. The Golden Kennedy was back. But looking closer, she could see new lines around his eyes and a hauntedness that never completely left his face. But still, he was beautiful. As always.

". . . the burning of paper instead of children . . ." Daniel Berrigan was saying. Bobby said nothing. It was intercut with footage of Philip Berrigan leading a prayer group in jail, where he had been forced to remain, determined by the court to be a potential fugitive from justice. A brief shot of bloodstained draft-board files, then back to the burning files, and the goose walked over her grave again. Not for the last time.

Her mother had called the next day. Her father was too ill to talk to her, Rose had said, so she was giving Eunice his message. Those damned showboat Berrigans and thank God they had a Kennedy in the government, un-quote, from her father.

Even if it's a woman, right, Mother? But she hadn't said that, only listened to the relaying of her father's instructions, knowing that if her father hadn't been incapacitated, he'd have done it himself without a word to her. The Kennedy machine was not finished yet. Perversely, she had to bite her lip to keep from laughing; her mother had a gentle voice that always sounded just a little bit puzzled, not made for the Joseph P. Kennedy kind of tough talk.

When she had finished, Rose asked her if she was getting enough rest. Eunice had to let herself laugh then. "Go to Church, Mother," she'd said, when she had recovered. "Just go to Church."

"I will," Rose had said, sincere. "I'll pray for you and Bobby and all of us."

She hadn't made any phone calls this time. Instead,

she'd gone in person directly to the governor's mansion in Maryland, without an appointment, and was ushered in immediately to see the man with the funny name. She had never thought much of him but, whatever he was, he wasn't dumb. Spiro Agnew had been expecting her.

When she left, she was sure she had left her soul behind along with her promises. And she hadn't even sold it herself, she reflected later. Her father had sold it for her, without a second thought. Not for her, not even really for Bobby, but for some ancient and mysterious force called *Kennedy*, the word that was interchangeable, in his vocabulary, with *God*.

The hell of it was, she hadn't thought it would fly. Like so many others, Agnew had been working from his own agenda. His conditions—*demands*—had been so absurd, she had come too close to laughing in his face. But it was all absurd to begin with. Her father had sent her on a fool's errand. There would be no Kennedy dynasty, not in this generation, and if Jean's or Jackie's or Ted's children had any political aspirations, the members that made up the old Kennedy machine would be long gone and forgotten by the time they reached their majority. Who knew what politics would look like then, anyway? Ronald Reagan was making noises; maybe in twenty years, the White House would be relocated in Hollywood. *Make movies, not war.*

There could be no beneficiary of Joe Kennedy's manipulations unless it was herself, and she doubted that her father would have gone to such trouble just for her. Maybe he wanted her to believe differently, but she knew better. A dead frog's leg—she decided finally, during the course of another long, sleepless night—with the name *Kennedy* as the current that made it jump. Joe was doing it for himself, to show that he still could wield that influence and power, to show that he was and always would be stronger than any forces that opposed him, whether it was his own ill health, or her feminism, or Bobby's priesthood, or Teddy's latest paternity suit.

Agnew surprised her; the initial results were swift. Only a week later, it had been announced that Father Kennedy would be tried separately from the rest of the Catonsville activists. Due to the fame and notoriety of this one defendant, it was felt that neither he nor the other eight could receive a fair trial. The Catonsville Eight would be tried right there in Catonsville, while Father Kennedy would have a change of venue, perhaps to New York State, which was his actual state of residence. In the meantime, he would stay with his parents while awaiting trial.

The screaming lasted for weeks and almost overshadowed the war itself in the news. There was no broadcast, no magazine, no newspaper, no bar, no smoke-filled back room that was not full of opinions, voiced at high volume, about this latest development with the Golden Kennedy. They were giving him preferential treatment because of his family; they were going to crucify him because of his family; he had bugged out on his brothers and sisters in the peace movement to keep from going to jail; his brothers and sisters in the peace movement had bugged out on him so they wouldn't have to share his stiff sentence. The theories were shouted, printed, broadcast, argued, analyzed, revised, discarded, restated, over and over, until it seemed as if the Vietnam War really would have to be put on hold until the matter was resolved.

Eunice accepted no more tranquilizers from Ethel, just sleeping pills. With sleeping pills, she didn't have to relive everything in her dreams.

She was tempted to take a few now. Just pop a few capsules and let herself nod off in the chair, instead of going upstairs to finish packing for the trip to her parents' home. They were expecting her to keep Bobby under a kind of house arrest and work on him about this anti-war business. And, not coincidentally, keep him buried while a Kennedy-approved lawyer filed motion after successful motion for delays, until so much time had passed between the actual crime and the start of his trial that it would be too much trouble to do anything more to him than put him on probation. That was her father's hope, anyway. With enough money and favors greasing the tracks, who knew but that Bobby's trial might even be delayed until the war was over? And then the charges might be dismissed altogether.

She had to laugh at that one. With Nixon in the White House? And *Agnew* as Vice President? Maybe her father had gone senile. With Nixon in charge, they'd be lucky if the war didn't last into the '80s. She wished she could have been a fly on the wall when Agnew had phoned Tricky Dick with the news: *I've got the election in my pocket, Mr. Nixon—can I call you Dick? Yes, I think I should, since we're going to be working together very closely . . .*

She wondered whose idea it had been to keep that one under wraps; speculation about anyone's running mate, including Nixon's, was still running wild. She was going to be watching the Republican National Convention on television for certain. While the Democratic one—she'd be lucky to get through it without getting addicted to Ethel's tranquilizers. She was still being pressured to go for the vice-president's spot and perversely, she could feel herself seriously considering it after all. If it was totally hopeless anyway, why not? She feared it might mark her as a loser . . . or it might, as Ethel kept insisting, shatter the last barrier to the acceptance of a woman candidate for the highest offices. No prisoners.

But Ethel didn't know about the deal. Not yet, anyway. She had been suspicious after Bobby's separation, but so far had said nothing. When the Nixon-Agnew ticket was announced, there was no telling what she would say. Or do. Eunice contemplated the resignation of her oldest and most trustworthy friend and confidante, and took more sleeping pills from her. Hell, maybe Ethel wouldn't quit until late in the evening of the first Tuesday in November.

Another idealist, Eunice mused. She had grown up around idealists and subsequently surrounded herself with idealists; now her own idealism had died a rather hideous death and there was nothing left to do but disillusion everyone. No prisoners.

Or was there?

Was there time to call the whole thing off? Who was going to object if the Catonsville Eight's lawyers managed to reverse the decision separating Bobby's trial, if it meant *more* money and favors changing hands? Besides Agnew, of course; he'd end up looking terrible, and good enough for him. Put it back the way it had been, let Bobby take his chances and let her father live with that and to hell with politics altogether—

No. Too late. Reversing the decision would probably only result in chaos and confusion and a trial that could drag on until God knew when . . . 1970, 1971, even. With the name *Kennedy* unfavorably in the news every night. That was her name, too, after all, and she had a right to keep it good.

Distantly, she heard Ethel calling her from upstairs and her first thought, as always, was that the house was just too damned big for one person and a few part-time live-in staffers. She should get herself a nice apartment somewhere . . . maybe in that Watergate complex . . . it was really nice . . .

"I *said*, will you for God's sakes come *up*stairs and decide what you're going to take with you of your personal stuff? I'm not a mind reader!"

Something in her voice made Eunice sit up and look at her. Ethel stood in silhouette, holding on to either side of the hallway entrance to the darkened living room. "In a minute," Eunice said thoughtfully. Ethel sounded like she needed one of her own tranquilizers.

"And turn off that television," the other woman added.

"Didn't anyone ever tell you you'd ruin your eyes watching TV in the dark?"

"Ethel?" Eunice asked, getting up.

"Turn off that television! Turn it off! *Turn it off!*" Ethel lunged for the TV set, but Eunice caught her and shoved her away. She collapsed on the sofa, burying her face in the cushions, but Eunice was already kneeling in front of the television, turning up the volume.

"... the scene at Catonsville not an hour ago when Father Robert F. Kennedy, the well-known Jesuit activist and brother to the slain JFK and Senator Eunice Kennedy of New York, drew a large crowd at the very spot where he and eight others were arrested for destruction of draft records two weeks ago. Our correspondent was there ..."

Cronkite's grave tones were replaced by the breathless voice of Connie Chung. "The crowds here are willingly staying behind the barricades that Father Kennedy apparently put in place all by himself before the press was called. It is unknown right now whether he called the press, or whether that was one of his confederates. To my right, you can see Daniel Berrigan and the rest of the Catonsville Eight—David Darst, John Hogan, Thomas Lewis, Marjorie and Thomas Melville, George Mische, and Mary Moylan—kneeling in prayer. They have rosaries and flowers— Daniel Berrigan is weeping openly—"

The camera remained fixed on Bobby. His face in the afternoon sunlight was happier than Eunice had ever seen it since the day of his ordination, but there was something more—

He was speaking, but the microphones couldn't seem to pick up all of what he was saying. "—left with no choice. To be co-opted by the machinery of death and destruction, of evil, or to stand before God and honor my commitment to His precepts. As a great man once said, 'Ask not what your country can do for you ...' And as an equally great woman once said: 'No quarter given, no compromise, and *no prisoners.*' "

He was *wet*, Eunice realized; he was dripping wet, drenched, as if he had taken a bath with all his clothes on. But she didn't get it, couldn't believe, until he struck the match.

The image on the television froze, but the sound continued. Connie Chung was saying something, but it was barely audible over the screams of the crowd. It cut off suddenly and Walter Cronkite's face was staring at her again.

And then there must have been some kind of terrible technical error at the network, because the sound and image from the Catonsville parking lot came back, and this time the image wasn't frozen. It lasted only five seconds before being cut off again, but it was enough.

Cronkite looked shaken. He was apologizing for the error that had just occurred with the further running of the footage, but Eunice wasn't listening. She stood up and moved away from the television set, still seeing it. The Golden Kennedy, engulfed in golden flames, by his own hand. She wasn't sure she would ever be able to see anything else.

For nothing, she thought. Nixon was going to be President, for nothing. The war would escalate, for nothing. The hysteria in the streets would escalate, for nothing. The Catonsville Eight would go to jail, for nothing. She would demand a spot on the Democratic ticket and either get it, or not get it, for nothing. The precepts of God would be honored, and they would be broken, for nothing.

Go to Church, she thought. Go to Church where all the answers are simple: you just burn Bobby. For nothing. For nothing. And for nothing. No prisoners.

In the back of her mind, she knew that in a week, or two weeks, or a month, she would pull herself together sufficiently to begin thinking about what she could do (for nothing—stop it! For Bobby.). Agnew would probably think he was home free after the swearing-in (for nothing—stop it!), but wouldn't it be something, wouldn't it just be devastating if something were to come out *after* the election ... something unsavory, something that smelled like corruption (for nothing—stop it!), and all done perfectly legally, if covertly ... After all, who could hide from the IRS? Nobody (for nothing—stop it!).

Ethel was sobbing now, but that was far away from her, like everything else in the world, except for the golden flames. The Berrigans would rot in jail, she decided. Their support would wither away. Whether they were right, whether Bobby was right, she would see that they paid, along with Nixon and Agnew, and Rose and Joe. And herself.

We'll all go together when we go, she told Bobby silently. *I hate you. I love you. No prisoners, no prisoners at all.*

I had a feeling that a lot of the writers would be turning in stories that featured Marilyn Monroe— so for my contribution to the book, I exercised an editor's prerogative and broke my own ground rule: instead of an alternate Kennedy story, I wrote an alternate Marilyn story, a story in which she's plain Norma Jean Baker, a Washington, D.C. waitress who has just had the most remarkable experience of her young life.

Lady in Waiting
by Mike Resnick

Her name is Norma Jean Baker, and she has been sitting by her telephone for four days and three nights.

It seems like only an hour ago that she was in the West Wing of the White House, her arms and legs wrapped around the President as he attacked his goal with his characteristic vigor. Then it was a glass of wine, a few shared words, and she was ushered out, down the elevator, through the basement, down a corridor, up another elevator, and out the door of the Executive Office Building to the waiting limousine.

You are the greatest, the President had said. *Baby, I've been around and you are the best. I've got to see you again.*

But you're a married man, Mr. President, she had replied.

Not for long, he said. *As soon as the election's over, she's history*. He smiled his charismatic smile. *Don't make any long-term plans, okay?*

When will I see you again? she asked.

Soon, he replied, lighting a cigar and starting to put his clothes on. *I'll call you tomorrow.*

She went home and spent the whole night thinking of the vistas that had opened up for her in the President's bedroom. There would be formal dinners and ball gowns, private concerts by Sinatra and the President's other Hollywood buddies, even parties by the swimming pools at the family compound in ... in *wherever* it was that they all lived when they weren't in Washington.

She'd have to watch her figure, of course. So many politicians' wives let themselves go to pot once their husbands started hitting the banquet circuit. She made up her mind that she wouldn't be one of them; she'd never give him reason to be embarrassed by her. She'd even go to the library and start reading all about politics and things like that, so they'd have interesting things to talk about. She was really going to work at being the kind of woman he needed, and she planned to tell him that as soon as he called her.

But the phone didn't ring. She had stayed in the apartment, afraid to go out for food, afraid even to leave the phone long enough to visit the bathroom. But the call hadn't come, and finally she turned on the television to see what crisis had developed to keep him away from the phone.

But there was nothing on the news. Martin Luther King had given another speech, Fidel Castro had made another threat, Sandy Koufax had pitched another shutout. The President was there, of course, welcoming the head of some African country, but that only took him a few minutes.

Still, he *was* the President, and if she was going to marry him, she would have to get used to the fact that Presidents had, well, presidential things to do.

She stayed up until midnight, then set the alarm for seven o'clock and went to bed.

She got up before the alarm went off and sat by the telephone. At nine in the morning she called the phone company to make sure her number was working. At eleven she realized that she had no food in the house, and paid a neighbor to watch the phone while she ran out to the store. She was back forty minutes later, and didn't really believe the neighbor when she informed her that there had been no calls.

What was the matter?

His wife must be back from that trip. Yes, she had decided, that must be it.

But how often does his wife visit the Oval Office?

But his secretary is there, and he doesn't want *her* to know.

But he's the President. He could order her to leave.

But there's his brother. Can he order *him* to leave?

But his brother has his own office at the Justice Department.

Then it must be his back, she decided. It had been bothering him when she had arrived. Probably he was in too much pain to call. Probably he was in bed, writhing in discomfort. The poor baby.

But he was on the television again that night, and his back didn't seem to be bothering him at all. He was giving a speech in New York, and of course that was why he hadn't called her.

She frowned.

The President of the United States couldn't make a phone call from New York?

People were watching him.

From the bedroom of his private suite?

He didn't have her number.

But he had only flown up there in late afternoon, and he was home already.

She looked at herself in the mirror. Approvingly. He

would call. After all, he had picked her out from all the women in Washington, and he wasn't just some horny middle-aged businessman looking for a quick roll in the hay: he was the President of the United States. He wasn't interested in an endless supply of bimbos; he had too much class for that. His marriage was in trouble, he had seen her, and something had just clicked.

You ought to dye your hair blonde, he had said. *Pose for some cheesecake shots, maybe go into movies.*

Norma Jean Baker isn't a movie star's name, she had pointed out.

So you'll change it, he replied. *Something catchy and al-literative.* Then he had smiled. *No one would dare say no to Norma Jean Kennedy.*

She waited by the phone until two in the morning, then fell asleep without setting the alarm. She slept until noon, then practically jumped out of her chair when the phone rang.

"I've been waiting for your call," she said in her breathiest voice.

But it had been a bored woman wanting to know if she needed her chimney cleaned at bargain rates, and she had slammed the phone down so hard that she thought for a moment she might have broken it, so she called the phone company again and insisted that they call her back, which they did half an hour later, startling her again as she was cooking some eggs.

At four o'clock she walked to her closet and began going through her wardrobe. The tight sweaters and tighter skirts were nice, very eye-catching, no question about it, but as the wife of a President she'd need something a little better, a little classier. Maybe she should start going through the Sears and Ward's catalogs. Some shirtwaists, perhaps, and a low-cut evening gown or two. After all, she would be making trips abroad as *his* representative, and she'd have to look her best.

She looked at her hair in the mirror. Maybe it *was* time

to go blonde. And to pick up a book or two on how to speak French and Spanish.

At six o'clock she called Weather, to make sure the phone was still functioning, then broke the connection for fear a call might be coming in from the White House at that very instant.

She turned on Walter Cronkite at seven o'clock. Usually the news bored her, but now things were different: she was going to have to learn who her husband's friends and enemies were, what countries we were courting and which ones we were threatening. And then there was the family. She would start by charming the Attorney General—he looked like the hardest case—and then, once she'd won him over, she'd meet all the sisters. She didn't know quite what she'd talk about with them, but one of them had married an actor, so they had *something* in common. She could discuss the current heartthrobs with the best of them.

At ten o'clock in the evening she called the White House.

"May I help you?" asked the operator.

What do I tell her?

She hung up without saying a word.

At 10:45 she called again.

"May I help you?"

"I'd like to speak to the President, please."

"The President isn't available. Where may I direct your call?"

"I've got to speak to him personally."

"What is the nature of your business?"

I want to know why he hasn't called me.

"It's personal."

"If you'll please leave your name and number . . ."

She hung up again.

He must have a private number. She could find it. There was that guy from the phone company who kept looking down her dress, what was his name, Paul? Yes, Paul. She could call Paul and get it from him.

Did people call the President? Did he have a private line in his bedroom, or only the hotline with Russia? And what if his wife picked it up?

She was still pondering her options when she fell asleep.

This morning she wakes up with the sun. For the first time since she left the White House she thinks about her job. Probably she'd already been fired. No great loss; she will never work as a waitress again.

She wonders idly what kind of job the President's current wife had when they met, whether she'll go back to work after he leaves her, whether later on they can become friends. There are so many things she has to learn about him, and about being a First Lady. It would be nice to have someone to ask, someone who's been through it all.

She realizes that she is chewing gum, and self-consciously takes it out of her mouth. That habit will have to go, she decides regretfully; you simply don't chew gum at all the state dinners and fancy parties a President's wife must attend.

She thinks back on her three hours in the West Wing, as she has done a hundred times since returning to her apartment. This is a classy man, this President. He carries himself so well, he dresses so elegantly, he knows all the right wines, the right things to say. His manners are impeccable, much more of a Clark Gable than a Humphrey Bogart or a John Wayne. He doesn't smoke in public, but he has a supply of very expensive Havanas in his room. Nothing second-rate about him.

Of course, he wasn't that great in bed; in truth he seemed more concerned with his own pleasure than hers, but he is the President, he carries the hopes and fears of the Free World on his broad shoulders, and she's sure that things will improve once they start sleeping together on a regular basis. He will learn to relax, not to be in such a hurry; she will see to it.

Their relationship will have to be kept secret for a while longer, she knows. He can't afford a scandal before he is reelected, and she will have to live with the situation. It won't be her first secret relationship; a lot of Washington businessmen and lawyers that she's known have had wives. Most of them, in fact.

But they never promised to marry her, and *he* did. At least, she *thinks* he did. *Don't make any long-term plans,* he had said. What else could that have meant? His wife will be history after the election. Those were his very words: *she's history.* Why shouldn't she believe him? What reason could he have to lie to her?

But he had also promised to call, and it's been more than three days.

He's the most important man in the world, she tells herself. *He'll call. He's surrounded by advisors and generals and things. He just has to get a moment alone.*

And if he's had second thoughts? If he doesn't want to marry her, just set her up as his mistress?

She considers the matter coldly. He's still the President. If that's what he wants, she can adjust to it. He's worth millions; a brownstone in Georgetown wouldn't be so hard to take. Diamonds now and then. A couple of charge cards at the better stores. Fine meals, fine wines, classy new friends who talk about politics and philosophy and opera and things like that.

Yes, she can live with it. All he has to do is call.

She stares at her phone.

It doesn't ring.

What is keeping you? she wants to know. *Don't you know I've been waiting for almost four days?*

She studies her face and figure in the mirror again, and now she reassures her unhappy image: *Smile, Norma Jean. You're not just some unimportant waitress anymore. The President of the United States thought enough of you to bring you to the White House itself. Can any other woman can make that claim?*

She reads a movie magazine, watches a quiz show, drinks a pair of beers. The sun begins going down. She realizes that she's very tense, very edgy. She ought to pop down to the drugstore and pick up some sleeping pills, but then she would have to leave the apartment.

She considers putting on her coat and going out, then shakes her head and sits down again by the phone.

"It'll ring," she says. "Any minute now, it'll ring. He'll tell me why he couldn't get away sooner, and then we'll make an arrangement to meet again."

At midnight she cannot keep her eyes open any longer.

"Tomorrow," she murmurs just before she falls into a restless sleep. "He'll call tomorrow."

Hugo nominee Michael Kube-McDowell has made a considerable reputation for himself as a writer of rigorously-reasoned "hard science" novels such as *Alternities* and *The Quiet Pools*, while at the same time turning out such realistic short pieces as "For I Shall Have a Flight to Glory."

In this story, he takes the affair between the youthful JFK and suspected Nazi spy Inga Arvad (who was known as Inga Fejos at the time), which has been historically documented—as were the FBI's interest, the Charleston tryst, the incriminating recording, and even the fact of Joe Senior making a pass at Inga—and creates a new tale with a most intriguing twist.

The Inga-Binga Affair
by Michael P. Kube-McDowell

The heavy burgundy drapes in Room 205 of the Fort Sumter Hotel were drawn snugly closed, shielding the two FBI men who occupied it against both the chill February night and the curiosity of the outside world.

So far, everything had gone smoothly, despite the haste forced on them by short notice. With the green-as-May-apples new agent behind the wheel most of the way, the surveillance team had tailed Mrs. Inga Arvad Fejos all the way from Washington to Charleston—eleven hours on U.S. 1 and two-lane South Carolina state highways—without a hitch.

The hotel manager had done his part, assigning "Mrs. Barbara White" (as Fejos was calling herself) to one of the Bureau's pre-bugged rooms and installing the agents in the adjoining suite. The new recorder that the veteran electronic intelligence specialist had brought with him was apparently behaving itself, hissing at them from the top of the credenza as its spools spun out and then collected the fragile ribbon.

And though they'd missed the call Fejos made when she arrived, they'd managed to get the recorder set up before the young beauty's gentlemen visitor joined her in Room 207.

"The spool's running out again, I think," said Special Agent Frederick Ayer, Jr., looking down at the machine. His accelerated training had included a quick course in wire recorders, but this beast was something else entirely.

"Kid, you don't know how lucky you are," the silver-haired ELINT man said, sighing as he traded places with Ayer, surrendering the headphones and the chair. "I must have been out on a thousand jobs for the Bureau, and they don't get any better than this. I mean, we've got here Miss blonde fucking Denmark, giving her all on a maximum goodwill tour. If this wasn't a special hand delivery to the Director ASAP, I wouldn't even give you a turn."

Deftly changing spools, the ELINT man took the used one across to the coffee table, where the portable Royal waited beside another spool and a half-written report. As the senior agent began to type, Ayer settled into the chair and placed the headphones over his ears.

He was instantly assaulted by a sybaritic chorus: a man grunting with passionate exertion, a woman crying out in animal abandon. Those raw melodies were punctuated by the rhythmic thumping of (Ayer thought) a headboard against a wall, and by the woman's frank and breathless urgings. On its own initiative, Ayer's mind busied itself constructing pictures to go with the sounds.

Looking up from his typing, the senior agent caught

the wide-eyed expression on Ayer's face and grinned crookedly. "You look like a fifteen-year-old at his first carnival strip show, kid. Little Inga-Binga's some kind of moaner, isn't she? I'd give my right nut to have a keyhole to look through. Your wife give you anything like that when she's doing her Saturday duty?"

"Hey, we're still newlyweds, but—" Ayer shook his head. "Jesus! I've never heard a woman make noises like this and sound like she meant 'em. Who is this guy, anyway?"

The senior agent grunted. "McKee didn't brief you worth a damn, did he?"

"There wasn't time to do more than draw a car from the pool and pick you up."

The agent shrugged. "Lieutenant Stud-puppy is an old friend of hers from Washington. I recognize his voice from the last time. Navy, Office of Naval Intelligence.

"Career's going downhill, though," he added, chuckling, his fingers flying over the keys. "You ask me, he's the real reason we're down here. Used to pull his duty in the ONI situation room in Washington. Got himself sent down here to Siberia for talking shop in bed—Pearl Harbor stuff. I don't wanna think about where they'll send him this time. I just hope they don't arrest *her* any too soon, and end my fun—"

Just then, Inga sweetly invited her partner to perform an act which Ayer's mind was ill equipped to picture. "Sweet Jesus, I can't believe they're still going at it!" Ayer said, his face red. "He's been in there almost three hours!"

"Huh? Oh, hell, no. He hasn't got that kind of stamina." The conversation was no apparent impediment to the ELINT man's typing. "That's the third time he's been in the saddle since he got here. With two showers, a back rub, and enough jaw-flapping in between to get any ordinary man cashiered."

"You're enjoying this, aren't you?" Ayer asked.

"Sure," said the ELINT man, pulling the sheet of paper out of the machine. "You gotta take your pleasures where you can, kid. Me, I don't mind seeing some Harvard blue blood who got a free commission on his father's clout brought down."

"I went to Harvard," Ayer said, bristling.

"Yeah, I know. Nothing personal." The report and two spools disappeared into a large envelope which had the code word JUNE written across it. "Tell you the truth, knowing what a bluenose they say the Director is, I'm also kind of enjoying thinking about him sitting there listening to Inga-Binga sing her favorite tune. Probably give him a hard-on and a heart attack at the same time."

Laughing at his own joke, he dropped the first envelope inside another, sealed it, and wrote across the top: TO THE DIRECTOR, FBI—PERSONAL AND CONFIDENTIAL.

"This one'll be a favorite in the back rooms, that's for sure," the agent said. "Can't you just see Clyde and the Director leading a solemn circle jerk in honor of Hitler's favorite Nordic beauty?" He guffawed and headed for the door. "I'm gonna take this over to the field office, turn it over to a courier. I'll bring back some burgers and coffee."

Ayer bristled at the ELINT man's disrespectful attitude, but bit back a rebuke. Out on his first surveillance, with barely six weeks' service to his credit, he hesitated to lecture an agent who had been with the Bureau for twenty-two years.

"Hey," he said, changing the subject, "aren't you going to tell me who this guy is?"

The ELINT man stared in mock disgust. "Where did Hoover *find* you war-corps kids? Unless you were lying to me on the way down here, you shoulda figured it out already."

"What? How?"

"Be back in an hour or so," said the ELINT man, waving away the questions. "They'll probably be going to sleep soon. But mind the machine, and keep a good log."

* * *

The senior agent had been right about the man's stamina (though surely quantity counted for something?). While Ayer had been distracted, the couple next door had finished their rites. They were talking quietly now—or she was, anyway, about someone named Kathleen. Making a note on his scratch pad, Ayer tried to listen while he searched his memory of the long hours in the car.

What had they talked about? Women, mostly. The woman they were following. The war. The ELINT man had gone on a tirade about Pearl Harbor being the War Department's fault, not the Japs—said someone needed to write a book called *Why America Slept*, but that no one ever would, because the truth would embarrass too many people.

And then Ayer had changed the subject, said that he'd known Jack Kennedy at Harvard, and did you know that *Why England Slept* was actually his senior thesis?

The man in Room 207 laughed nastily then, and Ayer's skin crawled.

"If you asked *him*, he'd say he was just saving me from myself—if you could get him to admit anything at all," said the man, his nasal Hyannisport accent clear for the first time. "But I'm dying of boredom. If I have to look out at one more auditorium of pie-faced defense workers and pretend I know all the secrets of German incendiary bombs—"

"The Ambassador usually gets what he wants," said Inga. "Look at us—having to sneak around like this. Look at how much he's taken from us already."

Kathleen? The Ambassador? It couldn't be!

"I'm getting out of here somehow," said the man. "You'll see, Inga-Binga. He hasn't won yet. I'm thinking about asking for a medical leave, inactive duty, to have my back looked at up in Boston—"

"But Jack, Boston won't put us any closer to each other—"

Boston? Ayer came to his feet with a start, forgetting the headphones. "Jesus! Jack? *Jack?*" he cried.

The headphone cable snapped taut and jerked the recorder toward the edge of the credenza. Ayer lunged forward in a panic, barely stopping it from falling to the floor. Then he slumped against the credenza, heart racing, hands trembling, the headphones down around his neck, as the truth slowly beat down his surprise.

Holy mother of Mary, there's a Nazi Mata Hari bouncing the bed with the son of the Ambassador—with my old classmate. We're bugging John fucking Kennedy!

It only took a few seconds for Ayer to collect himself sufficiently so he could pull himself up off the floor. But when he replaced the headphones over his ears, he heard only silence.

Had he broken the cable? Or given himself away with his outcry? He stared at the door, expecting to hear an angry knock—or worse. Spies had a nasty habit of carrying guns. *ONI officers, too, probably.* Ayer's right hand nervously sought the reassuring weight of his own holstered weapon.

I should have put in more hours on the range . . .

But no one came calling, and Ayer forced his attention back to the recorder. He tapped the headphones, ran his fingers along the cable, checked the binding posts. Silence. The spools kept turning, but Ayer could not tell if anything was being recorded.

God, I've screwed up good this time!

Dropping the headphones on the chair, Ayer nervously paced the room and wrestled with conflicting impulses.

Maybe they're falling asleep.

He could hope, anyway.

What a tangle it all was—no wonder the Bureau was interested. And no wonder Inga was such hot gossip. The ELINT man had seemed to know everything about Inga, and all of it was damning.

To start with, she wrote for the *Washington Times-Herald*, that Fascist mouthpiece. Ayer didn't read it himself, but any paper that would publish a secret American war plan had to be a nest of traitors and Nazi sympathizers—why, it was just three days after the *Times-Herald* told the world about the Rainbow War Plan that the Japs had flattened Pearl.

That wasn't the only bit of sabotage, either. Inga herself had embarrassed Clyde Tolson with a column so flattering that it sounded like she'd been sleeping with him, too—or would, if he'd just ask. And wouldn't that be fine, the Number Two man in the Bureau, Hoover's hand-picked factotum, compromised by a sexual liaison Hoover would never be able to forgive? What a perfect opportunity for blackmail . . .

It went on and on. Apparently Inga'd been a guest at Hermann Goering's wedding. Adolf Hitler himself had taken her to the 1936 Olympics, called her a perfect example of Nordic beauty—you could see them together in the newsreels.

And Inga's husband, Paul—she really *was* married, the ELINT man said, though the marriage wasn't slowing her down any—her husband was friends with a Swedish industrialist, Alex WennerGren, whom the State Department suspected of refueling U-boats from his yacht. Ayer had read about that in *Time* just last week.

Tolson, Goering, Hitler, WennerGren, and, now, Jack Kennedy.

That's some Christmas card list—

But what was her play? Did she want Jack, or his father? It had to be the latter. Ambassador Kennedy was a leading isolationist, a politically and financially powerful man. Some already thought he was leaning toward the Fascists. And now Jack was helping Inga push him right over.

I used to tell him not to think with his dick—

The ELINT man was right. If Jack hadn't been Joe Kennedy's son, the Navy would have deep-sixed him instead of sending him to Charleston. Rich hath its privileges. Not that Jack had learned anything from the break he'd been given—

Maybe he doesn't know.

Ayer stopped pacing. Jack and Inga'd been talking about—what, something about the Ambassador causing them problems, disapproving? It had *sounded* like Jack knew Inga was the reason he'd been reassigned—hadn't it? What other reason could there be for the "Barbara White" nonsense?

But if Jack thought it was his *father's* doing—if he didn't know Inga was being watched by the FBI—if he didn't even know there was a reason to watch her—

They're going to cut him off at the knees, and he won't even know why until it's too late.

It was a miserable dilemma. Ayer could not pretend that he and Jack had been close. But neither could he take delight, as the senior agent had, in the fate Jack was facing. There was a brotherhood of Harvard men, after all. Of *all* men, faced with women's deceit and trickery.

Their game, their rules, and the whole thing rigged from the start—

Frowning, Ayer put the headphones back on. Still silence. He glanced at the clock and tried to remember when the ELINT man had left. Could it only have been ten minutes? It already seemed like an hour.

Dammit, a man shouldn't lose everything just because he followed the wrong smile into the wrong bed!

Drawing a deep breath, Ayer slowly reached out and turned off the recorder. He waited until the hiss ceased, the spools stopped spinning. Then he left the room and started down the hallway to Room 207, before he could change his mind.

Ayer's knock was answered by an otherwise naked man with a royal-blue bath towel wrapped around him like a sarong.

"What can I— Freddy?" Jack Kennedy's face lit up with

an engaging smile, threaded with a touch of genuine surprise. "Freddy Ayer! Well, this is a hell of a note! What are you doing in Charleston?"

Glancing nervously toward the lobby stairs at the end of the hall, Ayer swallowed and shrank two inches. "Jack, we've got to talk."

"Freddy, I'm glad enough to see you, but your timing—"

"I know. You're with Inga. That's what we've got to talk about."

Jack knitted his brows quizzically, but stepped back to let Ayer into the room. "All right, then."

"No. Put some clothes on. We'll go somewhere." He looked past Jack and caught his first glimpse of Inga, sitting up in the middle of a sea of jumbled bedcovers. "Just the two of us," Ayer managed to croak.

She was being scandalously casual about covering herself, and Ayer's mind cheerfully began touching up the details of his imaginings. *You can't blame a man for being a man—*

"Why can't we talk here?"

"Because this room is bugged," Ayer blurted out.

Jack straightened up in surprise, blinking. Then he pointed at Ayer and silently mouthed "You?"

When Ayer nodded, Jack abruptly turned his back and retreated half a dozen steps into the room, his body vibrating with bottled anger.

"We're okay for the moment—there's no one monitoring right now—"

"Then get the hell in here and close the damned door," Jack said. He was looking at Inga as he spoke; Ayer could not see his expression.

Ayer's face crinkled unhappily. "But my partner's coming back—"

"Partner? What's this all about?" asked Inga. "Who are you watching, and why?"

"As if you didn't know," Ayer said coldly. He stepped into the room and closed the door behind him. "Look,

Jack, I'm way out on a limb here. I shouldn't even be talking to you. But you don't know what you're mixed up with, and I just can't let you walk off the edge of the cliff."

"Freddy, you think I don't know my father keeps files on my friends, Kathleen's, Bobby's?" Jack demanded, whirling around. "Nosy bastard's always done it—keeps a little legion of Irish detectives in beer money, watching over the kids. I just didn't know he'd started hiring my *friends* to do the spying—"

"Jack, this doesn't have anything to do with your father."

His mouth half open, Jack stared quizzically at the visitor.

Ayer swallowed hard, then went on. "I'm with the FBI now." He pointed at Inga without looking at her. "And the Bureau has her figured for a German spy."

Inexplicably, Jack and Inga looked at each other and laughed.

"This is no joke," Ayer said angrily. "Ask her. Ask her about Goering's wedding. Ask her about her buddy Adolf Hitler."

"Mother Mary—I know all about that," Jack said, his face still painted with amusement. "It's no secret. I've heard her tell those stories half a dozen times. Hell, Freddy, knowing Hitler socially doesn't make someone a German agent. You'd be surprised at some of the people who've had tea and biscuits with *der Führer*."

"Damn you, if you're not going to take me seriously— this was a mistake." Ayer gestured dismissively. "Forget it. If you want to be criminally stupid—"

"Freddy, Freddy. Calm yourself down." Jack looked toward the bed. "Inga-Binga, are you working for the Nazis?"

"No, Jack," she said brightly. "Ribbentrop asked, but I turned him down."

"There," said Jack with a nod. "Good enough for me."

Exasperated, Ayer strangled air with his hands. "Jack,

you damned fool, *listen* to me. Why do you think you're in Charleston? There's already one report in the Director's hands about you and Inga, from one of your Washington trysts. And by morning, Hoover's going to have the recordings we made earlier tonight."

"Did you have fun listening?" Inga asked sweetly.

Despite himself, Ayer blushed. "You've got exactly one chance, Jack. Arrest her yourself, tonight. Haul her down to the ONI and denounce her."

Jack sat down on the edge of the bed. "You don't understand, Freddy. I want to marry this woman. Tell him," he said to Inga.

"He wants to marry me," Inga echoed cheerfully.

"See?"

"But—his father won't let him," Inga added. "Something about my being a woman of dubious reputation. Personally, I'm insulted. My reputation should be secure by now. Say, since you were listening, perhaps I could use you as a reference?"

"You're a married woman," Ayer said disapprovingly. "Don't you have any shame?"

Inga clucked. "I keep forgetting—Americans do tend to consider being married the same as being dead below the waist, don't they?"

Jack laughed. "Mercifully, our family managed to escape that particular affliction of thought."

"Don't be so proud. There *is* such a thing as overdoing it." Inga leaned toward Ayer as though she were about to tell him a secret. He tried to keep his gaze from wandering south from her blue eyes.

"Jack and I went to Palm Beach for Christmas with the family," she said. "Every time Jack left the room, the Ambassador was after me. Apparently I'm not good enough to marry his son, but plenty good enough for the old coot to boff." She shuddered. "Disgusting man."

"You didn't tell me about this before," Jack said, wearing a hurt look.

"The weekend was miserable enough as it was, with you two fighting all the time," Inga said with a shrug. "What good would it have done? I handled it. I'm a big girl, Jack. I'm used to the come-ons—from men with a lot of class, and men with none, like the Ambassador. No one touches me unless I want them to."

Jack grinned unpleasantly. "Don't get me wrong—I think it's great that you left the old hypocrite blue-balled. I just wish I'd known, so I could have enjoyed watching him panting and begging."

Ayer listened to the exchange in a state of profound cognitive dissonance. How good an operative *was* she? Had she figured out what Ayer suspected, and cooked up this story to put him off the scent? Could it be that she really *wasn't* trying to get to Ambassador Kennedy?

What else could she be after? The ONI? But if she was bent on penetrating the ONI, Jack's usefulness should have ended the moment he was whisked out of Washington—so why this rendezvous?

Jesus, maybe she's really not *a spy. Maybe she really* does *love him, or something—*

And maybe "Mrs. Barbara White" was only trying to hide from Joe Kennedy's Irish detectives, not the FBI.

But who would believe it now? There wouldn't even have to be a trial. The headlines alone would convict them in the public's eyes.

And there wasn't one thing Ayer could do about it. *I've already tried to do too much.*

"Sweetheart, silly as it all is, we do have a problem," Inga was saying.

"I know," Jack said. "Two problems. Two busybodies who're making it their business to run my life."

"Look—I've got to go," Ayer said, edging nervously toward the door.

"Hold on, Freddy," Jack said. "I'm turning this all

around and I can't quite put the pieces together. See if you can help me."

"Jack—"

"Step one: The FBI takes notice of Inga-Binga here, starts to wonder if she might be a spy," Jack said, patting Inga's hand. "Maybe someone who heard those stories about Goering and Hitler didn't find them so amusing after December 7, and turns her in. Inga?"

"I can think of a few women at the paper who might have been happy to do it," she said, nodding. "Men have always treated me better than women do, with rare exceptions."

Jack nodded. "So the FBI starts following Inga, maybe taps her phone, bugs her apartment, checks her background, rummages through her lingerie drawer. What do they find? They turn up her good taste in lace, her bad taste in acquaintances, but no evidence of espionage—"

"Because there's none to find," said Inga.

"Right. But if they even *thought* they had something, they'd have picked you up by now."

Ayer said, "Unless the Director is biding his time, hoping to get some bigger fish, or at least more of them."

"Unless," said Jack. "But then why move me, and tip his hand?"

Shaking his head, Ayer said, "I don't know," and fell silent.

"All right. Now wandering in from stage left comes the young Lieutenant Kennedy, who turns out to know the dangerous Mrs. Fejos *very* well. This minor sensation goes right to the Director's desk. Hoover takes the news to— who? Captain Wilkinson? Captain Kingman? Someone high up at ONI ordered my reassignment. Who else? Biddle?"

"A tap would need the Attorney General's approval, I think," said Ayer. "He'd probably want a report."

"And if Biddle knows, chances are that President Roosevelt knows, too," mused Jack.

"Really!" said Inga. "I'm almost flattered, to have worried so many powerful men."

"Jack, I *have* to get back to my post!" Ayer said desperately. "I can't be found here!"

"Just hold on!" Jack said sharply. "This is the part that doesn't make sense. Why am I still in the Navy? Why didn't they bounce me all the way out? I mean, *I* know she's not a spy, and I'm not a traitor—but you were awfully sure about the first, and had your doubts about the second when you knocked on the door. Who went to bat for me?"

"Ambassador Kennedy," Ayer suggested.

Jack shook his head firmly. "No. Papa Joe never does you a favor without telling you what you owe him for it. And he never covers your screw-ups without taking an opportunity to let you know in colorful detail what a disappointment you are."

"Then it has to have been one of your father's friends," said Inga. "You're not the average Navy lieutenant, after all. You're the best-selling author of *Why England Slept.* You're the son of the Ambassador to the Court of St. James's. You're the 'boy with a future.' I should know—I wrote that column, after all. If the Navy sends Jack Kennedy back to civilian life under a cloud, that's a decision that carries a lot of consequences."

"Granted that I'm every bit as wonderful and famous as you say, Inga-Binga," said Jack with a faint smile. "But we're at war now. Captain Wilkinson wouldn't care about any of that. He's not a politician. He's Navy through and through."

"*I'm* confused now," said Ayer. "You think somebody protected you, and I can see that. But you've eliminated all the likely suspects. Who's left?"

"Who's in a position to soft-pedal the whole thing? To say to Wilkinson, 'Look, this isn't serious yet, but it could be—why don't you get this Kennedy kid out of harm's way?'"

Ayer's brow wrinkled. "The Director?"

"Who else?"

"But *why?*"

Jack pursed his lips and lowered his gaze to his hands. "Because Hoover collects obligations the way old women collect buttons—you never know when you'll need one just that size and color," he said slowly.

"Blackmail," said Inga.

"The polite word is *leverage*," Jack said. "I asked Papa Joe once why he worked so hard at cultivating a relationship with Hoover. He said it wasn't so much that he wanted to be Hoover's friend as he thought it wise to avoid becoming Hoover's enemy." He looked up at Ayer. "Freddy—what do you think?"

Ayer had been staring at the carpet while Jack spoke. "I think I should cut out my tongue rather than say this— but I think you could be right. You hear . . . rumors. About some of the things they keep downstairs, in the print shop. About how the Bureau makes friends in Congress."

"So what's Hoover going to do with those recordings?" asked Jack.

"I don't know," said Ayer. It was an honest answer.

"It's obvious to me," Inga said. "He's going to bank them—let them collect interest. They're not worth very much right now. They could be worth a lot more five years from now—or twenty-five."

Jack came to his feet. "That has to be it! Inga-Binga, that's the missing piece! If he used this now, all he could do is cause a big embarrassment for a couple of small-time celebrities. What does he gain? A few hero points, for defending the Republic? But if he sits on this—well, every successful blackmail begins with a juicy secret. Button-collecting. That's what he's doing." Jack shook his head. "Jesus, if he collects enough of the right color buttons, he could end up being Director of the FBI for life!"

"A scary thought," said Inga.

Jack clapped his hands together. "And I'll tell you this,

Inga-Binga—he doesn't believe for a minute that you're a German spy and I'm an American traitor. Whatever else he is, Hoover's a rabid patriot. He wouldn't look past real espionage and treason. No, he's got you figured for a slut and me for a chump."

"Well, he's half right, anyway," said Inga with a twinkle. "So what do we do? We can't very well get those recordings back. Hasn't he already won? How do we get out from under the cloud?"

"Jack, I *have* to leave!"

"Then leave, already." Rubbing the back of his neck with one strong hand, Jack said, "Inga, I'm not sure I want to. In fact, I wonder if I might not like it if this cloud started to rain."

"What?" Ayer stared, his feet still rooted.

"What are you seeing, Jack?" Inga asked, sliding to the edge of the bed.

"An opportunity, maybe," said Jack. "Look—Joe Jr. will get his wings in another couple months. The Ambassador'll make sure they send him somewhere hot, and he'll probably be a bloody hero, and more power to him. Papa Joe wants a standard-bearer, a Kennedy to run for office. Joe Jr.'s future's all planned for him. Me, I'm just a spare tire in case something happens to Joe."

She looked at him with a mixture of hope and wonder. "Are you thinking about letting the air out?"

"That's exactly what I'm thinking," Jack said. "If we can force Hoover's hand—"

"—we could be free of both of them, Hoover and your father. We could have our own life—the life *we* want!" Inga said. "Oh, Jack, I like it! I *despise* this sneaking around. I'd much rather just be shameless."

Jack smiled warmly at her. "Shameless—exactly. It's the only way to make what Hoover's holding worthless. Force him to use it. To hell with cowering in fear. A scandal is the *best* thing that could happen to us right now."

She joined him standing beside the bed, letting the

sheet fall away forgotten as she touched his elbow. "Jack, I want to believe—I know how you admire your sister Kathleen for standing up to him. But you know how hard it's been for you to resist him. It's his boys that really matter to him, after all. Are you sure?"

"I'm leaving now," Ayer said firmly, though he didn't move.

"I'm sure." Jack crossed his arms over his chest and scuffed his toes in the carpet. "Dammit, I don't want to be Papa Joe's goddamned Charlie McCarthy doll, turning on the Big Personality in command performance," he said. "Look at me, Inga-Binga. What the hell am I doing in the Navy, with this back, my asthma, the ulcer?"

"It wasn't your choice. It was the Ambassador's."

"It's a joke. I'll never qualify for sea duty—and if I do, it'll be a fraud." He dropped his arms and collected her hands in his own. "You know what I want? I want a quiet life, to do a little writing, a little teaching. I want to marry you—keep you out of trouble—"

"Ha!" Inga said, but the smile radiating up at him was warm and generous.

Jack went on, "I have a million dollars or so, trust money, royalties, that my father can't touch. We could live off what it brings in—couldn't we?"

"Of course we could."

He stopped and thought for a long moment, his lips drawn into a line. "You've been trying to help me see I need to break with my father instead of bowing to him. And I always knew you were right—but it *is* hard. If you'd only grown up in that house—it's *damned* hard—"

"I know."

"But Inga, this looks like the last chance, and I don't want to let it get away. Because if Papa Joe finds out about the FBI—and he will, sooner or later, one way or the other—it'll all be over. He'll have Forrestal ship me off to Hawaii, or worse, and it'll be too late. I'll be living the rest of my life for him, not for me. And I don't think I owe him that."

She nodded, smiling with eyes bright with tears. "You don't."

"Are you game, then? I can't do this without you. I don't have a reason without you. Shall we get me cash-iered—and then get ourselves married, shamelessly?"

Her laugh was as bright as her eyes. "I do love a good scandal. Let's do it!"

Squeezing her hands tight, he kissed her forehead. "Freddy, you still have something next door to record on—or with?"

Ayer nodded slowly. "I hope so."

"Then get it ready, Freddy. We're going to take a shower—and when we're done, we'll see if we can give J. Edgar something indigestible to chew on." He looked down at Inga. "We can make this work, can't we?"

"Even if I have to leak the story myself," Inga said. "We're going to be infamous, Jack. Count on it."

Ayer held his breath, closed his eyes in wordless prayer, then unlocked the door to Room 205 and slipped inside.

The clock told him an hour and ten minutes had passed—but everything was as he had left it. He was alone in the room.

Ayer hurried to the recorder, and saw almost immedi-ately what he had overlooked in his earlier panic—one lead of the microphone wire curled in midair, a quarter of an inch from the binding post. He realized it must have been pulled loose when he nearly jerked the recorder onto the floor—in fact, the microphone wire was probably what had saved the machine.

With clumsy fingers, he reattached the lead. When he tried the headphones, he was rewarded with the sounds of running water. For a brief moment, he imagined them in the shower together—her body beaded with rivulets of silver—

Then he angrily chased the image away, and let himself collapse in relief in the chair.

That was how the ELINT man found him, bare minutes later.

"What a town!" the senior agent grumbled, dropping a greasy paper bag on the side table at Ayer's elbow. "Nobody eats after midnight here, I guess. I had to drive all over to find a joint with a hot grill. And all they had was Coke and beer, so I got beer. And one looked lonely, so I got six. What's been going on here?"

"Been quiet," Ayer said with a swallow. "They've been napping, seems like. I turned the recorder off. One of them's in the shower now—Jack, I guess—"

"Oh, so you finally figured it out," the ELINT man said with a grin. "I won't ask how long it took you, so you won't have to lie."

"I felt pretty dumb, all right," Ayer said. "You'd have gotten a good laugh."

"Aw, you're all right, kid. I just can't let you know that yet." The senior agent held out a hand for the headphones. "Here, I'll take those, so you can eat—I was starving, I polished mine off in the car."

Ayer took the greasy bag and retreated to the couch. "Smells like they didn't spare the onions."

"Well, you didn't have a date tonight, did you? Hold on, the shower's stopped. Round four, coming up." The agent shook his head. "I tell you, I get tired just listening to them."

His mouth full, Ayer nodded. "You could almost envy the guy if you didn't know the ground was going to open up—"

The senior agent held up his hand. "Shhh," he said, and pressed one cup of the headphones more firmly against his ear. He listened for half a minute, then began to scratch something on the notepad with a stub pencil.

"False alarm," he tossed back over his shoulder to Ayer. "He should've listened to me, though, and stuffed her tit in his mouth. 'Cause what he's doing with it now is just digging a deeper hole for himself—for the both of them."

"What a chump," Ayer said.

"Yeah. You know, you've really missed all the good stuff tonight—the fine spectacle of a guy shooting himself in both feet and between the eyes, for good measure. You ought to hear some of this."

"It's okay," Ayer said carefully between bites. "I'll read about it in the papers."

The ELINT man chuckled and resumed writing. The spools kept turning, hissing like a snake that knew a secret.

Rick Katze, a Boston attorney appearing here with his second professional story, is understandably interested in Watergate, which probably ended more legal careers than any other scandal in American history.

I suggested that he might consider the implications had the break-in occurred in 1964 rather than 1972, and been masterminded by the Democrats rather than the Republicans. What if the Attorney General who obstructed justice was not President Nixon's friend but President Kennedy's brother? And, more to the point, just how successful would a cover-up of Bobbygate have been?

Here's his answer.

Bobbygate
by Rick Katze

The old man walked into the Oval Office, where his two sons were waiting for him. The President of the United States pulled up a chair for him; the Attorney General lit his cigar.

"You're underestimating him," said the old man.

"Underestimating who?" asked the President.

"Who the hell's running against you?" said the old man irritably.

"Goldwater?" said the Attorney General with a smile.

"He's a joke. I could pick a better candidate out of the phone book."

"Oh, you'll beat him, all right. But he's a party man, and he's going to be paying off a lot of IOUs during the campaign. You want to move this country? You can't just win the way you beat that bastard Nixon. The last three years should have taught you that much. You need a mandate, a goddamned landslide, and you're not going to get it if you don't start taking that little Arizona Jew seriously."

"He's not Jewish, Dad," said the President.

"Aren't you *listening* to me?" demanded the old man. "Who cares what the hell he is? I said you'd better start taking him seriously!" He glared at his sons. "*You're* too busy running the country, or so we'd like the press to think," he said to the President with a just a touch of contempt in his voice. He turned to the Attorney General. "That leaves it up to *you*."

"I'll take care of it, sir," promised the Attorney General.

"See that you do," said the old man, walking out of the Oval Office without looking either right or left. "I'm getting too old to run this fucking country by myself."

It was exactly sixty-seven days later that Sharon Thomas, a court reporter for the *Washington Traveler*, showed up for work in a foul mood. She'd left the house late due to a run in her hose, she'd hit rush-hour traffic, and when she arrived at the courthouse her private parking space had been taken. Two years of journalism school, a year on the paper, and she was still stuck here, watching junkies and wife-beaters explain why they were really great guys who were just misunderstood by an uncaring society.

She'd already missed two domestic beatings, both of which were continued, which meant that two more Washington wives would doubtless wind up in the hospital again before their husbands were locked away (or, more likely, given suspended sentences and told to go forth and never sin again). A liquor store holdup was up next, and she already knew that they would ask for a postponement and a change of venue, since this was the fourth time she could remember this particular teenager coming before this particular judge with wide innocent eyes and explaining that all black kids looked alike to white cops and that he had actually spent the whole day minding his nonexistent little sister.

Then a flurry of motion in the back of the courtroom caught her eye. Three very well-dressed men with expensive briefcases had just entered, and were speaking in low tones to a pair of policemen. She stared at them for a moment, blinked, and stared again.

What the hell were Collingworth, Fortwistle, and Kravets doing here? These guys spent most of their days rubbing shoulders with John Mitchell and Clark Clifford as they merged corporations and took over whole industries. They were boardroom lawyers, those three; they *never* appeared in court, and certainly not in criminal court.

She waited impatiently through two more domestic beatings and a drug bust, then sat up alertly as three young Latinos were brought before the bench, each with one of the lawyers in question. Even before the clerk could read the charges, the three attorneys were on their feet, waiving the reading, pleading not guilty for their clients, and requesting personal recognizance instead of cash bail. The prosecutor didn't even make a *pro forma* objection, and the judge merely nodded toward the attorneys.

At lunchtime she sought out a friendly bailiff.

"What the hell was that all about?" she asked.

"What was *what* all about?"

"All that muscle for the three Hispanics. What did they do, anyway? Shoot the President?"

"Some kind of prank, I suppose," was her answer.

"Tell me about it."

"They broke into 114 Washington Avenue."

"So?"

The bailiff grinned. "That's Republican party headquarters."

"You're back early," said Robert O'Malley, her lean, acerbic editor, when he found her rummaging through the file cabinets. "Did they run out of criminals?"

"Nope."

"Well, then?"

"Something is rotten in Denmark," said Sharon.

"Probably Danish blue cheese."

She turned to him. "What would you say if I told you that three Hispanic men were arraigned for breaking into Republican headquarters?"

"I'd say they were wasting their time. Goldwater's got more chance of running a three-minute mile than beating Kennedy."

"And," she continued, "what would you say if I told you that they were defended by Thomas Collingworth, Henry Fortwistle, and David Kravets?"

O'Malley stared at her. "You're sure?"

"I was there."

"I'd say it sounds like you've got some digging to do. Don't let me disturb you."

He turned on his heel and returned to his office.

The break-in got the closing twenty seconds on the Huntley-Brinkley broadcast, with David dryly wondering if they had broken into the wrong party's headquarters. Cronkite didn't mention it, and Howard K. Smith got it wrong; he had them breaking into the *Democratic* headquarters, a statement that was corrected on the eleven-o'clock news.

And that, so it seemed, was that.

It took her three weeks to tie one of the Hispanics to Sean McCormick, the young Harvard graduate who had been one of Bobby Kennedy's field men during the 1960 campaign. It took another nine days to tie McCormick to the Committee to Re-Elect President Kennedy.

Then things started to happen.

Her first contact with the man she referred to only as "Admiral X" had come in an underground parking lot. He had called her at her home and asked to meet her. She had no idea what he wanted to talk about, but she consented.

"You want a little fatherly advice, Miss Thomas?" he said after greeting her in the empty garage.

"I'd rather have some information."

"Take what's freely given and be grateful for it," he replied. "You are making some very important people very angry with you."

"I can't imagine why," she said. "I'm just a low-level court reporter."

"We both know what you're working on, Miss Thomas," he had said. "The difference is, *I* know where it leads and you don't. Take my advice and give it up."

"Give *what* up?" she persisted.

"Do you want me to say it?" he replied. "All right: the break-in. If you pursue it, you will bring some good men and women down, men and women we need in our government. Do you understand what I am saying to you?"

"Yes."

"And will you give it up?"

"I'll have to think about it."

"You do that, Miss Thomas. Think very carefully, and then we'll speak again."

"Let me get this straight," said O'Malley. "You want me to start running the series because this Admiral X warned you off?"

"That's right," said Sharon.

"And you won't tell me who he is?"

"That was my deal with him."

"But you want me to take your word for it that he's high enough up in the administration so that if he says major figures are going to fall, you believe him?"

"Yes," said Sharon.

"Did it ever occur to you that he might be lying?" suggested O'Malley. "That he might be trying to get you to overplay your hand, so that these three little creeps will go free while you're after bigger fish who don't know a damned thing about what happened?"

"No, it never did," said Sharon firmly. "Why would he care about them?"

"They can bring down Bobby's pal Sean McCormick. You make enough noise, their high-powered attorneys claim they can't get a fair trial, the Justice Department agrees, and they walk before they can implicate McCormick. You know how loyal Bobby is to his friends."

"I have a feeling this goes a lot higher than McCormick."

"I can't print feelings," said O'Malley. "Get me some facts and we'll talk again."

She had two more meetings with Admiral X. At the first one, he seemed genuinely concerned for her welfare. At the second, he was more concerned for his own.

Members of the administration had followed him to their last meeting, he said bitterly. He'd already been given his two weeks' notice, and a couple of threats that stopped just short of being actionable.

"Then why are you meeting with me?" she asked.

"Because I gave those bastards the best years of my life," he growled. "All I tried to do was warn you off, and those sons of bitches kicked me clear out of the government. And you know Bobby: by next week there won't be a company in the country that'll be willing to hire me."

"So what do you do now?" she asked.

"Now I extract my pound of flesh," he said, his eyes glazing over with hatred. "Get out your notebook."

* * *

The old man walked into the Oval Office.

"Some pair of geniuses I've raised!" he snarled. "Joe was the only worthwhile one of the lot, and he got his damn-fool head blown off in the war."

"What are you talking about?" asked the President.

"Your baby brother was supposed to prepare a campaign against the Arizona Jew," said the old man. "So what's the first thing he did? He authorized a break-in at the Republican headquarters."

"We needed material on Goldwater," said the Attorney General defensively. "We got it."

"You got more than you bargained for, boy!" snapped the old man. "You got a reporter who knows everything that happened and can trace the order all the way up the ladder to you."

"There's nothing to worry about," said the Attorney General. "We know about her. I told Sean to speak to her next week. He'll misdirect her."

"He'll probably have his ass indicted by next week!" bellowed the old man. He turned to the President. "And *you*! How many times have I told you that you only trust the family?"

"That's all I *do* trust," said the President.

"Then what the hell was"—the old man mentioned Admiral X's name—"doing, spilling his guts out to the reporter?"

"He was fired last week," said the President. "What harm can he do?"

"The man who runs your fucking White House security, who knows where your fucking tape machine is, and you want to know what harm he can do?"

"It wasn't *my* decision," said the President. "I didn't know anything about it."

"No," said the old man. "But when the boy genius here told you that the three spics got themselves caught, you told him to take care of it and make it go away, didn't you? Did you hold the fucking microphone in your hand while you said it, or did you just look in its direction?"

"Jesus!" said the President.

"I'll take care of it," said the Attorney General. "Let me make a couple of calls and—"

"You've taken care of enough," snarled the old man.

"What are we going to do?" asked the President.

"It's under control," said the old man disgustedly. "I'm going back to Hyannisport for a week. Just try not to get us into a war while I'm gone." He flared at his sons. "Do you think you can handle *that*?" he asked sarcastically.

Sharon Thomas and Robert O'Malley died in a car accident that afternoon. The hit-and-run driver of the other car was never apprehended.

"Admiral X" succumbed to an overdose of sleeping pills two days later. It was known that he was depressed since losing his job, and the coroner's official verdict was accidental suicide.

Eight months later, John F. Kennedy won reelection over Barry Goldwater by a margin of ninety-seven electoral votes. His first official act was to reappoint his brother, Robert F. Kennedy, to the post of Attorney General of the United States.

Their father spent election night in Massachusetts. He did not send a congratulatory telegram; his wife and daughters sadly agreed that he was becoming forgetful in his old age.

Jim Macdonald is back again, this time with Debra Doyle; the two, in tandem, have written the six-volume Circle of Magic series.

In this vignette, they choose as their subject matter the least-known Kennedy of all: Kathleen, who left her family and her religion behind her, married an Englishman, divorced him, and died when the plane she and her lover were flying crashed over the Rhone Valley.

Or did she/

Now And in the Hour
of Our Death

by Debra Doyle
and James D. Macdonald

In the summer of 1954, polio struck the village of Privas in the Rhone valley, and the sisters of the Carmelite convent came out into the world they had renounced to minister to the sick. Among them was Sister Marie Dives, who limped painfully as she tended the stricken children, so that many were convinced she had also suffered from polio in her youth.

That was the last time Sister Dives left the convent walls. But news from America travels fast, even into a foreign cloister if the news is bad enough, and late in the year 1963 Sister Dives asked to speak with the mother superior. She requested permission to travel to America, in order to attend the funeral of the slain American President.

"Sister," the mother superior asked, "what concern is it of yours?"

"He was a Catholic, Mother," Sister Dives replied.

"Pray for him. Return to your duties."

Sister Dives went to the chapel and prayed, thanking God for His mercy and praising His infinite wisdom. Then she prayed for humility, lest she think that she was favored by God. Pride had always been her greatest sin, so she gave herself a penance. Her legs pained her always, yet she accepted the pain, and scrubbed the convent's passageways on her knees, praising Christ's name with each dip of the brush into the bucket of cold water.

Later still, in the spring of 1978, Sister Marie Dives lay dying in her room of whitewashed plaster over stone. Père Rubeli, the convent's father confessor, sat at her bedside. Her gray hair was uncovered as she lay against the starched white pillow, and for the first time Père Rubeli saw the long, deep scar on her right cheek, where the wimple had hidden it.

"My daughter," the priest began, "I have come to bring you the comforts of the Church, to help you walk with Christ. Let me hear your confession."

"Bless me, Father, for I have sinned," Sister Dives began, speaking so quietly that Père Rubeli had to lean close to catch the words. "It has been thirty years since my last confession."

Père Rubeli did not speak, but he was startled. He had been coming to the convent now for more than ten years, and had heard from Sister Dives the usual sins that trouble nuns' thoughts: the pride, the anger, the inattention to the Daily Office, the temptations to sloth.

He hid his surprise. "Tell me," he said.

"I have not made a good confession since I came here,"

she replied. "For I have sinned, and I knew that I sinned, and I did not confess my sin. And I did not confess because I did not repent."

She was silent for a long time. When Père Rubeli looked from the corner of his eye toward her face, he saw that her eyes were closed. He wondered if he ought to continue with the rite, but before he could say the words of general absolution, she spoke again.

"For this reason, because I was in a state of sin, every time I received the Lord's Body, I committed sacrilege."

"What was the sin that you didn't confess?" Père Rubeli asked.

"I tempted others to sin, and they sinned. I endangered their souls, and I didn't repent."

"And the sin?"

"I asked them to lie for me."

"Who?"

"The townsmen who found me. After the plane crashed, and I lay all night in the storm with my legs broken and my face cut open. I was dying, and I was afraid—and I promised God I would give Him the rest of my life, if He would only let me live."

"What was the lie you asked the villagers to tell?"

"I asked them to tell my parents that I was dead."

"And you never repented?"

"Never."

"Do you repent now?"

"Father, I'm not sure."

"Do your parents still live?"

"I don't know."

"Let us pray to the Virgin together, that she may bring you the grace to find repentance."

Père Rubeli prayed aloud, and Sister Dives prayed with him: "Hail, Mary, full of Grace, the Lord is with thee. Blessed art thou among women, and blessed is the fruit of thy womb, Jesus. Holy Mary, mother of God, pray for us sinners, now and in the hour of our death, amen."

Sister Dives's voice faltered as she prayed, but Père Rubeli continued to the end. Then he saw that her eyes were open but the pupils were fixed and dilated, and he knew that she had died in the midst of the prayer.

"For these and all thy sins, I absolve thee," he said, making the sign of the cross in the air.

Thus passed Kathleen Kennedy, dead in an airplane crash in 1948, who was buried under the name Sister Marie Dives in a convent in France thirty years later. And she died in a state of grace.

Nancy Kress, author of *Brain Rose* and the forth-coming *Beggars in Spain*, is no stranger to the shorter forms of science fiction, having won a Neb-ula for her brilliant "Out of All Them Bright Stars."

In "Eoghan" she presents us with four genera-tions of Kennedys whose lives have been influ-enced by a very special coin from the Old Country.

Eoghan
by Nancy Kress

We thought you would not die—We were sure you
would not go:
And leave us in our utmost need to Cromwell's cruel
blow—
Sheep without a shepherd when the snow shuts out
the sky—
Oh, why did you leave us, Eoghan? Why did you die?

—Thomas Davis, "Ballad of Eoghan Ruadh O'Neill"

I

Cold evening mists lay heavily around the church at Bal-lykelly. Despite the blessing he had just received, the young man stumbling away from the church shivered. Already it was October. He should have left on his journey two months ago. Nay—three months ago, when the summer still lay fair on the Atlantic. "It's yer fault," Patrick Kennedy said bitterly. "Ye cursed, putrid demon! All yer fault!" He shook his left fist and spat. He was talking to a potato.

It was clutched in his right hand, wrapped in a bit of rag. The potato was black and stinking, fit for neither man nor beast. The priest had looked at it without surprise, his thin face—there was no one in Ballykelly whose face was not thin in that terrible summer of 1848—slack with resignation.

"Bless it, Father!" Patrick had demanded fiercely. "Three years and didn't the blight stay out of Dunganstown—God had to have some reason for sparing us so long! Bless it and drive out the demon!"

"Ye ask the impossible," said the priest, who had already seen too many potatoes, too many desperate young Patrick Kennedys. "Whatever part this blight serves in God's blessing, it's not within my power to change it."

"God's blessing!"

The priest looked Patrick steadily in the eye. "Ye are not so bad off as most. Ye have some corn, a bit of grain—"

"That must go to pay the rent to the English!"

"—a chance to earn wages, however small. In the south and west they're living in ditches, eating grasses, dying with their poor faces blacker than that potato. Be grateful for what ye have, my son, and don't be begging me for blessings on that stinking potato."

"Then bless me instead," Patrick cried, "for the only course left is for me to emigrate to America!"

"Ye won't be the first," the priest said, and gave the blessing without seeming to notice the young man's clenched fist.

On the road from Ballykelly to the tiny Kennedy cottage in Dunganstown, Patrick hurled the potato into the fields. Bitterness filled him, the brooding darkness that made men say in the public houses, "Don't cross a Kennedy, he'll never forget." Not that Patrick or his brothers or even his father had been in a public house this summer. There wasn't the coin for so much as a drop. The money from the grain crop had scarcely been warm in his father's hand before it had to be paid for the cruelly high rent on the farm.

Patrick wasn't ready to go home. He couldn't be taking this black mood into the tiny cottage, filled already with such worry. And he wasn't ready to face his mother with his decision. His mother, whom he suspected of starving herself so there would be more food for the rest. He stalked off the road towards a hummock where he could sit and brood.

The hummock was farther away than he had thought. Patrick stumbled towards it, his bootlaces tangling on grasses and rushes, while the sky darkened around him. The first stars came out. The hummock still retreated. Enraged now—the land had already cursed and mocked them enough, by God!—Patrick broke into a run. He was twenty-five, strong and fit. He leaped into the air, spreading his long legs wide, and landed on top of the hummock, on top of a large rat.

The rat screamed. Patrick screamed. He grabbed wildly. And then he was holding not the tail of a rat but the arm of an old woman, bent and hideous, who flailed at him with something hard and cold in her clawed fingers.

Patrick's heart pounded and his neck went hot. This must be a *sidi*, a sacred hill, and so then the old woman must be . . . He should let go of her immediately and run, run as hard as he could, before—

He was damned if he would! The old woman, despite her clawlike fingers and despite whatever she was, had a plump, sleek body. And the rat had been even fatter. *They* were eating, damn them, damn them all, while his poor mother— He suddenly saw what the hag was beating him with. A gold guinea, such as hadn't been struck in England in forty years, glinting in the starlight.

"I won't let ye go!" Patrick screamed. "Not until ye give me that guinea!"

The old woman stopped struggling at once. Trembling, Patrick stopped too. She stared at him. Her eyes, he saw, were the cold black of a rat, still. A shudder ran through him, along with all the terrible stories of mortals cursed by the *aes sidi*, the people of the hill. Sean na Banoige, who was blinded, and the girl whose children were all born dead, and the farmer whose manhood . . . but there were the other stories, too. Of the *aes sidi* tricked into giving protection. Or luck. Or riches.

"This guinea?" the old woman said. Her voice was shrill and unpleasant, almost a squeal. "Ye don't want it!"

"Give it to me!" Patrick shouted, in a perfect rage. She was no better than the English landlords, no better than the priest at Ballykelly, all grasping after what they could get for themselves, be it the Irishman's lifeblood or the bitter benefits of God's plan. There was no help anywhere, unless you took it for yourself and yours. His mother, thin and hollow-cheeked so that her sons could eat— "I need it for my people!"

"Yer people, then, is it?" the old woman jeered. "Ah, Patrick Kennedy, ye don't know what yer saying, ye fool!"

"Give it to me!"

She did. Abruptly Patrick was holding the coin, and the old woman was across the hummock from him, several feet away, her black eyes somehow glittering even in the darkness. "It's yers, then, Patrick Kennedy. Good fortune is yers, and yer sons', and yer sons' sons', so long as ye use yer power to the good of the people who look to ye. If not—" She shrugged. "Ye know who I am."

"No," Patrick said boldly, "I don't. Tell me who—"

"More fool, ye," the woman said contemptuously. "Ye don't recognize a thing when ye see it."

She vanished. A rat scampered off the hummock and away in the starlight.

Heart hammering, Patrick examined the coin. Gold, and maybe enough to pay for his passage to America. Now his mother wouldn't need to give him the little hoard so painfully saved over the years, she could use it to buy food ... Suddenly dizzy, he lowered his head between his knees. The coin slipped from his hand, fell to the grass, and disappeared.

Frantically he groped in the darkness for the touch of metal. All he found were grasses and old leaves. But all the ballads said the *aes sidi* kept their bargains, clung to them like life itself, said there was nought but truth in the Other World ... His hand closed on a dead leaf and it turned back into the coin.

Every time he let the coin leave his fingers, it became a dead leaf. Every time he closed his fingers around it, it became a coin. *"More fool ye, ye don't recognize a thing when ye see it—"*

He almost hurled the coin away, as he had hurled the potato. What good was it now, when he could never spend it? But, on the other hand, the rat woman was still of the *aes sidi*. He didn't want her angry at him. Patrick Kennedy, his temper cooling as he walked to Dunganstown in the chill and hungry dark, figured there were enough forces in the world ranged against him already. He kept the coin.

The three-hundred-ton packet ship pitched and rolled on the Atlantic, woefully outmatched. In steerage, Patrick Kennedy slumped over a bucket already foul with vomit. The roof was not high enough for him to stand.

The man next to him was dead. No one had come to remove the body. There was no fresh water; the shipowner had saved a shilling or two by storing the water in old wine casks, which had made it undrinkable. The air reeked of privies and disease.

By the time the ship docked, a third of the steerage passengers were dead. Patrick Kennedy staggered, weak-legged, down the gangplank and onto Noddle's Island, East Boston, before collapsing. A fellow passenger hauled him to his feet and supported him long enough to get him through Immigration. Afterwards, the stranger rewarded himself by going through the helpless man's pockets. He took three shillings, some hard biscuits, and a set of bootlaces. He left the brown, dead, curiously un-crumpled leaf. Then, whistling jauntily, one of the fortunate survivors, he left Patrick lying facedown in the mud and went looking for work in the thriving shipyards eager for able-bodied men.

The saloon was crowded. The Sons of County Wessex had rented it for the night, and brawny Irishmen drank, sang, boasted, and danced the jig with wild enthusiasm. Patrick Kennedy, at a corner table with his friends, sang as lustily as anyone, and threw his last pennies on the table. "Another round here!"

"And aren't ye the free-spending hero, Pat?" his friend Gerald jeered. "Anyone would think ye were getting ready to be a bridegroom!"

This sally brought explosive laughter; the banns had already been read for Patrick Kennedy and Bridget Murphy.

"A girl two years older than ye—she'll be leading ye by the apron strings for sure!"

"Hold yer tongue, Gerald O'Shea!" Patrick roared. "Or I'll hold it for ye!"

Gerald laughed. But the laugh ended abruptly when the saloon door slammed open and a gang of men stood there, faces grim.

The room quieted. The newcomers stared at the Sons of Wessex, who stared back. Finally the outsiders closed the door and went away.

"The Brotherhood of County Clare," Patrick said. "Taking the measure of us."

"It's trouble they'll be for us," Gerald said somberly. "They boast that County Clare has the best fighters in Ireland."

"Ah, 'tis the politics," Patrick said. "Ye can't trust County Clare. They're not like our own people."

"They better not come around here again," Gerald said, "or we'll show them just how much not like us they are!"

"I'll drink to that," someone else said, and they did.

Later, Patrick sat in his room in the East Boston boardinghouse, blearily counting the money he had saved. There wasn't much. But it would have to do. There wasn't going to be much more coming in in the future. And in two more weeks he would be a married man, with his dear Bridget to take care of. Now and for a long life, God willing. God and the shipyards of Boston.

Cholera raged in the slums of East Boston. Within days—sometimes hours—the stricken puked out their strength. Diarrhea and painful muscle cramps followed, while black-shawled women wailed and men smoked outside on the stoops, tight-eyed. The children died quickest, from this as from everything else. Six out of ten East Boston children never saw their fifth birthday.

Patrick Kennedy lay on the narrow iron bed he and Bridget had shared since their wedding. Three daughters they'd gotten on this bed, and then finally the beloved son, Patrick Joseph, sleeping now in his cradle across the room. The dying man lifted his head for a glimpse of the baby.

"Hush, now," Bridget Kennedy said. "Hush, Pat."

"Something . . . I have to show ye. For . . . the boy."

"Hush, dearest."

But he made her go to the cheap deal bureau and fetch his paper box, and to stop his fretting, she did. Inside was nothing but a dead leaf.

"Give it to me," Patrick gasped. "Ye must . . . tell Patrick Joseph . . . when he's old enough . . ."

She put the leaf in his hand, and gasped. A gold guinea lay there.

"Patrick Kennedy! Where would ye be getting such a thing!"

He told her, haltingly, clutching at the pain in his belly. Bridget Kennedy crossed herself as she listened. "Ah, Pat! Such a legacy for the little one!"

"And it hasn't helped . . . me . . . much . . ." Patrick said bitterly, just as another wave of cramps and diarrhea took him.

But later, after Bridget had tirelessly cleaned him up and he lay against the thin pillow too exhausted to thank her, he wondered. *Good fortune is yers, so long as ye use yer power to the good of the people who look to ye . . .* Wasn't that what she'd said, the old woman? There'd been more, about his son and his son's son—it was hard to remember the exact words. His head hurt so much, and it had been so long ago.

Ten hard years. He was thirty-five years old, and dying. *Good fortune is yers . . .*

But then again, maybe there was something to it after all. The *aes sidi* always kept their bargains. He had survived the crossing to America, hadn't he, when so many others died? And his four children, the three girls and little Patrick Joseph, all healthy and strong, thanks be to God, when he knew men without a surviving child. *So long as ye use yer power to the good of the people who look to ye . . .* Well, he had done that, and that was God's truth. Even if the only power he'd had was the strength in his back, he'd used it for Bridget and Mary and Margaret and Johanna and Patrick Joseph. No man could say different.

But it wasn't a man he saw sitting in the corner of the dreary room. It was an old woman, tossing a coin. She grinned at him, and it seemed to Patrick Kennedy that mists rose chill around her, and behind her stretched hills of vivid green ...

Bridget Kennedy closed her husband's eyes. For a moment she stood completely still. Then she took the gold guinea from his slack fingers and laid the brown leaf back in its paper box in the bureau.

II

P. J. Kennedy strode across Haymarket Square, which was full of wagons and shouting and pigs. The pigs had escaped from a farm wagon and ran squealing back and forth across the square, cheered by ragged lines of men who had stopped to watch the fun. Patrick Joseph Kennedy didn't stop. Women peeped at him from under their bonnet brims—he was fair and blue-eyed, well-muscled, not yet twenty-five—but women were another thing P.J. didn't stop for. Or at least not often.

He did pause, however, in front of a sign in a new business in Haymarket Square: HELP WANTED. NO IRISH. The sign itself wasn't unusual, you saw its like all over Boston, but not *here*, in the Haymarket. P.J. shook his head. Some men just had no business sense, and there it was, and nothing on God's green earth would change that. They'd be gone in three months.

He pushed open the door of a vacant saloon. He was early, but Mr. Smythe was already there, a stiff man dressed in a stiff black suit and even stiffer white collar. "Good day, Mr. Kennedy."

P.J. only nodded. This wasn't a social call, after all. He liked Ethan Smythe as little as Smythe liked him.

He inspected the saloon carefully. Smythe hadn't taken care of it. The walls needed repair, the long bar sagged, the floorboards had been ripped open. P.J. bent to examine them.

"Irish hooligans," Smythe said. "No proper respect for

a drinking establishment. But then, you'd know more about that than I, Mr. Kennedy."

P.J. didn't answer.

"You might think you're buying this place very cheap, Mr. Kennedy, but I assure you that running it without wanton destruction is very expensive."

Especially for you, P.J. thought. For himself, buying it was the expensive part. For years he had saved painfully from his wages as a stevedore, saved everything he could after putting money into his mother's hand each week. Buying the saloon would take the whole pile. He might lose it all.

But if he didn't buy the saloon, he might never get himself anything more to lose. He might end his days like his father, as poor as the day he walked down the gangway to Noddle's Island.

"I'll buy ye out," P. J. Kennedy said. "But at two-thirds the price we talked about."

Smythe flushed. "This establishment is already priced below what I paid for it!"

'That's my offer," Kennedy told him. "Accept it or not, just as ye choose."

The saloon door swung abruptly open. A terrified pig dashed inside, running straight for Mr. Smythe's legs. Smythe jumped nimbly onto the bar and crouched there while three Irishmen, whooping and yelling, raced in after the pig.

"I accept," the Yankee said.

P.J. nodded, careful not to smile, not to let his elation show. The pig, confused, scuttled behind the bar. One of the men yelled and dove after it, narrowly missing Smythe, who leaped down and stalked out the door. Finally P.J. let himself grin, gazing from his blue eyes around the shabby saloon, his right hand rubbing the gold guinea in his pocket.

* * *

A man ran into the saloon, waving a newspaper. "We won, lads! O'Brien won!"

Cheers erupted all over the saloon. Men rose and clapped each other on the back, yelling and laughing. Patrick Joseph Kennedy, behind the bar, grabbed at the newspaper.

It was true, then. Himself, Hugh O'Brien, had just been elected the first Irish mayor of Boston. Pat had had his doubts there were enough Irish votes to conquer the solid Protestant Yankee bloc in Boston. But here it was, in black and white. The Irish had seized the power. It had taken them until 1885.

Pat's mind raced. The city would be wide open now. He had already bought two more saloons, one of them across from a shipyard where the Irish workers thronged in morning and evening for a bit of drink and gossip. He was already a member of the "Board of Strategy," that group of influential Irishmen who gathered for lunch in Room 8 of the Quincy House, near Scollay Square, planning how the Irish would vote to their own best advantage. Joseph J. Corbett. James Donovan. The flamboyant John F. Fitzgerald, "Honey Fitz" himself. And Patrick Joseph Kennedy. He was one of them. He had already had so much good fortune—but now the city would be wide open.

"I did my part!" one man bawled. "I voted seventeen times!"

"A round of drinks for all o' ye!" Pat cried, and even over the din everyone heard him. They always did. A cheer went up, and Pat raised his own glass of lemonade, the strongest drink he took.

"Please, sir, and there's a man to see ye," his kitchen boy said. Pat nodded, gestured to the boy to take his place behind the bar, and slipped out. The boy began pulling pints; he was used to this. There was always somebody to see Mr. Kennedy.

The man waited in the kitchen, his clothes dirty and

torn, although it was obvious he had made some attempt at combing his hair and washing his face and hands. His West Country brogue was so thick Pat could hardly understand it. But he didn't need to hear much—from one look he knew the man's story. A month off the boat, a job in the shipyards but laid off in favor of some Yankee's cousin from the country, hadn't worked in two weeks and there was no coal in the house, no bread, his young wife big with child, someone had said to go see Mr. Kennedy ... The man looked at his boots and held his hat in his hand, his spine bent in the cringing posture of the peasant before his English landlord. Pat hated that posture. No Irishman should ever cringe like that again.

"Go see Gerald O'Rourke in Mackerel Street," he said crisply. "Tell him Pat Kennedy sent ye. Can ye read?"

The man shook his head.

"No matter. He'll give ye a job. Meantimes, here's a few dollars. Buy some coal and bread."

The man tried to stammer his thanks. Pat waved it away, "Now get yourself out front and raise a glass to our grand new Irish mayor!" As soon as the man stumbled out, the kitchen boy stuck his head in. "Another one, sir. Mrs. Dugan, it is."

Pat nodded. There was always another one. He was no Patrick Collins—President Cleveland's consul general in London, to say, "I love the land of my birth, but there are no longer any Irish voters among us. The moment the seal of the court was impressed upon our papers we ceased to be foreigners and became Americans." Not Pat Kennedy. He wrote every month to the family in Wessex, he had drunk the health of the revolutionaries who murdered the British Secretary for Ireland in 1882, he would be Irish until the day he died. These were his people. They looked to him.

He waited to hear what he could do for Mrs. Dugan.

* * *

Pat smiled down at his new son, nestled in the crook of his mother's arm as she lay in the wide white bed. Only a year a bride, and already she'd given him a son. "We'll call him Patrick Joseph."

"No," said Mary Hickey Kennedy, who had a spirit of her own, "that will cause confusion with you, dearest. We'll call him Joseph Patrick."

Pat nodded. She could call the baby anything she wanted, have anything of Patrick Kennedy she wanted. The baby was lusty and strong, his pretty Mary was the best wife a man ever had, and himself the most fortunate of men. He laughed out loud. Mary smiled.

"Mary—I must be showing ye something. I've waited till now."

From a locked drawer in his desk he took a wooden box. Outside the open window the endless parade of Merridan Street streamed by: milk wagons and beer wagons, shopkeepers and shoppers, Holy Sisters and policemen, one of whom might be his brother-in-law Jim Hickey, visiting from his neighboring precinct. On the desk lay a book of American history. Pat Kennedy, still a quiet man, liked to spend his evenings reading.

"Look, Mary."

"Why— 'Tis no more than a dead leaf!"

Pat picked the leaf from its box. It shone in his palm, a gold guinea.

Mary's eyes widened, and she hastily crossed herself. But it was 1888, and she was the daughter of a doctor. "How did you do that, Pat Kennedy? 'Tis a conjurer you are!"

"No," he said quietly.

"Then you've mesmerized me, like that French doctor at the lecture hall!"

"No, not that either. Listen, Mary. This comes straight from the auld sod. 'Tis for Joseph." He touched the baby, sleeping peacefully. "My father had it from one of the People of the Hill, just before he left Ireland. Only if a

Kennedy son holds it can ye see the gold. But it brings good fortune, for all that, so long as we use our power to the good of the people who look to us."

Mary looked skeptical. Pat tossed the coin into the air. There was a dead leaf, blowing sideways in the breeze from the window. Deftly he caught it, and a gold guinea glittered on his palm.

Mary shuddered. "Put the thing away!"

" 'Tis doubting ye are, Mary?"

"Are *you*?"

Pat answered slowly. "No. There are things in the auld sod we don't have here ..." After a moment he said, almost defiantly, "It's for Joseph. When he's old enough, 'tis myself who'll be telling him about it."

"You do what you must," Mary said austerely. In such moments Pat was reminded that the Hickeys were several social cuts above the Kennedys. Pat Kennedy might be a representative to the Massachusetts State Legislature, but he had left school at fourteen. Mary's father and brothers were educated men.

Pat didn't want anything to spoil the joy of this day. He locked the guinea back in his desk and took Mary's hand. " 'Tis proud of ye I am. Ye and my fine son. When he's finished at Assumption or Xaverian, we'll send him to Boston Latin School."

Mary looked at him in surprise; Boston Latin School was Protestant. Then her eyes began to gleam. Five signers of the Declaration of Independence had graduated from Boston Latin. It was a stronghold of the Yankee establishment. "Yes, Pat. Yes."

"And then Harvard," Pat Kennedy said, while the baby began to wake, waving his tiny fists and screwing up his tiny face to yell.

IRISH REBELS SEIZE DUBLIN, the headlines screamed. SINN FEIN PARTY COUP. MANY KILLED IN EASTER WEEK FIGHTING.

Pat Kennedy sat in a leather chair in his library, looking grave. The library, his favorite room in the big four-story house, overlooked Boston Harbor, but Pat didn't see the gray waves or the white sails braving the cold April waters. Instead he saw the bloody uprising in Ireland. The hand-to-hand fighting at the Dublin Post Office. The bodies sprawled on Stephen's Green. The Sinn Fein finally—finally!—in power, but the English by no means ready to give up. The newspaper account was maddeningly incomplete; the rebellion had begun only two days ago, Easter Monday. Had there been much fighting in Wessex? His cousins?

He wanted, suddenly, to talk to Joe. But Joe was always so busy . . . Well, the lad had to be. Married just two years to his Rose and already had a son and enough debts to choke a horse.

The wedding had been the talk of Irish Boston. Who would have thought that Pat Kennedy's boy, *Pat Kennedy* who had started as a stevedore in the Boston docks, would be married by Cardinal O'Connell himself in his private chapel? And to the daughter of Honey Fitz? For years the girl led young Joe a merry dance. But she was a sweet, womanly little thing for all that, and Fitzgerald had even had the good grace not to insist on singing his gaudy theme song, "Sweet Adeline," at the wedding.

But Joe had been spending a lot of money. He'd had to buy all those shares of Columbia Trust Company stock, in order to stave off the merger threat from First Ward National. Pat had turned over to Joe what money wasn't tied up in his other investments—coal, mining, real estate, all modest but doing well enough. But Joe had needed to borrow heavily, as well as rally proxy votes throughout East Boston. Of course, the lad's Harvard contacts had helped with both. Joe had saved the bank and ended up the youngest bank president in Massachusetts, but it had cost. And then there was more borrowing to buy the house for him and Rose in Brookline ... No, Joe had good reasons for seldom being home.

Besides, Joe had never been that interested in Ireland anyway. A hard truth, but there it was. When Pat had visited Ireland just before the War, Joe had declined to go. Nor had he gone when he and his college friends were in Europe in 1913. They toured Germany and France, but not Ireland.

Pat understood. Joe was Irish to his fingertips, and so was Pat's nine-month-old grandson, Joseph Patrick, Jr. Joe would never turn his back on his own people—look what he had done for that friend of Henry Siegal's, that poor lad whose job had gone and whose child died, and the poor boy not even able to bury it. Joe had paid his rent, buried the babe, given the man a job. No, Joe was sound. If he wasn't interested in Ireland, it was because he was an American. The people who looked to him—like that unfortunate lad, and the people Joe employed at Columbia Trust—weren't all Irish. They were American.

For just a second, Pat thought of the gold guinea in his desk drawer. It had been years since he had looked at it, years since he had shown it to Joe, then a wide-eyed child. *"As long as ye use yer power to the good of the people who look to ye—"*

Pat shook his head. He was tired; he had been up late last night, all of them had, waiting for more news from Ireland on the wireless. He was only fifty-eight, but he tired more easily than he used to.

Still, he couldn't take a nap. There was something he had to do first. He wouldn't put it off. He hadn't gotten this far in life by putting things off, and neither had Joe. "Young man in a hurry," the newspapers called his son.

Pat rose from his comfortable leather chair, picked up his stick and cane, and prepared to visit his broker with orders to buy whatever bonds were issued in Ireland, by whatever government was formed by the Sinn Fein, the very day any such bonds came on the market.

III

Joe Kennedy picked up the telephone. "Yes?"

"I want those two battleships, Kennedy, and I want them now!"

"Hello, Franklin," Joe said. He put his feet up on his desk at the Fore River Shipyard and prepared to fight. Someone had told him that before the war the young Assistant Secretary of the Navy, Franklin Delano Roosevelt, had been a diffident, scholarly man. He sure the hell wasn't now. He was the toughest man Joe had to deal with in the dizzying year since he'd taken over production for Bethlehem Ship. And he wasn't even Irish.

"Those ships are *finished*," Franklin said. "Finished and just sitting there and they belong to the Argentine government! Do you want to create an international incident?"

From his window, even with his feet up, Joe could see the frantic activity in the shipyard. The half-completed hull of a destroyer towered above its scaffolding. Tiny figures swarmed over it, working like sped-up movie frames.

"You're overlooking one little point, Franklin. They don't belong to the Argentine government until the Argentine government pays for them. And until the bastards do, I'm not releasing 'em!"

"Now you listen to me, Kennedy. You don't seem to acknowledge that there's a war on. I've offered you several compromises—"

"No, you listen to *me*," Joe said, slamming his feet back to the floor. Nobody exasperated him as much as Roosevelt. "I damn well *know* there's a war on! We've launched thirty destroyers in twenty-one months, starting from practically zero, not so much as roofs over the workers' heads! We delivered one ship to you in fortysix days—forty-six *days*, Franklin! Do you know how incredible that is? But I'll be damned if some foreign government is getting their hands on those two ships without paying hard American dollars for them!"

"You'll be damned either way, then, because if you don't release those two ships today I'm sending the Navy to come get them!"

"I thought the Navy was out fighting Germans!" Joe bellowed.

"And you," Roosevelt said, and hung up.

Kennedy didn't release the vessels. Two days later, Navy tugs steamed into Quincy Harbor and towed away the two battleships. Half the Fore River Shipyard of 22,000 men stopped work to watch. Joe Kennedy, gazing out his office window, muttered, "The bastard! The sneaking double-dealing Yankee bastard!"

He was impressed.

Edward F. Albee pushed his way past Kennedy's secretary. "I'm sorry, Mr. Albee," she said to the old man, "you can't go in there."

"Can't go in there!" Albee screamed. "You dizzy bitch, this is my company! Don't tell me where I can go or not go! You're fired!"

He slammed open the door. Joe Kennedy sat behind a huge teak desk, the KAO logo over his head and the brass sign Chairman burnished to a gleam. With him was Gloria Swanson, her hair gleaming like patent leather, her beautiful legs crossed in silk stockings the same creamy white as her dress. She gave him her cool, mocking, dazzling smile. Albee ignored her. He was so angry he trembled.

"You son of a bitch!" he said to Kennedy. "You fired my son!"

"That's a chairman's prerogative," Kennedy said. He watched Albee closely.

"I founded this company!" Albee shouted. "I built it up from nothing, I made it what it is, I—"

"You sold the controlling stock," Joe said coolly. "At

twenty-one dollars a share, when the market value was sixteen. Remember, Ed?"

"It's fifty now! And you dare—"

"It's fifty *because* I dare," Joe said, as coolly as before. "Including getting rid of deadwood like Reed."

"Reed—"

"Is gone. And so are you. Didn't you know, Ed? You're washed up. You're through."

Albee gaped at him.

"On your way out," Kennedy said, "be a good chap and tell my secretary she still works here."

Gloria Swanson smiled.

The pool sparkled blue in the sunlight at the bottom of the hill. Above, halfway to the Hyannisport mansion, the child hitched at the strap of her bulky black swimsuit and glared at her father.

"Kathleen says you won't take your swimming lesson, Eunice," Joe Kennedy said.

"I don't want to," Eunice said. She stuck out her lip, looking for a moment remarkably like her father.

"Why not?" Joe said. He knelt, to be level with the child.

"Because I don't want to go swimming."

"Then that's exactly the reason why you must go swimming."

Eunice looked confused. "What?"

"There are people," Joe said, "who can't ever make themselves do things they don't want to do. Those people are prisoners of themselves, just as surely as if they had on handcuffs. They can't ever win."

The child thought this over. "But I don't want to win anything."

"Yes, you do, Eunice. Winning is important. Winning is everything. For yourself and your family and the people who look to you."

Eunice looked unconvinced.

"Go get in the water," Joe said. "Now."

When she had left, still tugging at the strap of her bathing suit, Joe paused. His own words had triggered a memory. It took a moment to place it.

His father, who had died in the spring. But this was earlier, much earlier, when Joe had been a child. His father had showed him a leaf, some Irish talisman—Pat had been sentimental, always, about the land of his father's birth. The leaf had changed into a gold coin in Pat's hand. But, no, that wasn't possible—he must have misremembered. Or else it had been some trick, some of the famous Irish playfulness. His father's words, however, were clear enough in memory: "Good fortune is yours, and your sons', and your sons' sons', so long as you use your power to the good of the people who look to you."

And had he? Had the deals that had brought him important money been to the good of the people who looked to him? The displacing of Albee, who had died soon after, convinced he'd been betrayed? The FBO merger with RCA Photophone, which he'd arranged without consulting his partner, Guy Currier, who was still going around calling that a "betrayal"? Selling the market short just after the crash, operating from a desk at Halle and Stieglitz but routing his orders discreetly through a number of brokers? Had all that been to the "good of the people"?

Joe shook his head. It was the crash that was making him think like this. Nine months, and the market hadn't rallied. It was enough to upset any man. And he, Joe Kennedy, was hardly one to complain about the conduct of good fortune, with or without Old-Country talismans. He was significantly richer than he'd been even before the crash.

His father, God rest his soul. For all Pat Kennedy's financial savvy and all his love, he'd been just another superstitious Irishman.

Joe strolled down the hill to watch his children's swimming lesson.

* * *

"The market isn't rallying, Henry," Joe said to his old friend, Henry Morgenthau, at lunch. He picked up his crystal water glass, set it down without drinking, picked up his fork, set it down. His steak was untouched. "It's been over a year and it's not rallying."

"What are you afraid of, Joe?" Henry asked. "Your fortune's safe. You got out in plenty of time."

"It's not my current fortune I'm worried about," Joe said. "It's the future. The country is becoming desperate, Henry. Desperate men riot. They loot. They take by force what they can't get any other way. I have eight children. I would be willing to part with as much as half of everything I have if I could be sure of keeping—under law and order—the other half for the protection of my family."

Morgenthau looked thoughtful. "It may not come to that. There's someone willing to consider radical measures before it comes to that."

"Who?" Kennedy asked.

Morgenthau leaned across the lunch table. "Are you serious in saying that you would go along with some redistribution of wealth—even work for it—to avoid worse? Even if you were called a traitor to your own class?"

"It's my own class I'm thinking of," Joe said, a little impatiently. "Who do you think I'm concerned with—the working man? My grandfather and my father were working men, and they didn't need any handouts. But I know what desperate men can do to law and order, Henry. And I know that law and order serve the good of people like us."

"There's someone I'd like you to meet."

"So you already said. Who is this savior?" Joe knew his tone was sarcastic; he was uncomfortable revealing so much about himself. Only his profound pessimism about what the newspapers were already calling the Depression let him speak so frankly.

"Actually, you already know him," Morgenthau said.

"And you can do him a lot of good campaigning. Franklin Delano Roosevelt."

"Dad! Dad! You got it!" Jack Kennedy bounded through the Washington house, waving the *New York Times*. "You got the appointment!"

Joe Kennedy, in robe and slippers, looked slightly annoyed. Of course he already knew he'd got the appointment—the President had told Joe, in a tense meeting in the Oval Office, before it had been released to the press. Jack, at nearly seventeen, was old enough to realize how these things worked and not go whooping through the house as if it were a surprise. No question about it, Jack didn't have the political acumen of his brother, Joe Jr.

But then Joe's annoyance vanished. He was too pleased about the appointment, and too interested in the exhilarating controversy it would cause across the country. Joe Kennedy, Chairman of the brand-new Securities and Exchange Commission! Like letting Jesse James guard the bank vault!

"You earned it, Dad," Jack said warmly. "All that campaigning for Roosevelt, the contributions, the contacts you made for him . . . *You* made FDR president."

Joe allowed for youthful rhetoric. But neither did he deny Jack's statement. He had spent $75,000 and two years on Roosevelt's campaign. It was important, though, to see it in proper context. "I had to do what's best for our sort of people, Jack. They looked to me. The reformers are going to be running the show from now on. You can't tell the public to go to hell anymore."

Jack frowned briefly. Sometimes Joe wondered just what the boy's politics actually were. Not that it really mattered—Joe Jr. was going to be the politician.

On impulse, Joe told Jack about the talisman Pat Kennedy had shown him so long ago. Jack smiled. "A leaf?"

"It was."

"That turned into a gold coin?"

"So he said." Joe smiled, too. He preferred Jack in this guise: the skeptical cool young aristocrat.

"And where is this pocket miracle now?"

"Who knows? It disappeared, probably, when we moved houses so many times."

"Still," Jack said, thoughtful again, "it's interesting. 'To the good of the people who look to you—' "

"Just make sure you have your definitions of that straight," Joe Kennedy said to his son, and not even he was exactly sure what he meant.

An odd thing happened on the reviewing stand. Joe and Rose sat in a special place of honor, the first parents of a President-elect to both be present at an inauguration since Ulysses S. Grant. Everybody wore heavy coats; eight inches of snow had fallen the day before. Washington was bitter cold. Joe wrapped his muffler securely around his throat, bundling everything but his huge grin.

He had done it. A son in the White House. The lace-curtain Irish Kennedys, who had been blackballed at the Cohassaet Country Club when Jack was just a baby, had put that baby in the White House, at the helm of power.

"We observe today not as a victory of party but a celebration of freedom—" Jack's voice rang out strong and clear, the decisive voice of Joseph P. Kennedy's son.

The new President wore no overcoat. *Warmed by his own eloquence, his own inner fire,* Joe thought. The Kennedy fire. Boy didn't need an overcoat.

But then, incredibly, he thought he saw someone else without a coat. An old woman with plump bare arms and a long ratty face, sitting at the edge of the viewing stand, dangling her legs over the edge. She was looking right at Joe. How could—

He blinked, and she was gone.

"To those peoples in the huts and villages of half the globe struggling to break the bonds of mass misery," the new President said, "we pledge our best efforts to help them help themselves, for whatever period is required—"

IV

John Kennedy sat behind his desk, listening to his Vice President finish his oral report. The Oval Office had recently been painted white, from the bleak green Eisenhower had preferred. The air still smelled of paint. Above the mantel, the newly hung Constitution sailed towards its frame.

Lyndon Johnson was taking this report as high policy. Kennedy had sent him to Southeast Asia with the major stop in Vietnam, where Eisenhower had inexplicably sent American advisors to support the regime of Ngo Dinh Diem. Well, perhaps not inexplicably: Diem's was at least a native administration, unlike the French. As both a Congressman and a Senator, Kennedy had spoken against French colonialism, a view approved by his father. "Look at what colonialism did in Ireland," Joe Kennedy had said.

The Southeast Asia trip was supposed to be no more than a gesture of goodwill, a way of reassuring a weak and unsatisfactory ally that the United States still noticed him. It was also supposed to be a way of occupying the Vice President, who didn't have enough to do.

"And that's the substance of my observations," Johnson said, the Texas accent a bit too folksy to Kennedy's ears. "The details are all in the official report. But I'd be more than happy to answer any questions, Mr. President. Incidentally, your baby sister seemed to have a real good time on the trip."

"I'd glad Jean enjoyed herself," Kennedy said cordially. "Let me just go over a few points you raised. Diem doesn't seem eager to increase American presence in his country?"

"No, sir. I asked if he wanted American troops"—an aide made a choking sound—"but he said no. It'd look to his people too much like the French all over again. Also, it was my impression that he doesn't want to look any weaker to his own people than he has to. He's too damn dependent on us already, to his way of thinking."

"Did you really tell the press that Diem is—what was your phrase?—'the Winston Churchill of Southeast Asia'?"

Johnson grinned. He didn't yet understand what it meant when Kennedy asked a question to which he already knew the answer. "Mr. President, Diem's the only boy we got out there."

Kennedy twirled a piece of scrimshaw between his hands. The scrimshaw was a gift from his father. "But you, Lyndon—you think Vietnam is important to us."

Johnson's voice grew fervent. "If we're going to stop communism in Southeast Asia, it is. And communism can and must be stopped in Southeast Asia!"

"How?"

"By moving quickly and wisely. With creative management of our military aid program."

Kennedy was silent a minute. His aides glanced at each other, unable to tell what their young President was thinking.

"I see," Kennedy finally said.

"He backed down!" Bobby Kennedy said. "The Russian son of a bitch *backed down*!"

The Kennedy brothers sat in Jack's private study on the second floor of the White House. It was very late. Jackie had gone to bed; the aides had all left. Jack stretched out on a long sofa, his hands beneath his head, unable to sleep. The last thirteen days had left him taut as a racing sail. Bobby sat in a leather chair from which he had first removed Caroline's teddy bear.

" 'In order to eliminate as rapidly as possible the conflict which endangers the cause of peace,' " Bobby said, reading yet again from a translation of the Radio Moscow statement, " 'the Soviet government has given a new order to dismantle the arms which you described as offensive, and to return them to Soviet Russia' . . . You did it, Jack! You actually did it! He's taking every last missile out of Cuba!"

Jack looked up. Ordinarily Bobby addressed him as "Mr. President" whenever official business was being discussed, however informally. Jack grinned.

"Maybe this is the night I should go to the theater."

They both laughed uproariously. It was so easy to find anything funny, anything lighthearted. The world was not going to blow up after all. World War III was not going to start. Not this time.

Bobby finally said, wiping his eyes, "If you go to the theater, I go with you."

"Bobby," Jack said, sitting up, "did Dad ever tell you about the gold coin Gramps gave him?"

"Gold coin? No."

"It was supposed to be a prophecy, or a curse, or some such thing. That the Kennedys would only prosper so long as we use our power to the good of the people who look to us."

Bobby smiled. "Well, you did that today. Hell, we did it all summer." He fell silent. On his young face Jack saw the Freedom Riders, struggling to desegregate the South. He saw the President's personal envoy to the Governor of Alabama pulled from his car and beaten senseless by a racist mob. The bloody fight to admit James Meredith to the University of Mississippi. People had died. Bobby added, with some force, "The good of *all* the people who look to you."

"That's what I've been thinking," Jack said. "The entire last thirteen days. An American President has an obligation to the good of more people than Dad could ever recognize, let alone Gramps."

The mood had changed. Shortly afterwards, Bobby left.

Jack still couldn't sleep. He wandered out into the family sitting room and drew open the flowered drapes. Moonlight slid over the old green roof of the Treasury. A picture of Black Jack Bouvier in the uniform of a World War I lieutenant stared at him. Jack stared back.

He returned to his study and started a letter to Nikita Khrushchev. "We must give priority to questions relating to the proliferation of nuclear weapons, on earth and in outer space. We should work for a peace for *all* men, for *all* our children . . ."

The President's yacht, the *Honey Fitz*, was bright with lights, alive with music. Beautiful women with sprigs of holly in their hair climbed up and down ladders, hitching up their long silky gowns, or strolled on deck on the arms of men holding drinks. The yacht's wake churned silvery streamers on the glassy black surface of the water. In the distance, the lights of Palm Beach twinkled.

In the master cabin, the President finished reading the hastily typed report. His face grew redder and redder. Finally he looked up and snapped at Mike Mansfield, "Do you expect me to take this at face value?"

Mansfield, Senate Majority Leader and Kennedy's closest friend in the Senate, said, "You asked me to go out there."

"I asked you to find out the facts!"

"And that's what you're reading," Mansfield said evenly. "I'm sorry, Mr. President, if you don't like them."

Kennedy threw the report on a table and began to pace. There wasn't much pacing room in the cabin. "You're telling me nobody knows how many of the twenty thousand Vietcong killed last year were really innocent villagers. The Strategic Hamlet program is a failure. The people resent Diem and us as much—maybe more—than they resent the communists. The military figures I keep getting from McNamara are too optimistic, the figures I read in the *Times* are too pessimistic, the figures I get from State are inaccurate because they're barred from classified military information. You're telling me that we're headed toward fighting somebody else's war. And you're also telling me, in essence, that everything I hear from my chain of command is distorted, due to careerism or opportunism or incompetence."

Mansfield was silent. Kennedy stopped pacing. "Isn't that what you're telling me?"

"Mr. President," Mansfield said, choosing his words with great care, "I haven't accused anyone directly of incompetence. Or opportunism. I've only reported what I found over there. Our position in Vietnam is potentially disastrous. It's not at all clear how to improve it, despite the optimistic reports on the conduct of the war from the Joint Chiefs of Staff."

A burst of music sounded from the decks above. Kennedy ran a hand through his thick hair. Finally he said icily, "I'll read the report again."

Later, he was uncomfortable about how he'd snapped at Mike. It wasn't fair, or reasonable. He shouldn't have done it.

He'd had no idea Vietnam made him that angry.

"Thirty seconds, Mr. President," said the TV technician. Kennedy straightened his shoulders and faced the steady red light of the lead camera. He was an old hand at television, knew how to use it as no other politician ever had. You faced the camera steadily but naturally, and made your points with as much controlled charm as possible. Both the control and the charm were important. It wasn't really so different from bull sessions with his father.

"Five seconds, four, three . . ."

For just a second it seemed to Kennedy that he heard gunfire. But that was just his imagination; even if anything were happening out there, he wouldn't hear it. The studio was soundproofed and well away from downtown

Birmingham, where seven-hundred newly deputized Alabama state sheriffs stormed around, shoving blacks into doorways and snapping the safety catches of their pistols. Three thousand federal troops awaited Kennedy's orders at an air base outside Birmingham.

"Two, one . . ."

He was on the air. "The fires of frustration and discord are burning in every city where legal remedies are not at hand. This government will do whatever must be done to preserve order, to protect the lives of its citizens, and to uphold the law of the land."

He paused. An hour earlier a new batch of pictures had appeared in the newspapers, worse even than the one of the snarling police dog lunging at the terrified black woman, the one of the rubble left after the bombing of a desegregated hotel, the one of the fire hose turned on the black worshipers at the door of a white church. The Justice Department said the pictures would get worse yet.

"To protect the lives of *all* its citizens," he repeated, and looked directly into the camera, the technological witness to how earnestly he meant it.

The other photograph was on the first page of the newspaper, four columns wide. A young Buddhist monk, his head shaved, writhed in flames. His face twisted in agonizing pain. He had set himself on fire, the article said, to protest the attacks of the Diem regime on Buddhist pagodas, and the American presence in Vietnam.

Members of the National Security Council glanced at the photograph from time to time. It had been Bobby Kennedy, they suspected, who had put it in the exact center of the long, polished conference table. During the impassioned reports from both Joseph A. Mendenhall and Major General Victor Krulak, no one touched the photograph.

When the two men finished, Kennedy was the first to speak.

"You spent four days on your fact-finding trip in Vietnam," he said, his voice controlled as always.

"Yes, sir," Krulak answered. He stood at rigid attention, the shortest Marine in the Corps' history, whose nickname had been "Brute."

"You, too," Kennedy said to Mendenhall of the State Department.

"Yes, Mr. President."

"And now you tell me, General, that the war is on schedule. That if there is any dissent in the country, it's aimed at Nhu and not at Diem. That Diem is solid, and fully in accord with American efforts."

"Yes, sir!"

"And *you*," Kennedy said, turning to Mendenhall, "tell me that civilian morale has completely collapsed. That the cities are finally unified, and what they're unified against is the government and, by extension, us. That Americans are now more hated than the Vietcong because of the pain and suffering the war has inflicted on the people."

"Yes, Mr. President."

Kennedy burst out, "You two *did* visit the same country, didn't you?"

Nobody laughed.

"General Harkins wants defoliants," Kennedy said to Krulak. "Is that right? First it was napalm, now it's jets and defoliants and a free-fire zone."

"Yes, sir," Krulak said. His eyes never flickered towards the photograph.

"Harkins wants this 'Iron Triangle' to dump unused bombs on, so the pilots won't have to land with the bombs aboard. And he assures me there are no people in this Iron Triangle."

"That's correct, sir."

Bobby Kennedy said harshly, "No people, or no friendly people?"

Krulak didn't answer.

"What exactly is this war doing to those people?" Bobby said. "Maybe they *don't* want us there. What are we doing to the people of that little country?"

Robert McNamara, Secretary of Defense, began to answer. Bobby cut him off. "Maybe it's time we considered getting out completely."

A heavy silence hung in the room. No one else but the President's brother, they realized, would have said that sentence. Not at a meeting of the National Security Council. No one else could have.

But all Jack said, later and privately, was, "You know—when I first came to the White House, Ike never even briefed me on Vietnam."

The baby weighed less than five pounds. They had already moved him once; from Otis Air Force Base, where Jackie lay asleep after her ordeal, to Children's Hospital in Boston, where the little thing lay hooked to a respirator in a heated isolette. The President could look at his son only through glass. He touched the handwritten card on the isolette: PATRICK BOUVIER KENNEDY.

"In the name of the Father," the priest said, "and the Son, and the Holy Ghost ..." The respirator equipment rasped softly as the priest recited the last rites.

"Sir," his aide said, "you need to go now ... Sir?"

"My great-grandfather's name was Patrick," Kennedy said, to no one in particular. "He left Ireland in 1848."

"Yes, sir," the aide said.

"A stubborn people, the Irish," Kennedy said, and the aide saw that there were no tears in his eyes. "Fighters."

"Yes, sir."

He stayed that night at the Ritz-Carlton, to be near the baby. On the glossy desk of the hotel suite he spread out test-ban documents. The subject preoccupied him more and more. The scientists in New Mexico had shown him a huge crater, the result of an underground blast. They were very proud of it.

On this issue, he wrote, tapping the pencil against his teeth, *I must also act as President of generations unborn— and not just American generations. I must consider myself the President of all who look to the United States anywhere in this shrinking world. On this issue—*

The pencil dropped. For just a second it seemed there had been someone in the room with him, someone behind him. But when he turned around, no one was there.

Kennedys don't cry, Joe had always insisted. Jack said the same thing to his own children. *Kennedys don't cry.*

He resumed writing about the necessity of test-ban treaties to save all the children of the world.

The fighting went on all night and into the morning. Reports came regularly to the White House from the embassy in Saigon. Diem was trying to stage some sort of counter-coup, an insane move: The attacks of his troops on the remaining Buddhist pagodas only enflamed the Vietnamese people more. Finally the word came: Diem and his brother Nhu were gone. They'd slipped out of the city.

"Keep me informed," Kennedy said. His face was gray. He'd known about the coup days ago; he'd given permission for it weeks before that. Having crushed the Buddhists, the Diem government had attacked college students, moved against high-school students, arrested relatives of suspected plotters. No one knew how many people had been tortured or shot.

The rebels caught Diem and Nhu as the brothers were trying to leave the country. They ripped off the back of the armored personnel carrier and stabbed Diem and Nhu over and over. Madame Nhu, awakened in her room at the Beverly Hills Hotel and told of her husband's death, screamed, "Kennedy is to blame for this!"

"That's absurd," Jack said later to Bobby, as they walked in the Rose Garden.

"Of course," Bobby said. "But, Jack, there's something you should know. Lyndon is saying the same thing."

Jack didn't answer. Lyndon was an old problem. He pulled a leaf off a rose bush. It was already November; there were no blossoms.

"I think we should get out of Vietnam," Bobby said steadily. "Not just refuse to send combat troops. Get the fuck out."

"I'll think about it," Jack said.

The Mormon Tabernacle was packed. No one had expected such a turnout, not for what was supposed to be a speech on conservation. The crowd gave him a five-minute standing ovation as he walked in.

Kennedy stood looking out over the upturned faces. Around him white pillars soared to the domed ceiling. The temple was a majestic setting, large in more than space. He made the decision. He was not going to talk about conservation.

"The wisest course ahead of us," he said ringingly, "is to preserve and protect a world of diversity, in which no one power or combination of powers can threaten the security of the United States. We must commit ourselves to an enduring peace, not a *Pax Americana* enforced on the world by American weapons of war, not merely a peace for Americans, but a peace for all men; not merely peace in our time but peace for all time.

"To do this, we must accept the responsibility for limiting nuclear weapons, for avoiding the means to destroy our own children and those of the rest of the world. Above all, we must accept responsibility for using our power to the good of *all* who look to us, which means all the peoples of the world.

"I accept that responsibility. I pledge to you here, tonight, that that responsibility is mine."

They stood on the chairs to cheer him.

In his hotel room in Salt Lake City, after the reporters

and the aides had finally gone, Kennedy sat in a flowered chair and had a final, solitary drink. Elation filled him. He'd tapped some deep well in the American consciousness that he hadn't even been positive was there. He hadn't thought the people were ready to embrace diversity, test-ban treaties, peace. But the response tonight had been phenomenal.

He thought suddenly of his father, embracing FDR and the New Deal because it was politically expedient.

But it wasn't that way with him, he knew. He'd done for his people what he could because he believed in it. In civil rights, which in the three years of his presidency had brought Negroes out of the worst of their feudal serfdom, even though God knew there was still a long way to go. In Medicare, which even though Congress had defeated it, was going to be a major issue in next year's election. In the test-ban treaty. He didn't want to peer into any more holes in the New Mexico desert while cheerful scientists explained that soon they'd have bombs that made even bigger holes with even less dirt.

He was proud of what he'd accomplished. In a rare moment of theatrics, Jack Kennedy raised his glass and saluted himself.

The only failure was Vietnam. There was tremendous suffering there, tremendous pain to the people themselves. It wasn't enough to refuse to send combat troops. There were already 16,000 Americans in the country, and 108 of them had died. And how many more Vietnamese? Thousands. Hundreds of thousands. Bobby was right; he'd have to pull the military advisors out.

But not now. There was time. Next year was an election year; looking too soft in Vietnam would be a mistake until after the election. Not if he was going to push for a test-ban treaty as well. He couldn't risk the political fight until after the election, a year away.

But by that time ... how much more bombing and killing would have occurred? *We look to Kennedy!* the hysterical Madame Nhu had screamed after her husband's assassination.

Kennedy rose from his chair. He pushed Vietnam out of his mind. Nobody could do everything all at once. *The great thing,* Joe had always told his sons, *is to know what you can accomplish. And to get elected first. That above all.*

There was time to deal with Vietnam. After the election. What Bobby kept calling "the people of that little country" would just have to wait until then.

Kennedy brushed his teeth and took off his clothes. He was all of a sudden very weary. But when he went to climb into bed, he saw something odd: a dead, brown leaf lay on his pillow. It was November, the ground was covered with dead leaves, but how could it possibly have gotten inside?

He touched it, and under his fingers it crumpled into powder and dust.

This is Chuq Von Rospach's first professional science fiction sale, but he is hardly new to the field, having edited the Hugo-nominated *Other Realms* and worked as a reviewer for *Amazing Stories*, as well as having done yeoman duty for the Science Fiction Writers of America.

Most stories about John F. Kennedy end before or at the point of his death. Chuq takes you one step beyond, in this sardonic and ultimately moral little fable of a man obsessed.

'Til Death Do Us Part
by Charles Von Rospach

"Jack, is it safe for me to be here? What if Jackie finds out?"

The President rolled over onto his side. "Don't worry. She's in New York shopping. The guards don't keep logs for that entrance, and everyone on duty is loyal. Nothing can go wrong."

Washington, D.C. (API)—The capital was in an uproar today after the Washington Post *disclosed that it had obtained pictures of film star Marilyn Monroe leaving the White House last Tuesday at approximately 3:00 A.M. (EST). The pictures were printed in the Friday edition of the* Post.

The pictures were taken by Post *photographer Lance Jacobs, who claimed that he had received an anonymous*

*phone call telling him "to keep an eye on the President"
that night.*

White House spokesman Pierre Salinger announced that
there would be an official statement later in the day, but
noted that "The President is a very busy man, and it's not
unusual for him to have visitors at odd hours."

The First Lady, in New York to host a fund-raiser for the
Daughters of the American Revolution, declined to comment,
saying only "Jack is a good husband and a good Catholic.
I'm sure he has a logical explanation, because he would never
do anything to hurt me or his children."

Marilyn Monroe was not available for comment. According to Peter Lawford, a friend of Monroe's, she was on vacation in Bermuda for a few days before starting her next
picture.

President Kennedy sat at his desk in the Oval Office,
his head buried in his hands. "Can we stall them? Stonewall until something else comes up?"

"Jack, her face, among other things, was clearly visible."
Bobby Kennedy turned from the window and confronted
his brother. "You've seen the pictures! No stonewall in
the world will stop this. That would just give Stevenson
more time for leverage. We need a clean, quick out. What
it is, I have no idea."

"Bobby, call Hoover. He'll have some dirt on the *Post*.
He can shut them up."

The Attorney General sighed. "I did call Hoover. He
asked for prints."

A sound somewhere between a sigh and a gargle
erupted from the President. "Congress is going to rip out
my throat and leave the corpse for the voters to dance on
next election day."

"Jack, it's not that bad. It's not like they found out your
crew was asleep on that PT boat. If we can create a distraction and get the media to work with us, we can survive this. All we need is the right slant. Get your

mouthpiece working on that release before the dogs start digging through the garbage for something else. We'll be okay."

Washington, D.C. (API)—White House Press Secretary Pierre Salinger announced Thursday in a prepared statement that the reason for Miss Monroe's visit was "to discuss with the President plans for her upcoming USO tour of Southeast Asia and Europe. Because of their schedules, a late-evening meeting was the only practical time, and lasted until approximately 3:00 A.M. because of the many details that needed to be worked out."

Response from the Congress was immediate. Democratic Senator Adlai Stevenson announced that the Senate would be forming a special committee to investigate possible impeachment of the President, noting that, if the rumors were true, "Any man with morals as questionable as the President seems to have is not a fit person to be sitting in the Oval Office." An anonymous White House staff member labeled Stevenson a "sore loser" and said any investigation would prove the President's innocence.

The First Lady, in London to host a fund-raiser for the London Symphony, released the following statement: "I have all confidence in my loving husband and know in my heart that these baseless rumors were invented in the tawdry minds of the press. Jack and I love each other and he would never do anything to hurt me or our children. Every day that we are apart my heart cries out for him and I wish I could be with him in this time of crisis to support him as he supports me."

When asked when she plans to return to Washington, Mrs. Kennedy remarked that she had to fly to Monaco immediately after the performance to work with Princess Grace for the starving orphans of Monaco, and that she had no idea how long it would take to get them all fed and put to bed. "As soon as we have wiped out poverty in Monaco, I will be at my husband's side where I belong."

According to studio spokesmen, Marilyn Monroe was still on vacation and unavailable for contact.

"Bobby! Did you see what Jackie said? And who called Adlai a sore loser? He's going to hang on until I'm dead!" A paperweight crashed against the door with a thud.

"That wasn't supposed to be quoted. Whose idea was this late-night USO shit? That's so lame it hurts. Are you trying to get impeached?"

"*You* said that? I ought to kill you! The USO bit was *my* idea, and Norma Jean agreed to it. Nobody with a brain will believe it for a second—but nobody can shoot holes in it, either."

"You better hope so, Jack. You better get Jackie home, too. The longer she stay away, the worse it looks for you."

"Jackie won't come. She's going to sit over there and watch me twist in the wind. She never did forgive me for that nurse the night Caroline was born, and now she's getting even. This better calm down soon, or my career's dead. All for a couple of tits."

"Yeah, but what tits, Jack."

"Shut up, Bobby."

Hollywood (API)—In her first statement since her clandestine trip to the White House, actress Marilyn Monroe, back from vacation to start filming of Tom Jones *was quoted as saying "There is nothing between myself and the President. We're just good friends. I have nothing else to say, because there's nothing to talk about."*

In Washington, Senator Adlai Stevenson announced that the hearings on the All-Nighter Crisis, as it is now known, would begin in two weeks, on August 6. He also disclosed that all attempts to acquire the minutes of the meeting between the President and Monroe, as well as visitor logs for that evening, have been meet with silence. Stevenson declared that the White House could expect a subpoena for the records within the week.

* * *

"Jack?"

"Norma! It's not safe for you to call. I think Hoover has this phone bugged. I know Adlai's bugged yours. We can't talk."

"Jack, we have to do something. He wants me to testify! Jack, I miss you! I don't know what to do!"

"Norma, you're an actress. Lie."

There was a moan in the telephone. "I can't do that. I'll be under oath. That'd be illegal!"

"Norma, it's no more illegal than sneaking into the White House in the middle of the night and sleeping with a married President."

"Jack, when are you going to tell Jackie about the divorce?"

"I can't think of divorcing her until after the election. That's the worse thing we can do. You'll have to lie to Congress about us. If this blows up any worse, it'll cost me the election, and it won't do your career any good, either."

"I can't handle this! I tried to go to the bathroom last night and there was a man from the *Tribune* in my shower. They won't leave me alone. Peter's got me some more tranquilizers, but I can't sleep. We need to talk. I can't think straight. Can we get together? Oh, Jack—I need you!"

"We can't get together for a while. We shouldn't even be talking. The press would rip us to pieces. So would Adlai, if we gave him the chance."

"Jack, I don't know if I can do it. I'll try, but I'm afraid. Lonely and afraid. I need you."

"I need you, too. I wish I could be there, but we have to be apart a while longer. Do the best you can. Be strong. Don't talk to anybody you don't have to, and practice your story for Congress. Trust me, it's easier to lie to them than you think."

"Jack . . ."

"Norma, I have to go. The King of Belgium is in the

other room to talk about chocolate tariffs. I'll talk to you soon. I miss you."

"I love you, Jack. I'll try."

Kennedy hung up the phone, then threw it across the room.

"Bobby! Get in here!"

The door opened and the Attorney General ran in. "What, Jack?"

"That was Norma. She's cracking, the slut! We need to do something or she's going to spill to Adlai on national TV. Do you know of any place we can start a war? Blow up a couple of leaders and pin it on the revolution or something? We need a diversion, fast."

"Castro's up to something, but we don't have enough info to go public. Maybe we can scam something up in Vietnam. I'll find something."

"Vietnam? Where's that?"

"It's a rice paddy out in Asia. Nobody wants it, so we can bomb the shit out of it for a while without anyone getting hurt. Do you really think she'd going to crack?"

"She's cracking as we speak. She just doesn't realize it. Lawford's got her stuffed to the gills with tranquilizers, but that won't keep it bottled in long enough."

"Damn! You better talk to Giancana, then. See what he can do. I'd get one of my friends in the CIA to look at it, but Stevenson's got spies on our spies."

"Put out a hit with the Mafia on Marilyn Monroe? *Are you crazy?*"

"You got a better idea? If you do, I suggest you use it. Or do you like the idea of losing the election, getting divorced, and possibly being the first President of the United States to be impeached because of a morals charge?"

The President shuddered and rubbed his eyes. "Yeah. I'll have Judith call Sam and arrange a drop. *Jeezus!* Who would ever have guessed that a pair of tits could cause a national scandal?"

"Jack, these weren't just tits. They were Marilyn Monroe's tits."

"Bobby, don't remind me. Get out of my sight and go start a war."

Hollywood (API)—The film community is in shock tonight as one of the leading stars, Marilyn Monroe, was found dead in her Hollywood apartment of an apparent drug overdose. The police are investigating the death as an apparent suicide. She was found by a friend, actor Peter Lawford, who was visiting to talk to her about the script for her current film, Tom Jones. She had recently been involved in a controversy over a late-night meeting with President Kennedy at the White House and was scheduled to testify before Congress on Tuesday.

Monroe, 35, was the stage name of Norma Jean Baker. Her film credits include Gentlemen Prefer Blondes, Bus Stop, Some Like it Hot, and West Side Story.

"Jack, couldn't the Mafia have made it look like a fucking accident? Run the car off a cliff or something? Everyone's wondering if you had the CIA shut the bitch up."

"Giancana says it wasn't his hit. When his man got there, she was already gone. All he did was cover his tracks and get the hell out."

"You believe him? He's setting you up, Jack. Taking your money and leaving you to hang. He's never forgiven you for screwing him on that concrete deal."

"Bobby, what's worse: having the Mafia hanging around our neck for the rest of my life because they know I ordered a hit on Monroe, or having everyone wonder whether she's dead because I told the CIA to do it?"

"What's worse? Both. What if Giancana's lying, and decides to remind you of your 'debt' to him in, say, five years? You think you're safe now, but are you? Hell, maybe we should have had the CIA do it."

"Do you think they'd have any more luck with Monroe

than they're having with Castro? She's dead, and Stevenson's probe died with her. That's what we needed. We should be able to ride this one through now."

"Jack, at least *try* to sound unhappy that she's dead."

Washington, D.C. (API)—Senator Adlai Stevenson announced a delay in his hearings on the Kennedy-Monroe scandal because of the untimely death of Monroe. "Now is not the time to sully the memory of someone who is important to so many people in this country. This investigation can wait while we all grieve the loss of one of the shining lights of America. I can only hope that neither her involvement with the President nor these proceedings had anything to do with this final act of desperation."

"Bobby, did you see what that asshole said?"

"Jack, he can't hurt you now. The probe is dead and he knows it. You've won. Get Jackie home and maybe you've still got a shot at reelection."

"You think so? I'll call Jackie and try groveling again as soon as I get back from the funeral. Maybe if I let her redecorate the Lincoln Room." The President grimaced. "Again."

"Jack?"

The President sat up in bed, suddenly wide awake. "Who's that?"

"It's me, Jack—Marilyn."

"*Norma?* You're dead! Is this some kind of sick joke? Who is this?" The President turned and fumbled for the light.

"Jack, don't turn on the light. You won't see anything. I'm really dead, but I missed you so much. I had to be with you. I came back for you."

The light snapped on. The President stared at the empty room. "What's going on?"

The light turned itself back off. "I told you you wouldn't

see anything, Jack, and you won't." Something brushed the President's cheek in the dark. "You can *feel* me, though."

"*Norma!* What are you doing? Stop that! *You're dead!*"

"I'm dead, Jack, but I still need you. I need you badly. Love me, Jack. Love me with all your life."

"*Norma! No! Stop it!*"

"Jack, you look like hell. Your back bothering you again?"

"No, Bobby. Just having trouble sleeping. Nightmares."

"The PT boat again? Shall we call Dr. Stronton for some more tranquilizers?"

"No, not the PT boat. Norma. Damn, I wish Jackie would get back here! This sleeping alone crap is driving me crazy. I'd sleep better if she was with me."

"Still no luck bringing her home?"

"Nope. She wants me to fly out and grovel in person first. Come and bring her home."

"Do it, Jack."

"Huh? You kidding? She'd never let me live it down!"

"So? You won't live it down anyway. You need her, and she knows it. Besides, a vacation will do you good. Go spend a week in Monaco. Relax, play kissyface and get her back here. You haven't had a vacation for a while, anyway. What could go wrong?"

Washington, D.C. (API)—Secretary of Defense Robert Mc-Namara announced today that United States military intelligence had conclusive evidence that the Russians were building installations in Cuba for the purpose of housing nuclear missiles targeted at locations within the United States.

Showing a series of photographs taken by high-altitude reconnaissance flights, McNamara detailed what he claimed was a methodical military buildup of Russian troops and the creation of a series of missile silos and military bunkers.

The President, who has been on vacation in Monaco with

his wife since August 28th, cut short his trip and was return-
ing to Washington. White House Press Secretary Pierre Sal-
inger said that no further public statements would be
forthcoming until the President arrived and was briefed on
the situation.

"Bobby, if you ever say 'What could go wrong?' to me
again, remind me to have you killed. What happened?
This was supposed to be a nice, quiet, uneventful vacation and reunion with my wonderful, caring wife." The
President grimaced. "At least she's home. Hope you like
puce. That's the color of the wallpaper going in the Lincoln Room."

"Forget the wallpaper, Jack. Remember that war you
told me to start when we were looking for a distraction?
We forgot to call it off. Congratulations, Jack: We're now
the proud parents of a major nuclear crisis. You, me, and
Khrushchev."

"You set this up with the Russians?"

"No. He's doing it on his own. We're just blowing it up
onto the front page where everyone will see it, instead of
dealing with it quietly like we should have."

"Oh, Jesus, Bobby! He's a hard-nosed bastard. It's not
going to be easy to get him to back down. Nukes in Cuba!"
The President rubbed his eyes. "You don't suppose I could
get Adlai to impeach me now, could I?"

"Not a chance, Jack. You'll have to deal with this one."

"Damn. You know what's worse?"

"What could be worse than nukes in Cuba?"

"Jackie insisted on separate bedrooms."

"Jack. You're back. I missed you."

"Norma?"

"Yes, Jack. I'm glad you're back. I need you."

"Not tonight, Norma. Please."

"Love me, Jack. Love me."

"Norma, no. Norma. Stop that. Please, I need to . . . *Norma! Stop!*"

"Love me, Jack. Love me forever."

"Oh, Norma. Ohhhh . . ."

"Jack, why is Jackie pissed?"

"Don't ask, Bobby. You don't want to know."

"Jack, she was talking about painting the White House blue. I mean, the whole exterior."

"Shit! That woman will be the death of me."

"What did you do?"

"I . . . uh . . . I called her Norma."

"You *what?* Of all the stupid things you've done, Jack, that's the stupidest. *Why?*"

"It slipped. The nightmares are back, and Norma's in them. I wasn't thinking."

"You *never* fucking think! You and those gonads from Hell, Jack."

"Never mind that. How's the blockade going? Any word from Khrushchev?"

"Fuck Khrushchev. He'll wait. Go get Jackie settled before she ends up in fucking Monaco again."

"Fuck her, Bobby. Fuck being President. Let's give Nikita whatever he wants. We can bring in some broads and party until Adlai kicks us out and changes the locks. I don't give a damn anymore."

"Jack, Khrushchev wants out of this as badly as you do. We just need to find a way for everyone to save face. Let the diplomats do their job. You go talk to Jackie and then take a nap. I'll hold the fort."

"I don't want to sleep. All I see is Norma."

"Let me call the doctor and get you something to knock you out. You need to get some sleep. You look like shit."

"Jack?"

"Norma, please leave me alone. I can't handle it. I've *got* to get some sleep! Go away!"

"Jack, I can't go. I need you. You need me, too. You think of me, don't you? When you're with her? And the others?"

"Norma, go away. I'm crazy. You're dead. You're a figment of my imagination. You don't exist."

"I'm real, Jack. I may be dead, but could your imagination do *this* to you?"

"Norma, stop! Oh, God!. The best lay I've ever had and it's a fucking ghost!"

"A *fucking* ghost, Jack? Very funny. True, in its way. Don't think about it. Enjoy me. Love me. Be mine tonight. Be mine. Forever."

"Jack, did you get any sleep at all last night? You taking that stuff Dr. Stronton prescribed for you? It'd knock out an elephant."

"It makes me too stoned to think. I'm doing okay."

"Well, you look like hell. We need to announce the agreement on the missiles to the public in two hours, and you look like a fucking ghost."

The President giggled. "A fucking ghost. Right. Tell you what, Bobby. You get the speech finished and I'll go try to get a quick nap. Have someone come and get me so I can be made up in time for the speech."

"Jack?"

"Norma. I've tried. I can't live without you. What have you done to me?"

"Loved you, Jack. Loved you like you've never been loved by a real woman. Loved you like I never could when I was alive. As I will, as long as you sleep here."

"This room? What about when I'm not President anymore? What will we do then?"

"Then I'll be gone forever, Jack."

"No! You can't do that!"

"I can only visit you here, Jack. This is the only place we can be together, for as long as you live."

"But what if I lose the election? I've got to have you!"

"There is an alternative, Jack. We *can* be together. Forever."

"Forever?"

"Join me, Jack. We can be forever together. I'll never leave your side again."

"You mean, die? Kill myself?"

"Yes, Jack. If you want me forever, you have to join me."

"*No!* I can't do that! Suicide is a sin. I can't kill myself."

"You don't have to kill yourself, Jack. You have ... resources. I know."

"No. I don't want to die!"

"But you want me, Jack."

"Yes. I want you, Norma. But I don't want to die."

"Love me, Jack. Love me. Be mine. Be mine tonight. And forever."

"Norma, I love you. But I'm afraid."

"Don't be, Jack. I'll be there for you. Forever."

"I don't want to die."

"Love me, Jack."

Washington, D.C. (API)—In a speech televised nationwide, President John F. Kennedy today announced that he and Soviet Premier Nikita Khrushchev had come to agreement on the placement of Soviet troops and missiles on the island of Cuba. According to the President, all nuclear warheads and offensive missiles will be removed from the island, as well as Soviet troops and training personnel. In return, the United States will remove the blockade of the island and drop the economic embargo against the Castro regime, as well as cancel a CIA-run covert operation known as Mongoose. The United States will also be dismantling an unspecified number of Jupiter-class nuclear missiles currently stationed in Turkey.

Cuban premier Fidel Castro issued the following statement ...

* * *

"Jack?"

"Norma, I need you."

"Jack, if you had let them bomb the White House, we could have been together now. Forever."

"A nuclear war would have killed millions of innocent people!"

"So? They'll die sooner or later. I want to have you. I want you to join me now."

"Then come here. You can have me."

"No. I want you forever. Promise me you'll join me. Come to me soon."

"I don't want to die, Norma. I'm afraid."

"You'll have to make the choice soon. Life—or *me*? If you don't join me soon, I won't be able to be with you when you die. I don't have much time left. If you wait too long, you'll be alone forever."

"I need you, Norma! Give me a chance to work it out. I'll think of something. It can't be suicide."

"If you don't hurry, we'll lose each other. Join me, or lose me forever."

"I'll join you, as soon as I can work it out. Come here. Love me."

"Love me, Jack. With all your life. Forever."

"Mr. President. You run a great risk at being seen with me."

"Sometimes risks must be taken, Sam."

Sam Giancana absently removed his glasses and cleaned them on his tie. "So it seems. What is it that requires the President to come to me directly?"

"I need a hit. I can't do it with my people, and it can't be traceable back to me or my administration. It's too sensitive. I can't trust the CIA."

"That's a funny one, Jack. You'd rather deal with me than with your own family of spies. If you were anyone else, I'd think I was being set up."

"I'm offering permanent immunity for you, plus your fee. I'll make sure Justice leaves you alone as long as you live." The President pulled an envelope from under his jacket and tossed it on the desk. "That's the retainer. The other fifty percent on delivery."

"Who is this man who must die?"

"John Connally. Governor of Texas."

"A mere Governor? What did he do—sleep with Jackie?"

The President bristled. "Next spring he's going to announce Texas's secession from the United States. That has to be stopped before it goes public, or all hell will break loose. We might lose the entire South."

Giancana blinked. "Interesting. So he's a traitor."

"He can't be made a martyr. I can make sure there are holes in security that will allow your men to get in and out, but it has to be done when and where I tell you. They can't be caught. They can't miss."

"You ask a lot, Mr. President."

"You're up to it, Sam. We both know that."

"I will do it. For you, and for our country. A traitor. I think I will enjoy this."

"I'm scheduled to be in Dallas in November. That means the Secret Service will do security. I want you to get two or three men and get them positioned. I'll send you the location later, but they're to be told to take out everyone in the car with Connally. Everyone dies with him."

"We will do what you need. It is an honor to work for the country I love."

"And profitable, Sam. I am in your debt, and we both know it."

"Jack?"

"Norma! Where have you been? It's been days!"

"It is harder to visit you, Jack. The paths are dimming and I lose my strength. Soon we shall part forever, unless you join me."

"Hold on for a few more weeks, Norma. Just until Dallas. Then we'll be together. Forever."

"Jack. Together. Forever. You'll be mine. Forever."

"We'll be lovers for all eternity, Norma."

"We will be together, Jack. Now love me. Love me with all your life. Give me your strength until you join me."

Dallas (API)—A stunned country mourned the death of its First Family today, after an assassination claimed the life of President John F. Kennedy. Kennedy, in town for a fund-raising dinner later that evening, was attacked while his motorcade traveled through downtown Dallas. At least three gunmen opened fire on the President's car, killing the President; his wife, Jacqueline Kennedy; John Boucher, the driver; Jeremy Stark, a member of the Secret Service security team; and Pierre Salinger, the White House Press Secretary. Also riding in the car was Texas Governor John Connally, who was seriously injured but is expected to recover.

The gunmen opened fire at 12:45 P.M., firing at least forty rounds of ammunition into the car. All are still at large.

"Jack! You're here!"

"Norma! I've come to you!"

"Yes, Jack, you're here. And now you're mine."

"We belong to each other, now. Lovers forever."

Monroe chuckled. "No, Jack. Not lovers. Hell doesn't allow love."

"Hell? We're not in Hell!"

"We aren't? How did I die, Jack?"

"Giancana's man killed you."

"No, Jack, I was gone when he got there. I'm a suicide. Just like you."

"I didn't kill myself!"

"You didn't pull the trigger, but you killed yourself as surely as I did, Jack. Inspired piece of theater, that was, but you're still a suicide. By bringing you here, I've claimed a soul for Hell and so ended my own torments.

Your eternal torment is just beginning, Jack, and I am your tormentor. Welcome to Hell, and to your worst nightmares."

"Being with you for all eternity is a torment? Let's get started, Norma!"

"Started, Jack? With what?"

Marilyn Monroe pointed at the President's naked body and laughed. The President looked at himself—and saw the smooth, unbroken, and definitely unmanly skin between his legs.

His screams almost drowned out her laughter.

Brian Thomsen is back with another of the vignettes he does so well. In this one, Gloria Swanson, Joe Kennedy's former mistress, recalls a certain afternoon in 1929, and shows us the difference a single word can make.

Gloria Remembers
by Brian M. Thomsen

So you want to write the definitive Kennedy biography, warts and all as they say? Well, not having read your previous books, I'm not sure how I feel about that. The word is that you are quite the young hatchet lady, and one must admit that your proposed title of *The Dynasty That Failed* is a bit, how shall I say, judgmental. Still, it's not as if I would be revealing any secrets or anything. Joe and I did have an affair after all, and everyone knows it. I mean everyone was doing it back then. I'm not ashamed of it. You did read my book *Swanson on Swanson*, didn't you?

Oh, you want something that wasn't *in* my book, an exclusive as they say? Something that would play into the "like father like sons" theme you are trying to illustrate. Sins of the father sort of stuff.

Well, if it's the sins of the father you want to hear about, do I have an exclusive for you!—not that I think you're going to believe it or want to include it in your book. You see, it was Joe's fault all along. The boys never had a chance, at least not Joey, Jack, or Bobby. It was the sin of the father all right, and I remember it like it was yesterday.

It was early in the spring of 1929. Von Stroheim was directing me in a perfectly decadent epic of some sort, and Joe was flying in every other weekend for a Sabbath of passion. However, even a man of Joe's exceptional vigor needed an occasional respite from the enjoyable yet arduous rigors of sex, and therefore we would often spend the late afternoon and early evening of Saturday in less intense pursuits around town.

Now I don't need to tell you, dear, that Hollywood was quite a place back in those days. It was still the Roaring Twenties after all, and for the right price you could get, see, or do just about anything, any time of the day or night. It really was quite magical, though not all of the magic was necessarily white if you know what I mean. There was a dark underside to everything. People still hadn't gotten over the Arbuckle scandal, and several lost souls whose careers had not survived the death of the silents were still wandering around, desperately searching for something ... and where lost souls are prevalent, other, how shall I say, "entities," are sure to be around.

Now, Joe prided himself on not being scared of any man or devil, and scoffed at the rumors that Satan himself had set up an office in the shabby end of town. I had known several young ingenues who claimed to have sold their souls in pursuit of parts (those of us with talent never had to worry about such things), and had even received invitations to visit his office downtown. Joe thought it would be a hoot, so the two of us drove down there on that accursed Saturday afternoon.

Satan's office was in an abandoned storefront, as the rumors had said. Only one door wasn't boarded up, and coincidentally, a rather sleek young man was standing outside as if he were waiting for someone. As we approached he beckoned us to hurry.

"Why, Joe and Gloria, I've been waiting for you. Come step inside so we can talk. You can call me Lou," he said, quickly ushering us inside.

His office was decked out in red satin and black leather. Lou assumed his position behind a desk of the darkest oak I've ever seen, while Joe and I chose places on a plush loveseat.

"You two are in luck today. I've admired both of your past work. Today is not a day for deals. I wouldn't dare insult either of you with propositions involving your souls. No, today is a freebie day, so make a wish and I will grant it."

"What could you have that we could possibly want? Gloria is the biggest star in Hollywood, and I have wealth and power beyond even *your* wildest dreams. You may be able to work your magic for some second-rate chippies, but I'm afraid that we are way out of your league," said Joe in all of his Irish Catholic glory.

"Now, Joe, I know that there is nothing I can do for you personally, but what about your boys? Face it—you're not always going to be around. Sure, you've got wealth and power, but no matter how you look at it, you are still one of the new boys in Society, and not really respected besides. No, the Kennedy name will disappear from everyone's mind once you're gone, and what will your boys have then? The Kennedy name *needs* something, and they are the only ones who can do it. Don't you want the Kennedy name revered by posterity?"

Lou had instinctively known Joe's greatest weakness—he didn't trust his sons enough to believe that they would carry on the family name to fame and fortune.

"What are you offering me?" Joe asked.

"I can give the Kennedy name glory, and make it seem as if it was earned by your sons," he offered.

"Glory?"

"Glory," he said simply.

I wanted to leave, or at least tell Joe that I didn't like

the look in his eye, but I knew Joe, and kept silent. I knew it wouldn't do any good.

"I think I can accept your gift," Joe said carefully. "It is a gift after all—no strings attached?"

"That's right," said Lou with a satisfied grin. "I don't need to make any deals to get your soul. I'm more than willing to wait until the rightful time. The Kennedy name will get its glory through the lives of your sons. One as a war hero, one as a leader, and one as the hope for the future."

"You mean through the *deeds* of his sons," I corrected him.

"Same thing," said Joe.

"Almost identical," agreed Lou. . . .

. . . and with a puff of smoke Joe and I found ourselves standing outside, in front of the now boarded-up doorway.

I broke up with Joe soon after that. Rumor had it that he even started going to church regularly. Though we talked in the years that followed, we never again mentioned that Saturday afternoon. I think that both of us tried to forget what had transpired.

But then Joe Junior died a war hero back in '44, and Jack was shot in Dallas, and Bobby was killed before he could even make his mark. They had all brought glory to the family name, just as Lou had promised.

I sometimes wonder if Joe *still* thinks the words were identical. It is the only time I ever feel sorry for him.

In a field where humorous novels simply do not sell, Esther Friesner has been turning out such exceptions to the rule as *Hooray For Hellywood*, *Gnome Man's Land*, and *Harpy High* with startling regularity. Here she examines just what effect dealing with the Little People might have had on the career of our first Irish President.

Told You So
by Esther M. Friesner

He was strolling in the Rose Garden with Merlin when they met the leprechaun. Of course the wizard was instantly suspicious.

"Stand behind me, Mr. President, sir," the old one declared, spreading wide the black sleeves of his necromancer's robe like gorgeously embroidered bat wings. "I'll blast the treacherous atomy to Tir N'an Og's left hind tit!"

"Now just wait one minute, if you please." The President's clear, penetrating Harvard diction rang through the Rose Garden without benefit of microphone. "I don't see the need for such draconian measures."

Merlin snorted and cast a preliminary holding spell on the green-suited critter now trembling in the shade of the Queen Elizabeths. It was as if the President were invisible and inaudible.

The President did not much care for such treatment. It reminded him too much of home. "I believe," he forged on, "that you are allowing either professional jealousy of a fellow-creature of enchantment to cloud your judgment, or else you are acting out of an inappropriate sense of nationality. Merely because you are British and he is Irish—"

"That's all you know about such things," the wizard growled. "Sir. In my day, we didn't make so much of the Irish Question, largely because it didn't exist. We're all Celts under the skin on this bus."

"Then why not let him go?" the President asked. "He looks harmless."

"There are only two instances when a leprechaun is harmless: One, when you are in possession of the dinky bastard's pot o' gold, for the return of which trove it will move heaven and earth; and two, when it is *dead*." The President blanched at such ferocity. Merlin gave a short, nasty, superior laugh. "Your experience with the Seelie and Unseelie Courts is scant and sadly lacking. I, on the other hand—"

"You, on the other hand, were slapped shut inside that very oak"—here the President pointed at the venerable tree in question, incongruously plunked down smack dab in the middle of a patch of American Beauties—"by a member of the Seelie. Father told me so." He really did not like being lorded over, particularly since the wizard—beard excepted—did look *so* much like Father.

"Unseelie," Merlin muttered. "And it was a learning experience. Which proves that I know the tricksy ways of these slippery little buggers a damn sight better than you do. Or so your *father* believed when he brought me over!"

The President winced. Even now, in the first figurative hours of his triumph, he did not like to be reminded that it was his father's money and machinations that had done so much to turn the dream into the reality, almost like magic.

Almost? Exactly like. Old Joe had never been one to balk at employing a man or a method, however dubious, when it would mean the accomplishment of a goal. The President still recalled how his father's whoops of joy had made the welkin ring over much of Hyannis when he read that breakfast telegram informing him of the discovery of Merlin's oak. Old Joe had wasted less than no time jetting over to England, personally rousting the wizard from the sleep of centuries, and signing him up for the campaign trail and beyond.

Even now the more sensationalism-minded tabloids were shouting aloud what the *New York Times* only whispered ever so genteelly: Can an election seemingly won through the employment of the greatest wizard the world has ever known be valid? Was Nixon's sorry appearance during the televised debates due to Merlin's underhanded enchantments? Could anyone look that sneaky without the Dark Powers being at work? It didn't seem credible. Who could blame the defeated candidate for crying foul, or calling down Heaven's own retribution on the man who entered the White House via the sorcerer's equivalent of a broomstick? (It was a sleek, black Cadillac limousine, actually, but Mr. Nixon had had a very trying day.) And then there was the matter of the Chicago returns ... Father had said to ignore it all.

Father. The President stiffened his spine. His father was far from here, but even so it was oftentimes difficult to recall just *which* Kennedy had won the election. Once upon a time in the Pacific he had accomplished something on his own, without his father's money and power and sheer force of personality behind him, shoving. It would be a shame he would never get over if he had to spend his presidency on some deserted atoll in the middle of a vast ocean just to exercise a little independent action.

"Merlin ..." he said in those precise, clipped accents which a large portion of the female electorate had found so ... *enchanting* was exactly the word. "Tree."

The wizard made a face whose full measure of scorn

was mostly masked by his long white beard and mustache. "All right, I'll go," he said. "I could do with a nap. But you mark me well, Mr. President: Watch out. You'd do best not to touch the wight; you don't know where it's been, and nothing you ever learned at Harvard prepared you for this. I recognize the species. They can talk the skin off an apple. Whenever we spied one in Camelot, we got out the earplugs and the swatters. Oh, they're a canny lot, these leprechauns! Grab its pot o' gold, if you want it to deal honestly with you. If I were you I'd find out why White House security was lax enough to let such trash in. Someone wasn't doing his job, or else someone was doing his job *too* well, if you get my drift. Envy wears a thousand faces, some of them damned cute, and I ought to know. *Cave leprechaunem—*"

"Merlin . . ." the President reiterated. *"Quercus."*

Either it was using the Latin for "oak" that turned the trick, or else the old enchanter really did run out of steam. He slunk off to the tree and petulantly slammed the cleft shut behind him. The holding spell's power went with its master. The President was now free to kneel in the grass and speak kindly to the shivering sprite.

Only a little while later, the President came into the White House with a leprechaun perched jauntily on his right shoulder. He found his wife in one of the great State reception rooms, discussing redecorating ideas with her design consultant.

"Blue?" the fay shrieked, flying up until it was level with Jackie's nose. "You just said you didn't *like* blue!"

"I changed my mind," Jackie replied with as much courage as she could muster. The tiny being was twirling its sparkle-tipped wand in a threatening manner, much as if it were a cosh.

"Do you think I'm made of magic?" the fay demanded. "Every whim of yours that I turn into reality is a drain. I was six-foot-seven and two hundred seventy-five pounds' worth of raw sorcery when I first started out in the biz;

now look at me!" It fluttered its iridescent wings fast enough to set up a buzz like a wasp's nest.

"We can keep it blue if you like," Jackie ventured.

"Oh, sure, and then have you go running back to the boss, complaining you don't like the color scheme?" The fay crossed toothpick arms across its spool-sized chest. "No, thanks. It's not much of an unnatural life, but it's the only one I've got."

"I don't think Merlin would do anything too drastic to you over artistic differences with my wife," the President put in with an easygoing smile.

The smile vanished when the fay laughed sarcastically and said, "*Merlin?* You really think the boss is *Merlin?*" It collapsed into boisterous hilarity, crowing, "Boy-o-boy, wait'll I tell Old Joe *this* one!"

It was a cartload and a half past the last straw. The President glanced at the leprechaun. The leprechaun nodded. The President said, "I wish that you *and* Merlin *and* all personified manifestations of magic brought here *by* Merlin were right back where you were when my father's agent found you!"

There was no thunderclap, no puff of smoke, no special effects worth mentioning. Toys that crash-bam-tinkle when they are hauled out of nursery cupboards make precious little comparative ruckus when they are being tucked away neatly into their proper places. The fay vanished without preamble or epilogue. Out in the Rose Garden, the big oak tree zapped itself back to Britain, leaving the formerly overshadowed American Beauties to breathe easier in the restored sunlight. Jackie stood transfixed, staring at empty air. She turned to her husband and his diminutive passenger.

"Jack, what have you done?" she cried.

The President grinned. "Something I should have done long ago."

"Sure, an' very nicely done it was, too," the leprechaun agreed. He hopped down from the President's shoulder

and moseyed over to Jackie. Levitating smoothly, he took
her hand and raised it to his lips. "Deloighted."

"Darling, allow me to introduce Seamus FitzGerald,"
the President said. "I saved his life from Merlin's wrath
earlier, for which service he has agreed to grant my every
wish."

"That's nice," Jackie said, regarding the little man
askance. The leprechaun was dressed just as all the
Saint Patrick's Day decorations would lead one to believe leprechauns do dress: green derby, green swal-
lowtail coat, green knee-britches, green shoes of
eighteenth-century design with bright golden buckles.
There was even a short-stemmed white clay pipe
clenched between his teeth. His hair was red, the bridge
of his snub nose liberally sprinkled with freckles. His
eyes, how they twinkled; his dimples, how merry. He
was perfect.

Too perfect.

"Your . . . every wish?" Jackie repeated. Her family had
been intimate with money for long enough to know that
bad deals often sound like good bargains.

"Now, beggin' yer lordship's pardon an' all, but that
'tisn't entire what I said," Seamus said, wagging his finger.

"What?" The President was immediately on his guard.
"See here, FitzGerald, if you think you can back out of
an agreement, I've got a brother who's Attorney General
and—"

"Whist! Now why would I be wantin' t' back out o' anything atall, atall?" The leprechaun still held on to Jackie's
hand, which he gave a second kiss, this one longer and
more lingering. She tried to pull away, but he was remarkably strong for so small a creature. "Sure, an' I only
was meanin' t' correct yer misapprehensions, begorrah.
'Tis not mere yer wishes I'll be grantin', else I'll be leavin'
ye no more master o' yer own fate than yon gombeen
Merlin an' yer old man put t'gither. Nay, ye'll fast find

ye've no more need o' Seamus FitzGerald once ye know th' full scope o' me grateful gift t' ye."

"Which is?" the President inquired, gazing narrowly at the mannikin.

"Which is that *whatever ye choose t' say'll be so,* that's all," the leprechaun said with pronounced satisfaction. "Aye, from yer mouth t' God's ears 'twill be, an' no need fer callin' upon me anymore fer idle wishin's." He gave Jackie's hand one more nibble for the road and vanished.

As soon as she was free, Jackie dashed into her husband's arms. "This is awful! I don't trust that little man a bit. Something's wrong, I'm positive. From everything I've heard about leprechauns, they never give any gifts away freely; not unless you've got some kind of hold over them."

"Now, now, dear," the President said in the proper voice for calming skittish women. "You're acting as if there's a conspiracy afoot."

"Leprechauns just don't show up at the White House," Jackie protested.

"Well, he *is* a FitzGerald. And we were told that since Merlin's arrival, there might be some side effects. A magical irruption, spread by winds and waters and spells, could well engulf the great and the small, the rich and the poor, the committed and—"

"Bring back Merlin." Jackie was firm.

"Nonsense," the President replied. "This is Washington, not Camelot. I can manage perfectly well *on my own.*" He studied the half-decorated room and asked, "What color did you want it?"

Jackie remained silent, sulking, but at last grumped out the word: "Green."

"All right. Let's see if Seamus FitzGerald was on the level or not. This room is green," said the President, and so it was.

The walls were green, the floor was green, the ceiling

was green, the furniture was green, the lighting fixtures were green, the windowpanes were green—

And a very *ugly* shade of green, too.

The President soon got the hang of it. It took more than the demands of magical specificity to bulldoze a Harvard man. Despite his wife's objections, he accepted the leprechaun's gift with alacrity, tailoring his words to suit his desires, saying precisely what he meant. It was a far cry from politics.

Some called those the golden years. As an astonished world watched, the President of the United States said, "Ask not what your country can do for you; ask what you can do for your country," and Americans asked, and were told, and obeyed. He called for nuclear disarmament and the globe was deafened by the sound of missile silos being slammed shut forever while in Moscow powerful men stood around blinking at each other and uttering the deeply puzzled Russian equivalent of "I don't know why I signed it; I thought it was *your* idea!" He declared that the United States would no longer stand for racial segregation and everyone got a seat on the bus.

Objections? There were some. One man came to wrangle with the President over the matter of bus seats and water fountains and other imperiled bastions of national security. The President greeted him quite affably, saying, "So you're the Grand Dragon," and indeed he was. How fortunate, then, that the President had looked in his mirror that very morning and said, "If there are any dragons to slay, you are just the man for the job!"

Jackie was a bit upset about the rug, though.

The President said on. He said there would be peace, and there was peace. (Specifications: worldwide, long-lasting.) He said there would be plenty, and there was plenty. (Specifications: food, clothing, and shelter.) He said there would be an American on the moon, and there was. Next time he made sure to specify that the person in question went there while wearing a space suit. He wrote the widow a very nice personal letter and said she would soon find happiness again. She did.

"These things happen," he remarked to his wife that night as he prepared for his European tour.

"I still don't like this," Jackie replied.

"Well, you'd better get used to it," he told her.

"Why?" Jackie retorted. "What will you say about *me* if I don't?"

"I think I might say something like, 'How nice to see you again, Miss Monroe, and as usual you will remember nothing at all about this interlude when I return you to your original form,'" he replied, and spent a very pleasant few hours until it was time to put back his playthings and get to the plane.

Afterwards, every single living soul you asked would always be able to tell you right where he was at that fateful moment: June 26, 1963. The event was televised because the President had said it would be televised. It was on every television network at home and abroad because the President thought it would be a nice touch, in keeping with the universal-brotherhood-of-free-men theme of his speech. Immediately following it, he intended to say a few words about a certain wall coming down. He always did have a flair for the dramatic and a taste for things theatrical that didn't stop at actresses.

From the city hall of West Berlin, the President declared to the world, "All free men, wherever they may live, are citizens of Berlin." (Across the globe, a zillion passports changed; in Berlin proper the electoral records and the tax rolls burst their bookcovers and inundated scurrying hordes of helpless bureaucrats in a sea of fresh data.) "And therefore, as a free man, I take pride in the words—"

(In a low dive on the Potomac, a little man in green bounced up and down on his barstool as he elbowed his sullen companion and hissed eagerly, "This is it! This is it!")

"—*Ich bin ein Berliner!*"

"Pay me," said the little man in green as the television above the bar played the emergency inauguration of Lyndon Baines Johnson. The broadcast was interrupted only to post news flashes detailing a minor riot that had broken out among West Berlin bakers as to whose establishment should have the honor of providing the pastry box in which to ship home the Executive remains. One unlucky *Burger* whose grasp of English was on a par with the late President's fluency in German referred to these as the "leftovers" and was bludgeoned to death with strudel.

"Come on, get along wi' ye," said the leprechaun, pounding a walnut-sized fist on the bar. "I've done what ye asked o' me, an' now's the reckoning."

His comrade chuckled until his jowls shook, tiny eyes fixed greedily on the television screen. He ignored his teensy creditor, savoring the moment of triumph. "Only a matter of time now, just a matter of time before the American people get fed up with that Texas clod, and then— Oh, this is rich. *Rich!*"

"Sure, an' a *Berliner's* rich enough fer any man as cares fer jelly donuts. As fer meself, I much prefers a noice slab o' sody bread. *Which I'll be enjoyin' on me own sweet sod soon as a sartin party makes good on his promises,*" the leprechaun said pointedly.

"Here, take it, take it," said his companion, reaching into the bosom of his rumpled suit and producing a pot o' gold the size of a custard cup. "First the gift of his every word becoming real, then tampering with his speech—he never noticed the difference between *Ich bin Berliner* and *Ich bin ein Berliner*, for all his fancy Harvard education! Oh, it's too good, Seamus. You're crookeder than a dog's hind leg."

"Here now!" The leprechaun bridled. "I am not a crook!"

"I intended it as a compliment," his client replied, handing over the gold. "It was wonderful, magnificent, stupendous, astounding—!"

The leprechaun winked. "Piece o' cake, Mr. Nixon."

Ginjer Buchanan has spent her entire professional career in the field of science fiction as an editor. I did a little arm-twisting, and the result is her first sale as a science fiction writer.

Given the number of tragedies that have struck the nine Kennedy brothers and sisters, they must from time to time wonder if God has singled them out for catastrophe. In this offbeat little story, Ginjer suggests a very young, very enthusiastic alternative.

The End of the Summer, by the Great Sea
by Ginjer Buchanan

It was that time, that time of year, that time of life when the single most important thing in the entire wide universe was *to belong*.

But Peri had never belonged, not in the City, the only child of a woman alone, dark of skin and pale of eye in a world of lighter, brighter colors.

Even less did she belong here, at the edge of the Great Sea, in a house that seemed to be made of the purest crystal, a child taken in by the man her mother had chosen. (Say rather: the man who had chosen her mother, with Peri an extra, extraneous part of the deal, like a second nose or a fifth arm.)

Still, she never gave up hope. Perhaps today would be

the day she would swim in the great sea, like a smooth fish, impressing the others, the young ones, with her glides and turns.

(Memory: A scream. Thrashing. Peri, choking, spitting. Pulled from the water, limp and shaking—while the others stood on the hot sand, laughing.)

Still—perhaps today balls would go in nets and over holes. Perhaps . . .

"Puh-leese, Bren! Do we have to?"

"I know, Ro-an. I know. It's like, evil. But my old man and hers got some deal going, and he just says I must!"

"Sooo glad it's you that has to do it, and not me. I mean, I would be truly afraid that the call might get on my permanent file and like come back to haunt me just when I would be about to be crowned Queen of the World!"

"Real soon now." Bren snorted.

The two dissolved into prolonged giggles.

The end of the long, long summer at the edge of the Great Sea. Every year something was planned. Something for the young ones to remember during the equally long winter. An event of consequence, an event for the amusement of those who belonged.

Her mother frowned. "Are you sure, Peri, that you're dressed correctly?"

"Bren said, 'dress warm,'" Fana. I didn't think that meant fur and feathers."

"Peri! There is no need to use that kind of language! I'm only concerned about—well, I just wish I knew exactly what the event was going to be. Then I—we—could be certain . . ."

Peri knew that some of the old ones *did* know. They were the planners and arrangers, after all. Peri also knew that the truth was that Fana, despite the fact that she swam gracefully, and landed each and every ball in its correct place, did not belong. She was more tolerated than Peri, for her beauty, and the fact that she had been chosen. But Fana would never be asked to be a planner and arranger. She would never *know*. Sometimes Peri wondered if she truly realized it.

"It's going to be all night, the event, Bren said. So, well, don't worry or anything. Don't call the Club or anything."

Fana pursed her garnet lips and narrowed her mahogany eyes. "All right. You go on now, Peri dear. You know, your old man and I, we only want you to have a wonderful time. Just, don't—just, watch—well, be careful."

Peri headed down the sand, sparkling golden now in the light of the sun that was setting. "Be careful" meant "Don't trip over your own big feet. Don't spill, or stain, or laugh in the wrong places. Don't ruin the chance, this chance to belong. (Don't ruin *my* chance to belong.)"

She passed little ones, still laboring over intricate sandy constructions; runners, pelting along the golden shore, some followed by shaggy companions. She picked up a shell, pale blue, eight-chambered, the home of some long-gone creature from the Great Sea. She tossed it from hand to hand, then pitched it into the blackened fire pit as she walked by.

(Memory: Crackle of burning driftwood. Voices, off-key voices, raised in old songs, older chants. Peri, edging close, closer to the edge of the group. She takes the bottle being passed from hand to hand to hand. The liquid sweet, too sweet. She drinks, one swallow, another. And the sweet, suddenly sour liquid gushes from her gullet, onto the bare feet of Bren. She squeals, slaps Peri. The others laugh, and laugh even more as Bren says terrible things.)

Peri shivered, and hurried through the gathering dusk, toward the twinkling star that was the Club.

* * *

"Marag, like it's enough, isn't it, that he made me invite her. Now I have to be her partner! I. Will. Die."

"Bren, the pairings were done by blind lot. Your old man thought it the fairest way. You chose amethyst. Peri chose amethyst. That's that."

"Oh, and like he didn't maybe just kind of *help* the choices. Do a little quiet moving. F and F!"

"That's enough, Bren. More than enough." Morag regarded her daughter sternly. "You go and find Peri. Your *partner*, Peri. Now!"

Bren's old man, impeccably groomed, impossibly well-preserved for one who had fathered twenty, was running the event. No surprise there. But it was a surprise to Peri, a pleasant surprise, to find herself partnered with Bren. The luck of the lots, the others said. Luck. People who belonged had luck . . .

"All right, all right, boys and girls." He waved his arms wildly, as though he were splashing happily in the Great Sea. "Let us begin! In front of you, in the very middle of your viewtables, you will see a colored square. Press that magic button!"

Peri sat across from Bren, veiled in a cone of violet light. Through the haze, she could see six other cones dotting the luminescent white of the Club's dance floor. She hesitated, reached out her hand. Bren swept it aside and with one delicate finger firmly pressed the pulsating purple square. The table went dead black, then lightened as glowing purple letters appeared.

"The end of the summer event, boys and girls. A challenge for the mind and the heart. A race. A contest. And a test—of skill and luck!"

"F and F," Bren muttered. "What a hole he is!" Though her skin was a much lighter blue, and her eyes the deepest and most attractive ebony, when she pursed her lips and frowned, she reminded Peri so much of Fana.

"Still, this has, you know, possibilities."

Peri felt waves closing over her head. She blinked rapidly.

Bren tapped the viewtable with a long silver fingernail. "Just the sort of thing my old man would go for. So totally yesterday. But it could be—highly adequate."

Peri opened her mouth, half-expecting a ball to plop into it.

"In the Old Times, they'd play this game in the City. I've heard about it. There was much, much running around, usually after much, much drinking. Collecting stuff. Weird stuff. This is the same thing, only different."

Peri had spent several years trying very hard to have no memories of the Old Times in the City. She scanned the glowing purple words, searching for some clue or hint . . .

URTHOS, 376555. *One of the twelve private guards of Pattrap Poulos.*

GALADA, 527–520M.M. *A sacred fire manster from the innermost temple.*

"All right, all right. Team Scarlet, Goldenrod, Amethyst. Teal, Obsidian, Umber, and Emerald. Each of you have the same list. Each has until both suns rise to collect the six items on the list."

MARS, 6 Prime. *A crew member from the last ship to leave the planet before the great drought.*

MOOZ, 722201–722222 *One of the ten mates of zoraida greychin.*

Whistles of approval greeted the announcement of the prizes for the winners. "Not evil at all!" Bren said. "Almost like being Queen of the World." The old ones had certainly come through!

Peri, who had never even been to the past, felt a nervous thrill at the very thought of the hunt itself, never mind the prizes.

EARTH, 1940–1980. *One of the nine children of jose-phandrose kennedy.*

ANTARES, 42± *A herder from the lazute hill tribe.*

"Boys and girls. Hustle!" Bren's old man clapped his hands. Seven cones of colored light flared and dimmed. Fourteen young ones were no longer *there* on the white luminescent dance floor.

"Galada," Bren announced. "Like, there's a bunch more fire mansters than guards or kennedys."

Peri, her knees fairly atremble as they suddenly were *there* in the sultry quiet of the innermost temple, thought Bren's reasoning made sense.

Except—the fire mansters were sacred, so they were well-protected from any natural enemies. They were also incredibly inbred, slow, stupid, and quite lacking in aggression. Though Bren tried, they could not be moved to attack one another. Of course, it would have been relatively easy to move one to take a long drop from a tall tree, but, as Bren's old man had explained at some length, there were strict rules to the hunt, and strict penalties for breaking them.

Bren was disgusted. "Evil little holes! I'd wish I could . . ."

(Memory: Peri, walking alone along the pale yellow sand. Above her, the jutting deck of one of the biggest and most beautiful of the crystal houses at the edge of the Great Sea. She hears a tinkling giggle, sees a shadow, looks up—and meets a globe filled with foul-smelling liquid face-to-face.)

"Bren—wait!" Bren turned, ebony eyes dangerously dark. Peri swallowed. "See that fat old one sleeping in the shade? And look, at the roof, at the edge. The stones are loose. And there are little ones playing up there . . ."

It was not easy (*so* slow and stupid, even if they were sacred), but it worked. Bren moved (she would not let Peri help) and then quickly caught the life pattern of the old fire manster just as it was squooshed. Peri thought it rather pretty—a kind of drifting smoky red.

"Not evil, Team Amethyst!" Ro-an cheered. Peri fairly glowed under the praise; her indigo cheeks actually felt warm. Bren was less pleased. Team Teal—Ro-an and Nic—had collected not only a fire manster but also a kennedy.

"Like, there's some kind of big huge fighting going on on Earth in one nine four oh, and this kennedy was a soldier . . ."

"An air soldier, Ro," Nic interrupted. "A pilot, or something."

"Whatever. Anyway, he was supposed to do this special super secret mission thing, involving big booms. So we moved this machine person to cross a couple of wires, and—surprise boom!" She giggled.

The life pattern in the translucent globe was green and brown/gold, shooting sparks, constantly in motion. Peri thought the fire mansters far more attractive.

Team Goldenrod appeared. They'd been successful on both Mooz and Urthos. Bren shoved Peri roughly back to the cone of purple light.

"This fighting thing on Earth—if Ro and Nic can collect a kennedy there and then, so can we. Hustle, Missy P!"

"Was I right, or what?" Bren said. Team Amethyst hovered, none too patiently, waiting to move the crew of the ship beneath them to blow another, smaller ship to tiny bits. And on that other ship—their kennedy, ready to be collected!

"Bren, since we're—like—partners, maybe I could help. I could collect. I think . . ."

"Truly, truly. I'll just bet that when you lived in the City your old man, your actual old man, taught you all about moving and collecting. I'll just bet that I'm right about that too, Missy P."

Peri flinched, and dropped toward the Great Sea beneath her. (No, the ocean, the Pacific Ocean.) Bren was ready, steady, ready ...

And Team Goldenrod was suddenly *there*. Bren's concentration wavered—and their kennedy did not go boom satisfactorily.

"You, you *old things!*" Bren shrieked. Peri was impressed by her anger, and interested to see that when she was flushed, she too was almost indigo.

"Don't be evil, Bren. The boat did sink. The kennedy is down there, thrashing around in the Great Sea. So, just, like move a big fish or something to chomp him."

"No. Just—no."

"If you won't, maybe we will."

"Holes! Both of you!"

"Look, Missy B, you would have had your boom if you were a better mover."

"It wasn't Bren that lost it. It was me."

Team Goldenrod seemed to notice Peri for the first time. They laughed.

"That's makes better sense. About what to expect from you, who-knows-where-it's-been or what-it-is!"

"Never mind her." Bren did her best Queen of the World. "Listen, boys and girls, if you collect this kennedy now, I'll make sure my old man calls it a forfeit. Clear?"

"As houses." Team Goldenrod grumbled and was not *there*.

Peri waited, there above the strange sea, waited while she thought that maybe, just maybe, this time her ball had gone in the net. Bren had a very odd expression on her face, her ebony eyes almost opaque. Then she held out her hand. "Hustle, Peri. Team Amethyst to Mars."

On Mars, they collected the ship's navigator easily. Mooz was more fun. When they got *there*, zoraida greychin was already an outcast, said to be under a curse, which fell on her mates, one by one. The latest of them lived in daily terror. Bren actually let Peri do the moving, according to her plan. It was funny to see zoraida grey-chin's expression when her "carelessness" with the cook-fire claimed yet another of her mates (promptly collected by Bren). Team Amethyst giggled together. Now and then, Peri thought, now and then for a moment or two, she forgets who I am, who I'm not. Now and then she treats me as if I belong.

For a brief moment, they were all *there*, on the white luminescent dance floor. Team Teal, lagging after a strong start. Team Scarlet, Shera and Berg, with two fire mansters (no extra credit, but an especially striking life pattern). Team Goldenrod, who had finally collected a kennedy, a female, snatched from yet another exploding plane, after they had moved the pilot to fly directly into a very large mountain. Her globe glowed green and gold too, but the pattern was delicate and strong. It reminded Peri of the webs the iridescent insects spun in the fragrant bushes behind the house of the old man who had chosen her mother.

Team Amethyst was the first to collect a lazute herder. "Eee-ville!" Bren squealed. "I mean, this life pattern is so slimy you can like, feel it almost!" She passed the globe to Peri. "Here, partner, let's lose this, quick-quick!"

Partner. Team Amethyst in the familiar, comfortable cone of violet light. Bren was fairly dancing on the luminescent white floor with the excitement of the hunt.

But Team Scarlet, listlessly tossing a globe from hand to hand to hand, was not interested in their lazute.

"To hustle is to win, to win is to hustle," Bren said, gesturing wildly like her old man. Peri giggled.

Team Scarlet continued to ignore them, until Bren, moving with a grace, such a grace, perfection on land or in the Great Sea, caught the globe in midair.

"What in the names of the oldest of the old ones, is

this?" She held the globe up. Inside, a sickly yellow/green fluid settled to the bottom.

"Even slimier than the lazute," Peri said. Team Scarlet glared at her. (Careful, careful.)

"Well, boys and girls. I'm waiting."

"It's the kennedy Berg collected," Shera muttered.

"Berg collected? *We* collected, Missy S. And now *we* are forfeit!"

"Forfeit?" Nic asked, as Team Teal was suddenly *there*. He took the globe from Bren. "I gotta say, this is one dubious life pattern."

"Was it, like, sick or something?" Team Goldenrod joined in.

Berg and Shera were looking at each other less than happily. Peri could almost smell how they felt. It was a very familiar scent.

"All right, all right, boys and girls!" Bren did her old man again. "Tell all. You know I can find out."

"It's a *she*," Berg said, grabbing the globe from Nic, and shaking it. The green ooze stirred sluggishly. "She had some weird thing wrong in her head, and they were going to fix it and ..."

"This *hole*," Shera burst in, "was supposed to move the fixer to slip, and since the fixing needed very sharp pointy things, I was all set to collect, only the fixer, some stupid colorless biped with only two arms, was too strong for him."

"Don't let's forget the part, Missy S, where you collected, only what you collected was not what you would call your total life pattern, but there was no way to put it back, so we were stuck with it, and it's no good and we're forfeit!" He threw the globe at Shera, who ducked aside. It shattered on the white luminescent floor. Something trickled out slowly, a spreading stain.

"Boys and girls, boys and girls," Bren snickered.

"Completely evil," Ro offered.

"So, Mr. B, how about some moving lessons?" Nic said.

They giggled, the others giggled, Peri too. Team Scarlet flushed indigo, dark eyes hidden. The laughter grew. Peri joined in. She stood with the others and laughed at Shera and Berg.

It felt wonderful.

It was time, near time, time was almost up. Team Amethyst had collected all but their kennedy. Team Goldenrod was missing their lazute. Team Scarlet was forfeit, as was Team Emerald. Team Teal, Team Obsidian, Team Umber—no chance. The race was down to two.

"Hustle, partner. Team Amethyst to Earth."

Peri smiled, a smile that lit her odd pale eyes. "All right, partner. For the purple!"

Night. And fog. And the sound of the Great Sea. (No, the ocean. The Atlantic Ocean.) Peri was floating, a sweet bubble of a giggle caught in her gullet. They—she and Bren, Team Amethyst—were going to be winners! It was so close, all of it, including the prizes. Prizes. New things to wear. Credits of her own, to use for what she wanted. (Can you buy grace? Can you buy a name? No. But you can buy eyes. Ebony eyes, eyes exactly like Bren's.)

"All right, all right. Peri, I move and you collect. Got it? 'Cause if we do get it, we will be, like, Queens of the World!"

"Not evil, Bren." Peri responded. Team Amethyst shook hands and waited.

The vehicle could be heard but not yet seen. Bren was ready to move the driver, Peri to collect. Just as planned. The vehicle went fast, faster. (Bren at work.) The turn, the bridge. No muffled boom, and a very satisfactory major splash.

"Peri! Wait. The kennedy is ..."

The kennedy is collected! Peri thought gaily, as she moved quickly in and out, holding the globe, rising like the steam from the drowning machine. In the dark, in the

Sea (ocean) she heard thrashing. The driver, she supposed. No concern of Team Amethyst!

They stepped out of the violet cone of light onto the luminescent floor. Peri held the globe above her head, in two hands, like some offering to the Oldest of the Old Ones. Heartbeats passed. Time ended. Colored lights brightened, wavered, dimmed, as all the Teams were *there*. Team Goldenrod had their lazute. But Team Amethyst was returned first!

The cones of light winked out and the walls and ceiling winked on. A million billion stars twinkled at Peri and Bren. The others, even Teams Scarlet and Emerald, gathered round. There were hugs and kisses, and more hugs. (Oh, Fana, oh Fana. I did not trip and I did not spill and I laughed in all of the right places!) Peri hugged the globe to her chest with two hands, and reached out to Bren.

"We hustled, partner!" Bren smiled tightly. Peri thought she seemed strangely subdued. Ah well, winning was not that strange for the Brens of the world!

Bren's old man was suddenly there, too, crossing the glowing floor, waving his arms. "All right, all right, boys and girls! What a night, what a contest, what an adventure! Clear the way here, let me get in a hug or two. And make it official." He stepped between Peri and Bren and put arms around each of them. Peri shifted the globe. "And the winners are . . ." He paused, then pushed Peri away. "Girl," he said, pointing at the globe, "what—who— is *that*?"

Puzzled, Peri extended the translucent globe. Inside, the life pattern swirled, pastel pink, cloud-like, shot with pearly highlights. It was a she, but whoever she was, she was not a kennedy.

"I *told* her!" Bren said. "I told her the *passenger*, not the *driver*. But, like, she just got it all wrong. I mean, what can you expect from who knows where, who knows what?"

Bren's old man took the globe from Peri. "What's done is done. Team Amethyst is forfeit. The winner is Team Goldenrod!"

Peri walked slowly along the sand. Both suns were up now, and the Great Sea was already sparkling with points of light. In her mind, she said *You lied, Bren. You cheated. You tried to cheat.* But she knew that her answer would only be laughter, as deep as the sea, as long as the summer, as dark as ebony eyes.

Hugo and Nebula winner George Alec Effinger has excelled in a wide range of science fiction, from such famous and masterful novels as *When Gravity Fails* and *A Fire in the Sun* to his hilarious parodies of the field starring the one and only Maureen Birnbaum, Barbarian Swordsperson.

The one thing you can count on in an Effinger story is that it has never been told before. For example, who but George, when casting about for a Kennedy to write about, would hit upon Patrick Bouvier Kennedy, the son who died in infancy during JFK's presidency/

George grows him up and examines the path his life might have taken—with a tip of the hat to William Shakespeare.

Prince Pat
by George Alec Effinger

It was early in January in the magically numbered year 2000, the final year of the twentieth century, less than twelve months before the dawn of the twenty-first. In a large room in New York City's Carlyle Hotel, the same hotel where President John F. Kennedy had once kept a suite for himself, the Democratic party's kingmakers were meeting in urgent and desperate secrecy.

As a matter of fact, it had been quite some time since the party's kingmakers had actually *made* a king. If one considered Jimmy Carter a political aberration, a statistical fluctuation—and at the time of his presidency many people did—then the Republicans had owned the White House for almost two generations.

Meanwhile, some distance from the Carlyle Hotel down on the wintry street level, long-time political analyst Robert L. Jennings swore under his breath and stepped into the street to move around a clutch of tourists who were sluggishly gawking at all the tall buildings. He was frantically trying to traverse midtown Manhattan on foot during lunch hour. Attempting to keep up with Jennings was network news director Charles Harp, who had a number of questions to ask before they arrived at Jennings's favorite Italian restaurant at 59th and Lex. There would be plenty of reporters from his own network and others there, but Harp was after some exclusive information.

"So why," he asked, "hasn't the Democratic party been able to win the White House for so many years?"

"Simple answer, really," said Jennings, his breath making white puffs in the frigid air. "Years ago, the Democrats alienated their traditional power base. The Democrats had customarily been the party that united the poor and the middle classes. About the time of the first Ronald Reagan campaign, they lost the support of the middle class, which allied itself with the rich for the first time in recent memory. The Democrats, previously know as the party of the little guy, had endorsed policies which the middle class interpreted as taking money away from it, and giving it to the minority poor, who did not cast sufficient ballots."

Thanks for nothing, thought Harp, nearly ramming into a burly pedestrian who decided at the last instant to dodge in the same direction that Harp chose. *Let's try again.* "Now the growing feeling is that the Republican party may be in trouble, that it hasn't yet grasped the significance of the country's current demographic mix. It hasn't responded to the great growth of the Hispanic population, or the increased importance of the vote of Americans of Far Eastern ancestry, for two examples."

"I wouldn't disagree with any of that."

"So," Harp continued, "even though President Baker is just finishing up his first term in office, some of the high-level Democratic party strategists feel he's vulnerable, and that his re election is not a foregone conclusion."

They stopped for traffic at a crowded intersection, and Jennings took the opportunity to spell out his favorite personal theory. "The Republicans have occupied the White House from Richard Nixon's first election in 1968 through Gerald Ford, Ronald Reagan, George Bush, and the incumbent James Baker, finishing up his first term now in 2000. That's thirty-two years, minus the four-year Carter interregnum. Most unbiased political writers feel that's a long time for one party to be in power."

"In all those years," said Harp, stepping off the curb into the ankle-deep slush just before the traffic light changed, "the Democrats haven't even put up a good fight."

"They haven't put up a good candidate, that's the truth of the matter."

"Depending on how you feel about Humphrey, Carter, Dukakis, Clinton, and Matsunaga," said Harp. He paused to consider his next question. "The scandals attached to Baker's closest political and private connections, as well as to his staff members and appointees, may make his bid for reelection problematical. Also, while his foreign policy has been unassailable, his domestic programs have been disastrous. Do you think all that might add up to a Democratic victory in November?"

Jennings shrugged. They'd arrived at the restaurant. "Forget the clams here, but do try the veal parm. It's the best in the city."

"Pardon me?" said Harp.

Jennings waved in a dismissive manner. "I suppose the Democrats' task force believes that with the right ticket and a carefully written platform, they just might be able to wrest the Oval Office from the Republicans' decades-long grasp—but of course, they think so every fourth year. That's all I want to say about the situation. Let's go in where it's warm."

There were indeed a large number of print reporters and electronic media crews inside the restaurant. The reason for their presence was the appearance of quite a few members of the Kennedy family, some of whom hadn't been publicly visible in quite some time. It had been promised that the Kennedys would make themselves available to the press, but first they took the opportunity to hold a family meeting in one of the restaurant's private rooms.

Advising the Kennedys was the National Chairman of the Democratic party, Roslyn Carter. While she waited for the Kennedy family games and raucousness to calm down, she thought about what she'd say, and about the wisdom of their mutual decision. To beat James Baker, to defeat an incumbent president, the Democrats needed a special candidate. The Kennedy name had been tarnished by the revisionists—but there was still one Kennedy who could make the voters sit up and take notice.

He had been born while his father was in the White House, and had spent the first four months of his life in an incubator. The hourly bulletins concerning his condition were read and listened to around the world, and when he finally took his first unaided breath, it was as if he had two hundred million surrogate parents across the country who were as thrilled as John and Jackie were. His weakened condition had caused him to come down with every childhood disease, bar none, and he was three before his spindly legs were strong enough to carry him across the room without giving way . . . and two hundred million Americans lent him their spiritual strength as he overcame each obstacle that Fate had placed in his way.

This was no typical Kennedy, born with a silver spoon in his mouth, possessed of an almost unnatural health and vigor, this Patrick Bouvier Kennedy. This was a child who had to fight for every inch, who overcame enormous obstacles just to achieve normalcy ... and once he had achieved it, he left it far behind, gradually building his body to the point where he made the Yale football team. He wasn't big enough or strong enough to start—in point of fact, he was on the playing field for exactly eleven minutes during his four years as an undergraduate—but the public not only forgave him for this, they loved him all the more for it. Like his father before him, he'd sown his share of wild oats—but unlike his father, he had been completely discreet, and once he married Ruth, at age twenty-four, those days were forever behind him. It was when he passed his bar exams the first time, the same ones his older brother had flunked twice before passing, that it was acknowledged that should *any* Kennedy ever run for the nation's highest office, Patrick was the undisputed front-runner. The press had labeled him "The People's Kennedy" since the day he had first run for Congress at the age of twenty-five, and won by a landslide.

All three of Jack's children had shown up for the meeting, and there was a good turnout of Bobby's and Teddy's, but most of those sets were examining their silverware or trying to get the attention of the waiters. In addition, there were plenty of Shrivers, Townsends, Cuomos, Lawfords, Giffords, Smiths, and other collateral cousins present, but they weren't paying any closer attention. Aunt Rosemary's eldest daughter, Rose, started tossing rolls at the others as if she were still back at Wellesley, while Patrick, sitting in a corner with his wife, looked on the whole scene with the mild distaste of someone who'd been made to sit through the same entertainment too many times.

"Our candidate's had his fun," began Maria Shriver.

"As have we all," said Uncle Bobby's son, Edward. Everyone at the meeting laughed, some uncomfortably.

"But he's never been touched by scandal, and that's crucially important," said Paul Lawford.

"It's January of an election year," said Uncle Ted. "Not

even our potential candidate knew our plans. I firmly believe that he *still* doesn't know what we intend for him."

"Then it's about time he learned the truth," said Jacqueline Bouvier Kennedy Onassis, widow of both John F. Kennedy and Aristotle Onassis.

"Who do you all mean?" asked Uncle Ted's daughter, Bridget. "Who are you talking about?"

Paul Lawford laughed. "All right, it feels like an awards-show atmosphere, anyway. So the winner is—"

"Patrick Bouvier Kennedy, congressman from the great state of New York!" proclaimed Maria Shriver.

When his name was announced, Pat looked surprised and confused. He turned to his wife, Ruth, and said, "No, I won't have any part of it."

"We'll talk to you," said Uncle Ted. Everyone understood that the elder Kennedys would apply sufficient pressure that young Pat would be given little choice. He wouldn't even have a say in the matter.

Former First Lady Roslyn Carter realized that even though she was now party chairman, this back-room affair was primarily a family gathering. She was content to let the family speak for her. Jacqueline was the first to remark that Pat had matured, that he was no longer the fun-seeking son she'd watched grow up. Next, Uncle Ted pointed out that although he was only thirty-six years old, he was already the most popular and trusted of the Kennedys, and that he owed something to the memory of his father and his late uncle, and to the Democratic party, and to the electorate of the United States of America.

One by one, Pat's uncles and aunts spoke of where he had come from, who he was, and what he owed both his family and his country. Mostly, though, they argued forcefully that he was *electable*.

"Well, Pat?" asked Uncle Ted when each member of the family had spoken.

"I don't know if I can do it, Uncle Ted," said the young

man. "It's something I've never considered, not even for a moment."

Ted Kennedy put his hand on Pat's shoulder. "It's your time, Pat. And you'll have all the rest of this gigantic family helping you, as well as the resources of the party, which are not inconsiderable."

They talked some more, and finally Pat went back to his seat beside Ruth, a grim and worried expression on his face. In contrast, Uncle Ted raised a glass. "I give you a toast," he announced. "To the next President of the United States!"

Pat's brother John stood up and raised his glass. "To Prince Pat!" he said joyously. One by one, everyone got to his feet and joined in the toast.

The last to rise was Pat himself, but he did get up, and his acceptance of the family's support marked a change in him and a change in the Kennedys, too. It had been many years since they'd felt a sense of direction. "Thank you, Uncle Ted and John, for the toast. As you know, for years I've tried to keep in the background. Now, though, as unprepared as I feel for the huge job you ask of me, I'm honored and flattered and I feel the challenge deep in my heart. I want what you all want, and I'll do all I can to get us there."

"Look out, world!" said Uncle Ted's daughter, Siobhan. "The Kennedys are back!"

"The hell with the rest of the world!" said Aunt Rosemary's son, P.J. "I'd just like to be there when the *Republicans* find out!"

Pat held a meeting a few weeks later with his "Gang of Ten," as he called it, made up of himself, his brother and sister, his cousin Joe, Aunt Rosemary's son P.J., and Maria Shriver, who'd volunteered to represent him to the media. Uncle Ted was usually present as well, to offer the experience of his years of political infighting. Pat also relied on advice from three friends from his Yale years, Nate

Platt, Molly Kelly McCarthy, and Maurice Gonzales. Then, finally, when each meeting came to an end, Pat would go home and talk everything over with Ruth. At the kitchen table with her—that's where the genuine decision-making happened.

"I'll tell you one thing we're not going to have this time around," said P.J. earnestly. "We're not going to let the Republicans make us look like fools. We're not going to let them whip up some racist or sexist image that frightens away our voters."

"Not without a quick and honest response that exposes it as a fraud," said Gonzales. "When I was younger, I watched Ronald Reagan invent the 'welfare queen.' Our party sat on its collective ass, bewildered, and let him get away with it. I watched George Bush use that picture of— what was his name? Horton?—and again the Democrats couldn't defend themselves."

"That's when I realized how dirty a business politics really is," said Molly Kelly McCarthy. "That's when my youthful idealism died. When the Democrats let them get away with that."

"It's a very complicated issue, Molly," said Uncle Ted. "You can't—"

"You sure as hell can," said Pat, slamming his fist on the meeting-room table. "And I sure as hell will. No more of this 'Well, the Democrats are gonna give all this money to crack-dealing, gun-toting, shiftless scum who ain't nothing like you, but they gonna make you pay for it.' No, sir. We're not going to be packaged and sold, because when you start listening to the Madison Avenue guys, you start worrying about alienating this part of the voting public, or that part of the voting public. The next thing you know, you've sold away your ideals and your goals, and you just pray to God that you don't smell too bad."

"Democrats been smellin' bad for a long time," said Platt. "Even with the pretty packaging. You know the only time I ever seen a TV ad for a presidential candidate that *really* influenced me? It was more'n twenty years after the campaign, too. I watched it in a poli-sci class at Yale. Professor Lester, y'all remember him? It was the one Lyndon Johnson's media crew came up with, the spot with the little girl plucking petals off a daisy, and this cold voice counting down from ten.

"It really made the point that Barry Goldwater was a hawk, but the spot stirred up such a mess, they only ran it once and then pulled it. Never seen anything like that lately, not for power and persuasion on a gut level. Like Pat says, everybody's too afraid of turning off the blacks or the Hispanics or the Orientals or the gays or the Native Americans or the farmers or the blue-collar workers. So nothing gets said. Basically you sit on your thumbs and concede the football field to the other team. You can't score points if the opposition's got the ball all the time."

Uncle Ted stood up and started to pace. "I'm sorry, Nate," he said, "but you're all oversimplifying. In the days when you made speeches off the backs of trucks and trains it was one thing. Shaking hands with a thousand people and putting on an Indian war bonnet. It's not like that anymore, and you have to be right up to the minute with both your technology and your demographic analysis."

Pat looked furious. "The hell with your demographic analysis," he said in a quiet voice. "How far has it gotten the Democratic party since Lyndon Johnson? You want to get personal? What has it done for our family?"

Uncle Ted stopped suddenly and spun around, and for a moment the room was filled with tension.

"Hey," said Molly Kelly McCarthy, trying to defuse the situation. "Are we going to let the presidential nomination go down the tubes because of a little generation-gap thing?"

"He shouldn't have said—" Uncle Ted began.

Pat closed his eyes for a moment, then opened them again, "Uncle Ted, I'm sorry. I'm *truly* sorry. You've got to know that no one has more love and respect for my father, for Uncle Bobby, and for you than I do. I never for an instant intended to dishonor them or you. But the rules of national politics have changed, and maybe the reason the Democratic party has failed—has *failed*—is that it hasn't changed as well. Maybe it's time for a candidate to say what he believes, without being terrified that some fragment of the electorate will be offended."

"It sounds good," said Uncle Ted, "but it won't work. It *can't* work."

"I think I need a drink," said Pat. "Can I get something for anybody else?"

"Why *can't* it work, Uncle Ted?" asked Caroline.

Maria Shriver looked excited. "I think I understand how political attitudes would have prevented such a candidate from even getting nominated. Still, I like the idea. I like the challenge of getting that candidate's message across to the voters."

"And anyway," said Mary Kelly McCarthy, "wouldn't it be neat if, just once, some candidate would drop the pose and the carefully groomed look and the well-rehearsed responses, and say, 'Here I am. Here's what I think. Take it or leave it. But I want you all to know one thing: The other guys are trying to sell you a pig in a poke.' I'd like to have the chance to decide for myself, not wait for the surprises that happen after election day."

"It can't work," repeated Uncle Ted, shaking his head. "National politics is too big, too complicated."

Joe let out a deep breath. "We're just saying that maybe it doesn't *have* to be that way. That the person who ends up in the Oval Office doesn't have to be stamped '100% non-nutritive crude fiber.'"

"Maybe we should rent a truck and meet some people," said Platt. "One thing we got going for us is Pat himself. When he says he believes something, you know he ain't lyin'. So if he makes a speech to a group of Hispanics or Vietnamese or whatever—"

"Don't forget whites," said John Jr., smiling. "We still have some whites around, and they still vote, too."

"Yeah, you're right," said Platt, laughing. "What I meant was, we got ourselves a good candidate in Pat, a good symbol for the party."

Uncle Ted slammed his hand down. "Damn it, don't you see? That kind of politics went out with Huey Long. It doesn't *work* that way anymore. Now the nominees are chosen in independent primaries in states where you've spent maybe eight hours, if you're lucky. People will base their voting decisions on what they *think* you might say or do, or on what their downstairs neighbor believes about you, or according to some headline they glimpsed in a supermarket. So you have to manage everything with excruciating precision. You've got to have a gigantic machine working for you, because you can't be everywhere at once. You've got to build that machine and get it working, and in order to do that you can't afford to alienate the campaign workers, and that's months before the nominating convention, which is months before the actual election." He stopped and rubbed his forehead. "I'm trying to help you with the hard stuff," he said, "but you act as if you just don't want to hear it."

"We *do* appreciate all you're doing, Uncle Ted," said Pat. "And we're listening to everything you have to say. I just feel that the system hasn't been working for us, so maybe it wouldn't hurt to tinker a little with the system."

"And you're neglecting the possibilities of modern technology, Uncle Ted," said Maria Shriver. "You're not giving us credit where credit is due."

Ted Kennedy took a few deep breaths and forced himself to calm down a bit. "Yeah, okay, maybe you're right," he said to Maria. "Maybe it's the great Year 2000, and somewhere along the line I've lost touch. Maybe I belong in a museum somewhere, beside the last passenger pigeon. Still, I don't like to be told that everything I've learned, everything I know, all of that is wrong and that

I don't fit in anymore. That I'm useless. That I'm someone to laugh at when he leaves the room."

There was a horrible quiet in the room until Pat said, "Then it's a good thing that I didn't remind you what happened to Huey Long. I mean, *you* brought him up first." Caroline's eyes opened wider, and she turned to see how her uncle would respond. Uncle Ted sat up straight, then collapsed in laughter. It was the old Kennedy family laughter. It made everyone feel good to hear it again.

At what had been known for decades as "The Kennedy Compound" in Hyannis, it was time for another strategy session. The Gang of Ten acknowledged that they'd gotten off to a late start, and consequently missed the Iowa caucuses. Their two main opponents, at least this early in the campaign, were Arizona Senator Dennis DeConcini and Minnesota Congressman Hubert Horatio "Skip" Humphrey III.

"We can count on their campaigns to be slick and professional," said Molly Kelly McCarthy. "They're both experienced and well managed—"

"*Packaged,*" corrected Caroline.

McCarthy shrugged. "Just because we voiced a distaste for media packaging doesn't mean it doesn't work. It's something we'll have to overcome, and we're late already. Pat hasn't even given a major speech announcing his decision to run for the office, and he'd better do it soon. The New Hampshire primary is coming up fast."

Pat leaned back in his chair. "I know when I'll do it," he said.

"When?" asked Nate Platt. "And where?"

"In Chicago," said Pat. "Next Wednesday. Late afternoon. I've already scheduled a news conference in the Hyatt downtown."

P.J. laughed. "Forgive me for asking, but why next Wednesday, and why Chicago, of all places?"

" 'Cause I'm gonna be there anyway," said Pat. "Flying there to watch the Cubs play the Mets at a special local charity exhibition. I pulled a string and got a pass to sit in the Cubs' dugout. Always wanted to do that."

"You live in New York and you're going to root against the Mets?" asked Uncle Ted. "You could lose the New York vote. Are you sure that's prudent?"

Pat smiled broadly. "But I'll pick up the Chicago vote, which is pretty big itself. And the Cubs are on cable during the day."

Uncle Ted just shrugged. "There was a time when we were all Red Sox fans."

"Was a time when they didn't have no designated hitter, either," said Platt.

"Let's get serious," said Maurice Gonzales. "It's about time you picked one person to be your campaign manager. Who's it going to be?"

Pat turned to his right, toward his cousin. "Joe?"

Joe opened his mouth and closed it again. "I'd be honored, of course," he said. "Why me?"

"I'll tell you why," said Pat. "A thousand people are going to ask why, if there had to be a Kennedy in the race, it wasn't you, or John. You go ahead and field that one for me. I don't want to deal with it. I don't know what makes me more qualified to lead the country than you."

"You think *I* do?" asked Joe. "I have my own aspirations, you know."

"Wait your turn," said Uncle Ted. "We've got it all mapped out."

"That's the one thing I hate about this family," said Molly. "The way everybody and everything is always 'all mapped out.' "

"It's our greatest strength and the source of our weakness," said P.J. "You'll get the hang of it."

Hyannis staff members came in with platters of sandwiches and beverages. Joe grabbed a sandwich off the top of the pile. "You ask me to be your campaign manager, but you didn't even think that I might've wanted to sit beside you in the dugout. Goddamn!"

"Next time, Joe," said Pat easily. "When I drop into the broadcast booth, you'll be there, too."

"All right," said Joe, mollified. "As long as I get introduced first. I'm older, I'm better-looking, and we've got to start thinking about *my* bid for the White House."

"Not for eight years, Joe," said Pat confidently. He grabbed a sandwich, too.

Uncle Ted gave Pat some last-minute advice. "Make sure they see you eat a hot dog at the ballgame. And later on, some pierogies in an old neighborhood. And Chicago-style pizza."

"Wasn't it you who told me that kind of politics had gone out with Huey Long?" asked Pat.

Uncle Ted smiled. "Some things never change," he said. "Especially in Boston, New York, and Chicago. Now, go make that speech. I'll hover around for whatever good it will do."

"I appreciate it, Uncle Ted. I really do."

"Hell," said the senator, "we've got to get the White House back, so we can watch your wife and your mother fight over the redecorating."

"Oh, brother," muttered Pat. That was a nightmare he hadn't even thought of before.

Pat gave his first big speech just when he'd planned, after the Cubs smacked the Mets, 5–2 in "the friendly confines" of Wrigley Field. It was a fine speech, and the assembled reporters were receptive. It made good news to have a Kennedy in a presidential race again, and while there'd been rumors for a few weeks, no one connected to the family would confirm or deny.

In Chicago, Pat spoke directly to the people, not to the reporters and media crews. He spoke about wanting to get American back, the *idea* of America. He said that after years of cynicism and then cold pragmatism, it was time for a return to idealism. It was time for the young volunteers to get excited again. It was time for the retired voters to feel that they were a part of the decision-making system again. Pat spoke about working to *in*clude, not to systematically *ex*clude.

And then he told them what he felt. "I'm going to start out with the toughest question first," he said. "Abortion. Most other candidates won't even waltz around the subject. Here's where I stand on the matter. I am a member of the Roman Catholic Church, as was my father before me. I personally do not believe in the rightness of abortion. However. *However,* I also do not believe that anyone has the right to say yea or nay to a woman, that the decision concerning her choice is her own to make, and I will defend to the very end her right to make it. Even if her ultimate decision goes against my personal beliefs."

Cameras clicked in the hotel's meeting room. There were murmurs, some shocked, some very surprised, some angry, some pleased. No one said a word. They all waited for Pat to continue, and he did by detailing his feelings on a number of other important subjects. He concluded by saying, "I'll be the first to admit that I don't know absolutely everything about every crisis or conflict in this great nation of ours. I don't believe any single person can anymore. I'd like to acknowledge the support and advice of my Uncle Ted, who's helped me put together a first-rate advisory committee, so that I'll always be kept informed of what I need to know to perform my executive duties.

"If you remember the ancient stories of Arthurian legend, after the fall of Camelot King Arthur did not die, but was taken away to the Isle of Avalon, where he would sleep away the years until he was needed again. This, then, is the restoration of Camelot, the return from Avalon."

When he finished, the hardened, heard-it-all-before news correspondents stood up and cheered him.

And he hadn't eaten a single pierogi.

After the New Hampshire primary, which Pat took by a large margin, the press realized that the Chicago speech had been better than good: It had been *great*. And the phrase "Return from Avalon" had become the theme of his movement. Pat—with the other members of the Gang of Ten—had succeeded in giving his whole campaign a definite direction. The volunteer workers and voters of all descriptions *were* becoming excited, as they hadn't been in many years.

Nevertheless, some of President Baker's advisors refused to take Pat seriously. They expected to face De-Concini or, perhaps, Humphrey in November. They thought Patrick Kennedy too young, too inexperienced, too politically eccentric to be successful. One of Baker's staff members, someone so far down as to have no actual political influence, made a horrible mistake. Acting on a moment's whimsy, he purchased a racquetball racquet and sent it to Pat, with a note saying that Kennedy would be better advised to give up the difficult and hopeless presidential campaign, and get some exercise to keep his tummy flat.

"Let's get this in the newspapers," said Joe, outraged. He threw the racquet across the room in the suite at the Carlyle Hotel.

"No," said Pat. "That would make us look as if we're desperate for positive ink. We can't respond in kind. It would be completely against what I'm telling them I stand for."

"All right," said Caroline, just as angry as Joe, "I know you too well. You *are* going to do something. What do you have in mind?"

Pat allowed himself an evil grin. He walked across the room and retrieved the racquet. "I'm going to send this

back to them with a note. I'm going to write, 'Thank you
guys very much, but at Yale, racquetball was for wimps
who couldn't handle squash.' "

"Great!" said Nate Platt.

"I'll go along with that," said Molly Kelly McCarthy.

"And *then* we get the whole story into the news," said
Pat.

They all laughed. There was a lot of laughter at these
sessions. Running a campaign was an impossible amount
of work, but the ten of them were enjoying it immensely.
It did not hurt their mood that Pat began rising in the
pre-election polls, a trend that continued right up to the
national convention in August.

The Democratic National Convention was held in New
Orleans in 2000, in the Louisiana Superdome, still the
world's largest stadium. That fact hadn't had much influence on the party. What *had* influenced them was how
much fun the Republicans had had when they'd held their
national convention in the town in 1988.

Pat had warned them, but the on-site, behind-the-
scenes, back-room intrigues were more intense and more
dismaying than he'd ever believed. Delegates were
swapped like baseball cards. Last-minute deals were put
together that committed both sides for a decade or more
down the road. It all had an atmosphere of flesh-peddling
or patent-medicine-hawking, and Pat didn't like it at all.
Uncle Ted was there to guide him, though, and the elder
Kennedy said again and again that however much Pat
might not approve of what went on, it was absolutely vital
to jump into it and "keep their asses covered."

Pat spent most of his time in his Gang of Ten command center in the hotel connected to the Superdome,
while Uncle Ted, Joe, Maria, and Nate did the dirty work.
Meanwhile, John Jr., Caroline, and P.J. wandered about;
their job was to attract attention and make people "think
Kennedy." Molly Kelly McCarthy and Maurice Gonzales

were unknown to the press or to the other people on the convention floor wearing badges, and so were able to make quick progress from one state's delegation to another, making notes of who was locked in and who was still undecided.

The first and largest deal was engineered by Uncle Ted and Maria. Together they strolled in an apparently aimless path toward the Texas delegation. Texas represented the fourth-largest block of electoral votes, after California, New York, and Florida. What was so significant about the Texas delegation was that it hadn't yet been committed; the big bundle of electoral votes was still up for grabs. Uncle Ted and Maria Shriver went straight to the chairman of the delegation, retired Texas Governor Ann Richards, and started to charm her unmercifully. Richards, however, knew precisely why they were there. She had no illusions.

She cut Uncle Ted off in the middle of a rambling anecdote. "After our primary, we were committed to Christian Hunt, who, I'm sure you know, passed away a few weeks ago. So our delegates are free to make up their own minds. Here's what I say: You put a woman on the ticket, and I'll deliver the state's electoral votes to you."

"You just wait a second," said Maria. She plucked her small radio telephone from her belt and dialed Pat's secret number in the hotel room.

"Yeah?" he said impatiently.

"Here's how it stands," she said. "Ann Richards is prepared to hand over all of Texas' electoral votes, on the condition that you add a woman to the ticket. Who do we have on the short list?"

"No problem for me," said Pat. "I've been considering Louisiana Governor Channing Fouchet anyway. She comes from a strong political family—her father was a popular city assessor in New Orleans. She's got a solid background herself on the state level—state senator, lieutenant governor, then governor. She's physically attractive, which shouldn't be a qualification, but Uncle Ted will tell you it is, nevertheless. She's extremely bright, outgoing, and well spoken. As I said, the deal presents no problem for me."

"You just wait a minute," said Maria. She nodded to Ann Richards. "He says it's fine with him, too. He's thinking of Channing Fouchet."

Richards frowned. "Channing and I have been friends for years. I just wonder: Is Mary known that well outside of the Deep South?"

"By November we'll *make* her known, if we need to," said Uncle Ted. "That's what politics is all about."

"All right by me, then," said Richards. "Far as I'm concerned, it's a done deal."

Maria spoke again into her radio phone. "Pat? She says everything's set. You can count on the Texas bloc of votes."

"Wonderful, Maria. Thank Uncle Ted and Ann for me. Now I've got to locate Channing Fouchet and find out how interested she is in running for Vice President. And then I've got a million other things to do. I want to be there for Governor Bill Bradley's keynote speech. I've been an admirer of his since his days as a Senator from New Jersey. And I've watched hours of films from his playing days with the Knicks."

Maria Shriver made an impatient sound. "I'll convey your agreement to Richards," she said.

"Thanks ag—" Pat, the family's prince, the presidential hopeful, had been cut off by his own cousin.

After Pat won the Democratic party's nomination for President on the second ballot, the difficult work began in earnest. There were more months of tough campaigning; constant traveling which Pat and some of the others hated, but all had to endure; daily interviews that left him both physically and mentally exhausted by early evening; necessary separations from his wife, Ruth, that caused them both emotional pain; frequent meetings to redefine one plank or another in their platform; more deals; more demands for compromise which Pat resisted as much as possible.

Help from the Gang of Ten was often complete and ready before he even asked for it; they'd learned to think like Pat, to form ideas similarly and work as a unit that functioned with a simultaneity of an almost supernatural nature. Pat could rely on the Gang, on the family, on his old friends and political colleagues. He had, as promised, the resources of the entire Democratic party at his disposal. Still, the weeks leading up to the election were wearying beyond his imagining. On some bad days, he told Ruth that he wished he could just quit. He just wanted it all to be over, even if it meant his final failure.

The night before the election in November everything changed. While all around him there was anxiety and even hysteria, his own frame of mind became ever calmer. He found a wellspring of courage within him that overcame his doubts and temporary weaknesses. It was his mother, Jacqueline, who took him aside and told him that she'd never had any qualms about his candidacy, even though others of his generation might have had more political experience. "It has something to do with being a Kennedy," she said. "A *great* Kennedy, like your father, like your Uncle Bobby. There are literally dozens of family members roughly your own age, yet few besides you would ever be put in that class. A *Kennedy*." It was a serious responsibility, but it was also a unique honor. It was enough to see him through the next difficult twenty-four hours.

On the eve of the November election, Pat found it impossible to relax. Late at night, he went out and passed by groups of campaign workers in New York City. He planned to watch the returns the next day at home with

Ruth and his children and a number of his Gang of Ten and other Kennedy family members.

The volunteer workers, too, were extremely tired. It was near midnight and they had gone without sleep for many hours; but the personal contact with their candidate and his heartfelt thanks lifted their spirits. He also dropped in to see press representatives from all over the world.

"You know," said Charles Zewe, "the Republicans still feel that you're too young and inexperienced to make a viable candidate. With an incumbent President as their candidate, they're predicting a tremendous landslide victory. They've told us that the election itself will be the bloodiest, most lopsided race in American history. They've even suggested, only half in jest, that you concede now and prevent your humiliation tomorrow."

Pat laughed without humor. "I've just been out to give some encouragement to my volunteer workers. I told them that it was going to be a long night, and that the clock would move with unnatural slowness. I praised their labor on my behalf, and called them brothers and sisters, friends, and countrymen. I tried to hide my own worry and weariness, and put on the Kennedy confidence and cheerfulness."

"Did it work?" asked Harp.

"Every time," said Pat with a rueful smile. "I left them comforted and confident. Now if only someone would do the same for me."

"Go back home to Ruthie. You've got a sizable support group. You shouldn't be afraid."

"But I am."

Harp shrugged. "I know. I guess that's inevitable. Well, best of luck tomorrow."

"Thanks, Charlie. One thing, one favor."

"We'll see."

"Don't write me off too soon. I'll have my immediate family watching, and I'm standing in for my father and my uncles. Don't make me into a ridiculous figure."

Harp nodded. "You have my promise, but it's only good for my network, you know. I'll see if I can bully some of the others. I'll do my best for you, keeping in mind that I have to stay objective about it all, and that my reporters have to, too."

"I understand," said Pat. He reached out and shook Harp's hand. "Good night, Charlie."

The network news director laughed. "Not tonight, Pat, but I appreciate the wish. Good night to you, too."

Pat nodded. Then he went out to ride home.

Early the next morning, Pat got out of bed and took a shower, as usual. He continued to follow his daily routine—shaving, brushing his teeth, dressing, eating a light breakfast, scanning a stack of newspapers. Finally, the others began to assemble. His brother and sister arrived first, together. Then came Uncle Ted and some of the Gang of Ten and some of his close relatives. The rest rang Pat's doorbell every few minutes until they were all present. Ruth, Caroline, and Siobhan worked furiously with the kitchen staff to provide food for the horde. Pat sat alone amidst the nervous excitement, remembering his mother's words to him at the nominating convention, and experiencing an odd yet pleasurable peace.

"Well," said Joe, "what's going to happen today?"

"I'll tell you,' said Pat. "Years from now, those of us who've put in so many long hours, and our skillful and unparalleled campaign workers, will look back on this election. I predict each and every one them will say, 'You know, I was there when Pat Kennedy beat James Baker. I was manning the phones, or managing the press liaison,' or whatever. As the years go by, the deeds of people grown old get forgotten; but each year at election time, our crowd will remember, with added glory, what they accomplished today. The old folks will teach the young, and this election day will never be forgotten. We'll be remembered with astonishment. We few, we happy few, we great throng of brothers and sisters—within the family and without—will have much to recall. And those who didn't bother to participate will regret it to their dying days, that they weren't here with us, or at election headquarters, or at any of the other vital places. Today will be a momentous day in American history, and those who couldn't be bothered to help will hold themselves cheap when any of our workers tells how he helped us out on election day."

"Sounds pretty confident," said Molly Kelly McCarthy.

Pat smiled. "I am."

"Then you haven't seen or heard the polls," she said. "They all predict a huge Republican victory."

"Can I get coffee for anyone?" asked Pat. In a little while Nate turned on the television.

Soon after James Baker conceded defeat, Pat went to the Carlyle Hotel to make his acceptance speech and publicly thank his exhilarated campaign workers. He stood at a podium with his wife, Ruth, their children, and Uncle Ted, Jacqueline, Caroline and John Jr.

"Sometimes it's easier to be a gracious winner of a presidential race than a gracious loser," he began.

"I would've liked to discover that for myself," said Uncle Ted. There was loud laughter.

Pat went on. "First, I have to say that today's victory couldn't have been possible at all without the generous and unquestioning efforts of my campaign workers." Those in the Carlyle ballroom cheered long and loud. Pat waited patiently. "Second, I want to say that I hope I've made it clear that I have only the greatest respect for James Baker, and that he's set a precedent for me to live up to. Nevertheless, I have my own agenda, and I also hope that most of you know what's on it."

Pat waited for the applause to fade away. "I need to make it clear that my agenda cannot hope to succeed unless I have the cooperation of the other party. I've gotten to know President Baker, and I think he'll pass the word along that some of my ideas are worth supporting. What I'm trying to say is that I truly hope that we can grow beyond partisan politics and put America first. There's a lot that needs fixing. Let's fix those things, and not worry about whether the tasks benefit one party or the other. This has been a recurring theme in my campaign, and it wasn't just campaign rhetoric. I'm holding out my hand, not only to the Democrats, but also to the Republicans. I think we can work together and forget the distraction of partisan interests."

Pat spoke some more, and when he finished he made no self-congratulatory gestures. He merely thanked everyone again, smiled, and left the podium. It was for his sister, Caroline, to go to the microphone and say, "Yes, this is the Return from Avalon. Camelot is rebuilt. And Patrick Bouvier Kennedy will prove to be the ideal of what an American President should be."

After the cheering stopped, there were parties that lasted into the early hours of the morning. And everyone at those parties knew that Caroline had spoken truly.

Prince Pat had been crowned king.

I asked the book's editor for permission to append a short explanation of what I was attempting to do in "Prince Pat." As some readers may have recognized, the story is a parallel version of Shakespeare's *Henry V*, whom at least one critic called "Shakespeare's only hero." *Henry V* is my favorite play by Shakespeare, and what it's about is the change of Prince Hal, a drinking, gambling, wenching young man, into King Henry, the ideal British monarch. Some of the play's vital scenes are represented here, as well as two or three of the famous speeches. The major portion of the story, however, consists of character and story material that does not relate in any way to Shakespeare's play.

Why did I write "Prince Pat" this way/ Because my main theme was that the choices we're being given during presidential campaigns are so often marketed just as any other product, that a man with exceptional vision, with strong stands on controversial issues, has a difficult time making it through the nominating process. As Shakespeare said several times, I ask for your forbearance, as I had no intention to cause offense.

—GAE
New Orleans, 1991

Robert Sheckley, author of such classics as *Dimension of Miracles* and *Mindswap*, has long been acknowledged as perhaps the finest satirist ever to work in the field of science fiction.

Here he tells a story of Teddy Kennedy that, like most Sheckley tales, it almost impossible to define or describe, so I advise you to just plunge right in and read it.

The Disorder and Early Sorrow of Edward Moore Kennedy, Homunculus
by Robert Sheckley

It was another morning, this one in October. The time, as usual, was 6:00 A.M., and Teddy Kennedy's buzzer was sounding off. A stubby hand, manicured nails immaculate, slammed down on the alarm. Silence. Then a groan.

Two stubby hands rubbed the sleep from Kennedy's eyes—make that three. Monica, or was it Roxanne, ran a single slim index finger along the Senator's jowl-line. She seemed nonplussed when Kennedy ignored her, climbed from the bed, all white sheets and sky-blue blankets, and left the room.

The Senator began his routine, shaving off the hard bristles, combing his hair as only a Kennedy can. Dressing.

His clothes were pressed and laid out for him as always: designer silk boxer shorts, Armani trousers and coat, soft Gucci belt, monogramed shirt and silk tie. He slid the belt on with great effort, noticing the pull on the last notch. His tie constricted his neck. Damn.

And then the call.

It had somehow gotten through Kennedy's system. It was from a Mr. Smith. Smith, voice warm but firm, informed the Senator that they needed to talk. It was a matter, Smith insisted, of urgent business. "What is this business?" Kennedy asked impatiently, wanting eggs Benedict with a serving (make that two servings) of hollandaise.

"It's about our colony on Mars," Smith said. "We're interested in an intercolony population exchange between ourselves and Earth, Mr. Kennedy, and we've selected you as an appropriate Earth leader to, uh, assist us."

"Colony," Kennedy said, his voice rising. "What colony?"

"The Mars colony, sir."

"The United States does not have or maintain a Mars colony," Kennedy said.

"No, sir. But we of Mars have and maintain our own."

Kennedy slammed the phone down.

"Marie!" he yelled to his maid, not sure if that was her name, not sure if it mattered. "Marie, goddammit, some guy claiming to be a Martian just got through! Why aren't my calls being screened?"

This was not a good morning. Kennedy's driver was not to be found, so the Senator called for a taxi to take him to a morning Senate meeting. He forgot to say goodbye to Monica or Roxanne. Oh well, whichever one she was wouldn't be there tonight.

At the office, Kennedy's secretary greeting him warmly with a stack of reading material and the day's schedule. Kennedy asked her to order eggs Benedict with a side of extra hollandaise, which he proceeded to gorge on while reading newspapers, secret reports, Senate bills.

"Hold all my calls," he instructed the secretary. "There's an important meeting this morning and I can't be interrupted." Kennedy was aware, even as he shoved spoonfuls of albuminous egg between his Kennedy teeth, of the press of his stomach against his clothes and the lethargy from having overeaten.

More and more of late he experienced an exhaustion too profound to be mere lack of sleep. He knew what it was: he was old, tired; but life and all its demands went on. It was intolerable, but he also knew, paradoxically, that he was fortunate. What a bit of luck to be born a Kennedy: insulated from poverty, heir to a great name, lifelong recipient of a great time in the family funhouses, safe from all except the loneliness which was the common concomitant of fame.

Enough thinking. He had work to do.

In a room big enough to house every homeless person on the streets of Boston, Kennedy met with his colleagues. In serious tones the group discussed the plight of the poor, the need for more bureaucracy to provide for their needs and greater contribution from taxpayers to give them better tenements.

The meeting was dull, demanding, and left Kennedy more exhausted than when he walked in. Not that he showed it. He'd mastered the art of looking alert and enthusiastic when actually, inside the noble skull with its sculpted hair, he wanted to die. He returned to his office, deciding to skip lunch. He really needed to lighten the load against his belt.

Kennedy sat back in his chair for a moment of relaxation. He picked up the book again—*Robinson Crusoe*, a childhood favorite. The phone rang. His secretary, who usually announced callers, had somehow missed this one.

Kennedy lifted the receiver. The voice was familiar. English-sounding: Audrey Hepburn's lilt in a male voice.

"Mr. Kennedy, this is Mr. Smith again. We really must talk."

Kennedy controlled his irritation, forcing himself to see the light side of it all, concentrating on it until he was actually chuckling. "Mr. Smith, I am concerned about your interplanetary problems, please believe me," Kennedy said with a great sincerity, "but since I've just agreed to interplanetary meetings with beings from three other planets, I'm hard-pressed to see where I can fit you into my schedule. . . . Now, if you'll just call one of my colleagues . . ."

In good spirits now, planning his little joke, Kennedy fingered through his Rolodex, looking for the telephone number of one of his least-favored colleagues.

"You must take this seriously," Smith was saying. "We've chosen *you*, and I'm afraid in this case we have all the power cards. Now, if you'll just meet with me this afternoon at a mutually agreed-upon place . . ."

"Ah, yes, Strom Thurmond!" Kennedy said, grinning. "He's the man who deals with Martians."

Kennedy rattled off a phone number, replaced the phone and chuckled. The sudden pressure on his belly caused his pants button to snap. The Gucci belt, however, held tight. Thank God for high-class products. Kennedy reached into his desk for a safety pin and bolted his trousers back together.

He stopped laughing long enough to wonder: How did they get that call through? Kennedy walked out to the reception area. His secretary's glasses sat neatly on her desk. Her chair was empty. Where *was* the woman? Damned incompetents.

Kennedy walked back to his office. His phone was ringing again. Grabbing the receiver, holding back his annoyance, Kennedy began, "Look, you loony . . ." But the call was from his favorite deli. Would Kennedy like a delivery today, a young girl's voice asked. *Thank God someone's got some initiative!* Kennedy almost said yes—pastrami and rye seeme to be calling his name—but in a moment of caution he decided against it and went for a walk in the park.

The park looked nothing like the well-kept green lawns where Kennedy had played football as a boy. Here, the lawns were littered with bottles and papers. Smoke and soot fouled the air. No birds sang in the trees. Where, Kennedy wondered, are the damned birds? He thought about the office. God, he was so tired, and getting old, and soon . . . A bench. Kennedy lifted the pleats in his coat and carefully sat on a green park bench, knife-engraved with the words FUCK FUCK FUCK. He pulled the book from the pocket of his jacket, this tattered paperback copy of the adventures of Robinson Crusoe. Smiling to himself, Kennedy forgot the bleak reality of the park and slipped far away in time.

> September 30, 1659 . . . I, poor, miserable Robinson Crusoe, being shipwrecked during a dreadful storm in the offing, came onshore in this dismal unfortunate island, which I called "the Island of Despair," all the rest of the ship's company being drowned, and myself almost dead.

"Mr. Kennedy."

Kennedy looked up abruptly.

A man in a well-fitted suit sat down on his bench. The man was small, with short hair—didn't they call that a pixie haircut?—and polished shoes. Polished shoes, good suit. Well, he probably wasn't a mugger.

"Mr. Kennedy," the man repeated. Kennedy recognized the voice. The guy who had called earlier. The guy who called about the Martian colony. "So very glad you could 〈c〉ome to meet me." The nut had exquisite manners.

"〈I'〉m sorry, Mr. Smith," Kennedy said, "but I can't help 〈I'〉ve referred you to my colleague, uh, uh, a Mr. Thur-〈 〉nd now I really must . . ." Kennedy leaned for-〈 〉〈ri〉se and leave.

"It's you we want," Smith said, a little sadly. "Now, if you'll just be so kind as to come with me . . ."

The man placed his hand on Kennedy's knee. The hand felt . . . *alien*. Kennedy felt a moment of pain, like a pin-prick, then a rush of drug flooding his bloodstream. The heaviness of his mind lifted, euphoria slowly overtaking him. Why, the colors of the park were so beautiful; a pool, polluted before, now reflected greens and yellows and purples. And the flowers! Why hadn't he noticed before? He chuckled, then laughed.

"This way, Mr. Kennedy."

Kennedy awoke, this time without the nasal buzz of his alarm.

Nauseated, unrefreshed, he reached up, intending to massage his aching temples. His wrist did not respond to his mental command. For one terrifying moment he contemplated his last few memories. The phone calls, the park, the little man with the pixie cut, anxiety, anger and then joy. And now this headache.

"Where am I?" he asked. The room was dark. He thought he caught the shadow of a child, slipping out the door. No. "What time is it, what . . ." Kennedy focused on the throbbing in his head and decided the best thing was to focus out. Asleep again, he dreamed one of his favorite dreams: himself alone on a desert island with plenty of food and plenty of books and everything and nothing to do out of the ordinary: totally alive, he would have time, here, to think of how to build shelter, how to grow corn and wheat, how to make his own clothing.

How long does it take to get to Mars? Kennedy must have been asleep for weeks. As soon as he realized that, he awoke abruptly. "We're about to land, Mr. Kennedy," a proper voice said over the intercom. "Your chamber should protect you from the impact . . . We've taken every precaution ... Please inform us if you're having any difficulty."

"Diffi ..." Kennedy started angrily. "What is going on here?" he said with authority, despite the fact that he wasn't sure he was awake. Probably he was asleep, but best not to back off even from dream Martians. "There's no life on Mars," he continued, when there was no response to his demand.

"Correction," said the voice. "There's no life on the surface. There's plenty of life, but it's underground, beneath the surface. It has existed there for centuries."

"Why have you brought me here?" Kennedy asked.

There was no answer.

A terrible whirring noise filled the chamber, while a buzzing took over the intercom. Was this some amusement ride in hell? Kennedy began to sense crushing pressure against his being. Filled with nausea, he was conscious only of pain and fear of imminent implosion. And then it all stopped.

Kennedy lay bolted to a long tube in a dark room, angry as hell. The pain was gone. Apparently the ship had made a successful landing. On Mars. Oh, sure. Pretty soon he'd find out what was going on. He'd play along with these guys, whoever they were. His situation was absurd, but what the ...

He listened to a series of muffled noises. He heard several thumping sounds, like the automatic opening doors at a mini-mall. Then, whirring noises. The gizmo must be shutting itself down.

Aching, he sat up, rubbed his brow. The pain had left. His body had a lightness to it, an unbelievable lightness. Probably lost a few pounds, he mused to himself. Probably lost plenty. How long had it been? Moving through the dark room, he felt like he was navigating through water. He could breathe, but what was this atmosphere? Was this on the money? Were these guys really space beings and was he on another planet? Kennedy wondered for more than a few moments if he was about to die. God knows Earth was full of incompetents—did these guys know what he needed to live?

He wasn't walking. He was floating. It was wonderful. No more pain now. Kennedy distinctively heard voices. "We've brought you," the voices told him, "to bring a new dimension to our planet. Rather than learn about your culture, we've decided to absorb it. You, Mr. Kennedy, will bring a welcome change to Mars." Sounded to him like one of those crazy speeches he always listened to on the floor—lots of hyperbole, no substance.

"Welcome," the voices sang in squeaky tones. "Welcome, to you, to you."

This is silly, Kennedy thought, as he began to feel a force pulling him toward the chamber door. For the first time, about to meet his captors, Kennedy noticed that he was naked. Not a thing a man of his stature ordinarily overlooked, but he hadn't been in his right mind, it seemed, since the park . . .

Muffled voices rose outside the spaceship. Kennedy couldn't make out words. Sounds, yes. Moaning. Pain. Oh, God, what was happening? Kennedy wondered, suddenly terrified. The moaning grew louder. He was moving so slowly, sucked toward the chamber, and then into a tunnel, compressed again and in horrible pain. He tried to shriek but the pressure against his naked body was too intense. Christ. Jesus Christ. This is it, just let it be over fast, Kennedy thought. The moans grew louder. Were they his?

His body crashed through the tunnel.

And then he was in the blinding light, terrified, cold, naked. Crying like a baby.

The moaning had stopped.

An enormous being with a pointy face clapped its hands. Two enormous hands held Kennedy like a toy.

He had no control left in his body, his head falling to

the side, his hands clenching and releasing, clenching and releasing.

Edward Moore Kennedy threw his head back and screamed.

Then he forgot everything.

"Welcome, my new baby," said a pointy-faced woman who held the newborn to her chest. "Welcome," said her new husband, a smallish man with a pixie haircut. "Our new child. We shall call him John. John Smith."

Martha Soukup, Hugo and Nebula nominee and author of several brilliant works of imaginative fiction, didn't want to write this story. (Martha never wants to write any story I assign her.) So I nagged her and begged her and threatened her, just like I always do, and finally she relented, just like she always does, and turned in yet another memorable story, just like she always does.

Rosemary Kennedy is the sister no one ever talks about, the one who was lobotomized and locked away from the public, a mental infant to the end. In the true spirit of science-fictional speculation, Martha presents the same woman, similar surgery, and a startlingly different outcome.

Rosemary's Brain
by Martha Soukup

Rosemary had taken her bathroom mirror off its screws and propped it on the bed. It reflected her partnering her pink party dress around and around the room in a determined waltz. Her eyes never moved from the image.

The dress was leading.

Eddie Moore watched from the doorway. "Rose?" he said finally. "Rosemary?"

His goddaughter took a few more perfect turns around the room, as smooth as if she were moving on polished rails. Eddie thought of the thousands of hours of dance lessons, of tennis and swimming, she had been put through for twenty-one years. Rosemary had never really mastered any of them, though she tried like a Kennedy.

Whatever the doctors had transplanted into her frontal lobes had accomplished what dozens of patient tutors and family members had not.

Rosemary glided to a stop, folded the dress lengthwise, and laid it down carefully across the back of a hospital chair. "Uncle Eddie," she said. "How nice of you to come."

She seemed so sober. Not the girl who had lit up with pleasure every time he came to see her and give her a present, nor the frustrated, angry adolescent her father had had hospitalized before she could hurt anyone. Before she could get herself hurt, in her restless midnight walks alone.

"I saw this in a little shop on my way here," he said. He handed her the hatbox.

She opened it and pulled out a wide-brimmed hat. "Thank you, Uncle Eddie," she said. "This will be lovely when I get the bandages off."

He'd wanted to see her eyes glow the way they had when she was a little girl, and would throw her arms around her godfather. Instead she laid the hat gravely on the chair by the party dress. "It was foolish to bring you a hat, I guess," he said.

"It was sensible," she said, touching her bandages. "When these come off, I'll want as many wigs and hats as I can get, until my hair grows back."

Eddie removed his own hat and sat on the edge of her bed. "Tell me what you'd like next time I visit."

"Books," Rosemary said. "I've finished everything I have here. I need more books."

Now her godfather noticed the stacks of books on and under the little desk in the corner of the hospital room. There must have been dozens of them, not including a full, new encyclopedia set. She had only regained consciousness after her surgery a week ago.

"The encyclopedia, too?" he said, making it a joke.

"The encyclopedia first," she said. "I have a lot of catching up to do."

"Now, what would you want with all those dry books, Rose?" he said, picking up the volume marked G. "What could you learn from them?"

"Henry Grattan, 1746–1820," she said. "Irish statesman who helped obtain the vote for the Irish. Retired in 1797 when he failed to achieve the right for the Irish to sit in Parliament. Later sat in Parliament himself. Asa Gray, 1810–1888. American botanist. Taught at Harvard and revised Linnaeus's taxonomy. Author of *The Manual of Botany*, *Structural Botany*, and *The Elements of Botany*. Elisha Gray, 1835–1901, British poet and scholar—"

"My dear," Eddie said, a little dizzy. "My dear, is it wise to tax yourself this way? What does your doctor say?"

"Dr. Harper doesn't know." She moved the hat off the chair and sat down. "He gives me knowledge-retention tests, and I flub most of the questions. I let myself do a little better than I would have before. He thinks the operation is a success because I've calmed down. That's enough for them to think, since it's all they expected. Isn't it?"

"Isn't it what?"

"Isn't it all they expected? That this operation would perform the same function as a lobotomy, and calm me down, while perhaps slightly increasing my reasoning capacity?"

"Well—"

"But they didn't count on it making me smarter. It's all right, Uncle Eddie. I know they resigned themselves to my being the only imperfect Kennedy child years ago. The whole family has always been very nice about it. As long as I worked as hard as I could, and looked presentable in public, it was all right. The only person who couldn't accept it in the end, was me." She smiled. "Though I was so slow, it took me almost twenty years to really figure it out. Maybe that's why I took it so badly when I did figure it out."

Eddie said nothing. It was difficult for him to know how to talk to this young woman who had been a little girl her whole life, an angry, grown child consumed by violent tantrums for the past year. It was not just the turban of bandages swaddling her head that made her look like a different person. Rosemary looked eerily like her mother had when she was about her age, after she returned from the convent school which had made her so much more sober and thoughtful. As the secretary to Rosemary's grandfather, Eddie had seen many changes in circumstances for the Fitzgeralds, and then the Kennedys, but nothing as abrupt as this.

He missed his little goddaughter, but reminded himself that she had already changed beyond recognition before the operation.

"You're right, though," she said. "The books help, but I need to get out into the world if I'm going to understand it and learn to compete."

"Compete?"

"That's what it's all about, isn't it, Uncle Eddie? Every generation doing better than the last." She shook her bandaged head. "It won't be easy for our generation. Grandpa Fitzgerald went from being a newsboy to Mayor of Boston. Daddy went from being a saloon keeper's son to a millionaire and the Ambassador to Britain. It will be a challenge. I'll have to plan my priorities."

He doubted she'd even know the word "priorities" a month before.

"May I practice dancing with you? It's hard, without a partner."

"Of course. Let me sit awhile first."

"Social graces are my first priority. There's only so much one can learn from hospital orderlies. When I get out of here, I'm going to England with Kick. She has lots of boyfriends here, but she has even more there."

"What do Kathleen's boyfriends—?"

"Oh, don't worry, Uncle Eddie. I don't plan to steal my sister's boyfriends. She just has more than she knows what to do with, and she doesn't even kiss most of them. Mother's good Catholic training may not have taken on the boys, but Kick's a good girl." She paused. "That doesn't mean *I* have to be."

He rose to his feet. "Rosemary!"

She stood, took his hand, and sat him down again on the bed. "Uncle Eddie, I'll be careful. There's only so much one can learn from kissing orderlies, though, and one can't really go further with orderlies than kiss them. I need more experience, if I'm to make my mark on Hollywood."

"Hollywood?" Eddie said, weakly.

"Is there a better place for a woman to get a high profile? You always told me I was as pretty as a movie star, and from what I can tell from the orderlies and doctors, it wasn't all flattery. Not that all Hollywood stars are classically pretty. Character and confidence count for so much. Confidence shouldn't be hard to come by, when I can memorize a script with a single reading. I'll count on my bloodlines for the character."

"But this is so sudden—"

"I've thought about it for two days, Uncle Eddie," Rosemary said patiently, patting his hand. "I know that when Daddy was seeing Gloria Swanson—now, don't look shocked, I put that together the day after the operation, you must know he's always seen women—I know that she was making a fortune. If she'd had a financier's mind, she could have become one of the most powerful women in America. *I* can have a financier's mind. Bring me some books. Better still, I'll examine how Daddy has done it. There couldn't be a better course of study."

"Are you sure you want a career, Rose?"

"I know what you're thinking, Uncle Eddie. You're

thinking how hard it was for me, failing over and over all through my childhood."

He blinked.

"You're so easy to read. That's very sweet of you, but don't worry. I won't fail now."

She patted his hand again, stood up, and went over to her pile of books. She opened the closet door.

"I know how to work hard," she said, stacking the books inside the closet, "and now I'm smart enough to accomplish what I attempt. That's why I need to plan it so carefully, you see. I'll go to England for a year; I'll go to Hollywood for twelve years. It should be a good time for a woman to establish herself in Hollywood, with so many men going to war. After I star in a few movies I can start producing them, too. The acting is important, to get me in the public eye, and the producing is important, to show people what I can do. Though I expect I'll make more money investing in industry. After the war, there will be lots of money to be made."

Eddie watched the encyclopedia disappear into the closet. "Have you talked to the family about this?"

"Oh no. Daddy would have his own ideas. Mother would disapprove completely. I just want them to think I'm a happier girl who can look after herself a little. They'll see what I'm doing soon enough."

"Your family is always there for you, Rose."

"My parents are always traveling," Rosemary said. "But you're right. One way or another, they're always there. Loving me to death. Making me love them back. Trying to be what they wanted me to be *hurt*, Eddie. It hurt for years and years. Just because some fool doctor accidentally stumbled onto something that's given me twice their I.Q.'s doesn't mean I'm going to suddenly want to be what they want me to be."

Her voice was tight. "Do you know, I was happy in England? I might have been retarded, but I was happy. I was at that Montessori school, you know, and they let me read to the children every afternoon. The children loved me. They didn't think I was stupid. I was as good for them as any grown-up could be. And then they said I had to come home. What's home? We move all the time!"

She threw the last book, a *Physician's Desk Reference*, into the closet.

"Maybe they know best for Joe, and Jack, and Kathleen, and all the younger children. I'll do for myself. I'll do for myself. I'll do for myself." She slammed the closet door. It shook on its hinges.

"Rosemary," Eddie said nervously. He had seen her rages before the operation. She was a tall, strong young woman. He was always afraid she would hurt herself.

Rosemary stood, faced away from him. Her shoulders shook. He watched her, uncertain if he should go up and touch her. Before the operation, she had sometimes hit those who tried to comfort her.

He was about to open his mouth to say something—he didn't know what—when she turned. Her face was lit with a brilliant smile, disarming him.

"But I'll have no troubles, because, you see, I shall be an actress," she said. Her smile, her whole air, was Hollywood-dazzling. He had seen her sister Kathleen do that, but never to the dizzying degree Rosemary had already mastered.

"And do you know, Uncle Eddie, I think the future belongs to actors. Politicians who look and sound good in newsreels, they're the ones who'll have the edge. The books I've read convince me that television will work, too. By the time I'm ready, people will probably be able to see newsreels in their living rooms."

"Ready for what?" Eddie asked. He wanted to go home. He wanted to lie down. He felt as though he'd stepped right off the world he knew, and he wasn't sure if he liked it at all.

There was the sound of a man's hard shoes on the linoleum hallway floor outside. "That's Daddy," Rosemary said. She moved close to him and spoke rapidly and quietly. "You are never to mention a word to him. I love you like another father, and I want you to help me with my plans. Remember that I would never want to hurt you—but you don't want to find out how much I've learned about the skeletons in your political closet."

"Rose—"

"Politics," she said, "is the most interesting game of all. Daddy will just have to deal with it when Joe is not the one who wins for the highest stakes. He wants the first Irish Catholic President in the family? He'd never even think of playing with the odds against a woman."

Her smile was dazzling, but her eyes were hard. With an entire life in politics, he'd thought he understood how self-centered and cynical a politician could be. He'd always understood how his boss—Rosemary's grandfather, Mayor Fitzgerald, having grown up in wretched poverty and anti-Irish prejudice—loved the success more than any other thing. Her father was the same. The need was her heritage by blood and upbringing.

He had just never seen it so transparently displayed before.

After Rosemary perfected her performing style, he never would again. She could seduce a voting public with her new grace and her Kennedy charm and never look back. His stomach turned over with trepidation and love for his goddaughter.

"And you won't tell him a thing about it."

Joe Kennedy Senior, entered the room. Rosemary cried, *"Daddy!"* and ran into his arms for a perfect, childlike hug.

With trepidation, with love, Eddie said nothing.

There are a lot of hassles involved in editing: paperwork, contracts, payments, rights, permissions, and an endless stream of unpublishable stories. One of the things that makes it all seem worthwhile is when you receive a story from someone whose name is totally unfamiliar to you and who doesn't even know that this is a by-invitation-only anthology, you decide to glance at the first page before mailing it back to him, and suddenly you find yourself unable to put it down.

Which is precisely what happened when I received Nicholas A. DiChario's "The Winterberry." Nobody turns out a story like this the first time out of the box; surely he had been selling for years, probably under a pseudonym. (So much for keen editorial insight: It turns out that this was his second sale; his first story saw print a month after I purchased this one.)

This young man is going to be around for a long time, and he's only going to get better. That's almost frightening.

The Winterberry
by Nicholas A. DiChario

May, 1971

It was Uncle Teddy who taught me how to read and write. I think it took a long time but I'm not sure. I heard him arguing with Mother about it one night a few years ago when I wasn't supposed to be out of my room, but I was very excited with the next day being my birthday and I couldn't sleep.

"He can do it," Uncle Teddy had said.

And Mother said, "He doesn't care whether he reads or writes. It's you who cares. Why do you torture yourself? Let him be."

"He's fifty-four years old," Uncle Teddy said.

"Let him be!" Mother sounded very angry.

I listened to Uncle Teddy walk across the room. "If you feel that way," he said, "why didn't you just let him die?"

There was a long silence before Mother said, "I don't know," and another long silence after that.

Something in their voices frightened me so I returned to my room. I became very ill, and for several weeks Dr. Armbruster came to see me every day but he wouldn't let anyone else come in because he said I was too weak to have visitors.

But sometime after, when I was much better, Uncle Teddy came to visit and he brought a picture book with him which made me remember his talk with Mother. I'm glad Uncle Teddy got his way because now I read and write a lot even though I throw most of my writing away. I hide some of it though and keep it just for myself, and it's not because I'm being sneaky, it's more because some of the things I write are my own personal secrets and I don't want to tell anyone, just like people don't want to tell me things sometimes when I ask them questions.

December, 1977

I am very excited about Christmas almost being here. I am looking forward to Uncle Teddy's stay because he always has something fun in mind. Yesterday after he arrived he walked me through the house and showed me all of the decorations—wreaths and flowers and a huge Christmas tree near the front hall, strung with tinsel and candles. He brought with him several boxes full of gifts, all shapes and sizes, wrapped in bright colors—red and green and blue and silver with bows and ribbons—and I knew they were all for me because he put them under my tree upstairs.

Our house is very large. Mother calls it a mansion. She doesn't allow me to go anywhere except the room on my floor. She says I have everything I need right here.

That's why sometimes at night I'll walk around when everything is dark and everyone is asleep or in their rooms for the night. I don't think I'm being sneaky, it's just that I am very curious and if I ask about things no one tells me what I want to know. I've come to know this house very well. There are many hidden passageways behind the walls and I know them all by heart. I will hear things every once in a while that mother would not like me to hear.

There was a big happening in the house last night and the servants were very busy, although it did not look to be a planned thing because everyone appeared disorganized and Mother didn't come to lock me in my room.

I went through one of my passageways that led to the main entrance of the house and I peeked through a tiny opening in the wall and saw a very beautiful woman with dark hair standing inside the door. She was so beautiful that I held my breath. It must have been very cold outside because she was wearing a long black winter coat and there were flakes of snow on her hair. When she spoke, it was the most soft and delicate voice I had ever heard. She said, "Merry Christmas."

I wanted to stay and watch the woman forever but I knew that Mother would be up to check on me so I ran back to my room and pretended to be asleep. Mother came in and kissed my head and said, "Sleep well, child," like she did every night. I listened very closely for a long time hoping to hear the voice of the woman again, but next thing I knew it was morning, and she was gone.

October, 1982

I heard Mother and Dr. Armbruster arguing yesterday. They were just talking pleasantly for a while and I was listening in my passageway to the low, pleasant sound of their voices. The doctor was saying things I did not understand about sickness and diets and so on, when all of a sudden he said, "But John is doing fine," and Mother just about exploded with anger.

"His name is not John, do you understand me? Don't you ever call him by that name again! John is dead! *My* John is dead!" I had never heard Mother get so angry except for that one time with Uncle Teddy. She made the doctor leave right away and told him he could be replaced, but I hoped that she wouldn't do that because I sort of liked Dr. Armbruster.

I don't know who John is, but I felt very bad for Mother. I had never really thought about my own name before. Uncle Teddy and everyone calls me Sonny because it's short for Sonny Boy, and that's good enough for me. But it made me wonder how someone could get a name like John. Uncle Teddy was probably named after a teddy bear. Mother was just Mother.

May, 1987

Today was a very special day. It was my seventieth birthday. Uncle Teddy came to visit and I was very excited because I hadn't seen him in such a long time. We had a big cake and a lot of food and we played checkers for an hour. Then Uncle Teddy took me outside for a walk!

I'll never forget it as long as I live. I think Mother was not happy about it because she did not want to let me go at first, but Uncle Teddy talked her into it and we went outside surrounded by men in black suits and ties and shoes. Uncle Teddy asked me if I minded if his friends went with us, and of course I didn't care. They came to my party and they had a right to have fun. In fact, I told them that if they smiled more they might have a nicer time all around, but Uncle Teddy said they were usually very serious people and were happy that way.

It was a sunny day. The wind blew in my face and stung my eyes at first, but it felt good. Uncle Teddy took me all around the yard and into the garden where I smelled the roses and touched the bushes and the vines. I listened to the birds calling and the insects buzzing. I never dreamed they would sound so loud and so near.

I touched the winterberry hollies which were very special to me because I could always see their bright red berries from my window, even during the cold cold winters.

After a short time I caught a chill and had to go inside, and I was weak for the rest of the day. But I didn't care— I had such fun! I'll always remember it.

August, 1996

One night I entered a storage room through my passageway where there were a lot of tools and brooms and rags and buckets and things. I rummaged around in the dark and my hands found a flashlight. I thought this would be a wonderful thing to have so I took it with me hoping that no one would miss it. Now I can sit in bed at night and read and write as long as I like and not have to worry about someone seeing my light.

I have not seen Mother in a very long time. I wondered if she was angry with me even though I didn't think she knew about my passageways or my late-night writing. Mother would have yelled at me if she knew.

I've been seeing more and more of Uncle Teddy, so I asked him about Mother today and he said that she went away on a very long trip and I wouldn't be seeing her for a while.

I asked him how long that might be and he said not long, he said soon we'd all be seeing her and then maybe we'd find out whether we did the right thing, whether the choices we'd made over the years had been the proper ones. He looked very sad when he said this, and then he said, "I think there is such a place, Sonny Boy, a place where we learn why everything is the way it is."

I asked him if Dr. Armbruster had gone with Mother since I hadn't seen him in so long and I was seeing Dr. Morelande almost every day now, and Uncle Teddy told me yes.

I thought about how lucky Mother was to visit this place, a place where every time you asked a question you got an answer, and I could not blame her if she didn't want to come back for a while. I told Uncle Teddy so, and he seemed to cheer up. We played cards for the rest of the afternoon.

May, 1997

Today was my eightieth birthday. I have been very sick and I was afraid that I might not be able to have my party, but Dr. Morelande said it was OK so we had cake and games with Uncle Teddy and I had a very nice time even though I had to stay in bed.

It was after my party that I had a scare. I was very weak, and I probably should have just gone to sleep, but being so excited all day and not being allowed to get up, I turned restless after dark, so I decided to take a short walk through my passageways.

I followed a path that led to the back of a closet in Uncle Teddy's room, and I saw some light coming through the darkness so I went up to it. That's all I was going to do—peek and go away—until I saw Uncle Teddy crying. I'd never seen Uncle Teddy cry before. He was in bed. He had a large, green book on his lap, and every so often he would turn a page and cry some more.

I watched him for a while, waiting for him to be all right, but he didn't stop crying and I couldn't stand to watch him any longer, so I did a foolish thing and I entered his room through the closet.

"Sonny Boy," he said, "what are you doing here?"

I thought he might be angry with me so I wanted to say that I saw him crying, and that I only wanted to help him and be a friend, but before I could say anything he said, "So you know about the passages," and he didn't seem to be upset at all.

"Come over here, Sonny," he said.

I went and sat on the edge of his bed. He was looking at a photo album. Mother had shown me some photo albums years ago, and I thought they were interesting and we had a lot of fun even though I didn't recognize any of the faces. I don't ever remember crying over them. But Uncle Teddy's album was different. There were newspaper pictures, and headlines, and articles.

Uncle Teddy was looking at a picture of a man and a woman. The man seemed very serious-looking, and his right hand was raised like an Indian chief's, but he had on a suit and tie and no headdress. The man's eyes were closed.

The woman had short black hair with long bangs, and she was looking down.

And then all of a sudden I just about screamed. I knew that woman. I remembered her from . . . from somewhere.

Uncle Teddy said, "You know her, don't you? Think, Sonny Boy, think very hard. What do you remember?"

I did think very hard, and then I remembered where I had seen her. She was the beautiful black-haired woman I had seen at Christmastime in the main entrance of the house years ago.

But then there was more. As I looked at the woman in the picture something very strange came into my head. I had a passing thought of this same woman in a pretty white gown, with a white veil over her face. It was just a piece of a thought that I could not keep in my mind for very long, but I'll never forget it. I reached out and touched the picture.

"Always grand," Uncle Teddy said. "She was wearing a very dignified, raspberry-colored suit that day."

But that's not what I had seen. I had seen the white gown. I had seen something that happened before my room and my house and my passageways and Mother and Uncle Teddy. Was there anything before them? Yes, I think there was. It was more than a passing thought—it was a *memory*.

"Was I married, Uncle Teddy?" I asked him.

He smiled. "Yes, you were. You proposed to her by telegram, you know, from Paris."

I thought this was interesting, but nothing more than that. Uncle Teddy started to cry again.

"Please, don't cry," I said.

He held my hand then. "I'm sorry we couldn't tell her you were alive. We couldn't tell your children, not anyone, not even Father because we couldn't be sure of his reaction. Mother was adamant about that. No one could know. Just Bobby and Mother and myself—and the doctors, of course. Now there's just me.

"It was for the good of the country. Those were critical times. The eyes of the world were watching us. We could not afford hesitancy. We felt you would have wanted it that way. Do you understand?"

I didn't, but I nodded anyway to stop Uncle Teddy from crying. He was clutching my arm very hard.

He traced the newspaper picture with his finger. "She was a strong woman, Sonny Boy. You would have been proud of her. I remember her standing right next to Lyndon, solid as a rock, little more than an hour after you were pronounced dead."

I was very confused about Uncle Teddy calling me dead, and about what the woman in the picture had to do with any of it, so I closed the book and placed it on the floor. I remembered what Mother used to do to make me feel better, so I thought that maybe the same thing might help Uncle Teddy feel better too.

I pulled his bed covers up to his chin, brushed back his hair, kissed him on the forehead, and turned out his light. "Sleep well, child," I said, and then I went back to my room. I was sure Uncle Teddy would be just fine in the morning. It had always worked for me.

December, 2008

Dr. Morelande is the only one who comes to see me anymore. He says that Uncle Teddy is so busy he can't find time to stop by. But I don't think that's exactly true. I think Uncle Teddy went on vacation with Mother and Dr. Armbruster, and he is having so much fun that he is not coming back at all.

Dr. Morelande has tried very hard to make this a good Christmas, but I am sorry to say I am not very happy. I am tired all of the time, and I can't even move out of bed. Dr. Morelande asked me if I wanted anything for Christmas, but if I couldn't have Mother or Uncle Teddy, then there was nothing to ask for.

But then I thought about it and thought about it for a long time, and I remembered the pictures Uncle Teddy had shown me many years ago. I told Dr. Morelande about the green photo album in Uncle Teddy's room and asked him if he could find it for me. A little while later Dr. Morelande returned with the book.

Together we went through the pictures, and when we got to the one Uncle Teddy had shown me, the one with the man and the beautiful dark-haired woman, I made him stop.

"There *is* something I want for Christmas," I told him. "There is something I want very much."

I decided to tell Dr. Morelande about the passageways then. I didn't think that I would get in trouble. I made him put me in my wheelchair and take me for a walk behind the walls. He argued with me at first, but I refused to be put off.

I told him exactly which path to follow. He wheeled

me all the way down to the wall at the main entrance. I looked through the small opening. I was sure that the beautiful dark-haired woman would be standing at the door in her winter coat. I was disappointed that she wasn't there. I thought that if I waited long enough she would certainly show up—she would come back like the winterberry, bright and strong even in the cold cold winter. There would be snowflakes in her hair, and she would say "Merry Christmas" in her lovely voice. So we waited.

Finally Dr. Morelande said that if I agreed to go to bed, he would wait for the woman, and bring her directly to me as soon as she arrived. I thought that this would be a good idea since I was so tired.

When she arrives, we will have many things to discuss. I have decided to make her my new friend. I think I will show her my book of writings. I think I will ask her about the white gown to show her that I have not forgotten, and then I'll ask her about the children Uncle Teddy mentioned. I won't tell her about the vacation place where everyone has gone without me, and not because I'm being sneaky, but only because I am very lonely and I would like her to stay with me for a while.

What if...

... Benjamin Franklin had been elected the first president of the United States?

... Abraham Lincoln had lost the 1860 election, and became one of the great generals of the Civil War?

... Suffragist Victoria Clafin Woodhull had become president in 1872—and transformed the morals and mores of Gilded Age America?

... Adlai Stevenson had beaten Dwight D. Eisenhower twice in a row—only to be impeached?

... President Goldwater had used nuclear weapons in Vietnam?

ALTERNATE PRESIDENTS

28 Americas that never were...
but might have been
edited by
Mike Resnick
51192-11
$4.99/$5.99 in Canada

SF ADVENTURE FROM
MIKE RESNICK

THE BEST IN
SCIENCE FICTION

Buy them at your local bookstore or use this handy coupon:
Clip and mail this page with your order.

Publishers Book and Audio Mailing Service
P.O. Box 120159, Staten Island, NY 10312-0004

Please send me the book(s) I have checked above. I am enclosing $ _____
(Please add $1.25 for the first book, and $.25 for each additional book to cover postage and handling.
Send check or money order only—no CODs.)

Name _____
Address _____
City _____ State/Zip _____
Please allow six weeks for delivery. Prices subject to change without notice.